When Forever Comes

a novel

Anita Stansfield

Covenant Communications, Inc.

Published by Covenant Communications, Inc.
American Fork, Utah

Printed in the United States of America
First Printing: August 1998

05 04 03 02 01 00 99 98   10 9 8 7 6 5 4 3 2 1

ISBN 1-57734-300-X

To my children: John, Jake, Anna, and Steve.

No matter the obstacles that come into your path,
Remember who you are, and where you came from.

(Ether 12:27)

ACKNOWLEDGMENTS

I would like to express my appreciation to those of you who took the time to help me through this project. Especially to Art and Dallas, and John and Stephanie. *Your* stories inspired me and gave me faith. Also, to Dianne, for always having the right answer at the right time. And to Jenny, for bringing Kenny into our lives. And in loving memory, to my mother, for always being there for me.

PROLOGUE
Mount Pleasant, Utah

*W*hat a lousy day for a funeral. The rain hadn't ceased, even for a moment, since Hilary Smith had dragged herself from a sleepless bed. The large group of people gathered around the open grave were huddled beneath a mass of umbrellas, blanketed by a sky so dark and heavy that it felt as if heaven itself might turn inside out. Hilary had purposely left her umbrella in the limousine. The rain she had cursed earlier was now a blessing as it disguised the endless stream of tears that refused to be held back any longer.

Hilary scanned the faces of family and friends. Most of the people here meant little or nothing to her. There were relatives that she knew only by name; their faces had appeared in her life so rarely that it was difficult, if not impossible, to consider them close enough to care. There were ward members and people she knew from around town. And she had to give credit to those who had braved the rain to stay after the funeral service and show up here for the dedication of the grave.

Hilary's parents held to each other tightly, stone-faced and somber. She'd seen little beyond an occasional tear from either of them all day. Of course, they had both cried almost continually since news had come of the accident. She felt certain they were numb by now. And Hilary's siblings were all married; each of them had someone to cling to as they endured their varying degrees of emotion. Everyone here had cared for Jeffrey; their presence was evidence of that. But she felt certain that no one, *no one,* had any comprehension of what Jeffrey's loss meant to *her.*

There had been something special between the two of them as far back as she could remember. She was his only *little* sister. When they were children, she had followed him everywhere she possibly could. And, unlike most older brothers, Jeffrey had never treated her as a nuisance. He'd looked out for her, entertained her. He'd taught her to read and to ride a bicycle. He'd comforted her through everything from skinned knees to broken hearts. *And now he was gone.* She'd missed him dreadfully through his two-year absence, but he'd come home from his mission just when she'd needed him most. Jeffrey had almost made her believe that she could get beyond Leon's rejection. But now she wasn't certain she could get beyond anything.

Leon. Thoughts of him reminded her that he was there, standing a short distance away, his hands in the pockets of a long coat, his expression an exact replica of the dozens of people surrounding him. At least he'd come; she could give him some credit for that. But he'd come as a friend of the family, not as her personal support. And she resented it. They should have been engaged by now. She ached to feel his arm around her, to cry against his shoulder and know that he would be there for her as she endured the loss of her brother. But Leon was lost to her now.

She'd dated him since she'd been old enough to date, waited faithfully for him while he'd gone on his mission, never once even looked at another man. Everyone in town had taken for granted that the two of them would marry—especially her. But Leon had dumped her for some city girl who wore designer clothes, had her fingernails done professionally, and didn't have a clue about how to drive a tractor. Hilary had only met her once, at the drugstore, when Leon had so kindly introduced them. Beyond her perfect appearance, Hilary remembered little about her other than an annoying little giggle that had erupted two or three times a minute through their one brief encounter. And her name was Sunny, no less. Jeffrey had told Hilary that he'd never really liked Leon all that much anyway, and he knew she could find somebody better— someone *worthy* of her, he'd said. But now that Jeffrey was gone, Hilary wasn't certain if she could even find the strength to live, let alone make herself worthy of anyone or anything.

Well, at least Leon hadn't brought Sunny with him to the funeral. She caught his eye briefly a couple of times from where she stood at her mother's side. She sensed his compassion, perhaps even a degree of regret for the way he'd hurt her. But she quickly looked away, unable to feel anything that didn't create more pain.

When the dedication of the grave was finished, the crowd dispersed to their vehicles like mice scurrying away from the sudden appearance of a cat. Only Hilary's immediate family lingered—along with a couple standing some distance away beneath a black umbrella. They had previously been at the back of the crowd, out of Hilary's view. But she could tell they were watching her, and she sensed some kind of familiarity, though it was difficult to recognize their features through the continuing drizzle. As they began to approach, Hilary's heart quickened. The man she'd only met once, for just a moment, but the woman . . .

"Janna," she murmured under her breath and moved into her friend's embrace. She could never explain what it meant to know that Janna would take the time to drive more than an hour from Provo through this weather—for her.

Hilary had first met JannaLyn Trevor while she'd been waiting for Leon to return from his mission. She had been working at a mall in Utah Valley while attending Brigham Young University. At the time, Janna had been separated from her husband and going through some pretty tough challenges. They'd attended dance classes together, and in spite of their age difference, their friendship had grown deep. Janna was now reunited with her husband and doing well. But the last time they'd talked had been when Hilary had called to cry on Janna's shoulder over losing Leon.

An obvious question came to Hilary's mind, and she drew back to look into her friend's eyes. "How did you know?" she asked.

"Colin happened across the obituary," Janna said.

Hilary smiled toward Janna's husband, saying softly, "Perhaps that was an answer to my prayers. I'm so glad you came." Colin only smiled, and compassion radiated from his eyes.

"Are you all right?" Janna asked.

Hilary shook her head and bit her lip. "Not really, but . . ." She turned and noticed her family moving toward the waiting limousine. "Well, maybe we should get out of the weather. They're having a luncheon at the church building. Will you come and . . ."

"We'll see you there," Janna said, motioning for Hilary to join her family. Their reluctance to leave what remained of Jeffrey was finally overcome by the persistent rain, and they all huddled in the limousine, wet and eerily silent.

Hilary watched the rain drizzle over the car windows, her thoughts consumed with the reality that her future would be nothing like what she had expected it to be. The two people who meant the most to her in this world were gone. For her, there seemed little point in going on.

The minute she stepped out of the limousine, Janna was there to usher Hilary quickly inside the building. In a vacant hallway, Janna helped her friend out of her coat. "You're soaked. Just what you need, along with everything else, is to get sick."

"I hardly noticed, actually," Hilary admitted as Janna hung up the wet coat and put her hands on Hilary's shoulders.

"Well, at least it didn't soak through."

Hilary could hear the bustle of people in the nearby cultural hall, where the food was being served. She didn't know where Janna's husband had gone, but she was grateful they had some time alone. "Thank you for coming," Hilary said again, her voice cracking. "There's no way I can tell you what it means to know that someone was here for *me; just* for me."

Janna hugged Hilary tightly, whispering with emotion, "Maybe I do know."

They sat together on a sofa in the foyer and talked until Colin came to find them with the announcement that the food was getting cold. "There's nothing like a Mormon funeral luncheon," he said.

"Don't tell me. Don't tell me," Janna said lightly. "There are cheesy potato casseroles."

Hilary actually smiled as she added, "And ham."

"And rolls," Janna said.

"And dripper cakes. And Jell-O salads," Hilary added with a little laugh. "Mostly green."

Colin laughed softly. "You'd think they had put a menu in the Book of Mormon."

"But it always tastes good," Janna observed.

"Yes, it sure does." Colin glanced lovingly at his wife, and Hilary found it difficult to believe all the struggles they had been through.

She wondered if it would be possible for her to get beyond her own present struggles so valiantly. She seriously doubted it.

CHAPTER ONE
Three Months Later

*H*ilary got into the truck and slammed the door. The old blue pickup started fine, but the engine killed as she let up on the clutch too quickly. "Oh, garbage," she muttered under her breath and started it again. She *hated* driving with a clutch. But she had errands to run, and this was the only vehicle they had.

She backed the truck out of the long driveway, then drove up the short dirt road to the highway. The wind whipped at her dark blonde hair that hung well past her shoulders. It was straight and determined to stay that way, and wearing it long was the only way to manage it at all. At the stop sign, she hurried to pull her hair haphazardly into a scrunchie to keep it out of her eyes.

As soon as she pulled out onto the paved road, she noticed the gas gauge was nearly on empty. "Oh, *garbage*," she muttered more vehemently. It was an unreliable gauge, and ignoring it would be too risky. She usually went to the gas station on the south end of town, but she didn't even dare go that far. Pulling into the *other* gas station, she reached for the jockey box where her father kept a notebook to record the mileage each time he got gas. Pete Smith was a compulsive record keeper, and Hilary had learned at a young age that not keeping notes on her father's behalf made him very unhappy. She groaned at the little note posted to the jockey box. *Check oil,* it said. She could almost hear her father bellowing, "If ya got gas, why didn't ya check th' oil?"

Hilary climbed out of the truck and got the pump started before she went around to open the hood.

"Here, I got it," a masculine voice said, with just a hint of a southern drawl. A pair of tan arms took on the task, while Hilary felt more irritated than anything. She kept her attention on the hood as the service station attendant tried to open it. When he couldn't, she pushed on it just so, and it popped up.

"Well, now," he drawled, "I guess it takes a woman's touch."

"I just need to check the oil," she said, ignoring his flattery. "I can do it," she insisted without looking at him.

He ignored her and pulled out the dipstick, wiping it on a rag he'd retrieved from his back pocket. Hilary left him to it and decided to wash the windows instead. She was straining to reach the middle of the back window when that voice called, "How far have you driven?"

"I just came out of Mt. Pleasant," she called back.

He peered around the hood and flashed a wide, straight-toothed smile. "You're still *in* Mt. Pleasant."

Hilary finally looked at him, fighting back her irritation. "So I am," she said, tossing the squeegee back into the bucket next to the pump.

"Hey!" He pointed at her with the dipstick. "I know you!"

The pump clicked off, and Hilary turned her back to him to top off the tank. "In a town this size, that isn't too difficult."

"Your oil's fine," he said, closing the hood just as Hilary returned the pump and screwed on the gas cap.

"I didn't recognize you at first," he added, leaning against the side of the truck with his arms folded across his chest. The sleeves of his chambray shirt were rolled up high on his arms. She couldn't figure out why farm boys had to have their sleeves rolled up higher than the rest of the world, but she thought it looked tacky. As he smiled at her again, she quelled the urge to tell him to save his casual conversation for someone who might enjoy it.

"You look different," he added as she dug in her purse for a twenty. Hilary handed it to him, her irritation increasing. What he really meant was, *Your hair looks awful that way. You've put on twenty pounds.* And *you'd do better if you didn't go into public without wearing makeup.*

Before Hilary could ask for her change and make a quick getaway, he said, "I just got back from my mission. You've changed in two years."

She squinted to look at him closer. With his short-cropped brown hair, she figured he hadn't been home very long. He looked vaguely familiar; but then, everyone in this town did.

"Are you sure you know me?" she asked. "Maybe I just look like somebody you know, and—"

"Oh, no." He shook his head and laughed. "I'd never forget you. You're Jeff Smith's sister."

Hilary squeezed her eyes shut briefly as a memory began to stir. Her brother had had a number of obnoxious friends through his teen years. But only one had that Texas drawl, since his family had migrated from the Lone Star State. And he'd been the most obnoxious of all. She didn't remember his name, and she didn't want to have this conversation. But he didn't seem the least bit put off by her cold stare.

"Hilarious," he said, flipping the toothpick between his lips from one side of his mouth to the other. Then he laughed.

Hilary groaned and turned away. "That's what I hate about small towns," she snapped. "Can't a person ever live *anything* down?"

"What?" he laughed, still apparently unruffled by her animosity. "I always thought you liked your little nickname."

Hilary sighed, recalling how her brother's friends had incessantly teased her as a child. She had followed them around, doting on their attention, behaving like a clown. They'd found her antics more amusing than annoying. And this guy—whatever his name was—had been the one to first call her *Hilarious*—a simple change of pronunciation from Hilary S. And Hilary *hated* it.

While she was trying to think of an appropriate comeback, he grinned again. "Say, whatever happened to old Leon Phillips?" he asked. "The two of you were quite a thing for a long time. Although I never could understand what you saw in him."

Hilary's irritation rose several levels as she struggled to come up with an appropriate response. "He . . . uh . . . he's engaged to be married in November." She wished she could say it without hurting, but Leon was still very much a sore point. Since he'd let her go, she'd simply had no interest in herself whatsoever—a situation only made worse by Jeffrey's absence. But she had no desire to discuss it with anyone—especially this guy, who seemed bent on ruining her day. He smiled in response to the news about Leon, but she was relieved when he didn't question her further.

"You don't remember me, do you." He smirked with that toothpick tucked into the corner of his mouth.

"Oh, I remember you, all right," she said as she held out her hand. "Could I have my change? I need to get going."

"Oh, sure." He dug in his pocket and handed her a dollar and a quarter. "How is Jeff, anyway?" he asked as she opened the truck door. "I haven't seen him since I got back."

"That's understandable," she said. Their eyes met as he waited for an explanation. Hilary thought of a hundred different ways she could say it, but ninety-nine of them would evoke a heartache she was struggling not to feel. "Jeffrey is dead," she finally said and slammed the truck door.

Hilary glanced over as she turned the key. She could read the shock in his expression. For a moment, it was tempting to stay a minute longer and offer some kind of explanation. Maybe it would take away the obvious question in his countenance. But the mist that rose into his bright blue eyes was more than she could bear. If she stayed even another second, she'd end up crying herself, and she just couldn't take any more tears.

Hilary pulled out of the station, wishing with everything inside that she could just get out of this town, where reminders of her brother's absence assaulted her every time she turned around. The weeks remaining until she began another semester at BYU seemed like forever. But she had little choice; she'd have to endure them.

* * * * *

Jack Hayden stood where he was for a full minute after the old blue truck drove away. He finally forced himself to the moment and blinked back the emotion. *He couldn't believe it.* He and Jeff certainly hadn't been best friends, but Jeff was one of the few people who had taken him into the social circles and befriended him when he'd moved here from Texas at the impressionable age of thirteen. Jeff was just one of those people everybody loved to be around; he'd been fun and full of life. But he'd also had a spirit that radiated his beliefs, even at an age when most young men were more concerned with adventure and being cool. In fact, it was Jeff's testimony of the gospel, and his desire to serve a mission, that had helped keep Jack on the right path when the rest of his family was completely inactive.

Jack forced himself back to work when an older woman pulled into the station to get gas. He greeted her with a smile and unconsciously gnawed at the toothpick in his mouth as he helped her. But his mind was still trying to adjust to the shock. He wondered why he hadn't heard about the death before now. Of course, he'd not been home long; and in spite of living in a small town, his parents just didn't move in the same social circles that he did. They weren't much for writing letters, either.

The last time Jack saw Jeffrey Smith had been at his home following his mission farewell. Four months later, Jack had left on his own mission. And now, he wondered what had happened. By the end of the day, as he left the station and drove toward home, he had concluded that there was only one way to find out. And with any luck, he'd get a glimpse of Hilary Smith in the process.

* * * * *

Hilary was helping her mother put supper on the table while her father washed up at the kitchen sink. "I put gas in the truck," Hilary told him.

"Good. Thank you," Pete said. "Did ya check th' oil?"

"Yes, Dad. I checked the oil."

After the blessing had been said, Millie asked, "Have you found a ride to Provo yet? For school, I mean."

"I know what you mean, Mom. And, no, I haven't."

"Of course, we can take you up if we need to. It's just such a busy time, and we need the truck on the farm, and—"

"I know, Mom. I'll figure something out."

"What about Marla?" Millie pressed.

"Marla's going to Dixie College this year, Mom. It's the other direction."

"Well, isn't Janie—"

"Janie's going to Snow College so she can live at home."

"Now, there's an idea," Pete said, and Hilary forced herself to remain silent. They'd had this conversation a hundred times. Hilary was the youngest; the only one left at home since Jeffrey's death. And her parents wanted her company as much as her help. But she'd completed a full year at BYU, and she was already registered to continue. Not to mention the fact that she just couldn't stay here. But that was difficult for her parents to understand.

Hilary ignored her father's comment, grateful when her mother continued. "How about Lisa? Is she—"

"Lisa's getting married, Mother."

"Oh, that's right. Mildred says he's a fine young man. But they'll be living in Logan. It's too bad she couldn't have married someone from around here, so they could stay close to home."

Again Hilary bit her tongue. In her opinion, there was *nothing* worthwhile around here anymore—beyond her parents. Not since Jeffrey had . . .

A knock at the door brought Millie to her feet. "I wonder who that could be. The home teachers aren't supposed to be here for another hour or so."

Jack forced his nerves back and smiled as Mrs. Smith opened the door. For the last hour and a half, he had tried to come up with appropriate conversation ideas. What did you say to someone who had lost a son and a brother? Would his visit be appreciated, or would it only be a difficult reminder of Jeffrey's absence? Jack had finally given up on any prepared dialogue, and prayed instead. His heart was pounding painfully as he approached the big, old farmhouse and knocked at the door. But the glimmer of recognition in Millie Smith's eyes helped immediately.

"Remember me?" he asked.

"Well, of course I do." Millie beamed and opened the door wide, motioning him in. "Jack, isn't it?"

"That's right," he said as she closed the door. "I . . . uh . . . just wanted to stop by and see how you're doing."

"Well, come in. Come in."

Pete Smith appeared in the doorway to see who their visitor was. "Look who's here, Peter," Millie said. "It's Jeffrey's friend, Jack."

"Well, hello, young man." Pete smiled and offered a firm handshake, which eased Jack's nerves considerably. "We're just sittin' down to supper. You'd better come and have some, too."

"Oh, no, thank you." Jack put up a hand. "I didn't intend to intrude on you at mealtime. I can come back and—"

"Nonsense," Millie insisted. "You're not intruding. Come sit at the table with us, and we'll visit."

Pete took hold of Jack's arm and urged him firmly into the dining room.

"Have you eaten?" Millie asked.

"Well, no . . . but . . ."

"Then you timed it just right," she added, opening a cupboard to pull out an extra plate.

Jack's nerves escalated again as his eyes connected with Hilary's. There she sat, even more stone-faced than she'd been earlier at the station. She wasn't the lighthearted little teenager he remembered from two years ago. She'd matured into a beautiful young woman. Of course, he'd always thought she was beautiful. Even as a child, Hilary Smith had been someone he'd naturally gravitated toward. She'd been vibrant, happy, and full of life—not unlike her brother. Of course, Hilary had lost her brother, and Jack could well understand how difficult that must be. But there was a hard, cold look in her eyes that was absent in her parents' demeanor. Was her pain deeper than theirs?

"You remember Hilary?" Millie motioned toward her daughter as she set a plate on the table.

"Yes, of course," Jack said, showing Hilary a little smile. He added more intensely, "You really don't have to feed me. I just wanted to—"

"Now, I won't hear another word," Millie insisted. "It's a pleasure to have one of Jeffrey's friends with us."

Jack smiled at Millie, but a quick glance at Hilary made it evident she didn't agree.

"We've already blessed it," Pete said, passing the meatloaf to Jack. "So, dig in."

"Thank you," Jack said. "It looks delicious."

Millie bustled around a few minutes, making certain Jack had everything he needed to enjoy his meal. Then she sat down to eat. Jack was wondering how to make conversation when Pete said, "I guess you heard about Jeffrey."

Jack cleared his throat and glanced briefly at Hilary. "Just today," he said. "I . . . still can't quite believe it." He feared the subject would create tension, but only Hilary appeared to be affected.

"We can't quite believe it ourselves." Millie's voice picked up a sad lilt, although she was quick to add, "We miss him terribly, but there's great peace in knowing that we'll be with him again."

"Yes," Jack said. "I can't imagine having to deal with death and not having the gospel."

Pete and Millie exchanged a serene glance. Hilary just stared at her mashed potatoes while she gently mutilated them with her fork.

Jack hated to ask, but he had to know. "Forgive me," he began, "but . . . I can't help wondering . . . how . . ."

"My goodness," Millie said, not seeming the least bit upset. "I would think you'd have heard. It happened just two months after he got home from his mission. He was—"

"Excuse me," Hilary said as she stood abruptly and left the room.

"Hilary's havin' a rough time of it," Pete said gently.

"I can see that," Jack said. "I'm sorry if—"

"Oh, don't you worry about it," Millie said. "She'll come to terms with it in time."

"You seem to have come to terms with it," Jack said.

As if to contradict his statement, tears rose in Millie's eyes. But she just dabbed at them with her napkin and said, "Oh, don't think we aren't aching to have him with us. An hour doesn't pass without our thinking of him, and wishing . . . But, well . . . we know it was his time to go."

"There must be great peace in that," Jack said.

"There is, all right," Pete added. Then to his wife, "Tell him what happened, Millicent."

"Well, old Bill Jones was . . . you remember Bill?"

Jack nodded.

"Well, he had his first hay cutting down when he had an emergency surgery. It was his gall bladder, I believe. But anyway, they asked for help from the elders quorum to get his hay up and baled. Of course, you know Jeffrey. He was the first to volunteer." Millie dabbed at tears again. Pete took her hand across the table. "The details aren't important, really. He wasn't alone, at least. There were three or four of them out there, working together, stacking the hay on the wagon as soon as it was baled, and . . . well, something went wrong with the baler, and Jeffrey was trying to fix it. He was always so good with the equipment, you know."

Jack nodded again, fighting the lump in his throat.

While Millie quietly blew her nose, Pete added, "Jeffrey always said that most farm accidents were just plain stupidity. That's one of many things that makes me believe it was meant to be. No one can quite explain what went wrong." Pete sighed. "But he went helpin' somebody in need. That's the way it should be, I think."

"Amen," Jack croaked.

Following a moment of intense silence, Pete stood from the table. "I'll let Hilary know we're changin' the subject."

Pete and Hilary returned to the table a few minutes later. Jack knew that Hilary didn't want to talk about her brother, but he felt like he had to say something that she and her parents should know.

"I'm sorry," he said more to Hilary. "I didn't mean to ruin your supper. But I want you to know . . . all of you . . . that Jeff had a profound influence on my life." Jack looked down and cleared his throat as tears threatened. He wasn't prone to crying, and at first he felt ashamed. But something warm inside prompted him to realize that these people needed to know that he shared their pain, if only a degree of it.

Jack looked straight at Hilary as the tears streamed down his face. "He was the only kid in seventh grade who didn't tease me about my accent, and he made a point to include me in every activity. He always made it clear that he would do the right thing—even when it wasn't cool. And more than once he kept me on the straight and narrow when it would have been easy to stray." Jack wiped his face with the palm of his hand. "Going on a mission with no support from my family wasn't easy, but Jeff told me at least fifty times that if I did, I'd never regret it." He sniffled and wiped his nose with his napkin. "I must say he was right about that."

Silence descended again until Hilary said, "I thought we were going to change the subject."

Jack caught a quick glance from Hilary's parents, as if they meant to ask for his patience. He just smiled at Hilary and said, "Forgive me, Hilary. Why don't you tell me what *you're* doing these days. If my calculations are correct, you should have graduated from high school over a year ago."

Hilary said nothing. Millie finally spoke on her behalf. "That's right. She graduated with honors, and she went to BYU for a year on a scholarship. She's done very well."

"That's wonderful," Jack said. Then to Millie, "This meatloaf is great. There isn't a whole lot of home cooking at my house, and what I ate on my mission was, well . . . it was interesting." He laughed, then turned to Hilary. "So, what are you majoring in?"

When it became evident that no one else was going to answer, Hilary finally said, "I'm focusing mostly on dance at the moment."

Jack made a noise to indicate that he was impressed. "I didn't realize you had such an interest."

Hilary kept her attention on her meal, wishing Jack Hayden would just go home. It was difficult for her to define the uneasiness provoked by his presence. Maybe it was the way he sat there where Jeffrey used to sit. Maybe it was simply the irony of having one of Jeffrey's friends here, and not Jeffrey. Or maybe she just didn't like him. She knew his type well. Farm born and bred. The land was in his blood, and life began and ended with it. Her father was the same way, as were most of the men she knew around here. And Hilary was just plain tired of it. She hated the lifestyle. She hated the mentality. She hated the way that working the land had killed Jeffrey. And she just wanted to get out of here.

"Hilary," Millie said, "Jack is talking to you."

"I'm sorry," she said, even though she wasn't. "I've always been interested in dance. There just wasn't much opportunity for such things around here. I'm trying to make up for that now."

"What kind of dance?" Jack asked.

"You name it."

"Hilary has taught dance, as well," Pete bragged with a grin. "We peeked in on her once when she had a room full of little teeny girls. It was just the cutest thing."

Jack grinned. "I bet it was." He took a bite of mashed potatoes smothered in butter and added, "So, I assume you're continuing at BYU this fall."

"Yes," she said.

"If she can figure out a way to get there," Millie interjected. Hilary sighed, fighting off the embarrassment. She really didn't appreciate having her dilemmas aired with company at the table. But Jack looked at Millie with interest as she continued. "Of course, Jeffrey was planning to go to BYU this fall, and Hillie was going to ride up and back with him. We had a car that she used last year, and they were going to share it, but . . . well, we had to sell it . . . with the funeral expenses and all."

Hilary sighed again. Now her mother was airing their financial circumstances, too. She wondered how many times she'd told her mother that it wasn't necessary for the entire city of Mt. Pleasant to know that Jeffrey's hospital and funeral expenses—with no insurance—had put them deeply into debt. Hilary had offered to give up her tuition money to help, but her parents had adamantly refused. Still, they'd had to sell the car and a number of other things just to put the debts at a level where they could afford the monthly payments.

"Of course," Millie went on, "we can drive Hillie up ourselves in the truck if we have to. Or rather," she chuckled, "Pete could take her. I don't do well driving that far. It's just such a busy time, and—"

"She could ride up with me," Jack interrupted, and Hilary's head shot up. He just grinned at her and added, "I'll be going to BYU myself this fall."

"I don't know if . . ." Hilary began, trying to think of some appropriate protest. But nothing came.

"Don't think a thing of it," Jack insisted. "It would be a pleasure." Then he pulled a toothpick out of his shirt pocket and stuck it neatly into the corner of his lips, leaning back in his chair as if he'd just been awarded some great prize.

"Oh, that would be perfect," Millie declared. She sighed loudly. "That takes a big worry off my mind."

Hilary hadn't realized it was such an enormous issue, but she would far rather have her father take a few hours out of his day to go to Provo and back, than to have to ride with Jack Hayden *anywhere*.

"Would you like some more meatloaf?" Millie asked Jack.

He held up a hand. "No, thank you. It was great."

Hilary helped clear the table, but she managed to escape the room when Jack insisted on helping with the dishes. Millie and Pete talked and laughed with him as if . . . Hilary didn't even want to think it. But it was true . . . as if he were their own son. Was that why they were so glad to have him here? The thought disgusted her, and she kept to her room until the home teachers came and Millie hollered up the stairs for her to join them. She was dismayed to realize that Jack was still there, leaning back in a corner of the couch as if he were in his own home. And everyone seemed to be enjoying his company— except her. He was drilled with questions about his mission, while Hilary kept thinking of Jeffrey. She finally excused herself and escaped out the back door.

Needing something to keep her busy, Hilary went out to the garden, enjoying the slight evening breeze as she knelt to pull weeds. After half an hour of vigorous work, she almost had Jack Hayden out of her system. Then she looked up to see him standing just on the other side of the squash plants, his hands in the back pockets of his jeans, pushing the toe of his cowboy boot back and forth in the dirt. The toothpick in his mouth was practically in shreds.

"Can I help?" he asked.

"No," she replied, quite serious. But he laughed.

"I get the impression you don't like me," he said, bending over to pull some weeds.

"At least you're perceptive," she retorted.

"Do you want to tell me why?" he asked.

"No," she said again.

"Will you anyway?"

"Are you always this way?"

"What way?"

"Pushy and obnoxious."

Jack laughed again. "Am I? I always thought of it more as straight-forward and witty."

Hilary gave him a glare of disgust. Jack sobered his expression and asked, "Are *you* always this way?"

"What way?"

"Cold and arrogant."

Hilary's glare deepened. She attempted to stare him down, but he won and she looked away, concentrating on her work. "Listen," she finally said, just hoping to get this encounter over with so he would go home. "All I remember of you is your incessant teasing. You were always calling me ridiculous names like . . . like . . ."

"Hilarious," he provided.

"Yes, and . . . you'd pull my hair, and hide my toys, and—"

"I get the point," he interrupted with a chuckle. "I have matured some since then, or hadn't you noticed?" Hilary observed the way his T-shirt stretched over his shoulder muscles, and the obvious stubble on his face. But she said nothing, so he added, "You know what they say about boys who pull girls' pigtails, don't you?"

"No, what?"

Jack laughed. "You need to get out more, Hilary. I thought everybody knew the pigtail theory."

"Sorry, I missed that one."

"Well, maybe you'll figure it out one of these days."

Hilary's disgust increased when she realized he wasn't going to tell her. Then she scolded herself inwardly for displaying any curiosity at all.

Jack continued to pull weeds in silence. He blew the shredded toothpick into the pile of weeds, then he began to whistle . . . *Dixie,* no less. After he'd gone through it three times, Hilary demanded, "Don't you know anything else?"

He grinned and started whistling *My Darling Clementine.* She wanted to ask him if he'd been trained in whistling obnoxious tunes in his Texas childhood, or if it was something he'd acquired in Utah. But she kept her mouth shut, even when he went on to a lively rendition of *She'll Be Coming Around the Mountain.* At least the weeds were getting pulled, she thought.

They worked until the sun had gone down and it was difficult to see. Jack helped her gather the weeds into the wheelbarrow before he said, "Well, it looks a mite better."

"A mite," she repeated with subtle sarcasm, resisting the urge to call him a *hick,* the way he used to call her *Hilarious.*

"I'd best be gettin' on home," he drawled, and she could almost swear his accent had thickened since he'd come outside. "I'll see you in the mornin'."

"In the morning?" she squeaked.

"Your daddy said he was haulin' hay, six sharp. I figured I could get a few hours in."

Hilary said nothing, for fear of making a fool of herself. She didn't like him, and she didn't want him around; but spouting off about it wasn't going to do any good. She had to admit she was grateful to know they'd have some help. Her father tired quickly lifting the heavy bales onto the wagon, and she wasn't strong enough to do it. She just wondered if she was strong enough to endure Jack Hayden.

CHAPTER TWO

$\mathcal{T}$he following morning, Hilary had just climbed onto the tractor and started it when Jack Hayden drove up and got out of his truck, pulling leather gloves onto his hands. She recognized the truck as one he'd driven in high school, although it had a new paint job and looked well cared for. He waved and grinned, then pulled off his baseball cap, pushed a hand through his short-cropped hair, and replaced the cap. Hilary waited for her father's signal before she put the tractor in low gear and moved it forward. As she drove it up and down the long rows, Jack and her father hoisted the bales onto the wagon. Then her father got on the wagon and stacked them while Jack threw them up to him. Hilary could vaguely hear them talking and laughing over the dull roar of the tractor engine. She attempted to ignore them while her mind wandered with trivial thoughts.

When the wagon was carrying its limit, Jack jumped onto the hub over the tractor wheel. Hilary ignored him and increased speed to take their load to its destination.

"What is this?" he asked, pulling at the blue bandanna she had tied around her nose and mouth. He laughed. "The tractor-driving bandito?"

"Don't touch that," she warned, readjusting the scarf. "I'm allergic to alfalfa."

Jack laughed so hard she thought he was going to fall off the tractor. "It's not funny!"

"No, I guess it's not, but . . . it's ironic that a woman living on two hundred acres of alfalfa would be *allergic* to it."

"Well, I certainly don't intend to make it my life's profession. So don't get too worried about me, Hayden."

"What time is it?" he asked, touching her arm to look at her watch.

"Don't touch me!" she snapped.

"What?" He lifted both hands high.

"I break out in hives if I get it on my skin, and you've practically been swimming in it."

"Whoa, girl, you should have been born in the city."

"My thoughts exactly."

Hilary managed to evade his attempts at clever conversation until they arrived at the haystack, where Pete was waiting. When the wagon was unloaded, Jack had to leave to get to work on time. Hilary was glad to be free of him for the remainder of the day, but she had to admit that the work went much slower without him, and she was concerned for her father.

The next morning, Jack came again. And early that evening, when Hilary and her father were driving back to the house, they noticed Jack out working in his father's fields. Hilary wondered how many hours a day he was putting in at the gas station, in addition to working on two farms. He came the next day to help again, and Pete invited him to dinner. This began a routine that Hilary wasn't terribly fond of. Jack helped on the farm nearly every day, and ate at their house almost as often. The most popular topic of conversation between Jack and her father was the glory of round balers. The bales were bigger and more efficient, and didn't have to be hauled by hand. They even talked about possibly investing in one together. Hilary wasn't terribly thrilled with the idea of merging business interests with Jack Hayden; but then, school would be starting soon, and for her the farm would be put on a back burner until next summer. And only heaven knew where she might be by then.

On a day when Pete drove to Moroni to take care of some business, Hilary was forced to work alone with Jack. Everything was fine until she parked the wagon at the stack for him to unload it. "Hey, Hilarious," he said as she jumped down from the tractor, "I think you and I need to have a little talk."

Hilary steeled herself to not let him rile her. But she had a feeling this wasn't going to be good as he pulled off his gloves and folded his arms across his chest. "What do you need?" she asked.

"I need to know why you find my company so difficult to swallow. Did I wrong you somewhere? I mean . . . I don't figure how a little teasing warrants such a cold shoulder. If we're going to be working together, I think we could at least be friends, and—"

"We're not *working* together, Jack," she interrupted. "Your little service project is greatly appreciated, but the fields are nearly cleared and summer is just about over. Once you drop me off at my apartment in Provo, I don't expect to see you again for a very long time—which makes this conversation practically irrelevant."

"On the contrary," Jack said coolly, "your dad's asked me to check up on you. He worries about you all alone in the city. Can't say that I blame him, but—"

"I can assure you that I don't need looking after," she snarled. But he only smiled. She realized that one of the things she really disliked about Jack Hayden was the way he never seemed the least bit ruffled. No matter how sassy she got with him, he just smiled and took it. And she hated him for it.

"So, what is it, Hillie?" he asked, sticking to his original purpose. "What is it about me that offends you so deeply?"

"Everything," she snapped.

"Come on, Hil. Don't beat around the bush. Let me have it."

"Okay, I will. You're annoying. You smile when things aren't funny. You whistle stupid songs. And you always have a toothpick or some weed in your mouth." He grinned, and she pointed at him. "See, you're doing it again. You're smiling. There is nothing amusing or pleasant about this."

"That's a matter of opinion. Go on."

"I do not appreciate the farm-town mentality, and you are *reeking* of it."

"Is that the . . . uh, same farm-town mentality of your parents, and forgive me, your brother?"

"I can tolerate it in my family, but I can choose my friends."

"And I take it you wouldn't choose *me,* even if I were the last person capable of conversation on the face of the earth."

"You're perceptive, as always."

"And, I ask again, what is it about me that you find so offensive?"

"Everything. Don't you get it?"

"Apparently not."

"I don't like the way you wear your clothes, the way you live your life. And I hate that pathetic little southern drawl you have that's—"

"Oh, so it's bigotry. Is that the problem?"

"Maybe it is." Hilary turned to leave, but he grabbed her arm to stop her. She looked down at his hand, then into his eyes, with hatred blazing in her expression.

"Well, you know what, Hilary? I don't think you're a bigot. And I don't think you're so stupid that you can't look past *farm-town mentality* and find the true worth in a person. Because that's not the way you were when I left on my mission, and I don't think you've changed so much that—"

"You have no idea who or what I really am, Jack Hayden. I'm not a little girl you can tease and torment anymore. I've grown up."

"You haven't grown up, Hilary. You've grown *old*. Old and hard and cold. And I think there's only one reason you really want to get out of this town—because it's haunted. Because you can't face the fact that Jeffrey is gone, and everywhere you turn his memories are haunting you. And that's why you don't want me around, because it reminds you of something that hurts, and—"

"You could *never* replace my brother," Hilary snapped, hating the way he'd hit so close to the truth. He really was perceptive—one more reason to dislike his company.

"I'm not trying to," he said.

"The hell you aren't," she shouted. "You're doing his job, sitting in his chair, monopolizing his parents with—"

"Is that how you see it? Is that all my effort means to you? What's the truth of it, Hilary? Why do you hate me so much?"

All her defensiveness and anger came to the surface as she shouted, "Because he's dead and you're not!"

Hilary heard the words come back to her and felt warmth rise in her face. She turned her back to him, angry at him for manipulating her feelings into the open like that—and embarrassed at the way she'd fallen for it. She expected him to respond with anger, and she didn't know how to react when he gripped her shoulders and whispered behind her ear, "For your sake, Hilary, I wish it could be the other way around."

Hilary turned to look at him, determined to find some lack of sincerity or sarcasm that could justify her anger. But she saw nothing in his eyes except genuine concern.

"I don't know what you think my motives are, Hilary. But for the record, I just want you to know where I'm coming from. If it hadn't been for Jeffrey Smith, I'd probably be riding around this country on a Harley with a bunch of drug-addicted losers. I'm attempting, in some small way, to repay a very big debt. Jeff died serving his fellow man, and by all I hold dear, I will live doing the same. I can't replace him, but I can share the burden of the work he would have done. And I can fill some empty hours for your parents. But don't get me wrong; it's not completely selfless. I've always loved being in your home, Hilary, because there's a spirit there that simply never existed in my own home. My parents are good people. They're honest, and they did their best to raise me well. But they want nothing to do with the Church, and the atmosphere they create is less than desirable. As I see it, that makes this puzzle fit together very nicely at the moment. Is there a problem with that, Hilary? Would you prefer that I just go away and let your father haul his own hay? Would it be better if I left your parents to get by on *your* wit and bubbling personality?"

The last sentence had a subtle bite of sarcasm—and it only took Hilary a moment to realize she deserved it. She looked at the ground, searching for something to say that could somehow rebuild a bridge she had burned the minute he'd checked the oil in the truck for her.

"Hey, Hil," he said, "all I'm asking is that you tolerate me. I know what you're going through must be tough, and I don't claim to understand it, but . . ."

He seemed at a loss for words, so Hilary forced out a squeaky, "I'm sorry, Jack. I really do appreciate the help you've given us, and it's evident that my parents adore you. I guess I . . . well, I must admit, you remind me of Jeffrey. Not in appearance, really, but . . ." She looked into his eyes as if they might help her explain it. "You're just so much like him."

Jack smiled. "Except he didn't have that horrible southern drawl you loathe."

Hilary gave an embarrassed chuckle. "I guess that really sounded awful. I just . . ."

"It's okay," he said, giving her a quick hug.

Nothing more was said as Jack got busy unloading the wagon, and Hilary left for the house before he was finished. At Pete's insistence,

Jack joined them for dinner that evening. He'd been there for about twenty minutes when he finally asked, "Where's Hilary?"

"Oh, she's not feeling well," Millie explained. "She must have gotten too close to the hay. It always does her in."

"Does her in?" he questioned.

"Well, actually it's that medicine she takes to get rid of the hives. That's what puts her to sleep."

Jack felt suddenly guilt-ridden as he put the pieces together. Since he had hugged her after hauling hay, he felt relatively certain that he was the reason for her hives. He apologized the next day, but she said little. She wasn't belligerent; she was simply indifferent. And he didn't know which was worse.

The remainder of the summer passed quickly, and Hilary was counting down the hours until she could go back to Provo. The only problem was getting there. She kept hoping some alternative transportation would pop up, but it didn't. And her parents were thrilled that Jack would be seeing that their "baby girl got to school safely."

On the morning they were supposed to leave, Jack arrived right on time. He took one look at the luggage and boxes by the door and bellowed, "Whoa, girl, how long are you stayin'?"

"All year," she said with no sign of humor.

Jack just grinned and started carrying her belongings out to his truck. She followed him out with a large suitcase; he took it from her and settled it next to his own luggage. "It's a good thing I got a truck, eh?" he said.

"I wouldn't expect you to drive anything else," she retorted, and he laughed.

Jack waited patiently while Hilary exchanged farewells with her parents. He was touched by their obvious emotion and their reluctance to have their daughter going away. Jack could understand that. Hilary was a little teary when she finally climbed into the truck. He just reminded her to fasten her seat belt, then headed toward the highway while Pete and Millie waved from the front lawn.

After several miles of silence, Jack started asking Hilary questions about where she would be living and working, and which classes she would be taking. She explained briefly that she would be living in an apartment with three other girls, one of whom she knew well and another with whom she was acquainted. She would be working at the same dance studio where she had worked before summer vacation.

"So, you must be quite a dancer, huh?" Jack said.

"It's hard to say," she replied dryly.

He wasn't certain how to take that. "But you enjoy it, right?"

"I used to, but . . ."

"But?" he pressed.

Hilary turned to look at him, reminding herself that he wasn't being pushy or obnoxious, and he knew of her loss. "I don't know. I just . . . don't seem to enjoy much of anything since . . . we lost Jeffrey. At this point, I'm continuing with dance because it's already established. I have a job. I'm already registered. But I'm really not very excited about it."

Jack thought through his response carefully. "If dance is something you love, don't you think Jeffrey would want you to continue loving it?"

Hilary didn't answer, but it gave her something to think about for the next twenty miles.

"Where to?" Jack asked.

Startled from her thoughts, Hilary realized they had just exited the freeway on University Avenue in Provo. She told him the address and he flashed her a brief, nonchalant smile. She concluded that he had a nice smile—if it weren't for the constant presence of that stupid toothpick!

Jack drove Hilary to her apartment and helped her carry all of her belongings up the two flights of stairs. He seemed hesitant to leave after the last box was deposited on the front room floor of her apartment.

"Thank you . . . for everything," she said. "I appreciate it . . . really."

"I'm glad I could help," he insisted. After an awkward moment he added, "Is there anything else I can do, or—"

"No," she said. "Thanks anyway."

"Well, I'll . . ." He backed toward the door. "I'll keep . . . in touch."

Hilary really didn't want to keep in touch. She just smiled and opened the door for him. "Thanks again," she said, and blew out a long sigh when he was finally gone.

Hilary enjoyed settling into her apartment and getting reacquainted with two of her three roommates. Becky and Kim were fun girls, and they had a great deal in common. Lorie, their third roommate, was Kim's younger sister, who was just starting her freshman year. Hilary didn't know Lorie well, but she seemed a little more headstrong and less friendly than her sister. But since Hilary was sharing a bedroom with Becky, she doubted that her path would cross Lorie's often enough to be a problem.

Hilary was so busy the first few weeks of school that she didn't have time to think about the losses in her life. Except on Sundays, when her parents called to see how she was doing. The calls never lasted long, since they had to be careful not to run up the phone bill. But their loneliness was evident, and it tore at Hilary. Of course, if Jeffrey had been away at school, they would still be lonely. But it just wasn't the same.

Long after she had hung up from talking to her parents on a particularly difficult Sunday afternoon, Hilary lay on her bed, staring out the window. Her roommates had all gone to the missionary farewell of a friend Hilary wasn't acquainted with. A pleasant breeze rustled the leaves of a tall tree and teased at the curtains. Hilary closed her eyes, reminded of home. How could she ever forget the lazy afternoons in her bedroom, when autumn breezes would rummage through the branches of the huge oak that loomed outside her bedroom window? Every once in a while, Jeffrey would climb up the tree and throw pebbles at her window until she'd snarl at him and he'd slide down the trunk, laughing and . . .

"Oh, help," Hilary muttered and sat up abruptly, searching her room for something to occupy her mind. *Anything* to keep her from thinking of Jeffrey. She was rummaging through a stack of Becky's magazines when the doorbell rang. She was tempted to ignore it, since the visitor was likely one of Lorie's many male admirers. Hilary couldn't recall having anyone come to see *her* since she'd come to Provo.

A minute after the ringing of the doorbell, there was an irritating knock at the door. Hilary resigned herself to answering it, if only to be left in peace.

"Jack!" she blurted out, wishing she hadn't sounded so enthusiastic.

He smiled widely and flipped a toothpick into the corner of his mouth. "Well, if you ain't sunshine personified," he said in a drawl much thicker than she'd remembered.

"What are you doing here?" she asked.

"I was just seein' if you were okay," he stated. When she didn't respond he added, "Can I come in, or—"

"Oh, sure." She motioned him inside, unable to deny that she was glad to see him.

Their conversation was stilted and dry, but rather than feeling annoyed by the way he reminded her of Jeffrey, she found some comfort in it. Jack Hayden wasn't really her type, but she had to admit he was a nice guy; and she was grateful for his company, if only to distract her from depressing thoughts.

He stayed nearly an hour, then insisted he had to go. "But hey," he took hold of the doorknob, "would you like to go get something to eat with me . . . sometime this week?"

Hilary was caught off guard and said nothing for a full minute. She finally responded to his expectant gaze with a strained chuckle. "I really appreciate your checking on me, Jack. You've been really sweet, but . . ."

"But?" he pressed.

Hilary glanced at the floor and cleared her throat much louder than she'd intended. "It's just that . . ."

"You have a boyfriend?" he asked with a subtle edge to his voice, and very little evidence of any accent.

"No, of course not." She laughed at the absurdity. Was he blind?

"Well, then . . ."

"Jack, it's just that . . ."

"You already said that. If you don't want to go out with me, just say so. It's only something to eat."

"I'm just . . . not dating, Jack. I'm just . . . not interested in . . . well . . . anything *romantic* . . . right now."

"It's just something to eat, Hil."

Hilary watched his eyes a moment before asking, "Nothing romantic?"

"Nah," he said easily, "just a burger or something."

"Okay," she agreed, somewhat reluctantly. "That sounds nice. But I work every evening except Friday."

"Okay, we'll make it Friday. How about six, then?"

"That sounds great."

The week went quickly for Hilary. School during the days, teaching dance in the evenings, and studying every minute in between. She didn't give Jack Hayden another thought, and would have forgotten about their date if he hadn't called Thursday evening to confirm it.

"Did my dad put you up to this?" she asked before he could hang up the phone.

"What?" He was obviously baffled.

"That's why you're taking me out, right? Because my dad wanted you to—"

"Hilary, Hilary," he said with a drawl that grated her nerves. "Your dad asked me to check up on you, but I could certainly do that without buying you a hamburger. Is there a problem?"

"No, of course not," she insisted. "Just remember it's not—"

"Romantic. Yes, I know. I'll see you tomorrow."

Hilary got home a little before five on Friday. As always, Lorie was getting ready for a date. Some guy she'd just met last week was taking her to a concert, and she made a point of letting Hilary know that the tickets had cost nearly thirty dollars apiece. Kim and Becky were going to a movie together, and they invited Hilary to go along.

"No, thanks," she said. "I've got other plans."

"Like what?" Lorie asked with a giggle that Hilary found annoying. "Are you going to wash your hair, or splurge and rent a video?"

Hilary turned to look at Lorie's seemingly innocent expression and resisted the urge to slap her. What was Lorie implying? That she had no life? That she was too homely to get a date? "Actually, no," she stated in a calm voice.

"Come with us," Becky urged. "It'll be fun."

Hilary couldn't define her reasons for not wanting to spend the evening with Becky and Kim. She was grateful to be able to say, "Thanks, but . . . I've got a date."

They all looked so surprised that Hilary wondered what kind of unspoken messages she had been giving these girls she lived with.

"That's great!" Becky said with far too much enthusiasm.

"Where did you meet him?" Kim asked.

"He was a friend of my brother's."

"Oooh," Lorie said, "the boy next door."

"We're just friends," Hilary insisted and escaped to the bathroom to shower.

At three minutes to six, the doorbell rang. Hilary was just smoothing her hair into a long pony-tail and was glad to hear someone else answering the door. When she entered the little front room, Lorie was telling Jack something about herself with great animation. Becky leaned toward Hilary and whispered, "He's adorable. Just friends, huh?"

"Yes," Hilary said firmly. Jack looked her way, apparently relieved at being rescued from Lorie's monologue. He smiled, and Hilary had to admit that Becky was right. He really was adorable. As much as she disliked western boots and jeans, Jack Hayden had a way of wearing them that certainly did them justice. He wore a white, collarless button-up shirt, a stark contrast to his tan face and hands. But even as good as he looked, Hilary knew she could never feel anything romantic for Jack Hayden. He simply wasn't her type.

The evening actually turned out to be enjoyable. They ate and played a round of miniature golf, talking and laughing as if they'd known each other forever. Hilary reasoned on the way home that they *had* known each other since she was a little girl.

At the door Hilary turned to Jack, saying with genuine warmth, "Thank you. It was really nice to get out."

He grinned and shifted the toothpick between his lips. "It was nice for me, too." As Hilary turned the doorknob he added, "You have my phone number. Be sure and call me if you need anything. Okay?"

Hilary nodded. "Thanks, Jack."

"I'll be going home next weekend. If you want a ride, let me know."

"I might do that. Thanks again."

Hilary slept better that night than she had in a long time, and she had to admit being grateful for Jack's friendship.

On Tuesday morning, Hilary overslept and missed the bus that would get her to classes on time. Her roommates were already gone, so impulsively she dialed Jack's number. She caught him on his way out, and he eagerly came by to give her a ride. In an attempt to express her gratitude, she took him a plate of homemade peanut butter cookies Wednesday evening. A guy she'd never seen before answered the door and left her standing in the untidy front room while he went to get Jack. He appeared wearing slacks and a white shirt and tie, so obviously pleased to see her that she almost felt embarrassed.

"Hi!" He grinned, motioning toward the old sofa. It was the first time she'd seen him without a weed or a toothpick between his lips. "What brings you here?"

"Oh, I can't stay." She pushed the plate of cookies toward him. "I just wanted to thank you for the ride yesterday morning." She laughed softly. "You saved me."

"Well, it was no problem, but . . ." He sniffed the cookies dramatically. "Thank you. This is great."

A brief silence intensified her embarrassment. "So, where are you off to?"

He glanced down at himself as if he'd forgotten. "Oh, just going home teaching."

"Well, I won't keep you," she said, opening the door.

"Call me anytime you need a ride . . . or anything else," he insisted. "And you don't have to bring me cookies."

"Thanks. You're sweet." Hilary started out the door, then turned back. "Oh, are you still going home this weekend?"

"Yeah. I need to help my dad on Saturday."

"Could I go along then? I need to spend some time with my parents."

"I'd love the company," he said. "I'm leaving Friday night about six. Will that be all right?"

"Fine. I'll see you then."

When Friday arrived, Hilary found she wasn't dreading the journey at all, unlike her initial trip to Provo with Jack. They chatted casually, and he carried her overnight bag into the house when they arrived. After her parents greeted her with an embrace, they did the same to Jack.

"Are you hungry?" Millie asked right off.

"Nah," Jack said, "I ate before I left."

"Well, I've made some chocolate cake. Surely you can find room for that."

Jack grinned and flipped that toothpick with his tongue. "You don't have to beg me to eat your chocolate cake, Millie."

While Millie was getting Jack a piece of cake, Hilary stepped outside with her father, admiring his pumpkin patch while they chatted about insignificant things, absorbing the multi-colored leaves of the trees surrounding the house, inhaling the coziness of home.

She had to admit that it was good to be here, as long as she knew she could leave again on Sunday.

When Hilary went back into the house, her mother was laughing over something Jack had told her. Turning to her daughter, she said, "Oh, Hilary, I just got an invitation for the two of us to go to a wedding shower. But it's next Saturday afternoon. You wouldn't be able to come home two weekends in a row, would you?"

"Sure she can," Jack piped in with his mouth full of cake.

Hilary scowled at him, and he chuckled. "Who's it for, Mother?"

"Why, it's for that sweet little thing who's marrying Leon. I believe her name is—"

"Sunny," Hilary snarled. She bit back a sudden rush of anger. She couldn't believe her mother would be so insensitive as to think she would actually go to *Sunny's* wedding shower. And if Jack hadn't been in the room, she would have told her so. Instead she simply stated, "I can't come home next weekend, Mother."

"I'd be happy to give you a ride," Jack insisted.

Hilary glared at him and repeated, "I can't come home next weekend." Then she went to her room, forcing thoughts of it out of her mind for fear of ruining her entire weekend.

For the most part, Hilary enjoyed Saturday. She helped her father in the yard, and her mother with some extra cleaning. As long as she kept busy, she didn't think too much about Jeffrey's absence—or Leon's. But when she went downtown on a few errands for her mother, the memories assaulted her. She choked out a few tears on the way home, then forced herself to appear happy before going inside the house.

On Sunday, Hilary went to church with her parents, then helped prepare dinner. At her parents' insistence, Jack came to eat with them before they started back to Provo. He helped wash up the dishes, and they were on their way by late afternoon.

"You okay?" Jack asked after they'd traveled the first thirty miles in silence.

"Sure, why?"

Jack glanced at her then back to the road. "It's hard for you to go home, isn't it?"

While Hilary was trying to digest the accuracy of his perception, she noticed that at times his accent was almost nonexistent.

When she said nothing, he added, "Come on, Hil, I thought we'd become friends. I'm not trying to be obnoxious. I'm just concerned, that's all."

"Yes," she admitted, "it's tough."

"You miss Jeffrey," he said with certainty.

"Yes." Hilary looked out the window and forced back a rise of emotion.

"And Leon?" he guessed.

Hilary snapped her head around to glare at him.

"Ooh," he chuckled, "that hit a nerve."

Hilary reminded herself not to say something stupid and make a fool of herself. "I refuse to discuss this with you."

"Why?" He turned his toothpick over to chew on the other end. "Is there something wrong with admitting that he hurt you? He's a jackass, if you ask me, and—"

"I didn't ask you."

"Well, I'm telling you anyway." He turned his attention away from the road just long enough to say, "You deserve better, Hilary." The intensity in his eyes gave her a sudden chill as he turned back to look at the road, saying in a softer voice, "But I know that doesn't take away the fact that he hurt you."

"What makes you so sure he hurt me?"

"I'd swear, girl, you think that because I'm a farm boy I'm stupid or something? You think I can't see what happens in your eyes when anything comes up about him—or . . . what's her name? *Sunny?* Whoa. You need to get out more."

"What's that supposed to mean?" she retorted.

"If you're pining over a man like Leon Phillips, then I'd say you've got a pretty narrow perspective on life."

"I am not pining over Leon. I'm just—"

"Bull-pucky! Have you ever dated anyone—*anyone*—besides Leon Phillips?"

It was tempting to get defensive. But Hilary just blew out a long breath and forced herself to admit, "I went out with you last week."

Jack snorted in disbelief and shook his head. "Like I said, you need to get out more."

"Well, maybe I do," Hilary said, her eyes focused on the stretches of farmland passing by the truck window. "But I'm not sure I know where to start. I can see now that I made a mistake. I should have dated more. But I didn't. And the fact is, I centered my whole life on him—and he dumped me. And then when Jeffrey . . ." Emotion prevented her from continuing.

Jack took her hand and squeezed it. "Hey, you got every right in the world to miss your brother. But Jeffrey would want you to get past that Leon creep and get on with your life."

Hilary said nothing. She knew he was right, but she also knew it was easier said than done.

CHAPTER THREE

$\mathcal{J}$ack said nothing for several minutes, and Hilary was hoping the subject had been dropped. "Can I ask you something?" he said with a thoughtful drawl, dashing her hopes.

"Sure," she said, wondering if she could take it.

"What's the real reason you don't want to go to that shower? Is it hurt? Jealousy? What?"

Hilary glared at him again, but he only said, "I'm just trying to help!"

"Well, maybe I don't need any help."

"I assume, then, that you are perfectly content to spend the rest of your life teaching dance lessons and avoiding life in general."

Her scowl deepened but she said nothing. Jack knew he was on the right track, and at the risk of alienating her eternally, he intended to keep on pushing.

"Just answer the question, girl. Why don't you want to go to the party? I mean . . . it's not such a big deal, is it? The bride-to-be opens a few silly, useless presents, then everybody eats little frosted cakes and pink punch, right? So why don't you want to go?"

Hilary sighed and resigned herself to having this conversation. Perhaps it really would do her some good to talk about it. "Maybe it's a little bit of everything."

"You're hurt."

"Yes. I have to admit it. Maybe it wouldn't have been so bad if he'd let me down easy. But . . . I really thought we were going to get married. And then . . . poof! Sunny shows up in his life, and I'm history. He basically told me I'm not his type and—"

"His *type?*" Jack questioned, lifting his brows comically. "Oh, you mean arrogant and cocky? Is that what you mean?"

Hilary might have bristled at the remark, but instead she was overcome with chills. Jeffrey had used those exact words to describe Leon just a few days before he died. She turned to Jack and asked, "Do you really think so?"

"Yes, ma'am," he drawled with a little smirk. "In fact, everybody I know, who knows him, would probably agree with me. Everyone but you, that is."

Hilary sighed. "Maybe love is blind."

"Maybe so, but hey . . . you're tough. You're adorable. You can get over it."

Again Hilary was astonished. She didn't even think before she blurted out, "Maybe *you're* blind."

"What's that supposed to mean?"

"Have you taken a good look at me lately?"

Jack smirked again. "Actually, I have."

"And?"

"And what?"

Hilary stopped a moment to realize where this conversation had come, and she felt momentarily embarrassed. "Never mind," she insisted.

"No, I'm not going to never mind. What?"

Hilary turned to the window, feeling her cheeks burn.

"Oh, I get it," he said. "Since Leon dumped you, you just figure there's no point in trying anymore. I get the impression you don't give a hill of beans about the way you look, and that's why you don't want to go to the party."

Without looking at him, Hilary snapped, "You don't know what you're talking about."

"Don't I? Well, maybe not. But I'll tell you what I do know. You are not the girl I knew before I left on my mission. And I can only see one reason for it: you don't care. There is no woman on the face of the earth who can't look and feel beautiful with whatever God gave her. Now personally, I don't care how you look. If you blimped out to two hundred pounds, I'd still think you were cute. But I care how you feel about yourself. And I'm no psychologist, but I believe the way people feel about themselves shows in their face. It's that simple. So if I were you, I'd—"

"You know what, Jack," Hilary interrupted tersely, "you're not me. And you have no idea what's going on in my head. So why don't you just leave me alone?"

"Because I'm not going to stand back and watch you ruin yourself over some imbecile who didn't deserve you to begin with. If you—"

"And what makes you think this is just about Leon? I lost my brother, Jack, and I'm not sure there's anything left in this world worth caring about."

"You think that's what Jeffrey would want? You're fooling yourself, Hilary, if you think you can somehow stop living and become a martyr to his death. And if he were here, he'd be saying exactly what I'm saying. So you can hate me if you want to, Hilary Smith, but I'm going to say it anyway. The best thing you could do with your life right now is to start caring. And I think you'd feel a whole lot better about yourself if you just march into that party, or shower, or whatever they call it, and let old what's-her-name know that you don't give a flying flip about Leon!"

Hilary made absolutely no response. In fact, nothing more was said through the rest of the trip. Jack had no idea if she was hurt by what he'd said, or just plain angry. When he pulled up in front of her apartment, she grabbed her bag and got out, saying tersely, "Thanks for the ride."

Jack winced when she slammed the door, then he watched her walk toward her apartment, praying silently that she would grasp even a little bit of what he'd said. It was simply a shame for someone as adorable and talented as Hilary Smith to stop living in the prime of her life.

* * * * *

Hilary walked in the door to find Lorie peering between the blinds. "Ooh, was that Jack?"

"Yes, why?"

Lorie turned as the truck drove away and took a long look at Hilary's overnight bag. Then she grinned. "You spent the weekend with Jack?"

Hilary was so appalled by the insinuation that it took her a moment to respond. "No, I did not. I've told you before, we come from the same town. He gave me a ride home for the weekend."

"And that's all?" Lorie looked as if she might die if she didn't get some juicy piece of gossip to share with their other roommates. It wasn't the first time she had said things that made Hilary wonder what kind of morals this girl had—or rather, didn't have.

"I told you," Hilary managed to say in a steady voice, "we're just friends."

"Well, in that case," Lorie plopped down on the couch and pushed a hand through her short, dark hair, "maybe you could line us up. He's adorable."

Hilary sighed with disgust. "I don't do matchmaking. You're on your own." She hurried off to her room before the conversation could go any further.

That night, Hilary slept little as Jack's speech kept bouncing around in her mind like a self-propelled ping-pong ball. He was right, and she knew it. And it made her *angry*. She got up somewhere around three in the morning, went into the bathroom, and stared at herself in the mirror. She'd always considered herself pretty—at least until Leon had brushed her aside. Since then, she'd become obsessed with a nose that was too thin, lips that were not symmetrical, and eyes that couldn't decide if they were blue or green. Her hair was bone-straight and stubborn, and she'd indulged in far too many foods that contributed nothing to her health—and a great deal to her hips. And standing here in worn-out pajamas in the middle of the night didn't do much for her self-worth.

Hilary went back to bed and forced herself not to think about it. She dragged through school and dance classes the following day, and she'd barely come home when her mother called, wondering if there was any way she could come to the shower. Hilary felt irritated, knowing her mother's biggest motive was to socialize, and she wasn't terribly fussy about who she might socialize with. Still, there was something genuine in the way Millie said, "I know it's hard, Hilary, but I do think it would be good for you."

She wondered for a moment if, in spite of her mother's sheltered life, she somehow understood something Hilary didn't. Could it possibly be the same thing Jack had lectured her about? "Maybe it would," she admitted. "I'll see what I can do," she added noncommittally, but Millie seemed elated at the thought.

Hilary sat down on the edge of her bed, absently watching Becky rummage through her dresser drawers in search of something. She'd always liked her roommate, and they'd had a lot of fun together. At the moment, she longed to spill all that was troubling her, but she just couldn't bring herself to do it. Becky was a cute girl, but she always had a good supply of junk food kicking around, and as a result, she continued to slowly put on weight. She never wore makeup, and her hair was short-cropped and straight, requiring no effort beyond keeping it clean. Becky and Kim often joked about their lack of dating opportunities, as if there simply wasn't a man out there worth going out with. But Hilary could easily see the truth. They both wanted to date as much as any single woman, but neither of them seemed to grasp the connection between their lack of available suitors and their lack of attention to their appearance.

And then there was Lorie, who certainly *did* care about her appearance—which was one of many things that made her a stark contrast to her sister, Kim. The problem was that Lorie cared about nothing *but* her appearance. It seemed that her entire life was centered around conquering men's hearts and using them at will. Hilary could no more relate to Lorie as a friend than she could fly to the moon.

As Becky left the room, Hilary lowered her head into her hands and resisted the urge to cry. She needed a good, firm shoulder to lean on—someone who would give her a listening ear and some sound advice. What she needed right now was a *true* friend. Ironically, the first person who came to mind was Jack. She had to admit that they had become friends—sort of. But he'd already told her what *he* thought. And he was a man, for crying out loud.

"Oh, garbage," she muttered under her breath. Then, like firelight appearing in the midst of a bitter cold night, Hilary realized she *did* have such a friend. "Janna," she murmured and hurried to flip through her planner in search of the phone number.

When Hilary and Janna had first met, Leon had been on his mission, and Janna had been struggling through some incredible challenges. Hilary had done little beyond just being there for her, but she recalled now that it had been Janna who appeared at Jeffrey's funeral, when not one of her college or high school friends had bothered to attend.

"Oh, please be home," Hilary prayed aloud as she punched in the number and listened to it ringing on the other end. Just as a male voice answered, she recalled that it was Monday evening, and Janna was likely involved with her family.

"Hello," she said. "Is Janna there?"

"Just a minute, and I'll—"

"If this is a bad time, I can call back," Hilary hurried to add.

"Oh, no, she's right here."

Hilary felt terribly nervous as Janna said, "Hello."

"Hi," Hilary said quickly, "this is Hilary, and—"

"Hilary!" Janna's obvious delight put her at ease. "It's so good to hear from you."

"I just realized it's Monday. I hope I didn't interrupt your family night, or—"

"Oh, no," Janna insisted, "we finished early so Matthew could work on a school project. What's up?"

"Well . . . I must confess, I need a friend." Hilary wasn't prepared for the emotion that bubbled out as she said it.

"What's wrong?" She could hear Janna's concern. "Are you—"

"Oh, it's nothing that serious. I just . . . well, do you think we could talk?"

"Sure. Hold on just a second."

Hilary could hear muffled conversation on the other end of the phone, as if Janna had put her hand over the mouthpiece. She came back on and said, "Colin said he wouldn't mind putting the kids to bed. How about if I come by and pick you up?"

"Oh, that would be great." Hilary knew her enthusiasm was readily apparent, but she had no reason to be pretentious with Janna. Twenty minutes later, she heard a horn honking outside. She grabbed a sweater and hurried out, climbing into the little convertible Janna was driving. Janna laughed and hugged her before she even had a chance to buckle her seat belt.

"It's so good to see you," Janna said with an eagerness that made Hilary feel better already.

"So, what are you up to these days?" Hilary began as Janna drove.

"Well, I'm glad you asked," Janna said, "because I've gone back to school—and I'm loving it."

"That's great. What are you majoring in?"

"That's the interesting part, I guess. I never would have believed in a million years that I would do something like this, but . . . well . . ."

"Go on," Hilary prodded.

"Nursing," she provided. "I want to be an LPN."

"Really?" Hilary couldn't help being surprised. "Forgive my asking, but . . . why? I mean, Colin's a successful lawyer. He makes good money. So you obviously don't need a second income."

"Well, no . . . not right now, at least. I mean, you never know when something might happen to change your life. Colin's got a really good life insurance policy, so if he were to die, we'd be fine. But if he became disabled or something, I might need to work to support the family, and it's good to have something to fall back on. But actually, my initial reasons for doing it had nothing to do with that."

"Tell me," Hilary said, already enjoying a level of conversation that she'd not shared with a friend since . . . well, since the last time she'd been with Janna.

Janna parked the car next to a fast-food place where they had often gone together in the past. "Are you hungry?"

"Actually, yes," Hilary said, realizing she'd not eaten since lunch.

"Well, I had dinner with the family, but I can always tolerate a chocolate malt." When they were inside, Janna added, "Have whatever you like. It's on me."

"Oh, you don't have to—"

"I know, but I want to. I know what it's like to be struggling, and I can afford it, okay?"

"Okay. And thank you."

After they had ordered and found a booth in a quiet corner, Hilary returned to their conversation. "So tell me what prompted you to get into this nursing thing."

"Well, not long after Colin and I got back together, I was called as a counselor in the Relief Society presidency."

"Wow. That must be a challenge."

"Yes, but I really do enjoy it. The thing is, we have so many sisters in our ward who have medical needs. It's amazing. There are a couple of diabetics, a woman with MS, and another who is paralyzed. We also have quite a few elderly women, and they have a variety of health problems. It seemed that two or three times a week I was called upon to help with something, and I was continually getting frustrated because of the trouble we'd have just getting a simple question answered, or having a simple medical procedure done. A couple of times I thought, 'if I had the skill to do this, it would save so much trouble.' Then one night, after I said my prayers, I just had this over-whelming feeling that I should pursue a degree in nursing. I'd been thinking about going back to school anyway, but the more I thought about it, the more I knew this was right for me."

"And what did Colin think?"

"Oh, he thinks it's great. He's been very supportive. It's been a challenge to rearrange our schedules to be with the kids, but we're managing, and I really believe it will be worth it."

"That's great," Hilary said, loving the enthusiasm and positive atti-tude she was gleaning from Janna just by being in her presence. She found it an interesting contrast to the way Janna had been when they'd first met. She'd been recovering from an emotional breakdown at the time, struggling to believe in herself. But Hilary had seen this woman move steadily onward and upward, continually working to improve herself.

Which brought Hilary back to the reason she had wanted to see Janna to begin with. She was wondering how to begin when Janna asked, "So, what's up with *you?*"

It took Hilary a few minutes to build up some momentum and get to the heart of the problem. Their order came to the table, and Hilary talked continually between taking bites of her hamburger. She often felt as if she was rambling, but Janna showed genuine interest and didn't seem the least bit impatient. Hilary talked about the way Leon's rejection had affected her, and how it had all become worse with Jeffrey's death. She talked about her apathy toward life in general, and especially toward herself. She finally got around to Jack and the things he'd said just yesterday on their way home from Mt. Pleasant.

"He sounds like a pretty neat guy," Janna said. "I'd like to meet him."

"Well, I'm sure that could be arranged, but don't go making some-thing of it. We have *nothing* in common. He's very nice, but it could never be romantic."

Janna smiled with mischief. "Never say never."

Hilary laughed softly. "I mean *never*! He's really not my type."

"Okay, so he's not your type. But he obviously cares about you, and he had some good insights. Do you think what he said was true?"

"Yes, I suppose it is. Maybe that's what's so hard . . . to admit he's right. I guess I just don't know where to start. I know you've been through some pretty tough things, and I was hoping maybe you could help me get back on track. I mean . . . I know I can live without Leon, and I want to be happy without him. But I'm just having a rough time with it right here." She pressed a hand over her heart. "Jack said the best thing I could do with my life would be to start caring about myself again. He said I'd feel better about myself if I just went to the bridal shower feeling confident and letting them know—indirectly, of course—that I don't care about Leon. Does that make sense?"

"Yes," Janna said, "and I agree with him. You're right when you say I've been through some pretty heavy struggles. But one of the most important things I learned is that I didn't need anybody else to make me who and what I am. My strength had to come from inside me. Even as much as I loved Colin, I had to find my own value apart from him before I could be a good wife. I don't really think you're so bad off, Hilary. Maybe you just need a little shot in the arm."

Janna told Hilary to get out her planner and begin a list. They talked about eating correctly, transferring the principles of the Word of Wisdom into modern, practical terms. With Janna's help, Hilary wrote a tentative eating plan that would help her have healthy meals in spite of her busy schedule. They talked about exercise, and Hilary admitted that even though she kept moving in her dance classes and the lessons she taught, she wasn't putting much energy into it. Janna challenged her to take some time when she was in the studio to work up a good sweat in order to keep herself healthier—the way she used to.

They also talked about spiritual matters, and Janna suggested that she put more purpose into her prayer and scripture study. Hilary knew this would help, but there was still something that bothered her. She told herself she should talk to Janna about it, but the time just didn't seem right.

"So, when is this wedding shower?" Janna asked.

"Saturday afternoon."

"Are you going?"

"I'd like to, but . . . well, quite honestly, I can hardly fit into most of my clothes, and I just don't want to go feeling fat and—"

"Hey, you can get down to your normal size with a little time and work, but you can't do it too quickly or it will only make you sick— and then you'll gain it right back. In the meantime, you can treat yourself to a few new things to wear that make you feel good. If your money's tight, I'd be happy to loan you some or—"

"Oh, I've got some put away," Hilary admitted, attempting to digest the idea. "Maybe I should, but . . . it's been so long since I've bought myself anything new to wear, I'm not sure I'd know where to begin."

Janna smiled. "I know how that can feel, but I once had a friend teach me a thing or two about shopping for just the right outfit. I'd be happy to pass it along."

Hilary went home feeling a little overwhelmed, but determined to take the steps Janna had challenged her to take. The following afternoon, they met at the mall and shopped store after store. Hilary tried on a number of things and began to get an idea of what would disguise her temporary figure problems.

While they were rummaging through the sale racks at the back of an elite clothing store, Hilary asked Janna, "Who is this friend who helped you learn how to shop for the right clothes?"

"My mother-in-law."

"Really?" Hilary chuckled in surprise.

"I'm serious. She's incredible. You see, I had to go to this hearing because I was pressing criminal charges against my first husband, Russell. I was staying with Colin's mother at the time, and she took me shopping. She said sometimes the right outfit just gives a woman that extra something that helps her feel better about herself. And I think she was right. Of course, in the long run, it all has to come from within. But we have to use the tools we've been given, too."

Hilary realized that Janna was right when she finally tried on a print skirt and a short-sleeved burgundy sweater that complemented her complexion and actually made her look several pounds lighter. She also bought a pair of jeans in a bigger size to get her by. She could still wear most of her shirts and blouses—which helped, considering her budget. She also found a pair of shoes for under ten dollars that worked with either pants or skirts.

Hilary figured they were finished shopping when, by chance, they came across a suit on a sale rack that was so perfect it almost felt eerie. "It's amazing how the Holy Ghost can go shopping with you," Janna commented matter-of-factly as she surveyed Hilary wearing the deep green suit.

"What do you mean by that?" Hilary asked, certain she was joking.

"I prayed that we could find just the right things for the right prices and—voilá!" She laughed softly. "You look incredible in that. You've got to get it."

Hilary loved the suit, and had no doubt she'd get a lot of good use out of it. It came with both pants and a skirt, and with a long jacket, cut to accentuate her figure. But even at its incredibly low price, she just wasn't certain if she dared spend any more. She was contemplating how to tell Janna that she just couldn't do it when her friend said firmly, "I am buying that suit for you. You've got to have it."

Hilary tried to protest, but Janna insisted, gently reminding her to be gracious and enjoy it. "Do you remember all those breaks we took together when we worked at the mall?" Janna asked as they walked out of the store with the suit in a shopping bag.

"Yes."

"Do you remember how you paid for what I got most of the time, because I was trying so hard to support myself and get Christmas for my kids? Do you remember how you took me out to eat once when I was really down, and how you insisted on paying for it?"

"Actually, I'd forgotten," Hilary admitted.

"Well, I haven't forgotten. Now I have an opportunity to return the favor."

Hilary had to get to the studio and teach her dance lessons, but she went to Janna's house later that evening, and they sat in her bedroom for over an hour, trying different things with Hilary's hair and makeup. She realized then that Janna had some real skill in what she put on her face. She never looked made up, but she always looked beautiful. Hilary learned a great deal about what to do for her face, but Janna declared with a laugh that Hilary's hair wasn't going to do anything but hang straight.

"I know. I hate it," Hilary insisted.

"Actually, it's very beautiful," Janna said firmly. "I've often longed for smooth, straight hair."

"Well, I've longed for curls—like yours."

Janna chuckled. "My, my; it seems we've got a case of *the grass is greener on the other side of the fence.* But if you want curls, why don't you get a perm?"

"I tried that once. It was horrible."

"How long ago was that?"

"I was fifteen."

"Well, maybe it was just a horrible perm. Maybe you should try again. It's up to you, of course, and I like your hair the way it is. Maybe you should pray about it."

It wasn't until later that night, while Hilary was trying to sleep, that she contemplated some of the things Janna had said. Praying about whether or not to perm your hair? Asking the Holy Ghost to help you find the right clothes? It seemed almost ridiculous. She'd always believed in God, but she felt certain he wasn't the least bit concerned about her hair and clothes. Yet Janna had seemed so matter-of-fact about it, as if she truly believed it. Of course, Hilary hadn't felt very good about her relationship with God for quite some time now. She'd continued going to church, and a part of her knew there were things she just didn't understand. But it was difficult to admit aloud that she resented God for taking Jeffrey. Her brother had never shown malice toward anyone; in fact, he'd been serving when the accident happened. And it just didn't seem fair.

Forcing her mind away from thoughts that only brought pain, Hilary concentrated on all Janna had taught her the last few days. Already she felt better about herself, and was finding some hope in her future.

Recalling that she'd forgotten to read her scriptures as Janna had challenged, Hilary tiptoed out to the front room where she could turn on the light without disturbing Becky. She couldn't remember the last time she'd read in the Book of Mormon, and she opened it to where the marker had been left. Alma, chapter thirty-two. As Hilary read about experimenting with faith compared to planting a seed, Janna's comments came back to her. She finished reading the chapter, then got on her knees and told her Father in Heaven she wanted to feel better about herself. She expressed gratitude for Janna's friendship and willingness to share. She then asked, a bit reluctantly, if it would be better to leave her hair as it was, or if there was something she could do with it that might make her feel better about herself.

Hilary finished her prayer and went off to bed, feeling a bit silly. She slept well, and when morning came, she enjoyed putting on new clothes. Wearing makeup, earrings, and a touch of perfume for the first time in months, she walked out of the apartment feeling almost like a new person.

Hilary didn't give her hair a moment's thought until she overheard some girls talking at the next table in the cafeteria. It took great self-restraint to keep her jaw from hanging open at the coincidence. While she ate her lunch, she heard every detail of how this young woman had hated her long, straight hair, but she'd been afraid to perm it for fear of ruining it. She told her friend how she'd gone to a cosmetology school to get a perm that cost very little. It was given to her by a girl named Jody, and she loved it.

When the girls left, Hilary found herself asking in silent prayer if that was just a coincidence, or if it had truly been evidence that her Father in Heaven was mindful of her. She didn't hear any thunderbolts, but in her heart she believed her prayers had been heard. At the first opportunity, she made a call and discovered an opening for a perm with a girl named Jody.

"Do you have more than one Jody working there?" she inquired.

"No," the receptionist answered.

Hilary nearly called her mother to tell her she would be coming to the shower, but she decided to wait and see how the perm turned out. It was a somewhat miserable experience, but when she looked at the final results in the mirror, she had to admit she liked it. And with some suggestions from Jody on caring for it, she realized it would be relatively maintenance-free.

On the way home, Hilary impulsively stopped by Jack's apartment. She was surprised to see his truck parked there, knowing he had a busy schedule working construction while going to school full time. She was doubly surprised when he answered the door personally, as there were several guys sharing the apartment.

Hilary's heart began to pound before she could even say hello. His eyes widened, then they sparkled, and she had to admit she'd never felt more beautiful than she did at that moment. Without a word, Jack fell backward onto the floor, pretending to faint.

"Oh, stop that!" she insisted, fighting her sudden embarrassment. But he didn't move.

"Jack!" she said, but nothing happened. She nudged him gently with her shoe and he smirked subtly, but his eyes remained closed. "Get up off the floor," she snapped.

"I won't wake up until the most beautiful woman in the world kisses me," he whispered.

"Well, you're out of luck."

He opened his eyes but didn't get up. "But . . . here you are. All you have to do is—"

"Beautiful or not, I won't be kissing you, Jack Hayden. So get up off the floor."

He exaggerated a sulky expression that made her laugh as he came to his feet. Then he put his hands on his hips and just looked her up and down, shaking his head slowly. "You look incredible, Hilary."

"Well, I guess you said some things that got me thinking."

"And I thought you'd never speak to me again."

"Well, that did cross my mind," she said, then they both laughed.

Hilary felt suddenly uncomfortable beneath his lingering gaze. She cleared her throat and asked what she'd come to find out. "I was just wondering if you were still going to Mt. Pleasant this weekend. I'd like to go to that shower if—"

"Oh, I'll be going. No problem there."

They discussed what time he would pick her up, then Hilary went home and called her mother, realizing she was actually excited to go to the shower. Perhaps life was looking up a little.

CHAPTER FOUR

*H*ilary ended up enjoying Sunny's wedding shower, but not for the reasons she'd expected. Just as Jack had predicted, she felt so good about herself that the reality of losing Leon to another woman felt suddenly less important. The surprise came in realizing that Sunny was not someone she could ever like. And in all honesty, it had nothing to do with jealousy. For all of Sunny's beauty, she was shallow and trite. While she opened her gifts, showing little if any graciousness, she made silly jokes that in Hilary's opinion were not even remotely funny.

Before the shower ended, Leon showed up to be teased by the women in attendance. While he made a fuss over Sunny's gifts, Hilary observed them interacting. Any hint of jealousy Hilary felt was quickly replaced by something close to nausea. They were so syrupy toward each other that she wanted to gag. It was easy for Hilary to congratulate them and be on her way, towing her mother along.

That night, lying in her own bedroom at home, Hilary contemplated what she had observed in Leon. Had he changed? Or had she just been too blinded by love to see him for what he really was? As if to answer the questions she hardly dared say aloud, memories assaulted her. Jack had told her that he didn't know anyone who liked Leon Phillips. And Hilary knew that Jeffrey hadn't liked Leon; he'd just been too sweet to say anything until Leon had finally dumped her. Had she been so blind? So stupid?

About two o'clock in the morning, she finally came to the conclusion that it really didn't matter. Leon was marrying Sunny, and she was relieved to note that she didn't care.

Jack picked her up about ten the following morning to start back to Provo, since he had a meeting to attend. "So, how did it go?" he asked as soon as they pulled out on the highway.

"Good," she admitted. "They deserve each other—and I told them so."

Jack laughed ridiculously loud. "You did, really?"

"Yes, I did." She laughed with him.

"Well, tell me."

"Leon showed up near the end, and they were absolutely revolting together. So I excused myself politely. I just smiled at them and said with great enthusiasm that I was happy for them, and they deserved each other."

Jack laughed again, then he reached for her hand and his tone became serious. "I'm proud of you, Hillie."

"Thanks," was all she said, and the conversation turned to things that Hilary could care less about—balers, cows, and the price of grain. But she remained polite and concluded that being in his presence wasn't entirely miserable. He told her that his father had purchased a round baler, and next summer Jack intended to help her father bale his hay with it. "Then it can be loaded with a fork on the tractor, instead of by hand, and your dad won't get so worn out."

"That sounds great," Hilary said. She couldn't share his enthusiasm over balers, but she was all for anything that would help her parents. "But Dad doesn't have a fork on his tractor," she told him as if he didn't know.

"We're working on that, too," he said and flipped the toothpick in his mouth from one end to the other. "My dad does a little welding on the side; he's taught me a thing or two. It doesn't take much to weld a few pieces together and make a tractor fork."

"You're very good to my father," Hilary had to admit.

"Nah," Jack shook his head humbly, "he's good to me."

"Hey," she said when they were nearly to Provo, "would you have a few minutes to stop at the studio where I work? I left something there, and—"

"No problem. Where is it?"

Hilary gave him directions and quickly jumped out of the truck when they arrived. She came back a minute later, and he took her home. "Thanks, Jack," she said as she got out of the truck. "You really are good to me."

"It's no problem," he said with a smile that warmed her.

Over the next few weeks, Hilary became so busy that she hardly gave Jack or Leon a second thought. As she followed through on the goals that Janna had helped her set, she felt better physically and mentally than she had since long before Jeffrey's death. Through exercise and eating better, her muscles began to tone up and those extra pounds gradually fell away. Her grades improved, and she began to enjoy teaching again.

Hilary began to appreciate life like she never had before, which made her realize that her mind had been clouded with Leon Phillips since she'd been old enough to think of herself as a woman. And she was pleasantly surprised at the sudden increase in dating opportunities. Nearly every weekend was filled as she went out with a number of different men, until she became rather fond of a young man named Robert. He'd recently returned from a mission to Canada, and he was attending BYU. After just a couple of dates, she found that she enjoyed his company very much, and she hoped something good might come of it.

Jack called occasionally to ask her out, but she told him what she'd told him to begin with: she just wasn't interested in anything romantic. She knew she'd given him the impression she wasn't dating at all, but she didn't see that it mattered. And there was no problem— until Jack called to ask if she was going to Leon's wedding reception.

"I've hardly thought about it," she admitted.

"That's good, isn't it?"

"Yes, I suppose it is."

"Well, I was planning on going and wondered if you'd like to come along."

"That would be fine, I suppose," Hilary said without enthusiasm.

"The reception is here in Provo on Thursday, and there's an open house in Mt. Pleasant on Saturday. Which would you rather—"

"Oh, Mt. Pleasant," she said quickly, afraid that Robert might think she was going out with somebody else.

"Okay," Jack said, "I'll probably go down Friday evening. I'll pick you up about—"

"Uh," she interrupted, "I've got plans Friday evening. Could we go Saturday early?"

Jack was silent a long moment. "I guess we can. Do you mind if I ask what you're doing?"

"What is this? Are you being my daddy's spy again?"

"I'm just curious, Hilary. You don't have to tell me."

"Well, I have a date, Jack, okay? He's a returned missionary, and I find him terribly attractive. Is that all right with you?"

Again Jack was silent until Hilary said, "Jack? Are you with me?"

"Yeah," he said tonelessly. "I'll pick you up Saturday morning about eight."

"I'll be ready."

Jack hung up without a good-bye, and Hilary wondered what was eating at him. Reminding herself that Jack and his life were none of her concern, she didn't give it another thought.

When he picked her up Saturday morning, Hilary noticed that his hair had grown significantly since he'd returned from his mission. Thick and curly, it hung over the top of his collar and was combed back off his face. While she was momentarily distracted with the thought that Jack Hayden was actually rather attractive, he said with a smirk, "You're looking great these days, Hil."

"Thanks," was all she said as he opened the truck door for her and took her overnight bag.

They drove in silence until Jack said, "So how was your date?"

"It was fun, actually."

"What did you do? . . . if you don't mind my asking."

"We went to a movie and—"

"A movie?" he echoed with that southern drawl coming out prominently.

"And," she continued in an attempt to ignore him, "we went out to dinner." She looked at him hard and added, "It was a good movie."

"Okay, but it's such a . . . *dating* kind of thing."

Hilary glared at him. "So?"

"I was just under the impression that you weren't dating—at all."

He almost looked angry and she said, "I thought you were my friend, Jack. Is there a reason you think I shouldn't date?"

Jack reminded himself that he *was* her friend, and he needed to act like it. He forced a smile, then added, "I take it you're over Leon now."

"Yes, I suppose I am."

"So, what's his name?"

"It's Robert. Is there a point to this?"

"I'm just curious."

"Well, there's nothing to tell."

"You like him, I take it."

"Yes, I like him, but we've only gone out a few times. Could we change the subject?"

"Okay, what do you want to talk about?"

"Anything but farm equipment. I get enough about the latest in round balers from my father."

"Okay, let's talk about dancing."

Hilary was surprised. "What about it?"

"I was always kind of a crummy dancer. I hated those school dances and stuff, but . . . well, you must be pretty good, eh?"

"I suppose I am. But I don't really do much couple dancing."

"Oh, you do the performing kind of stuff."

"Well," she laughed softly, "I'm not much of a performer, either. I mean, I've been in a few school and local productions, but I really enjoy teaching . . . and well, what I really enjoy is . . ." She hesitated, realizing how personal she was becoming.

"What?" he pressed.

"Oh, it's not important."

"Come on, just tell me. What is it you really enjoy?"

"Well," Hilary looked out the window to avoid embarrassment, "I just like to dance . . . all by myself. After classes are over, I turn out the lights in the studio and turn the music up really loud and just . . . dance. I think that's what really makes teaching worthwhile—to have that opportunity to be there all alone. It's like . . . well, the music just becomes a part of me, or I become the music, or . . . it's hard to explain." She laughed softly. "That sounds really silly, doesn't it."

"Silly? No," he said. "I think it sounds . . . well . . . it makes me wish I *could* dance. Do you teach old awkward people like me?"

"Old?" she laughed.

"Well, I'm older than those little teeny girls you teach, I'm sure."

"Yes, but . . ."

"And I *am* awkward, trust me."

"I guess we'd just have to see."

"Does that mean you'd give me a lesson or two?"

"You're serious," Hilary said.

"Yes, I'm serious."

"Well, I must confess I've never taught a man *anything.*"

"There's always a first time," he said. Then he laughed.

Jack dropped her off at home, then came back that evening to get her for the open house.

"You look great, Hil," he said when they were on their way to the church building. "Are you nervous?"

"No, not in the slightest."

"That's good," he said, "'cause I sure am."

"Why on earth should you be nervous?"

"I'm showing up with his gorgeous ex-girlfriend. He's gonna take one look at you and wonder where he went wrong."

Hilary laughed and slugged him playfully on the shoulder. As they stepped into the church building, Jack helped Hilary out of her coat and hung it up for her. "Ooh," he said, noticing her dress, "black. It's appropriate, I'd say."

"I thought so," she murmured, and realized her heart was pounding. Impulsively she took hold of Jack's hand. He looked at her in question and she simply said, "I'm nervous." He smirked and she added, "Of course, if you don't want to be seen holding my hand, then . . ."

Jack laughed and put his arm around her shoulders as they walked into the cultural hall. They signed their names in the guest book, then moved to stand in line. "Wow," she said, "it looks like the whole town is here."

"Could be."

Hilary glanced up at him and asked, "So, why did you get invited, anyway?"

"Heck if I know. We were in the same grade in school, but I didn't think he knew me from Adam. He probably invited his entire graduating class."

"But why did you come?" she asked.

"Besides to hold you up, you mean?" He squeezed subtly where his arm was around her shoulders. Hilary nodded. "I came to get a good look at *Sunny.*" He snorted a little laugh. "I bet she snores like a train and bites her fingernails. And she probably can't dance worth beans."

Hilary laughed and nudged him with her elbow as they moved closer to the receiving line. "She is beautiful," Hilary commented, glad to realize it didn't bother her in the least.

Jack craned his neck to look over the crowd. "That's a matter of opinion, I suppose. She looks like somebody who'd advertise laundry detergent on television."

As they went through the line together, Hilary knew that people would assume she and Jack were dating. But she really didn't care what anybody in this town thought, and she was grateful for his support and laughter through a difficult moment. With Jack by her side, she was able to shake Leon's hand and congratulate him with sincerity. While she was greeting the new Mrs. Phillips, Jack's description of Sunny appeared in her mind, and it took great self-control to not burst out laughing. A tiny giggle erupted, but she quickly swallowed it and moved away.

"Not laundry detergent," she whispered to Jack. "Toothpaste."

He chuckled. "Maybe both . . . at the same time."

Jack and Hilary sat in the truck and talked for nearly an hour before she went into the house. On their way back to Provo the following day, she made a point to say, "Thank you, Jack."

"For what?"

"For helping me through."

"Through what?" he asked. She felt certain he knew what she meant, but he wanted her to clarify it.

"For helping me get through getting over Leon."

"Did I do that?" he asked with an exaggerated air of enlightenment.

"Indirectly, yes. I really appreciate your taking me last night, and for making me laugh."

"It was my pleasure," he said with a smile. Then his eyes turned serious, and he focused intently on the road as he drove. "I know what it's like to be in love with someone you can't have. Sometimes laughing is the only thing you can do."

Hilary was taken aback as she considered something that had simply never occurred to her. There was obviously a lot about Jack Hayden that she didn't know. She couldn't resist saying, "You never told me you were in love with someone."

"It's really not relevant," he said, seeming suddenly nervous.

"Sure it is. We're always talking about me. Maybe we should talk about *you* for a change. Who are you in love with, Jack?"

He turned to look at her for a long moment, then his gaze went back to the road. "It doesn't matter, Hil."

His tone was so serious that again she was taken off guard. "Okay. If you don't want to talk about it, then—"

"I don't want to talk about it."

Hilary said nothing more, but she found herself wondering who might have broken Jack Hayden's heart. It couldn't be somebody in Mt. Pleasant, because very little happened that she didn't hear about. Had he met someone at BYU? Was it before his mission? Or since? Or maybe both? Had someone waited for him and then let him go? Is that why he was so compassionate about Leon? Is that why he had so much insight into the things that had helped her get over him?

"Hey," he said, interrupting her thoughts, "there's something I've been meaning to ask you, but I never think about it when we're together."

"Okay."

"Did Jeffrey ever keep a journal or anything?"

Hilary hated the way her insides reacted at just hearing Jeffrey's name. She tried to cover her emotions and simply said, "I think he did. You'd have to ask my mother. I don't know anything about it."

"Okay," Jack said. Then she looked out the window to avoid his questioning gaze. "One more question. Why do you always look like you want to bite somebody—specifically me—when Jeffrey's name comes up?"

"Because you're the one who always brings him up."

"You can't talk about your brother without getting upset?"

"No, I can't."

"Why not? Don't you have fond memories? Isn't there a lot of good you can think about, or—"

"Jack, please. I refuse to discuss this."

Jack was surprised by the intensity of her reaction. She wasn't any more comfortable with Jeffrey's death now than she had been the day he'd first learned about it. He felt compelled to ask, "Is there a reason why this is so hard for you?" She gave him that biting look he'd just described. "Don't get defensive, just answer the question."

Hilary's thoughts ran in circles. She had no desire to share with him her deepest thoughts and feelings. He'd helped her get over Leon, but she doubted he could help her get over Jeffrey. Nothing could do that. How could she possibly explain the disconcerting thoughts that had plagued her since Jeffrey's death? She had a testimony of the gospel, and she knew God was real, but a part of her felt somehow betrayed. If Jeffrey had been such a good person, giving so much of himself, why would God take him like that? Hilary didn't understand, and she didn't want to talk about it. So she simply said, "I can't talk about it, Jack. That's all." Jack said nothing more, and Hilary forced it out of her mind.

Once they were back in Provo, she didn't give Jack much thought as the week became busy, and every spare minute was spent with Robert. Her attraction to him grew steadily in proportion to the amount of time she spent with him. He invited her to spend Thanksgiving with his family in Ogden, and even though Hilary knew her parents would be terribly disappointed by her absence, she accepted his invitation. She wasn't ready to say that he could be a part of her future, but at this point she felt like the possibility was fairly high.

Jack called the Sunday before Thanksgiving to tell her when he'd be going home on Wednesday.

"Uh . . . I won't be going," she told him.

"It's Thanksgiving, Hilary," he said as if she didn't know.

"I'm well aware of what it is, Jack. I'll be spending Thanksgiving with a friend."

He made a noise of disbelief and she sighed, reminding herself to be patient. "What about your parents?" he questioned. "Are you just going to leave them alone to—"

"They'll have other family members there. It's not like—"

"Hilary, it's not the same. What kind of friend is more important than spending Thanksgiving with your family?"

"You know, Jack, this is really none of your business. It's not like—"

"It's a guy, isn't it. You're going home with some guy to meet his family. Criminantly, girl, it's not another Leon, is it?"

"No, of course not! He's a wonderful man, and—"

"I really don't want to know, thank you very much."

After Hilary hung up the phone, she had to ask herself why Jack was so upset over something like this. Was he so concerned for her parents? Or was there more?

On Tuesday evening, Robert took Hilary to a movie and she had a great time. They went out for ice cream afterward, talking and laughing as if they'd always been friends.

When Robert took her home, he pulled his car into the apartment parking lot, put it into park, and turned out the lights. She expected him to get out and open the door for her, but he turned in his seat and touched her face, saying gently, "You know, Hilary, I've never met a woman like you. You're smart. You're beautiful. And you just make me feel, well . . . it's so hard to explain. He bent to kiss her, and Hilary closed her eyes. It wasn't the first time Robert had kissed her, but she wasn't prepared for the way it turned subtly insistent.

"Robert," she said, "I really should go inside. I'm sure it's not a good idea to—"

He interrupted her with another kiss that wasn't subtle at all. A distinct uneasiness prickled at the back of her neck. She had the urge to just get out of the car, but she found herself in his arms, not certain how she'd gotten there. He kissed her hard, behaving as if he expected her to enjoy it and get caught up in the moment.

Reminding herself to be appropriately assertive, she eased back, saying firmly, "Robert, please. I'm really not comfortable with this. We hardly know each other when it comes right down to it, and—"

Robert interrupted her with some syrupy and irrelevant comments about his feelings for her that apparently were meant to ease her misgivings.

"Robert," she persisted, "I need to go inside. I . . . oh, my gosh!" she exclaimed far louder than she'd intended, realizing that his hand was on her leg. Her attempt to squirm away made it evident just how powerless she was, and his strong hold was hurting her. Stories she'd heard of date rape and sexual assault flashed through her mind. Then, in response to her fear, she could hear some oft-repeated advice from her father, as clearly as if he was with her: *When somebody's bein' obnoxious, don't worry about bein' polite, just do whatever it takes to be safe.*

In a desperate move, Hilary drew one arm back and slapped Robert as hard as she could. He drew back in shock, murmuring, "I can't believe you'd do that!"

"Yeah, well, that makes two of us," Hilary retorted, scrambling out of the car.

By the time Hilary got to the apartment door, she was shaking and could barely find her key. She desperately wished one of her room-mates would be there, but all three had left that afternoon to go home for the holiday weekend. Before she got inside and closed the door, she could almost imagine Robert, who knew she would be alone tonight, coming up behind her to finish what he'd started. And she thought she had known him so well.

"Oh, help," she murmured, securely locking the door. But that didn't take away the fear she'd just experienced. Maybe he'd had no intention of forcing himself on her. Maybe she'd overreacted; maybe she hadn't. Either way, she was upset. Without hesitating, she grabbed the phone and dialed Jack's number. She didn't even think about what time it might be, or what she'd say to him until it started ringing. When someone answered, she forced a steady voice and said, "I'm sorry to call so late. Is Jack still up, or—"

"He's right here."

"Hello," Jack said.

"Hi, it's Hillie. Sorry to call so late, but—"

"We're just watching a movie. What's up? Did you decide to go home tomorrow, or—"

"Actually yes, but . . ." What little composure she'd managed to maintain suddenly crumbled. "Would it be silly if I asked you to come over here for a little while?" She started to cry and wondered if he had even understood what she'd said.

"Are you okay?" he questioned. "What happened?"

"I'm okay . . . I think . . . I just. . ."

"I'll be right over," he said.

Hilary hung up the phone and began to pace, trying to convince herself that she *had* overreacted, and that she was being silly to call Jack. He would probably tease her and make light of it, just making the whole thing worse.

The knock at the door actually made her jump. Her relief was more intense than she dared admit, but as she reached for the door-knob, it occurred to her that perhaps Robert had come back to . . .

"Who is it?" she asked, forcing a firm voice.

"It's Jack," came the voice of reason and strength from the other side of the door.

She opened it only far enough for him to slip inside, then she quickly closed and relocked it. "What's wrong?" he demanded, wearing a new beard that amounted to just enough hair on his face to enhance his already rugged features.

Suddenly flustered and embarrassed, Hilary blurted, "I went out on this date, and . . . when he brought me home . . . we were in the car and . . . and he . . . he . . ." She started to cry and shook her head in frustration.

Hilary could almost literally feel Jack's anger as he grasped her shoulders and bent down to look into her eyes. "What did he do, Hil? What?"

Again she just shook her head, unable to speak.

"Hilary, look at me!" he demanded gently, urging her to sit beside him on the couch. "Calm down and tell me . . . Did he hurt you? Did he—"

Hilary shook her head more vehemently, taking a deep breath. "No," she said, "but . . . I thought he was . . . going to . . . I just . . . got scared . . . and I was here all alone . . . and . . ."

While she was feeling flustered and embarrassed, Jack urged her head to his shoulder and put his arms around her, holding her as he might a hurt child. "It's okay," he said. "Everything's okay."

Hilary clung to him, grateful beyond words for the safety and security he represented. "I'm sorry to bother you like this," she murmured. "I know it's silly, but—"

"It's not silly, Hilary," he insisted. "I'm glad you called."

"So am I," she admitted. And then she just cried. And he just held her.

Jack relaxed into the corner of the couch and closed his eyes, relishing this opportunity to hold Hilary close and feel her need for him, wishing it would last. When she finally calmed down, he asked quietly, "Are you going to be okay?"

Hilary sniffled and nodded, but she felt reluctant to remove herself from the comfortable haven surrounding her.

"Are you sure he didn't hurt you?" Jack asked.

"No, he didn't hurt me . . . not physically, anyway."

Jack waited patiently for her to explain, unconsciously smoothing her hair with one hand.

"I thought he was a nice guy, Jack. I was really learning to care for him. Am I that stupid?"

"Anybody can be deceived by the way something appears to be, Hilary. I guess the trick is learning from mistakes and listening to the Spirit."

"Yeah, well, I'm not sure I've ever been very good at either one."

"Sure you are."

"No, I'm not. I mean, look at Leon, for instance."

"Well . . . ," he chuckled, "I wasn't going to say anything, but . . . you sure know how to pick 'em."

"Yeah," she said with sarcasm, "I sure do."

"But you learned something, didn't you?"

"Yes, I did. But I think I've learned more in the last hour than I ever learned from Leon."

"Like what?"

"Well, maybe it's more like . . . there are things I've struggled with for a long time that are just beginning to make sense."

"I'm listening," he said when she hesitated.

As Hilary began talking about her relationship with Leon, she found herself saying things she'd never said to anyone before. And as she talked, the puzzle pieces began to fall into place and make sense. She realized that she had always struggled with a certain lack of self-worth, and Leon had taken advantage of it. Hilary didn't even think before she spilled confessions of the challenges she'd had with Leon. With a great deal of emotion, she told him of the immorality problems they'd developed after dating for a couple of years. She realized as she talked that with Leon she had been completely passive, willing to do anything to keep him, and she admitted how wrong she had been. She expressed relief that Leon's fear of her getting pregnant had kept it from going too far, because she was certain that she wouldn't have had the willpower to resist him. She told Jack she had talked to the bishop about it a long time ago, at the same time Leon had been preparing for a mission and was putting his own life in order. Technically the sins were taken care of, but in her heart Hilary had suffered a great deal of guilt over the situation. As she talked it all out, with Jack listening compassionately, Hilary realized that part of the reason she'd had trouble getting over Leon was perhaps her belief that marrying him would somehow wipe away her guilt and make the things they had done all right.

When Hilary had nothing more to say, Jack reminded her of her self-worth and her inner strengths. He talked to her about the beauty of the gospel, and how she always had the chance to make a fresh start. He talked of repentance in a way that actually made her believe for the first time that the mistakes of her youth were truly washed clean. Then he challenged her to fast and pray to gain a personal assurance that the Lord had forgiven her.

Their conversation was interrupted by a knock at the door. Hilary met Jack's eyes with alarm, then glanced at the clock. "It's well past one in morning," she whispered. "Who on earth . . ."

"Just ask," he whispered back.

"Who is it?" she called.

"Is that you, Hilary? It's Robert. Can we talk?"

Hilary's heart began to pound, and she wondered what she might have done if she'd been alone. She looked to Jack, and he nodded. "Go ahead and open it. I'd like to meet him."

Hilary didn't question Jack as he stepped quietly behind the door, signaling for her to go ahead. She had no desire to ever see Robert again, and if Jack could help guarantee that, she was all for it.

Hilary took a deep breath and opened the door to see Robert looking rather sheepish. "Hey," he said, "I'm really sorry about that. I just . . . got carried away."

With a discreet glance, Hilary noticed Jack rolling his eyes. "Yes, you certainly did," she said firmly.

"We're still on for tomorrow, aren't we?" he asked. "I mean . . . I just wanted to be sure this hadn't changed anything between us, and—"

"I'm going home for Thanksgiving," she said without apology. "And it changes everything. It's obvious you don't respect me, and I've got better things to do with my life than—"

"Don't respect you?" Robert echoed with a sarcastic lilt in his voice. "Oh, come on, Hilary. I got a little carried away. It doesn't have anything to do with respect."

"If that's the way you see it, then we obviously have nothing in common."

"We have a lot in common, Hilary," Robert argued. "Except that you don't seem to have much concern for a man's needs. I must say, I'm surprised at your insensitivity when it comes to—"

"Insensitivity?" she nearly shrieked, almost forgetting that Jack was there. "Is that it? We go out for a few weeks, and I'm supposed to be sensitive to your *needs*? I assume from your behavior that you're not talking about supporting you as a priesthood holder; as if you could even claim to—"

Hilary stopped when Robert's eyes turned hard and he reached above her head to push the door open farther. Her heart began to pound with fear until she remembered that Jack was behind the door. She took a step back as Robert stepped inside, and in a split second, Jack was standing between them. Robert gasped and his eyes shot upward, betraying his dismay at facing a man who was obviously taller and bigger. "Who are you?" he snapped, quickly covering his brief lack of confidence.

"I'm Hilary's brother, and if you ever come anywhere near her again, I will hunt you down and teach you a whole new meaning of the word *respect*. Now, get out of here, before I lose my temper."

Robert glared briefly at Jack, then at Hilary, then he turned and walked away. Jack waved comically toward Robert's retreating form, then he closed the door and leaned against it.

"Like I said," his voice picked up that light drawl he was famous for, "you sure know how to pick 'em."

Hilary sighed and willed her heart to slow down. "Yeah, I guess I do."

"He's a nerd, Hil," Jack added. "He's probably never had grease under his fingernails, and I'd wager he can't change the oil in his own car. What kind of a man is that?"

Hilary realized he was teasing her—but not entirely. Responding to his lighter mood, she said, "Of course, a *real* man changes the oil in his own car, and knows how to get good and dirty, right?"

Jack smirked. "Of course."

"And the really *great* real men come from Texas, right?"

"Hmm-mm." Jack nodded.

"And the best ones always wear cowboy boots and chew on toothpicks, right?"

Jack reached into his shirt pocket and put a toothpick in his mouth as if to demonstrate, his grin deepening. "Yep."

"Well, you know what?"

"What?"

"I think a real man has a sensitive heart and a listening ear. A real man is someone who can respect a woman, even if he doesn't agree with her. And it doesn't matter whether he can change the oil, or drive a tractor. It doesn't matter what he wears, or how he talks, or what he does for a living." Her voice became as serious as her eyes. "And that, in my opinion, is what makes you a real man, Jack."

The intensity in his eyes made her suddenly uncomfortable. She laughed softly to break the mood, and added, "You're really not my type, but I'm sure grateful to have you as a friend."

Jack swallowed hard and glanced down, blinking back an unexpected rush of emotion. He cleared his throat and looked up again. "It's my pleasure, Hil. I'm here for you . . . any time. And I mean that."

"By the way," she said, lightening the mood again, "I've often wondered why your accent seems to fluctuate depending on your mood."

Jack grinned and laid the drawl on thickly. "I just like to *rile* certain young ladies with my hickish ways."

Hilary laughed. "You're serious. You do it just to annoy me? Just *me?*"

"There's nobody else I know who would even notice."

"I think you're a rogue, Jack Hayden."

"Maybe I am. Or maybe it has more to do with the pigtail theory."

Hilary held up her hands. "I don't even want to know."

Jack spent the night on the couch, which gave Hilary a lot more comfort than she dared admit. She'd insisted he didn't need to, but he apparently saw through to her real feelings and stayed anyway. The following morning he went home long enough to shower and pack a few things, then he came back to get her for the trip to Mt. Pleasant.

When they had gone several miles with nothing but small talk, Hilary blurted out of nowhere, "Lorie thinks you're cute."

"Who?" Jack's eyes narrowed.

"My roommate, Lorie. She thinks you're cute. Maybe you should ask her out." Hilary lifted her brows mischievously, then she giggled.

Jack chuckled, but only because he loved it when Hilary acted silly. The thought of dating one of her roommates held no interest for him.

"Well?" Hilary pressed when he said nothing.

"I don't even know who she is. Why would I want to take her out?"

"She's the one with dark hair. She's cute, don't you think?" Hilary didn't add that she thought Lorie was basically an idiot. Maybe she hoped Jack would take her out and hate her, which would validate her own feelings.

Jack glanced at Hilary's expectant expression. He could almost feel her baiting him. If only to gauge her reaction, he said, "Okay, so maybe she's cute. Although I barely remember her. You're her roommate. Tell me about her."

"I hardly know her, to be honest. Becky and I are good friends. Kim is Becky's friend. They grew up together. And Lorie is Kim's sister. She's not around much. So, what is there to tell? It couldn't be any worse than a blind date. If you don't want to take her out, fine."

"Okay, fine," he said, and the subject was dropped. Hilary's indifference was evident, which bothered him more than he wanted to admit.

A couple of hours after Jack dropped Hilary off at her house, he came back. Hilary was already busy helping her mother make pies when Pete went to answer the door. From the kitchen she could hear her father say, "Jack. Come in. Come in. The girls are makin' pies for the big feast tomorrow. Come on back here."

"Thank you," Jack said and followed Pete into the kitchen.

"Long time no see," Hilary said, rubbing her nose with the back of her hand to keep from getting flour on her face. Then she continued to roll out pie crusts with a rolling pin.

"Yeah," Jack smirked, "I missed you."

"Oh, it's always good to see you, Jack," Millie said. "How are you?"

"I'm good . . . I think."

"What's wrong?" Millie asked, as if she were acting in a melodrama.

"Nothing, really. I just came to bribe you."

"Oh, I like a good bribe," Pete said. "What's up?"

"Well, I was wondering if I could inflict myself on you for Thanksgiving dinner, if I was willing to peel potatoes or something."

"Oh," Millie laughed, "you know you're always welcome."

"That's nice to know, since my family up and left town."

"Really?" Hilary was surprised. "Didn't they let you know or—"

"Well, I tried to call a few times yesterday and got no answer, but I didn't think much of it. Nobody's there, and Fred next door said they went to Arizona for the holiday."

"Arizona?" Millie echoed.

"I have a couple of aunts down there. It's nice for them to get away," Jack said, "but I'm certainly not excited about spending Thanksgiving alone." He didn't add that he was glad for an excuse to be here instead of home, and he was grateful to know that he was welcome enough to invite himself.

Jack came early on Thanksgiving Day, and in spite of Millie's protests, he *did* peel potatoes, and a few yams as well. He helped move the table into the front room and put the extra leaves in it, carried chairs up from the basement, then he moved gracefully into the background as Hilary's siblings began arriving with their families. He enjoyed listening to their chatter and watching them interact, longing to be part of such a family—more specifically, to be a part of Hilary's life in a much more personal way. But he simply wasn't prepared to admit it—to anyone, especially not Hilary. He wondered, as he often did, if his hesitance to be honest with her about his feelings somehow stemmed from his mother's attitudes that he'd grown up with. Whatever it was, he simply wasn't ready or willing to bare his heart to a woman who had made it clear that he was not her type.

Jack hung around a lot through the remainder of the long weekend, helping Pete with some repairs around the house and teasing Millie in the kitchen. On Saturday afternoon, he asked Hilary if she wanted to get out of the house and go for a ride. "Sure," she said without hesitation, but she was surprised when he drove to his house and parked the truck just outside one of the barns.

"Come on," he said. She followed him into the barn, where he left the big door open and sat on a large four-wheeler, pulling on a heavy pair of gloves. "Well, come on," he said with a little laugh. "You said you wanted to go for a ride."

"Yes, but . . ."

"I'll be very careful, I promise."

"Oh, it's not that."

"What is it, then?"

"I've just never done this before."

"Just get on," he laughed.

Hilary zipped up her coat and reached into her pockets for her gloves. She sat behind him and felt a rush of excitement as she put her hands at his waist to hold on, certain that her reaction was merely a response to this new adventure as he backed the machine slowly out of its resting place and drove it into the open air. He picked up speed as they headed out into the snow-covered fields that flourished with alfalfa in the summer months. Hilary instinctively pushed her arms tightly around him and buried her face against his back. He laughed and let out a whoop like some cowboy riding in a rodeo.

Jack drove the four-wheeler across the fields, loving the way the snow flew behind them— almost as much as he loved the way Hilary held to him for dear life. "Are you scared or having fun?" he hollered back at her. She just laughed and bravely peeked up over his shoulder, feeling every bit as secure as she had Tuesday night when he had held her in his arms and let her cry.

They rode the acres that belonged to his father for better than an hour, then returned and went into the back door of his parents' home, where he put some water on to boil and dug in the cupboard for hot chocolate mix. Hilary was surprised at the surroundings he'd grown up in. The house was so immaculate that she was afraid to touch anything, yet it was filled with clutter and paraphernalia that seemed a stark contrast. A heavy scent of cigarette smoke filled the house, as if every piece of drapery and furniture had been saturated with it.

"Sorry about the smell," Jack said as he set two cups on the table. "I get used to it, but, well . . . it's kind of embarrassing."

"There's no need for that," she said, realizing how very little she knew about Jack and his upbringing. While stirring the powdered mix into her cup, she said, "I take it your parents are not active in the Church."

He snorted a laugh, as if it was the stupidest question he'd ever heard.

"I'm sorry," she said. "I just didn't know, so—"

"It's fine." Jack leaned his elbows on the table, with his cup wrapped firmly in his hands. "I don't mind telling you. I just thought everyone knew just how *inactive* my parents are. They're both baptized members—technically. But I don't think either of them have gone to church since they were kids. My grandparents on my father's side are actually pretty strong in the Church. But my parents were married when they were both seventeen . . . about five months before my brother was born. They were both originally from this area, then moved away right after they were married and my dad went into the military. They finally settled in Texas, then came back here when my mother had the chance to buy her grandfather's farm for practically nothing. They're good people as far as . . . well, they're honest and hardworking. My father put a great deal of effort into teaching me right and wrong. And I always knew he loved me."

"And your mother?"

It was subtle, but Hilary noticed an uneasiness in Jack's eyes. "She loves Dad very much. She'd do anything to please him. But she pretty much left the child-rearing up to him, grateful that she only had sons. And she and I have simply never had much to say since I made it clear that I was adopting a value system that she wanted nothing to do with. She often drinks too much and makes a fool of herself when she does. But Dad just laughs it off and helps her to bed. He takes good care of her. Dad's the smoker. He can go through a pack a day easy, and occasionally he has a beer. But he's a lot more levelheaded."

"That must be hard for you," Hilary said, and it took Jack a moment to swallow the fact that she was showing some genuine interest in him—and some compassion on his behalf.

"Yeah, it's been hard. I'm just grateful that I have something they don't have. I only wish I could share it with them."

"You mean the gospel."

"Yeah, I mean the gospel . . . and everything that goes along with it."

"I would imagine you've attempted to share it with them."

"Oh, yeah," Jack chuckled cynically, "to the point that I had to just shut up or jeopardize my relationship with them. Dad wasn't very happy about my going on a mission. He wanted me to work on the farm, and he wasn't willing to give up any money to support me in something so 'unprofitable,' as he put it. But in the end he told me I had to follow what was in my heart, and if that's what I wanted, he'd stand behind me. He even ended up contributing a hundred dollars a month, and ward members came up with the rest. Your parents even helped some."

"They did?" Hilary was genuinely surprised.

"Now, Mom, on the other hand, was completely against my going. She told me it was foolish and stupid, and she was pretty sure I'd come home with some horrible disease and contaminate the family."

"Where did you go on your mission?" she asked.

"Africa."

"Really? Wow, that's out there."

Jack laughed. "Yeah, it's out there."

They talked for another hour about his mission and his love of the country and the culture. Then he took Hilary home and stayed at her house until nearly eleven o'clock. Together with her parents they played a game of *Monopoly*, with Pete winning by a landslide.

Sunday afternoon, as Jack let Hilary off at her apartment in Provo, she hesitated before closing the truck door.

"Thanks, Jack."

"Hey, I'm always available for cheap taxi service."

"I was under the impression it was free," she said with a smile. "Are you keeping a running tab?"

"Nah," he chuckled. "For you, it's free."

"Well, I appreciate the taxi service, but . . . that's not what I was saying thanks for."

"Okay," Jack drawled and flipped over the toothpick in his mouth. "What, then?"

"Thanks for being my friend, Jack. You've saved me from Leon. And you've saved me from Robert. And well . . . you've just been there for me. You've given me things I didn't even know I needed. You're kind of like . . . well, like my protector. Thanks for looking out for me." Hilary fought back her emotion and admitted something she felt compelled to say. "In a way, you're like the big brother I lost. And I'm really grateful for all you do for me."

Jack swallowed slowly, but he couldn't force his eyes away from her. "It's my pleasure, Hil. You call me anytime."

"Thanks," she said. "The same goes for you."

Jack nodded, and Hilary closed the truck door. He watched her walk away, her overnight bag slung over her shoulder, and he wondered if there might be just the tiniest chance that Hilary Smith might one day see something in him beyond the farm boy. He sighed and drove away, forcing back thoughts that seemed fruitless.

The following week, Jack's construction work was slow due to bad weather, so he took advantage of it to catch up on his studies and do some cleaning around the apartment. He also had the opportunity to spend some one-on-one time with his boss, Ammon Mitchell.

The first thing Jack had noticed about Ammon when he'd been interviewed for the job was his striking appearance. He was tall and dark-skinned, but it was impossible to look at him and guess which race he belonged to. When Jack had become more comfortable with Ammon, he'd come right out and asked. With a great deal of pride in his heritage, Ammon had told him about his mother's parents, who were Mexican and Native-American, and his father's parents, who were Polynesian and African-American. But there was no mistaking his strong testimony of the gospel and deep sense of integrity that made working with him a privilege.

Although Ammon was a little older than Jack, married with a couple of small children, they hit it off and worked together well. Ammon had a college degree in business management, and had incorporated it into his love of building homes. He had a well-established construction business with several employees, but he gravitated toward Jack when it came to discussing problems or sharing lunch. Jack figured that was likely because most of his other employees were a little rough around the edges and didn't share the same value system. Whatever it was, he appreciated Ammon's friendship, even if it rarely went beyond working hours.

A week after Thanksgiving, while the snow drifted outside, Jack and Ammon sat in the cluttered business office, trying to deal with a computer problem that was holding up some paperwork Ammon needed to get out. Jack had volunteered to help, since he'd done fairly well in his computer classes. When Jack solved the problem with little trouble, Ammon laughed and slapped him on the shoulder. "You're pretty good at that, kid. Maybe you should consider a change in profession. Pounding nails and driving a backhoe could be wasting your talents."

Jack snorted. "I'd die being stuck behind a desk. I'll stick to lumber and concrete, thank you very much."

Ammon took Jack to lunch at a nearby pizza-video place where a bunch of high school students were hanging out. Then they went to the recreation center and played basketball for a couple of hours. They talked about their families and interests. After Ammon had told Jack a little about how he and his wife, Allison, had come together, he asked, "So, tell me. You must have some love interest somewhere."

Jack stole the ball from him and dribbled it casually. They were both getting tired, so he knew Ammon wouldn't try too hard to steal it back—at least not for a minute or two. "I'm afraid you won't hear any great romantic stories from me. The only girl I've ever cared to look at twice swears by all she holds dear that I'm not her *type.*"

"Do tell," Ammon said with a little chuckle, then stole the ball back after Jack attempted a shot and missed.

Jack briefly told Ammon his history with Hilary and where it stood presently. "Oh, man," Ammon responded, holding the ball under his arm and wiping sweat from his face, "I know what you mean. At first Allison would give me this *you're just like a brother to me* thing. Drove me nuts."

"So, what did you do?"

"One day I just told her I had no desire to be her brother. It blew her away initially, I think. But we were engaged not long after that. Of course, women are different." He mimicked some kind of guru, saying, "One can never tell how a woman will respond."

"And that's what's really scary," Jack said, stealing the ball to make one last shot before they gave up and went to the locker room to shower.

Jack thought a great deal about what Ammon had said, and wondered if he should just tell Hilary how he really felt. He didn't know if it was fear that held him back, or perhaps some instinctive belief that she would only throw it back at him. She'd come a long way since he'd come back into her life last summer, but he knew there were still struggles going on inside her—most specifically, the struggle over Jeffrey's death. And maybe Hilary just needed to grow up a little bit more before she could comprehend the things going on inside of him. If only he could be patient that long.

CHAPTER FIVE

*T*hrough the following weeks, Hilary's friendship with Jack deepened. They went out nearly every weekend, while she continually made it clear in a joking manner that he wasn't her type and she had no intention of ever having a romantic relationship with him. He took it all in good humor, never even holding her hand unless they were crossing a busy street or moving through a crowd.

Hilary occasionally went out with other men, but never more than once or twice. And while she teased Jack incessantly about his "farm-boy mentality," she couldn't deny the way he made her feel her worth. He treated her with respect and showed genuine interest in her—something Leon had never done.

As she became increasingly comfortable with Jack, Hilary found that she was also becoming more comfortable with herself. She often contemplated the things Jack had challenged her to do—not only in regard to feeling better about herself, but also in strengthening her relationship with her Father in Heaven. While thoughts of Jeffrey's death were still difficult, she couldn't deny a softening of her heart— even if she didn't fully understand.

Not long after the holidays, Hilary stayed late at the dance studio, as she often did, just to have some time to herself. Her apartment was always overflowing with her roommates and their friends; but here she could be herself and let out all her pent-up energy.

She turned off the lights and put in a tape she had recorded of her favorite dancing songs; music she had collected over many years. Some were slow and gently rhythmic, others were powerful with strong beats and vibrant melodies. But every piece on the tape had the ability to touch the deepest part of her and motivate her. The huge room was lit only by a neon sign across the street, beaming softly through high, lightly curtained windows, barely illuminating the polished wood floor. One wall was solid with mirrors, and the other walls were lined with handrails on different levels that were used for ballet bars.

As the music moved through the floor, Hilary danced as if there was nothing more to life than this. From one song to another, she didn't want to give up this feeling. Only absolute exhaustion could stop her, and she wouldn't give up until she absolutely had to.

* * * * *

Feeling an urge to see Hilary, but knowing she was at work, Jack waited until he knew her classes would be over, then went to the studio. She'd told him she usually caught a bus that stopped close by, and he hoped to intercept her and give her a ride home. He saw through the curtained windows that the lights were off, and he waited, certain she would come out any minute. When several minutes passed and she didn't appear, he wondered where she might be. Was there a back door? Even if there was, she would still have to walk past him to get to the bus stop.

Jack finally got out of the truck and went inside to investigate. As he approached the door, he could hear music playing—rather loudly. He walked stealthily inside and saw nothing, but the door was open to a connecting room and he realized there were two studios. His heart quickened as he moved into the doorway, and what he saw took his breath away.

He had known that Hilary was a dancer. She'd talked about it frequently, but in a way that made it seem unremarkable. But now, to music that was moderately slow and faintly poignant, Hilary flowed around the room. It was as if she were somehow an extension of the music, bringing it to life. Not wanting her to see him and stop what she was doing, he slipped into the shadows of the corner near the door, leaning against the wall. After a few minutes, he felt so moved that he slid to the floor and just sat there, feeling somehow weak.

That song ended and another began, this time with a hard, strong beat that he could feel through the floor. She accommodated herself to the music so fluidly that he couldn't help being fascinated. Now she was jumping—no, *leaping*—as if she were weightless. She spun and twirled on feet that moved so fast he could hardly see them. He wondered if he would feel so touched by this experience if he didn't care for her the way he did. Knowing such a thought was irrelevant, he just leaned back and absorbed it, feeling as if he were in some French museum, observing centuries-old art.

Most of the lyrics were difficult to understand, and it wasn't the kind of music he generally listened to. But he caught a few phrases that only added to the ethereal quality of the moment.

Locking rhythms to the beat of her heart, changing movement into life. She has danced into the danger zone, where the dancer becomes the dance. She's dancing like she's never danced before . . . never stopping with her head against the wind.

Jack kept thinking she would stop, and then he would make his presence known. But she danced to two songs, then three and four. On the fifth, she walked to a corner of the room and pulled something out of a bag on the floor. She sat down, and he could barely discern that she was changing her shoes, wrapping ribbons around her ankles and tying them. Then she went to the tape player and stopped it. The room became eerily silent until she pushed a button, and an entirely different kind of music began. She moved to the side of the room and lifted a leg onto a bar, stretching over it as if she could fold right in half. She did the same with the other leg, then she moved to the center of the room and began to dance. He understood the change of shoes when she went up on her toes. Jack actually caught his breath to see her do that. He'd seen a little ballet on TV, and it had certainly been intriguing, although he'd never bothered with it for more than a minute or two. But this was *Hilary*, and she was *incredible*.

When the music ended, nothing more followed. Hilary stood in the ensuing silence, her hands on her hips, her entire upper body moving with each breath. She wiped a sleeve over her face, then put her hand back on her hip. Jack got quietly to his feet and stepped toward her.

Hilary gasped and turned when she sensed more than heard movement behind her. "Oh, Jack!" She laughed and sat abruptly on the floor. "You scared me. How long have you been here?"

"Since you turned the lights out," he said.

Hilary looked up at him. "You're serious."

"Yes, I'm serious."

"Why didn't you say something?"

"I was enjoying myself. I was afraid you'd stop if you knew I was here."

"I certainly would have," she said, seeming embarrassed. "What are you doing here, anyway?"

"Just . . . needed a friend, I guess. And I thought maybe you'd prefer a ride home to the bus."

"Oh, that would be nice, but . . . why do you need a friend? Is something wrong?"

"No, just . . . lonely, I guess."

There was silence.

"Now that I'm here," he finally said, "maybe I could get that dance lesson . . . just something simple. I don't think I want to do the toe thing."

Hilary laughed and held out her hand for Jack to help her to her feet. "Men don't do the toe thing."

"What a relief," he chuckled. "What *do* men do?"

"Well, actually, when they dance with a woman, they kind of just stand there and hold her up. But really, Jack, I don't think ballet is up your alley."

"I can stand there and hold you up," he insisted. "Show me."

Hilary laughed, startled by his seriousness. "Okay," she finally said, putting her hand into his. Then she went up on one toe, using his hand as she would the bar, lifting her other leg high in front of her, then gracefully pushing it behind into an arabesque. She bent forward, consequently lifting her leg until her toe nearly pointed toward the ceiling. Jack's grip remained firm and steady until she slowly lowered her leg to meet the other one.

"Okay, now take my waist," she said, and he did. "Keep your hands there, but don't hold too tight, so I can move."

"I'm with you," he said in a voice that was almost dazed.

Hilary spun on one toe and ended in another arabesque. Then she abruptly stepped down, and the spell was broken.

"Very good, Hayden," she said. "Maybe ballet *is* your thing. But I'm not sure you'd appreciate the wardrobe."

"Probably not," he smirked. "Although . . . it looks good on you."

Hilary sat on the floor to remove her point shoes.

"Hey, what about my dance lesson?"

"Don't get all uptight. I'm just changing my shoes."

Hilary felt tense and conspicuous as she turned on the music and attempted to show Jack some basic dance steps that he could use at any social dance. But she quickly relaxed as he followed her lead easily and kept her laughing. She was surprised by his natural rhythm, and even more so by how much fun she was having. After an adequate lesson, a song began to play on the tape that was perfect for slow dancing. Hilary put Jack's hand at her waist, and took the other into hers. They moved together without much trouble. She smiled and said, "Ooh, you're good."

"Yeah, this two-step thing takes lots o' talent."

"Yes, it does, actually. You told me you were awkward."

"I always thought I was."

"Well," she smiled, "I disagree."

Hilary felt a little unnerved by the way he watched her so closely as they danced. She pressed her head to his shoulder, if only to avoid his gaze.

Jack closed his eyes and inhaled her nearness, as if he could keep it forever. The lyrics settled into him as he pressed his arm just a little further around her waist.

. . . And when I need to see you again, all I have to do is close my eyes. . . . I'll be here where the heart is . . . I'll wait for you.

Jack became lost in the music, indulging himself in a fantasy that just seemed too good to be true. The song's ending startled him to reality, and Hilary took a step back. "Oh, my gosh," she gasped, glancing at her watch. "It's past eleven o'clock. I've got classes early in the morning."

"I'm sorry," he said.

"Oh, don't apologize," she insisted, gathering up her things and turning off the stereo. "I had a good time. I didn't realize you were so talented."

Jack laughed. "Hey, you ain't seen nothin' yet. Me and Gene Kelly, we go way back."

Hilary laughed and locked up the door while he held her bag. Then he drove her home, saying as she got out of the truck, "Thanks, Hil. It was fun."

"It was my pleasure," she said as he often did. "Thanks for the ride."

Winter moved into spring while Hilary remained terribly busy. She pulled favorable grades in her classes, and her love for teaching dance grew steadily. She continued to see Jack regularly, and dated others here and there. All in all, she felt that her life was good. There was only one thing that nagged at her, but she felt certain it always would. Jeffrey's absence in her life, and the way she'd lost him, continued to haunt her. But it was something she tried not to think about—and she never talked about it. The only people she *could* talk to were her parents and Jack. While her folks missed Jeffrey, they seemed to have come to terms with his death a long time ago. And for some reason, it was just too sensitive an issue to discuss with Jack. So she simply didn't talk about it, hoping that one day she would be free of the nagging doubts that made it difficult for her to have the kind of relationship with God that she really wanted. As long as Hilary didn't think too hard about Jeffrey, life seemed to be pretty good, and she couldn't find any reason to complain.

On a rainy April morning, Jack called when she was barely out of bed. "Is something wrong?" she asked.

He was silent for a moment. "I just wanted to let you know that I'm going to Mt. Pleasant for a few days. I didn't want you to wonder where I was if you needed something."

"Okay, but . . . why? What's up?"

Again he was silent.

"Jack?"

He cleared his throat. "Uh . . . my mother called a couple of hours ago. My dad died last night."

"Oh, Jack, no. What happened?"

She could tell that he was struggling for composure. "Uh . . . he . . . well, I guess it was a heart attack."

"Are you okay?" Hilary asked gently.

"No, not really. But I'm sure I'll make it through. I'm certainly not the first person alive to lose a father."

"No, but . . . it's got to be tough."

"Yeah," his voice broke, "it's tough."

"My heart is with you."

"Thanks, Hil. That means more than you know."

For several minutes after Hilary hung up the phone, she sat staring at it. Could she miss classes for a couple of days? Could she get someone to cover for her at the studio? It would only take a minute to find out.

Everything worked out so easily that when she called Jack only ten minutes after he'd called her, she felt confident she was doing the right thing. "Hi," she said. "When are you leaving?"

"In about ten minutes."

"Can I go with you, or is that not a good idea?"

"Hilary, don't think that you have to—"

"I just want to go, Jack. I've been through a death before, remember? I figured you could use a friend. I'll stay out of the way and—"

"It's not that, Hilary. I just—"

"If you don't want me to go, Jack, say so. If you're not comfortable with it, okay. I'm just telling you I'd like to come along. Funerals and viewings and everything that goes along with them can get pretty long and difficult."

Jack tried to swallow the knot in his throat, but his voice betrayed his emotion. "I'd like nothing more than to have you with me, Hilary."

"Good. I'll be ready in ten minutes."

When Jack came to the door, Hilary put her arms around him with a tight embrace. He held her with a desperation that betrayed his emotion.

"Oh, my." They both heard and turned to see Lorie standing in the hallway, wearing a very short nightshirt. "What is this?"

"Nothing," Hilary said. "Why don't you go put some clothes on?"

Lorie lightly called Hilary a prude and disappeared down the hall.

"Sorry," Hilary said, but Jack only picked up her bag and they walked out to the truck beneath an umbrella.

Through the drive, Hilary asked questions about Jack's father and got him talking about pleasant memories. Occasionally he stopped to control his emotion, and more than once a stray tear trickled down his cheek. "I've told you," he said, "that most of my family isn't active. In fact, my brothers are a lot like Mom. They drink a little too much, and they can be pretty belligerent." Hilary nodded. "But we have some extended family that are active. The thing is, I know it's going to be up to me to plan the funeral, and I want it to be a good one. He may not have been a religious man, but he was a good man, and I want tribute paid to him appropriately—according to my beliefs."

"I think that's wonderful," Hilary said quietly.

"Well, I'm not so sure I can pull it off without resistance. I'm afraid my mother will accuse me of shoving religion down their throats, and my brothers will back her up. You know, me and Dad, we were always close. He was always in my corner, so to speak. Now it's me against them."

"Well, just do what you feel is right, and do the best you can. Concede to them on some things that don't matter, and I'm sure it will work out. It doesn't have to be really religious to be spiritual, does it? If you get up and talk about the relationship you had with your father, and bear your testimony of life after death, what would that hurt?"

Jack absorbed her advice and felt warmed. "Yeah, I'm sure you're right. Thanks, Hil. I'm glad you came."

"Me too. How many brothers do you have?"

"Two. They're both older."

"And no sisters?"

"Nope." He smiled. "Just you."

Following a brief silence, Hilary admitted, "I feel a little guilty."

"Why?"

"I've never even met your family. And now I'll never meet your father. I just . . . wish I had."

"You will . . . one day."

"Yes," she took his hand, "maybe I will."

Jack glanced down at their clasped hands and looked back to the road with a little smile.

"What?" she asked.

"You're holding my hand. You'd better be careful; I might get the idea you like me or something."

"I do like you," she said lightly, "but don't go making something of it."

Jack smiled and tried to convince himself that they would never be more than friends. But Hilary continued to hold his hand. She went to his home and washed dirty dishes while Jack tried to console his mother. She called the Relief Society president and informed her of the situation, letting her know that this would be a good service opportunity that might leave an impression on Judy Hayden, since she'd just lost her husband and could use some friendship and support. Then she went to the mortuary with Jack and sat with him as he made the funeral arrangements, since his brothers didn't seem to care one way or the other, and his mother was too absorbed in grief to think.

Hilary was there when the bishopric came to visit the family. Judy barely came out of her bedroom for a few minutes, but she thanked them for their visit. A meal arrived from the Relief Society, and Hilary helped serve it and clean up afterward. She was there to oversee the meals that arrived the following two days. She ordered flowers and wrote up the obituary and got it to the newspaper.

Jack was surprised by how many people came to the viewing, and he realized that his father had been a prominent figure around town, as well as a respected farmer, even if he hadn't gone to church. He marveled at Hilary's endless support; he only had to glance up and see her somewhere in the room at any given time. He had to admit that whether she ever saw anything romantic in him or not, she'd become a true friend, and he was grateful for that. She held his hand through the funeral and rode with him in the limousine to the cemetery, where the grave was dedicated.

When the service was over and everyone had headed back to their cars, Jack noticed tears streaming down Hilary's cheeks. "What is it?" he asked quietly, handing her a tissue out of his suit coat pocket.

"I was just thinking about Jeffrey's funeral."

"You've probably been thinking about it a lot the last few days."

"Yes, actually, I have."

"I wish I had been there."

"Me too," she said and walked back toward the car.

They returned to the church building for a luncheon prepared by the Relief Society. Jack was amazed at the love and support of the ward members, especially when his parents had been so inactive—and his mother had been downright difficult. He recalled more than once hearing her tell the visiting teachers to go to hell and never come back.

As Hilary hovered close to Jack through the luncheon, she realized that gossip would probably get started about them. But she didn't care; she had no intention of ever living in this town again, anyway. What these people thought simply didn't concern her.

Hilary was nearly finished with her meal when one of Jack's brothers whispered to him, "I'm taking Mom home. I think she's had it."

"Okay, I'll be there as soon as things wind down here."

When they had gone, Hilary whispered, "Your brothers have actually done pretty well."

"Yes, they have, I must admit . . . and I'm grateful. I couldn't handle her on my own. My dad has been the center of her life since she was a teenager. He's taken care of her every need and catered to her every whim. I'm not sure she'll make it without him."

Hilary went back to Jack's home with him to see if anything needed to be done. Judy rarely even acknowledged Hilary's presence, but she just helped around the house anyway. She'd only been there a while when Jack was called into his mother's room. Hilary could hear his mother sobbing and screaming, and it made her heart ache. Finally, Jack came out to call the family doctor. He then said to Hilary, "I'm going down to the drugstore to pick up a prescription. We've got to get her to calm down."

Hilary volunteered, "Let me go get it. You stay with her."

"Thanks. You've been wonderful."

"It's my pleasure," she said, and took the keys to his truck.

Standing at the drug counter while the pharmacist hurried to finish preparing the prescription, Hilary heard a voice say, "Well, hello, Hilary. How are you?"

Hilary turned to see a girl she'd gone to school with—Lizzie Rae Peterson. She was even more obese than she'd been when they'd graduated. And the snippy attitude she'd been famous for was still evident in the tone of her voice.

"I'm okay. How are you?"

"I noticed you at the viewing last night. I hear you and Jack have become quite a thing."

"You hear the strangest things in these small towns."

"Well, it's a little obvious, isn't it? You're with him all the time. He must be your boyfriend."

"We're friends," Hilary said without elaborating.

Lizzie looked like the cat attempting to swallow the canary. "Yeah, I'm sure you are. I must say it's a relief to know he's got a girl. We were all beginning to wonder if he was gay or something."

By *we*, Hilary knew she meant her tacky little group of friends who were too homely or obnoxious to get dates, so they spent their time gossiping about and criticizing the *rest* of single society in this town. Hilary looked directly at Lizzie and said firmly, "That is the most disgusting, ridiculous thing I have ever heard. Why don't you find something productive to do with your life?"

The pharmacist interjected, "Here it is; prescription for Judy Hayden." Hilary paid for it, aware of Lizzie's snide expression—as if this was one more piece of evidence to favor her theory.

"So, is he your boyfriend or not?" Lizzie asked, walking with Hilary toward the door. "I mean, he must be something for you to be hanging on him all through the funeral like that, and—"

"You know, Lizzie, Jack Hayden is one of the most decent people I know outside of my own family. Our relationship, whatever it might be, is quite frankly none of your business. If you don't see any wedding announcements, then there's nothing to talk about."

Hilary walked out of the store and got into Jack's truck. She was annoyed by Lizzie's attitude, mostly because she knew there were others in this town who shared her mentality. It was one of many things about small towns that she disliked. She reminded herself that she could find that kind of mentality anywhere, but it didn't lessen her desire to find a life elsewhere.

By the time Hilary had returned to Jack's house, she'd forgotten all about Lizzie. While Jack didn't leave his mother's side, she realized there was nothing more she could do to help, so she discreetly called her father and asked him to come and get her. She left Jack a note and went home.

The following morning was Sunday, and Hilary went to church with her parents. Sacrament meeting came last, and the opening song had barely begun when Jack slipped onto the bench beside her. "My ward meets later, and I didn't want to miss church," he said. "I want to leave about two or three so I can take care of some things when I get back. Is that okay?"

Hilary nodded and whispered, "Are you all right?"

"I think so. Once we got Mom drugged, she was out for the night. This morning she seems depressed, but she's calm. She basically told me to go away, so I guess that's my signal to leave town."

He said it tonelessly, but Hilary sensed the hurt. She squeezed his hand and turned her attention to the meeting. Jack went to her house for dinner at Millie's insistence, but on the way Hilary noticed that his bags were already in the back of the truck, ready to leave for Provo. He changed his clothes before dinner, then helped with the dishes afterward. Hilary noticed her mother talking quietly with him near the sink, then she hugged him tightly and he discreetly wiped his eyes.

After they left the house, Jack asked, "Would you mind if we stop by the cemetery before we leave town?"

"No, not at all," she said.

They walked together toward his father's grave. The freshly turned earth that covered it was a startling contrast to the green lawn surrounding them. A wide array of flowers were laid over the ground that Hilary knew would soon be covered with sod, and in a few weeks the headstone would be set in place. Jack cried as he stood beside his father's grave, and Hilary just put her arms around him. "Sorry I'm so short," she said.

"You're not short."

"Okay, you're tall. Either way, my shoulder isn't very accessible when we're standing up."

"That's okay." He rested his chin on top of her head for a moment. "You're still right where I need you." He sighed and added, "Hilary, I can't thank you enough for being with me through this. You were amazing. I don't know what I would have done."

"It felt good to be helping somebody. I'm glad I was there."

They stood in silence for several minutes. She knew Jack felt hesitant to leave, and she understood. She'd felt what he was feeling.

"I guess we should go," he finally said.

"I'm not in any hurry."

A few minutes later, he tugged on her hand. "Come on."

Hilary tugged back and stopped him. "Would it be okay if we go to Jeffrey's grave before we leave?"

"Sure," Jack said, wishing he had thought of it.

Hilary went straight to the headstone and stood looking down at it. Jack put his arm around her shoulders. "I wish I would have been here."

"Yeah, me too."

"I would have liked to see him one last time."

"None of us saw him," she said. "It was a closed-casket funeral. The accident was . . . well, you know what I mean."

Jack nodded and squeezed his eyes shut. Tears that were already too close to the surface ran down his face as he considered an aspect of his friend's death that he'd never thought of before.

Hilary cried herself, oblivious to Jack's tears. She ached to feel the kind of peace that she knew her parents and most of her siblings felt. She wondered what was wrong with her, that she couldn't get past it. She expected to miss him—but she wasn't certain she could live with this lingering anger inside her that erupted every time she thought about it. She wondered if she could actually talk to Jack, now that they'd become so much closer. But death was too close to him right now. Perhaps, with time, they could both come to terms with it.

Without a word, Hilary started back toward the truck and he followed. She walked slowly, not anxious to leave, grateful for Jack's arm around her shoulders.

"I wish I would have been there for you when Jeffrey died, the way you've been there for me the last few days."

"You've been there for me a great deal since then, Jack, and I'm grateful. You were where you were supposed to be."

Jack said nothing more, but Hilary's mind tallied all he had done for her since last summer, when he'd shown up in her life and refused to go away. A thought struck her, and she felt compelled to ask, "Why have you been so good to me, Jack?"

He chuckled tensely. "There are a lot of reasons. I cared for Jeffrey. He got me through a lot. Your parents are practically like family to me. I just—"

"No." She stopped walking and made him do the same, turning to face him. "Why have you been so good to *me*? I haven't always been kind to you, but you've always been there for me. Why?" He glanced down and gave a tight, nervous laugh. "Have you got some ulterior motive or something? You look downright guilty."

Jack looked at her briefly and glanced away, unnerved by her perception. Then his eyes were drawn back to hers.

"What?" she pressed, her heart quickening when she saw the intensity in his eyes. She almost felt scared.

Jack watched Hilary's expression, and his heart began to pound. Could he tell her the truth? Well, he certainly couldn't lie. It just wasn't in him to deceive her. But the thought of facing the truth of his feelings for her was frightening. He knew how *she* felt, and he believed there was nothing he could say or do to change that.

"Jack," she said when the intensity of his expression only deepened, "you're scaring me."

"No need for that," he said.

"Okay, so tell me what's on your mind. I just asked a simple question, but . . . obviously it doesn't have a simple answer."

Jack shook his head. "Hilary," he said, "I guess it's time I was completely honest with you." He took a deep breath and drew back his shoulders, drawing the courage to look directly at her as he said it. "I have loved you for so long, I don't remember what it was like not to love you."

Hilary looked into his eyes, searching for some evidence that he was joking. *But he wasn't.*

Jack's heart began to pound through the raw silence that followed his confession. He felt as if he'd just held out a hand to a man-eating crocodile. Instead he had exposed his heart, knowing fully that Hilary Smith had no such feelings for him. He saw her brow furrow and her eyes go narrow. She took a step back, then turned away.

Hilary tried to find some words to fill the persistent silence. She finally had to admit, "I don't know what to say."

Jack cleared his throat. "I would hope you'd be honest. I wouldn't expect anything less of you."

Hilary chuckled with no humor.

"Just tell me what you feel, Hilary." He set his hands on her shoulders and felt her bristle at his touch.

She spoke slowly and deliberately. "I feel . . . I feel like you're destroying our friendship by trying to turn it into something romantic."

Jack turned her to face him, holding her shoulders in his hands. "I'm not *trying* to do anything, Hilary. I'm telling you how I *feel.*

We're two adults, who should be mature enough to discuss our feelings and act on them appropriately."

While Hilary was searching for the words to tell him that she didn't feel *anything,* Jack tightened his grip on her shoulders and whispered fervently, "Talk to me, Hilary."

Seeing the intensity in his eyes, it was tempting to smooth it over; to tell him what he wanted to hear. His vulnerability was painfully evident. His father's grave wasn't even cold yet. But honesty was the only option, and she prayed inwardly for help in finding the right words.

"Jack," she finally said, "I care for you. I am grateful beyond words for all you've done for me. Our friendship really means something to me, and I don't want to lose that. But . . ."

"But?" he pressed when she didn't finish.

"We're just not . . . compatible, Jack."

Jack didn't agree, but he only said, "How is that?"

"Well . . . ," she floundered, "like . . . our goals, and . . ."

"Our goals?" he questioned. "Like getting married in the temple? Living the gospel? Raising a family? Doing our best to get back to where we came from? Are those not your goals, too?"

"That's not what I mean."

"Oh." He pushed his hands into his pockets and forced his voice to remain steady. "What you mean, then, are temporal goals. Where to live, career choices—things like that."

"Yes," Hilary said, "that's what I mean."

Jack wanted to add to the list her goal to not marry a farm boy and live in a small town, because she knew he loved the farm life and he'd come back here to stay in a minute. He knew that was a lot of it, and the thought made him angry—that her prejudice might come between them. But bringing it up would only make *her* angry. And he'd already pressed this further than he had the strength to handle right now.

"Hilary," Jack said gently, "I've always believed that love could overcome any earthly struggle."

He saw her eyes harden, and he knew what was going through her mind. He could almost feel the words on the edge of her thoughts. *But I don't love you, Jack.* He understood why it would be difficult for her to say it. He took a deep breath and reminded himself that if he was any kind of a man, he would not coerce her into saying something she didn't want to say. Wondering how they'd even gotten into this conversation, he struggled to find a way to get out of it and save face for both of them. He swallowed hard and said, "But if you don't love me, Hilary . . . if the feeling isn't there, then . . ."

Hilary watched Jack's eyes and felt the urge to cry. She wished she could tell him she loved him. But she couldn't. And they both knew it. Still, he had left a bridge between them, and she had to have the courage to walk across it.

"Jack," she touched his face, "it just . . . isn't there. Please understand, and . . . don't let it come between us. I need you."

Jack briefly tried to comprehend what that meant. Did being her friend mean standing on the sidelines while she continued to date other men, and eventually married someone else? Could he bear it? Would it be better to just end it now, and spare himself any more misery? But could he bear not being a part of her life at all? He'd grown to depend on her. He needed her.

The reality culminated in a sudden rush of emotion. Perhaps if he hadn't just buried his father, the tears wouldn't have been so close to the surface. But they fell down his face before he even had a chance to think about holding them back.

"Jack," she cried, "you're breaking my heart."

She pushed her arms around him, and he eagerly accepted her embrace. "There's no need for that." He forced out a little laugh, if only to avoid sobbing. He didn't bother adding that his heart was breaking enough for both of them. Struggling to cope, he forced thoughts of their conversation out of his head. But all he could replace them with was the reality that his father was gone.

Without a word he walked toward the truck, keeping his arm around her, fighting with everything he had not to just break down and sob. His head was pounding and his throat was tight. They drove for several miles while he managed to maintain his composure, then he pulled off to the side of the road when his vision blurred and he couldn't drive.

"What is it?" Hilary asked as he hung his head and the tears oozed out like hot lava bubbling out of a volcano that was threatening to blow any second. He shook his head, unable to speak. "Do you want to talk about it?" He shook his head again. "Do you want me to drive?" He nodded.

Hilary got out and walked around the truck. Jack slid over as she got in and fastened her seat belt. She was keenly aware of his emotion as she adjusted the mirrors and pulled out onto the highway, but she felt helpless. Were these tears for her, or for his father? Or both?

"You can cry, Jack," she said, sensing that he was holding back. "You're not going to embarrass me."

He wanted to tell her that it wasn't her he was worried about embarrassing, but he couldn't speak. Instead he just let it out, as if her permission was all he needed. Unable to sit up straight, he put his head down on the seat and just cried, vaguely aware of Hilary's hand on his shoulder, gently reminding him of her presence.

Hilary shed a few tears of her own as she observed the evidence of Jack's mourning, while her mind replayed his confession of love. She thought of the time they'd spent together, their conversations, all he'd done for her. Had he been feeling this way all along? The thought was alarming, yet touching somehow.

When his emotion finally settled into silence, Hilary asked, "Are you going to be okay?"

"Eventually."

At the risk of jumping back into their difficult conversation of earlier, Hilary said, "Talk to me, Jack."

"I just can't believe he's gone. I just can't believe it."

Hilary sighed. "I know what you mean."

"Yes, I know you do. Maybe that's why I can cry like a baby with you around."

"My dad always said it took a lot of courage to cry. He cried a great deal when we lost Jeffrey. Personally, I think real men aren't afraid to cry when it hurts. It's the fake men who think they're too macho to shed a tear."

"Like Leon," he said with a chagrin that took on new meaning in light of his recent confessions.

"Yes, like Leon," she said, trying to pretend that nothing was any different between them.

As the weeks passed, Hilary was relieved to see that for the most part, nothing tangible had changed between them. He seemed more somber, but she attributed that to the death of his father. Occasionally she would catch something in his eyes—that same something she had seen when he had confessed his love to her. And she knew that in spite of whatever pretense he might show, his feelings for her went much deeper than the friendship they shared. But she tried to ignore it and appreciate their relationship for what it was, hoping that Jack would eventually be able to do the same.

On the positive side, because they had shared honesty on such a difficult level, it became easier for them to talk about deeper feelings. Their relationship took a new shift as they had long, deep spiritual discussions. They talked about self-worth, faith, and the Atonement. They talked about life and death and principles related to them that Hilary had never considered before. As she took the time to hear what Jack had to say, and to study her scriptures and discuss what she learned with him, she was amazed that the things troubling her began to take on a new perspective. When she admitted to having trouble dealing with Jeffrey's death, Jack challenged her to take what she'd learned, then fast and pray that she might have peace. "And you might want to read this," he said, giving her a folder thick with white pages.

"What is it?" she asked.

"It's from your brother's journals. Your mother let me borrow them a while back, and I asked her if I could make copies of some segments that meant a lot to me. I must confess, it's gotten me through some difficult feelings."

Hilary admitted that she was nearly afraid to read what Jeffrey had written. But she took on Jack's challenge—all of it. And with time, the answers came. Hilary knew beyond any doubt that it had truly been Jeffrey's time to go; otherwise the Lord would have warned him, or protected him, because he was a righteous man. She came to understand through the whisperings of the Spirit that Jeffrey had a mission to be filled on the other side of the veil, and he was busy and happy where he was now. And through Jeffrey's own writings, she knew he had instinctively been prepared for his death; something in his spirit had known, if only subconsciously. It came through in the thoughts he'd written through the final weeks of his life.

As Hilary shared her newfound peace with Jack, she believed it helped him come to terms with his father's death. He said he'd like to hope his father was embracing the gospel on the other side, and when a year had passed, he intended to do his father's temple work.

Hilary was aware that the situation with Jack's mother wasn't good. She was drinking more than ever, and only knowing that Jack's brother was living with her gave Jack any peace. He knew there was nothing he could do, but he was concerned about the farm and how to keep it going, knowing that neither of his brothers would do anything with it. The decision was made to lease the land, so they wouldn't have to worry about working it. Jack knew it was the best thing, at least until he finished school and was ready to settle down. But it was difficult for him to see someone else working his father's land.

All of his father's equipment was divided among the brothers. The other two promptly sold what they'd been given, but Jack fought to get the round baler, and he asked Hilary's father to keep it for the time being and use it as much as he needed.

When summer came, Hilary stayed in Provo to continue teaching. The studio she worked for had many summer activities planned for the students, and she enjoyed her work and wanted to be involved. By putting more hours in she was able to get a car, and she appreciated the independence it gave her.

Jack went to Mt. Pleasant for the summer, staying with his mother. He and his brother, Don, stayed out of each other's way as much as possible. Don sat around the house and took care of Judy. Jack worked at the gas station some every day, kept the house and yard maintained, repaired fence lines on the land they were leasing, and even helped the farmer who was leasing the land a bit here and there. He also spent a great deal of time with Hilary's parents, helping on their farm and around the house. More and more, he preferred their home over his own. Occasionally he just slept in the spare bedroom and didn't even bother going home. All in all, he stayed too busy to miss Hilary—but he did anyway.

Through the summer, Hilary found her thoughts and feelings leading her in a direction that was completely unexpected. In coming to terms with Jeffrey's death, she had learned things about herself and the gospel that she had never considered before. Putting the pieces together, and seeing where she was in her life, new desires began to blossom in her. Needing some sound feedback, she made arrangements to go home for a weekend. She left after classes ended on a Thursday evening and pulled up in front of the house in Mt. Pleasant at about ten-thirty. The front room lights were on, but the rest of the house was dark. Hilary knew her father had likely gone to bed, but her mother would be up reading for another little while.

The door was locked, and Millie laughed when she opened it to see Hilary standing there.

"What are you doing here?" she asked, ushering her daughter into the house. "Not that I'm complaining. It's good to see you."

"It's good to see you, too, Mom."

They sat and shared some small talk, then Hilary slipped into her parents' bedroom to kiss her father good night. She talked to him a few minutes, then left him to go to sleep and went to the phone. She knew it was late, but Jack had told her that his mother usually slept half the day and stayed awake until two or three in the morning watching TV.

"Is Jack there?" she asked when his brother answered.

"Nope," he said through a yawn. "Haven't seen him all day."

"Do you know where he is?"

"Nope," he repeated.

Hilary sighed, actually feeling worried. "Okay, thank you."

"Who are you trying to call at this hour?" Millie asked as she walked in the kitchen to find Hilary hanging up the phone.

"I wanted to talk to Jack, but they don't know where he is, and—"

"Well, I know where he is. You should have asked me first."

"Okay, Mother," Hilary smiled. "Where's Jack?"

"He's upstairs in the spare bedroom."

"Oh, really." Her smiled widened.

"He just walked up the stairs about five minutes before you came."

"Well, then I think I'll just go talk to him. We'll visit more tomorrow, okay, Mom?"

"I'll look forward to it," Millie said, and they exchanged a hug and a kiss.

Hilary went quietly up the stairs, past the room that used to be Jeffrey's, past her own room, and stopped at the third bedroom that had been used to house guests ever since the oldest two children had left home. She took a deep breath and knocked lightly at the door.

"Yeah?" she heard him call.

"Are you decent?" she called back.

"No, but I'm under the covers." Jack leaned over to turn on the bedside lamp as the door swung open. He'd expected it to be Millie, but he wasn't disappointed at all to see Hilary. "What are you doing here?" he laughed and sat up, leaning against the headboard.

"I was about to ask you the same. Moving in, eh?"

"It beats the heck out of living with Mt. Pleasant's greatest alcoholic."

"Things aren't too good, huh?"

"No, but . . . well, sit down." He patted the side of the bed. "What brings you home this time of day?"

"Well, there's something I've been thinking about, Jack. I need to talk to my parents about it, but I wanted to talk to you first. I'm so glad you're here. Maybe that was an answer to my prayers."

Jack smiled, then he realized she was nervous. "What is it, Hil? Is something wrong?"

"No, I mean . . . not really. I would hope you'd be happy for me, but . . ."

Jack's heart began to pound. Was she going to tell him she'd met someone? Was she getting married? Could he bear it?

"Well, out with it," he insisted, unable to tolerate the suspense.

"Jack, I never thought this was something I'd do. I mean . . . I just thought Leon would come home from his mission and marry me, and I'd be having babies by now."

"Well, I'm glad you're not . . . at least not his babies."

"Yeah, me too," she admitted eagerly.

"So, what is it?"

"Jack, I want to go on a mission."

Jack's relief in knowing that she wasn't talking about a love interest was nothing compared to the warmth that filled him as he observed her countenance and the conviction in her eyes. He marveled at how far she had come, but he couldn't find the words to express it.

"Well," she began to ramble, "I'll be twenty-one in November, and if I start working on my papers now and get them sent in, I could probably go right after my birthday. What do you think? Is it crazy?"

Jack shook his head and couldn't resist the urge to hug her. "No, Hilary," he said close to her ear, "it's not crazy. I think it's wonderful."

She pulled back and looked into his eyes. "You do? Really?"

"Really. There's nothing better you can do with your life at this point, Hilary. If you go, you'll never regret it." He sighed and added, "That's what Jeffrey told me."

In that moment, Hilary had to acknowledge that in nearly every way, Jack had become the brother she had lost. When he'd first shown up in their lives, she'd resented his presence, fearing he would try to replace Jeffrey. Now she could see that he was a blessing from God who had helped her and her parents to cope with Jeffrey's loss, and to somehow compensate for his absence.

"Oh, that's what I needed to hear, Jack." She hugged him again. "I prayed that you would support me in this." She eased back and tucked her feet beneath her on the bed. "But I'm afraid my parents won't be happy about it."

"Why wouldn't they be?"

"Oh, I don't know. They've just always been so protective of me. It's different sending a daughter out, isn't it? And the money . . . you know how tight it's been since Jeffrey's death. I just don't know if they can handle it."

"The Church will help, Hillie. They helped me. Ward members donated. And I can pay a hundred dollars a month."

Hilary was almost speechless. "You would do that?"

"Of course. I would consider it an honor."

"Oh, Jack," she hugged him again, "you're the best friend a girl could ever ask for—even if you are a redneck."

Jack laughed, then with comical indignation he insisted, "I am *not* a redneck. I have not ever—nor will I ever—wear my name anywhere on my belt."

Hilary laughed and had to admit, "No, you're not a redneck. In spite of everything, you're really a very classy guy. And I love the way you let me tease you without getting offended."

"That works both ways," he said. "I used to tease you mercilessly when you were a little girl, and you always took it pretty well."

"When I was a little girl?" she asked lightly. "I wasn't aware that it had stopped."

"It's the pigtail theory," he said.

She ignored him and finished her thought. "You still put on this hick routine just to *rile* me. Isn't that how you put it?"

Jack chuckled, then his eyes became serious. "I knew it bothered you, and I just wanted to be sure you liked me for who I really am."

"A redneck," she said, attempting to be serious. Then she laughed as he mocked hurt feelings.

"Hilarious," he said, lifting his brows to draw attention to the double meaning.

"Hey," she leaned against the footboard of the bed, "what exactly *is* the pigtail theory?"

"Whoa, girl, you need to get out more."

"That's what you said the first time it came up. Tell me."

"You honestly don't know what it means when little boys tease little girls and pull their pigtails to make them cry?"

"No."

"Take a psychology class or something," he said.

"Just tell me!"

"They do it because they really *like* the girl. They're just too immature to know how to express it appropriately, so . . ."

The light mood surrounding them settled into something almost painfully uncomfortable as Hilary recalled Jack's confession. *I have loved you for so long, I don't remember what it was like not to love you.* Is that why Jack had incessantly teased her as a child—and since? Because he'd always felt drawn to her; because he'd always felt something for her that was difficult to express in any other way?

Jack watched Hilary's expression as she grasped the implication, then her eyes turned away as she obviously didn't know what to say. What could she say? Still, he was glad he'd said it. As uncomfortable as it was, he wanted her to know how he felt. And maybe, one day . . .

Taking the conversation back to a less sensitive point, Jack said earnestly, "I'm proud of you for deciding to go on a mission, Hil. I'm with you all the way."

"Thank you," she said, relieved that he wasn't going to talk any more about the pigtail theory. "With you behind me, I might actually be able to get there."

The following morning, Hilary was just sitting down at the breakfast table with her parents when Jack appeared and joined them. Following the blessing, Jack blurted out, "So, Hilary, have you told your parents the good news?"

"Uh . . ." She was caught so off guard she didn't know where to begin. "No, I just got here."

"What good news, sweetheart?" Pete asked.

"Uh . . . ," Hilary stammered, "I don't know where to start. Uh . . ." She looked at Jack and figured since he'd brought it up, he could handle it. "Why don't you tell them, Jack."

"I'd love to." He grinned and leaned back. "Hilary's going on a mission."

While Hilary had expected some kind of dismay or uncertainty, both her parents nearly flew out of their seats with excitement. They didn't seem concerned in the least about the money, and Hilary marveled at their faith. They rattled on with questions and speculations so long that their hot cereal turned cold. Jack just stood up and put their bowls into the microwave oven one at a time.

Hilary enjoyed her weekend at home, visiting with her parents and spending time with Jack. There were moments when the love in his eyes was evident, and it nearly broke her heart. A part of her wanted to love him the way he loved her. But in spite of how badly things had turned out with Leon, she would not marry someone who didn't evoke the kinds of feelings in her that she'd felt for Leon. And it simply wasn't there with Jack.

On Sunday, she returned to Provo and made an appointment with her bishop to get started on the necessary preparations for a mission. He told her the ward would be able to help some with the money, but he advised her to see what she could come up with on her own. This troubled her somewhat, but she reminded herself of her parents' faith—and Jack's—and she put it into the Lord's hands.

The following Saturday, Hilary called Janna and asked if she could come over because she had some news. Janna was thrilled and invited her to have lunch with the family. Hilary was literally on her way out the door when Jack showed up. "What are you doing here?" she asked.

"Just had to come up north to get some things, and thought I'd stop by. Where are you headed?"

"To visit a friend." Impulsively she asked, "Want to come?"

"Oh, I don't want to intrude," he said, relieved that it wasn't a male friend, or she wouldn't have invited him.

"Hold on," she said, and went into the bedroom where she called Janna to tell her a friend had just stopped by.

"Well, bring him, too," Janna insisted. "We'd love to meet him."

"I was hoping you'd say that," Hilary said, then she marched into the front room and ushered Jack out the door. "Come along," she said, "we're having lunch at Janna's house."

"Yes, ma'am," he drawled, and she laughed.

They went in Hilary's car, but she made Jack drive. When they pulled into the driveway, he commented, "Wow, nice house."

"Well, her husband's a pretty good attorney, from what I understand. But they've had more than their fair share of struggles."

"Ah, yes," Jack said, "this is the friend you met after she'd had an emotional breakdown."

"That's right. But, uh . . . we'll just keep quiet about that."

"Oh, yeah," Jack said firmly as they walked toward the door. He didn't know any more than that about Janna's situation, and he really didn't want to. He yanked the toothpick out of his mouth and stuck it in his pocket, muttering, "Wouldn't want to embarrass you."

Hilary only smiled at him. Janna rushed out before they even had a chance to knock, embracing Hilary enthusiastically. "Oh, it's so good to see you. And this must be Jack." She shook his hand firmly. "It's nice to finally meet you."

"And you," he said.

"Come in. Come in."

They stepped inside, and Janna introduced her husband, Colin, who shook Jack's hand firmly, then said to Hilary, "It's good to see you again."

"Well, lunch is ready. Come on into the kitchen," Janna urged.

As they were sitting down, Jack and Hilary were introduced to Janna's children. Hilary marveled that she had known Janna for as long as she had without ever meeting them. Matthew was fourteen years old and the spitting image of his father. And Caitlin and Mallory, ages six and five, hardly even looked like sisters, although they each had obvious features that belonged to their parents. Mallory, especially, favored her mother.

Hilary thoroughly enjoyed her time in Janna's home, and was relieved to see that Jack seemed relaxed and at ease. He and Colin actually exchanged some serious conversation, and Hilary found the contrast between the two men ironic.

When lunch was over and cleaned up, the adults went into the family room to visit. When Hilary announced her plans to go on a mission, Jack beamed, Janna got tears in her eyes, and Colin took his wife's hand as if to show empathy for her emotion.

Hilary nearly brought up the matter of money, since it was a prevalent concern, but she didn't want to make it sound as if her visit had been for the purpose of soliciting funds. After they had talked for another half an hour, Colin inquired, "How are you fixed financially for this mission, Hilary? Can we help?"

Again Jack beamed. Hilary got tears in her eyes. And Janna looked at her husband with so much warmth and admiration that it practically permeated the room.

When Hilary was overcome with emotion, Colin went on. "We were donating quite a bit to the mission fund in the ward for a long time. But most of our missionaries have come home; right now we only have two."

"One," Janna corrected. "The Wilkinson boy came home last month."

"Oh, that's right. One. And his family's rather well off, so they're doing fine. We've always considered such things a blessing, and we'd be more than happy to help."

Hilary was still too emotional to speak. She looked at Jack, and he took it as a cue to explain. "Hilary's parents are thrilled that she's going, but their financial resources are . . . well, actually they don't have any. When Hilary's brother died there wasn't any insurance, and it set them way back. I told Hilary I could cover a hundred a month, and I'm sure I can manage that. But the ward Hilary lives in has limited resources, and well . . . we've been praying she'd find the means to go. Apparently you're the answer to prayers."

Hilary nodded and finally managed to say, "Yeah, that's what I wanted to tell you."

"Well, how about if we cover two hundred a month?" Colin asked. Then to Janna, "Can we handle that? It might be a little tight, but—"

"We can handle it," she said firmly. "I think it's perfect."

Hilary went away from Janna's home feeling very loved and deeply humble. She called her parents as soon as they got back to her apartment and told them the good news. They felt certain that with whatever her ward would contribute, they could make up the difference and consider it a privilege.

Time flew for Hilary as she started school again and sent her papers in to Church headquarters. Since Jack had returned to Provo for school, she called him as soon as she got her mission call in the mail.

"Have you opened it?"

"No, of course not. I can't do it alone. Do you think we could fit in a quick drive to Mt. Pleasant and get back this evening? I want to be with Mom and Dad, but I can't wait."

"I'll pick you up in half an hour."

Hilary had butterflies in her stomach through the entire drive, and Jack kept laughing at her as she'd wrap her arms around her middle and moan. Since Pete and Millie had been warned with a phone call, they were waiting anxiously. With her audience present, Hilary opened the envelope and scanned the letter quickly. Her heart beat hard and fast as she absorbed it, then she said aloud, "I'm going to Bulgaria."

Jack knew he had the same thoughts go through his head as her parents. They couldn't help being happy, and they had to have faith that everything would be all right for Hilary. But *Bulgaria*? He was already worried about her. And oh, he was going to miss her!

Hilary felt both scared and excited as she prepared to go into the Missionary Training Center. The time flew, and before she knew it, it was time for her to go through the temple as part of her preparation. Most of the adults in her family were meeting to go through with her, and she was glad her parents had invited Jack to come, as well.

Jack enjoyed being in the temple with Hilary and her family, but for him it was an experience filled with mixed emotions. He was thrilled to see her going on a mission for many reasons, one of them being that it was far better than seeing her marry somebody else. And just maybe, a little time might change her feelings toward him. But seeing her wearing temple robes, within temple walls, made him ache to have her as his wife. For now, all he could do was hope and pray that she would be cared for through the next eighteen months, and that their lives would work out peacefully—whether it be separately or together.

The night before Hilary was to be set apart as a missionary, Jack insisted on taking her out for a nice dinner. After they had finished their salads, he stared at her across the table and smiled serenely.

"What?" She laughed softly.

"You're practically glowing. You're excited about this, aren't you."

Hilary sighed. "Yes, I am. And scared. But . . . I know it's the right thing to do."

Jack took her hand across the table. "You've come a long way."

Hilary nodded. "And I owe a great deal of my progress to you." He glanced down shyly, but she continued. "I'm serious, Jack. I don't think I ever really had a testimony before Jeffrey died. And I know I never really believed in myself; never believed I was capable of accomplishing anything great—of making a difference in somebody's life."

Jack looked into her eyes. "Well, you've made a difference in mine. And I'm proud of you for doing this. I'll write every week—I promise."

Hilary appreciated his efforts, but there was something she needed to say. "Jack, I don't want you to wait for me. I need your support, I know. But you need to get on with your life. You once got after me for pining away over something fruitless and meaningless. Now listen to me when I tell you that you can find happiness without me." He said nothing, but his lack of expression was obviously an attempt to avoid getting emotional. She could see it in his eyes. Hoping to lighten the mood, she leaned back and smiled. "You just need to find some cute little thing who can drive a tractor and marry her." He showed no response and she added, "But whatever you do, don't wait for me. You need to be dating and enjoying your life."

Jack tried to come up with the words to tell her that he truly believed they were meant to be together. But he knew in his heart that all his desires would never take away her free agency. His voice was hoarse when he finally said, "I'll do my best, Hil. You don't need to worry about me. You just get out there and change some lives, okay?"

Hilary nodded, and the tension lightened through the remainder of the meal. It was dark but relatively warm for November when they left the restaurant. Jack drove Hilary home, then asked if they could walk together for a while before they said good night. Hilary enjoyed their stroll and felt completely comfortable, even when Jack put his arm around her shoulders. The conversation was genial and added to the anticipation Hilary was feeling. Her thoughts were consumed with embarking on her mission as a warm silence fell over them and they continued to walk.

"Hilary," Jack said in a tone that let her know he was about to say something serious, "I have a favor to ask you. If you're not comfortable with it, all you have to do is say so."

"Okay. I'm listening."

Jack stopped walking and turned to face her, putting his hands on her shoulders. She could barely make out his expression from the glow of a street lamp farther up the block. "All I want is a kiss, Hilary. For all we've been through together, for whatever the future may bring . . . just let me kiss you good-bye."

Hilary couldn't think of any reason to protest that he didn't already know. Jack was well aware of where her feelings stood. And she was leaving for a very long time. She figured a kiss couldn't hurt any under the circumstances. She nodded slightly and saw relief flood his countenance. He reached out a hand to touch her face, and she caught her breath. The gesture surprised her as much as her own reaction. With his fingers, he slowly traced her features as if he were blind. There was something completely genuine in his touch; it was so adoring. She'd known for a long time that his feelings for her ran deep, but she'd never even begun to comprehend that depth until now. A part of her wished that she *did* love him; that it might be possible to spend the rest of her life with him and be content. But she reminded herself she was going on a mission, and any future beyond that simply didn't matter right now.

Hilary felt her heart quicken as his face moved slowly toward hers and he closed his eyes. And again she was surprised. She'd expected his kiss to be something she would politely endure. But the moment his lips made contact with hers, something inside her began to tingle. She felt herself respond at the same time his hand pressed into her hair. Just when she began to wish it could last forever, Jack eased away and pressed his forehead to hers, as if he could somehow absorb her thoughts. Or perhaps he wanted her to absorb his.

"I love you, Hilary," he murmured. While she was wondering how to respond, and attempting to quell the tingling inside her that still lingered from his kiss, Jack sighed deeply and stepped back. "Come on," he said, taking her hand, "you'd better get some sleep."

CHAPTER SIX

*J*ack went with the family to escort Hilary into the Missionary Training Center. It was an emotional experience for everyone, but Jack wondered if her family had any idea how he really felt about her. He suspected that her parents might. Or perhaps they just took it for granted, as Hilary did, that they were friends—like a brother and sister.

Hilary had only been away for a matter of hours when Jack sat down to write her a letter. There wasn't much to say that she didn't already know, but he did it anyway. He wrote faithfully at least once a week, and was relieved when letters came from her almost as often. He knew she was busy; he'd been through it himself. The fact that she took the time to write to him meant a great deal.

Through the following weeks, Jack kept extremely busy. But he still missed her, and it was difficult not to feel discouraged. He reminded himself that she was on a mission; he couldn't want anything more for her than this. He also reminded himself of the things she'd said before she left. *Don't wait for me. Find some cute little thing who can drive a tractor and marry her.* Logically, he knew her advice was probably good; but emotionally he just couldn't digest it, at least not yet. Perhaps, in that respect, her absence would be good for him. So he just kept busy and tried not to think about her.

Hilary experienced a combination of excitement and fear as she completed her training at the MTC, and her family met her at the airport to see her off to Bulgaria. Jack came, too. He hovered in the background and kept his distance, but Hilary felt the warmth of his presence, and she was grateful he'd come. When it came time to say good-bye, he was the last in line to hug her, and for some reason, it was difficult for her to let go. Jack's love for her was evident in his eyes, and it was the memory of his expression that brought her to tears once she was settled on the plane. Drawing on faith, Hilary tuned her thoughts in to what lay ahead and concentrated on filling her mission.

Through the first couple of months that Hilary was in Bulgaria, Jack's feelings continued to spiral downward for reasons he didn't understand. He missed her, yes. But he found a certain hopelessness in trying to imagine her returning and putting an end to the ache he felt. According to Hilary, she would return to seek a future elsewhere. She'd never been anything but honest about her feelings for him—or the lack thereof. In truth, she had been brutally honest. He appreciated knowing where he stood, instead of having to guess. But he did wonder if it was time he got on with his life. He missed her *so* much. But would missing her get him anywhere? She'd told him not to wait for her, and she'd made it repeatedly clear that, for all their friendship, she simply had no romantic interest in him. Was he being a fool to continue hoping for something that would never come to pass? If he looked at the situation logically, the answer was easy. *Yes,* he was being a fool.

Knowing the answers he needed were more spiritual in nature, he fasted and prayed for guidance. The only answer he could get that made any sense was to simply have patience. But patience for what? Patience to wait for her to come home and then come around? Maybe. But thinking it through logically, he doubted she would ever come around.

Looking at his life, Jack realized that he had little beyond Hilary and her family. The members of his own family seemed more like casual acquaintances than relatives. He was making progress in his schooling, and he enjoyed his job for the most part. His relationship with Ammon helped keep up his spirits, and they played basketball occasionally together to get some exercise. But Ammon had a wife and children. And beyond Ammon, Jack simply didn't have any good friends. The guys he roomed with were nice enough, but he'd just never connected with any of them beyond an occasional movie or pizza. Was there something wrong with him? he wondered. Had his upbringing somehow made him different from most of the people he knew, the same way his gravitation to Mormonism had drawn him away from his family?

Jack often spent time with Hilary's parents on the weekends, helping out where he was needed. He felt so close to them, and so warmed by their company, that he began to wonder if his attachment to Hilary was partly due to his desire to be a part of her family. Of course, in essence he was. He didn't need Hilary around to feel the love her parents had for him. Pete and Millie made up for the lack of his own mother's love and the absence of his father.

Jack was feeling particularly low on a Saturday afternoon in late January when he stopped by to see if Pete and Millie needed anything. He was sitting in the kitchen, eating from a bowl of popcorn Millie had made the previous evening, when he noticed a letter from Hilary lying on the table. "May I read this?" he asked.

"Oh, sure," Pete said, "but I doubt it says much different than what she writes to you."

"Probably not," Jack said, but he just wanted to read something she'd written—as if doing so here, in the home where she'd grown up, might make her feel closer.

Even though he'd heard it all before, he enjoyed hearing little details of the life she was living halfway around the world. Combining this letter with his memories of her previous letters, he could easily imagine her living in the center of town above a pastry shop. He could see her walking with her companion along a street lined with sidewalk cafes, her hair pulled back into a long ponytail. She'd told him how strongly the sister missionaries stood out, being taller than even most of the men, as well as distinctive in the way they dressed. And she'd told him how they could never be out after dark unless they were with the elders. He tried not to think about the dangers she might be in, and concentrated instead on the way she shared her experiences with the people they met.

As he read, Jack wondered if he was only inflicting misery upon himself; after all, reading this letter made him miss her all the more. But he was totally unprepared to read something that she had completely excluded from his letters—something that made his heart fall with a hard thud.

You remember the gypsy family I told you about. They were baptized yesterday, and it was probably the most incredible experience of my life. The oldest son in the family, who is about twenty-five, I think, is the one

I told you about, who bore his testimony at the town meeting they called after we did that service project in the village. Beyond being incredibly handsome, there's something about him that just stirs me. I know I told you about him already, but I just can't seem to get him out of my head. I've been praying hard about it and reminding myself hourly that I'm a missionary. But I could almost wonder, at moments, if there's something in the future for us. I know he feels much the same way, but he's made it clear that he understands the requirements of my being a missionary. I've never felt the way he makes me feel, but rest assured, Mother, I'm doing my best to be a good missionary and keep my thoughts in perspective. Didn't Rachel what's-her-name meet her husband on her mission? I guess you never know.

Knowing that Pete and Millie were in the room, Jack fought with everything he had to keep from screaming or breaking into tears. He'd certainly experienced jealousy before when it came to Hilary; she'd dated many other men, and he'd done his best to accept it. But what he felt now was more like an irreparable crack through the middle of his heart. Whether she ended up marrying a Bulgarian gypsy or not, Jack felt certain Hilary was lost to him.

A week later, he was still not doing any better. It was difficult for him to find anyone or anything he could connect with enough to make sense of his thoughts and feelings. Of course, he had the gospel, and he was grateful for its stability. But even that seemed difficult for him to grasp. He knew he wasn't putting into it what he should, but he found it hard to be motivated in anything.

Jack ran a few errands Saturday morning, which included picking up some things his mother had called and asked him to get. Recalling that he'd overlooked breakfast, he pulled into a burger place on the University Parkway to get an early lunch. He was standing with his hands in his back pockets, staring up at the menu, when a feminine voice startled him.

"Jack, isn't it?"

He turned to see a face, framed by dark, semi-long hair, that looked vaguely familiar. Not certain how he knew this woman, he simply said, "Yes, that's right."

"I thought so." She smiled, and Jack felt something tingle inside of him. He became speechless for reasons quite apart from not knowing what to say to her. He had no idea how she knew who he was, but he was definitely glad to be standing here right now.

At his continued silence she added, "I was Hilary's roommate for a while."

"Oh, of course," he said. "Your hair's different."

"I've been growing it out," she remarked, glancing down shyly.

"I'm sorry," he said, "but I don't remember your name."

"Lorie Walker." She held her hand out in greeting and he took it for a moment, squeezing more than shaking it.

"It's good to see you again, Lorie," he said, trying to remember what Hilary had told him about this woman.

"Uh . . . are you here alone?" She glanced behind him.

"Yeah, I, uh . . ."

"Well, I am, too. Would it be too presumptuous if I joined you?"

"That would be fine," he said.

The girl behind the counter called out a number and Lorie said, "Oh, that's mine. I'll save you a seat."

Jack nodded and moved to the counter to order. He sat across from Lorie to wait for his food. She smiled as she dipped a fry and asked, "So, how's Hilary these days? I know the two of you were quite a thing."

Jack cleared his throat. "She's on a mission, actually."

"Really?" Lorie laughed. "That's great . . . I mean . . . I never expected her to do that. But I think it's great."

"Yeah, it is."

"So, are you waiting for her, or—"

"Oh, no," he chuckled as if it was no big deal. "We were just friends. We keep in touch, and I'm helping out with the money a little. But that's as far as it goes. I see her parents quite a bit. Actually, she's more like a sister to me."

Lorie smiled even wider. "Oh, that's nice."

"There's my number," Jack said, and stood up to get his food. While he ate, Lorie regaled him with everything she was doing. She nearly had her degree, and was currently working as an office assistant for a large corporation in Provo. She talked about how much she enjoyed her work; there were many opportunities for moving up in the company for someone with her education. But she also said that her work was only something to keep her going until she could settle down and have a family. Jack watched her closely and found it difficult to imagine her as a mother. She was so well put together and so beautiful, he could more easily see her walking down a runway wearing the latest fashions. But she talked about her desire for children with such intensity that he found the contrast intriguing.

"Now, is Jack your real name?" she asked. "Be honest. Do people really name their sons *Jack?*"

Jack chuckled. "Well, I've always been Jack, but my birth certificate actually says Jonathan Stewart Hayden. Stewart was my mother's maiden name."

"Ooh, I like that," she said. "Somehow I think you look more like a Jonathan than a Jack to me, but I guess that's a matter of opinion. So, tell me more about you," she continued. "Sometimes I talk too much, and—"

"Oh, no, I've enjoyed it," he admitted, realizing how pleasant adult conversation was with a peer. "There's not much to tell about me, really. I was born in Texas and lived there until I was thirteen. I've always lived on a farm; I really love the farm life, and hope to go back and work my father's land when I'm finished with school."

Lorie continued asking Jack questions, coaxing his thoughts and dreams into the open. He was surprised to learn that she had also grown up on a farm. He laughed as he asked her, "Can you drive a tractor?"

"Yes," she said. "Is that funny?"

Jack shook his head, and they talked for over an hour after they had finished eating. He told her about his upbringing, and the difficulties of having an alcoholic mother. He talked about his father, and the admiration he had for him. And while he talked, he felt something warm happening inside of him. He couldn't recall ever feeling this way with any woman—except Hilary. But there was a look in Lorie's eyes that he'd never seen in Hilary. Was this how it felt to be with a woman who was actually *attracted* to him?

Jack felt nearly panicked when she glanced at her watch. "Oh, my gosh, look at the time."

"Do you need to be somewhere?"

"No, not really. I just . . ." He looked directly at her. "It hardly seems like ten minutes have passed, and look at us."

Their eyes met for a time-stopping moment. Jack was trying to think of a way to say that he didn't want to leave her, when she said, "Do you have plans, or . . ."

"Or what?"

"Well, I was wondering about a movie or something. There's always a choice of matinees at Movies Eight. It's not too far from here, but . . . well . . ." She glanced down and laughed softly. "I'm being awfully pushy, aren't I."

"I'm not complaining," he said, thinking perhaps he needed a woman who could give him a good, hard push. "A movie sounds great."

She looked up at him, so obviously happy that he couldn't help laughing.

Jack helped her into the truck, and they drove the short distance to the theater. He took her hand to help her out, and she didn't let go. They were glad to find an appropriately rated movie they could both enjoy. Jack bought the tickets and Lorie bought the popcorn. After the movie they went to the mall, where they could walk and not freeze. They talked so much that Jack's voice began to turn dry. Again they shared a meal, eating slowly and sharing conversation so invigorating to Jack that he began to dread their imminent separation. When he took her back to her car, they stood next to it for several minutes until she began to shiver. "You'd better get in," he said. "You're freezing."

"Yeah," she chuckled, "but I don't particularly want to."

As Jack met her eyes for the hundredth time that day, he realized the warmth that rose inside him had become familiar through these hours together. Impulsively he put his arms around her to keep her warm. He feared that perhaps *he* was being too forward, but she nuzzled her face against his shoulder, murmuring softly, "I have a confession to make, Jack."

He pulled back enough to look into her face, nearly expecting her to tell him that she already had a boyfriend and this had to stop here. The thought scared him. But she smiled serenely and said, "I think I had a crush on you the first time I saw you; the first time I saw you come by the apartment to get Hilary."

Jack took a minute to absorb that. Unwilling to admit to his feelings, he said, "I seem to recall Hilary suggesting more than once that I should take you out."

Lorie laughed softly. "Well, you should have listened to her."

Jack looked into her eyes long and hard, wondering if his obsession with Hilary had kept him blinded all these years. Had he just completely missed Lorie? What else had he missed? She touched his face tentatively with fingers that had been kept warm in her pocket. She closed her eyes and sighed, and no power on earth could keep him from kissing her. He enjoyed it so much that he was startled to recall that this was a first date, and he hardly knew this woman. But then, they had shared enough conversation today to equal four or five dates.

"You'd better go home," he whispered close to her ear. "It's getting late."

"You'll call me?" she asked.

"Only if you give me your phone number."

Lorie scrambled to get a pen out of her purse, and Jack held out his hand. She wrote her number there, then kissed where she'd written it. "Thanks for a great day, Jack," she said, easing away.

"It was my pleasure," he assured her, already counting the hours until he could feasibly talk to her again.

The following day, Jack called Lorie the minute he got home from church. They went to a fireside together, and began the week by arranging opportunities to see each other whenever it would fit in. Within a month, Jack couldn't comprehend life without Lorie. He was in love and not afraid to admit it. She had a way of saying and doing all the things that made him feel good—about himself, about life, and about her. He considered the future carefully, realizing that he desperately wanted her to be a part of it. Even though they had both grown up on farms, he could see that her interests were much different from his. In that way, she was much like Hilary. But they differed in the respect that Lorie didn't have a problem with settling down in a small town. In fact, as he talked of his goals and desires for the future, hers coincided so closely that it was almost difficult to believe.

Jack often thought of Hilary, and something ached inside of him. He couldn't deny that his feelings for her had not gone away in spite of his feelings for Lorie. But he knew his love for Lorie would help him get beyond this fruitless obsession he'd had for Hilary. He knew they would always be close, and their friendship would forever mean something to him. But it was as he'd told Lorie: Hilary was more like a sister to him. And for the first time in his life, he believed he could be content with that. Everything with Lorie just seemed too good to be true. So, what could he do but marry her?

Through the weeks he and Lorie were dating, Jack thought of Hilary less and less. As a result, his letters to her became less frequent, and so did those she sent in return. She rationalized that she was terribly busy, and he did the same. He told her nothing about Lorie, knowing from little things she'd told him that Hilary had never been terribly fond of Lorie. He doubted Hilary would be happy about this relationship; but then, he figured it really wasn't any of her business. Lorie spoke occasionally of Hilary, and alluded to some misunderstandings they'd had as roommates. Jack concluded that some personalities just didn't go well together. All he cared about was the way Lorie's personality made him feel. She was almost like a drug to him. She soothed him and lifted him—without any hangover. And he was addicted.

Jack pretty much let Lorie plan the wedding. With her eager mother and three sisters, he didn't stand a chance at having an opinion anyway. They set the date for March, in the Provo Temple, with an open house in Provo, where they both knew many people. The main reception would be in the town where she'd grown up. She asked if he wanted an open house in Mt. Pleasant, but he really didn't. There simply weren't that many people there he cared about, and he didn't figure it was worth the effort and expense.

As the wedding drew closer, Lorie was continually buying Jack gifts. She bought him clothes and shoes, and purchased household items that she said would be theirs when they were married. Much of what she bought really wasn't his style, but he enjoyed humoring her and the way it made her so happy. She bought him CDs of music she liked, sharing her thoughts and feelings about them. Often it wasn't what he would have preferred, but again he did his best to learn to like what she liked. And even when she began calling him Jon more than Jack, he just smiled and told her how much he loved her, and how happy she had made him.

When Jack realized that announcements were being printed, he knew he had to write Hilary and tell her what was happening in his life. The letter was more difficult than he'd expected it to be. In spite of his happiness, he still wasn't completely free of a formless heartache regarding Hilary. At this point, his feelings for her didn't make sense; so he just tried not to think about it. He felt certain in a few years he'd wonder why he had ever cared for Hilary in any way beyond friendship. Jack didn't really intend to omit his fiancée's name in the letter, but when he'd finished and it wasn't there, he didn't bother going back to fix it. He figured Hilary would know soon enough.

A few weeks before the wedding, Jack went home on a weekend to check on his mother and take care of a few things. He stopped in to see Pete and Millie, and they laughed and hugged him as if he'd been off to war or something. They all sat down at the kitchen table, where Millie began drilling him with questions. "What's going on, Jack? We've hardly seen you. I know you're busy, but even Hilary said in her letters that you haven't been writing as often and she's concerned. Is everything all right? Are you well? Are you—"

"Whoa there, Millie," Pete interrupted. "He can't answer a question when you're asking twelve more."

Millie giggled. "Sorry. I do run on."

"That's okay," Jack said, relishing the feel of home surrounding him. "I love the way you run on." He thought briefly of the time he'd spent in the home of Lorie's parents. They seemed to be good, conservative people, and she never stopped talking about how wonderful they were, and how good her upbringing had been. But Jack had trouble feeling as comfortable there as he did here. Of course, it would take time, he reminded himself. He felt certain that everything would work out with time.

"So, what have you been doing?" Millie repeated.

"Well, I guess that's what I've come to tell you." He took a deep breath. "I'm getting married."

Following a taut moment of silence, Pete smiled and said, "Well, that's great, Jack." But his eyes told the truth. He wasn't happy at all.

Jack looked at Millie, who looked as if she might cry. He knew he could pretend everything was okay and move on, but he didn't want to. "I get the feeling you're not very happy about this."

"Well," Pete cleared his throat, looking suddenly guilty, "it's not that we don't want you to . . . I mean . . . of course we . . ."

"Come on, Pete," Jack said, "we're too much like family to pretend. Just tell me what you think. It's okay."

Pete looked directly at Jack, saying quietly, "We must admit, we'd always had hopes for you and Hilary. I'm just a little disappointed, that's all. And I'm sure Millie is, too."

Millie nodded, still looking as if she might cry.

Jack cleared his throat. "Well, I must admit I had hopes for me and Hilary, too. But I just don't think it would have worked out. Hilary just didn't feel that way about me. And I can't change that."

The silence dragged on uncomfortably while Millie sniffled occasionally. Pete finally broke in with a cheerful, "So, tell us about her. She must be something, eh?"

"Yeah," Jack admitted, "she's pretty incredible."

Jack answered their questions and told them everything he could think to tell about Lorie, feeling warm inside as he did.

"So, what are your plans?" Millie asked.

"Well, we're going to finish out this semester at BYU, then we're coming to Mt. Pleasant the end of April. I'm going to run my father's land this year, rather than leasing it out."

"Oh, then we'll get to see you more," Millie declared.

"Yes, I hope so," Jack said.

"At the end of the summer, we'll move back to Provo so I can keep working toward my degree."

"And after that?" Pete asked.

"We're planning on settling right here. I want to buy out my brothers on the farm. They have no interest in it. But it will take time for me to get the money together."

"That sounds great, Jack," Pete said. "I'm sure you'll do real good."

They went on to talk about the wedding plans, then the conversation shifted to neighborhood gossip and the farming industry. When Jack was leaving, Pete and Millie assured him they were happy for him. But he left with a knot in his stomach. For the first time since he'd laid eyes on Lorie, he wondered if he was doing the right thing. Driving back to Provo, he considered the reality that their relationship had developed very quickly. He believed that marrying her was the right thing to do. It just *felt* right. But he'd never actually fasted and prayed about it. And he wondered if they were just moving too fast. He geared himself up to talk to Lorie about it, but he arrived at her apartment to find her addressing wedding announcements. She bubbled with excitement, and he couldn't help getting caught up in her happiness. He was certain that everything would work out with time.

"What do you think?" she asked, shoving a printed announcement into his hands as he sat on the couch.

"The picture's nice," he said, "but only because you make me look good."

Lorie laughed. "Oh, no, Jon. You look good all by yourself."

"But I look better with you next to me," he said, diverting his attention long enough to kiss her.

"Well, read it," she said with enthusiasm.

Jack glanced over the announcement and felt his uneasiness returning. "What is this?" he asked.

"It's your name," she said so matter-of-factly that he had to stop and wonder why this was bothering him so much. Reading the announcement again, it clearly said that Lorie Walker was marrying Jonathan Stewart Hayden. When he said nothing more, she interjected, "I'm sorry if you don't like it. I just wanted the announcements to sound really formal, and it's such a nice name. We can't possibly afford to have them reprinted, but if you—"

"It's okay," Jack said. "It's not a big deal."

Lorie laughed and hugged him. "You're so sweet." She gave him a long kiss, then looked into his eyes. "I can't wait to be your wife. I'm counting down the minutes."

Jack smiled and resisted the urge to hold her unrespectably close. "Yeah, me too," he said and kissed her again.

* * * * *

Hilary had been in Bulgaria for about four months when the letter arrived. She had just followed her companion, Maria, downstairs from the tiny apartment they shared above a pastry shop, when the assistant to the mission president met them with their mail. It had been over two weeks since they'd received anything, and the stack of letters was thick.

Hilary quickly separated her letters from Maria's and glanced through them, but they were on their way to an appointment and there was no time to open anything.

For some reason, Hilary's mind stayed with Jack's letter. His letters had become sparse and thin lately. She'd not heard from him at all for weeks, and she was aching to open it and read about the happenings in his life. But the day was busy, and it remained tucked into her bag along with her books and several letters from family members. During their tracting, Hilary recalled the many times Jack's letters had filled her with warmth and given her hope. She longed for that feeling now and couldn't wait to get home and read it.

It was late before Hilary finally found the time to sit down and read her mail by the glow of a dim lamp.

Dear Hilary, I hope things are going well for you. I think about you a lot, and I'm sorry for taking so long to write, but I've been pretty busy. Which brings me to the news. Something big has happened in my life, and I hope you'll be happy for me.

Hilary felt an uneasy chill, suddenly fearing that she would lose her best friend to marriage. Of course, she'd anticipated it. She'd told him to find someone and get married. Still, the thought of not having him available to talk to and lean on was disconcerting. Taking a deep breath, she read on.

It really feels strange to be telling you this. After all we've shared together, and the feelings I've had for you, this is hard for me. Of course, you'll probably be relieved to know that I won't be pestering you when you come home. I guess that pretty much gives it away, so I'll get to the point. I'm getting married, Hil.

Hilary wasn't prepared for the sudden rush of tears, making it impossible to keep reading.

"Bad news?" Maria asked in Bulgarian. It was their only common language.

Hilary tried to explain away her tears as homesickness, but Maria wasn't convinced. She finally told Maria about her friendship with Jack, and how it was hard to have him getting married while she wasn't there, and to know her friend wouldn't be there for her when she returned. Maria accepted the explanation and returned to reading her own mail.

Hilary blew her nose and finished the letter, which was nothing but some trivial notes about Jack seeing her parents occasionally, and how his job and schooling were going well. There was nothing about this woman who had claimed his heart; not even her name.

Through the following days, Hilary's mind was often with Jack as she attempted to digest the reality of his upcoming marriage. Maria was patient with her sour mood for the first few days, but she finally sat Hilary down and forced her to talk about it.

"What's bothering you?" she insisted. "We can't accomplish what we're here to do if you don't get over this."

"I don't know, really . . . it's just this thing about Jack getting married."

"I thought you didn't love him."

"He's a good friend. I suppose I'm just afraid of losing that friendship."

Maria gently reminded Hilary that she had to accept the agency of others, and she needed to have the faith that things would all work out. Maria took Hilary's hand and said kindly, "You must remember that your mission is the most important thing right now, and you shouldn't be so concerned with things at home that you lose sight of your reason for being here."

Hilary appreciated Maria's insight and kindness, and she worked very hard to keep her mind and heart where they belonged. But she couldn't deny feeling uneasy at the idea of Jack getting married. And she didn't understand why. She knew now, as much as she ever had, that marriage simply wasn't in their future. So why couldn't she feel happy about Jack getting married?

The wedding announcement arrived with the very next mail delivery. Hilary held it for several minutes before she found the courage to open it. Unfolding the fine parchment, her focus was drawn to the picture, and something inside her turned cold.

"No," she murmured, and suddenly found it difficult to breathe. Certain this woman just bore a startling resemblance to Lorie Walker, she scanned the announcement quickly, only to find the name there, as plain as day. *She couldn't believe it.* Then the coldness inside her intensified as she read his name.

"Jonathan Stewart?" she shrieked aloud. "Who in the world is Jonathan Stewart Hayden?" Maria looked up quizzically from her reading. Hilary just motioned for her to continue reading while her mind spun like a tornado.

"Oh, help," she cried, actually feeling faint.

"What is it?" Maria asked.

Hilary handed her the announcement, muttering over and over, "I can't believe it. I just can't believe it."

Hilary spent the next two hours crying and attempting to explain to Maria why this was so awful. With their language barrier it was a challenge, but of all her companions, Maria seemed to have a sixth sense about emotional things. Maria suggested that Hilary quickly write to Jack and express her feelings concerning the things she'd observed that indicated a lack of integrity in Lorie. At first, Hilary was determined not to do it. It was Jack's life, she reasoned, and he deserved to live it as he pleased. She told Maria what she thought, but Maria simply observed, "You should do your part, and what he does with the information is up to him."

Following some serious prayer, Hilary knew that Maria was right. She stayed up half the night, writing a carefully thought out letter, praying it would arrive before the wedding. She felt a little better after it was mailed off, but she couldn't deny the heartache she felt. Maria teased her, saying that she obviously loved Jack a lot more than she was willing to admit. Hilary argued the point, insisting he was only a friend and she was concerned. But every once in a while, she would recall how it had felt to be kissed by Jack Hayden. And the thought of Lorie Walker spending the rest of her life being kissed by Jack Hayden was more than she could bear. She prayed for peace and kept her focus on her work, but a piece of her heart was with Jack—and afraid on his behalf.

* * * * *

Two days before the wedding, Jack received a letter from Hilary. He felt almost afraid to open it, then almost wished he hadn't. There was nothing critical or judgmental in the words she'd written, but she very strongly expressed her concern over his marrying Lorie. Of course, he'd expected as much; he knew from Lorie that they hadn't necessarily seen eye to eye. But he felt certain Hilary had no idea what the real Lorie was like. Hilary gave a couple of specific examples of things she had seen Lorie do that showed an apparent lack of integrity and morals. She wrote that Lorie seemed to be the kind of person who always wanted what she couldn't have, and her life was a series of conquests. Once she got to the grass on the other side of the fence, she moved on to conquer something else. But Jack reasoned that he had to accept Lorie for who and what she was now, not what she might have been before he met her.

Hilary concluded by writing: *What you choose to do with your life is up to you, Jack. Please don't think that I'm trying to control you. I was concerned and felt like I needed to let you know. If you do marry her, I wish you every happiness. No one deserves it like you do. I only wish I could be there for the wedding.*

Jack folded up the letter and put it away. Determined to see this marriage through, he pushed thoughts of Hilary away, and longed to have Lorie as his wife. He felt certain that everything would be perfect.

Through his wedding day, Jack felt as if he were in the calm eye of a tornado that was whirling around him. Each event moved like clockwork, and every aspect of it was beautiful—most especially his wife.

Their wedding night was incredible, except for the brief, unsettling feeling he had that she knew what she was doing and he didn't. But he quickly became caught up in the experience and didn't give it another thought. Later, as she slept in his arms, he told himself that whatever mistakes she might have made prior to meeting him simply didn't matter. She had been worthy to go through the temple today, and she was his wife. He knew that everything would be all right.

Jack's marriage to Lorie was everything he dreamed it would be—for about five days. They had barely returned from their honeymoon when she erupted over something he considered petty and insignificant. Reasoning that marriage was a big adjustment, he smoothed it over, feeling certain that with time their relationship would settle into something deeper and more comfortable. But as the weeks passed, he steadily became more disconcerted. There were so many little things about their relationship that concerned him, he didn't know which to worry about the most. Overall, Lorie seemed much more concerned about her friends than she did about him. He concluded that once they moved to Mt. Pleasant, that particular issue would improve. He found a nice little apartment to rent and tried to make it as comfortable as possible.

About the time they moved, Lorie told Jack that the company she was working for really needed her for a while longer. "They've just had a hard time finding the right person to replace me," she said. "As soon as I help finish up this project, then I can quit."

What could Jack do but support her? She commuted to Provo every day, coming home so late that he nearly felt like he was still single. Then she began staying over with friends so she wouldn't have to make the drive every day. By mid-summer, she was only coming home on weekends, and then she was so "burned out" that she slept most of the time.

When Jack found his patience wearing thin, he sat Lorie down and talked to her. But their conversation quickly turned angry, just as he'd expected. He took a deep breath and reminded himself that getting caught in this endless cycle of arguing would accomplish nothing. "Okay, Lorie," he said calmly, "there's something I need to understand. Can we just cool the anger and talk?"

"Fine," she said, but her voice sounded even more angry.

"Just hear me out, okay?"

"Fine," she repeated in the same tone.

"Maybe we should just get past all the muck and get to the heart of the problem. I was under the impression, when I married you, that we were extremely compatible. In fact, as I recall, you spent a great deal of time convincing me that we *were* compatible." She looked dubious but determined to let him finish. "Did you or did you not put a great deal of effort into telling me that you had grown up on a farm, that you loved the farm life? Did you not say to me many times that all you really wanted was to settle down, live a quiet life, and raise a family?"

The anger in Lorie's eyes deepened. But it was a defensive look; he knew he'd hit the truth. And she obviously knew it, too.

"Well, is that not what you told me? Am I wrong to have expected that from you?"

Through the ensuing silence, Jack ached to have her tell him that he was right, that she needed to rethink her priorities and remember the promises she'd made to him. He wanted to hold her in his arms and hear her tell him she loved him, and she'd do whatever it might take to put their relationship back in order. Of course, he knew it was probably unrealistic to expect everything to fall into place so easily. But he could go a long way on hope—if only he had some evidence that she could see her part in the problem and make a step toward resolving it.

Lorie abruptly turned her head the other way, as if she suddenly couldn't look at him. Was she crying, or . . . ?

"Okay, Jack. You're right. It's obvious I was wrong."

Jack's heart beat painfully hard. He squeezed his eyes shut briefly to absorb it. Then she turned back to face him, and he saw a hardness in her expression that didn't mesh with what he believed she was saying. It all made sense when she added, "It would seem I didn't know myself as well as I thought I did. I thought I could do whatever you wanted of me and be happy. I guess I was wrong."

"What are you saying?" he asked breathily. His already pounding heart nearly burst right out of him.

"I'm saying that maybe we're not so compatible after all. You have this cozy little picture of me waiting at home for you, wearing an apron, with a baby on my hip and bread in the oven. And it's just not going to happen."

Jack tried to find the words to tell her that her description was grossly exaggerated, but his tongue had frozen. And somehow he knew it wouldn't make any difference.

"I'm not sure I'm ready for children," Lorie blurted, erupting to her feet. "And I'm absolutely certain that I can't spend the rest of my life in this wretched little town."

"So, what are you saying?" he finally managed to ask.

"I'm saying we should move back to Provo, where I can work and be able to see my friends."

When Jack expressed his commitment to taking care of the farm and his need to be living where he was, Lorie told him he was being insensitive and controlling, and if he loved her he would make the sacrifice. She finished with a harsh tirade, then grabbed the toothpick out of his mouth and tossed it, shouting, "And why do you have to chew on these stupid things? I hate it!"

Lorie went to work early the next morning. Jack made some calls and found that getting someone to take over the land wasn't as difficult as he'd expected it to be. Lorie was ecstatic when he told her they were moving back to Provo, and Ammon was only too happy to have him come back to work, since the construction business was booming. Jack felt certain that this would bring back the relationship he'd shared with Lorie before they were married.

But very little changed. She still spent long hours at work and with friends, and her homemaking efforts were little to nonexistent. Jack often lay awake at night, with Lorie sleeping beside him, apparently oblivious to his concerns. He prayed for help and guidance, but somehow felt as if he'd fallen into a big, black hole by his own doing, and he was going to have to get out of it himself.

One morning, after a particularly bad night, Jack was the first to arrive at the construction site. He quickly went to work, appreciating the opportunity to pound out his frustrations. He tried not to think about Lorie, but fragmented arguments stormed through his mind over and over until he felt so weak that he had to sit down. He was leaning in a corner with his head in his hands when Ammon startled him. "It's not like you to sit down on the job," he joked.

"Sorry," Jack said, missing the humor. He started to get up, but Ammon stopped him with a hand on his shoulder.

"What's up?" Ammon asked, sitting beside him on the concrete floor.

Jack took a deep breath. He didn't really want to talk about this, but Ammon was the closest thing he had to a friend.

"I think I'm in trouble, Ammon. *Big* trouble."

"What? You've been gambling or something?" Ammon chuckled. "You've been embezzling from me, is that it?"

"Nothing so exciting, I'm afraid." Still Jack didn't respond to Ammon's humor. "It's Lorie."

"Uh-oh, marriage problems."

"You know about marriage problems?"

"Not directly, thank heaven. But I've heard about a few in quite a bit of detail."

"From who?"

"My mother-in-law, mostly."

"Really? Does that make your father-in-law a jerk?"

"Not exactly," Ammon chuckled. "My wife's blood father died when she was nine. Her mother has married again, but there are still some pretty difficult memories from that first marriage. And Emily admits that even in her second marriage, as much as they love each other, it hasn't always been easy. Allie and I have learned a lot about handling our own problems from the things Emily has taught us."

"Emily?"

"My mother-in-law. She's an amazing woman."

Jack nodded, and his mind wandered back to Lorie.

"Hey," Ammon nudged him, "you still haven't told me about this big trouble you're in."

"She's not the woman I thought I married, Ammon. By the end of the honeymoon I was feeling uncomfortable, but I just figured that some time and effort would smooth things out. Well, it hasn't. The problem is only getting steadily worse, and quite frankly, I'm scared." He blew out a long, slow breath. "I've wondered if my love for Hilary has somehow subconsciously affected the marriage. But I know in my heart, Ammon, that I've committed myself to Lorie completely." He sighed loudly. "So, what would Emily tell me to do?"

Ammon was thoughtful for a moment. "Well, I remember hearing her say that she knew, in her case, it had been the right thing to marry who she had married; it was like the Lord wanted her to learn something, and to grow. She told me she had learned how to stick up for herself, and to believe in herself, in spite of whatever he might say or do. And she said her personal belief, when it comes to a tough marriage situation, is that you do everything you possibly can to make it work, and if it doesn't, then you can put it behind you and have peace with the Lord."

"Whoa," Jack said, "I think that was a two-hour sermon in thirty-five seconds."

"Well, maybe something I said might help. But think about it. If you want to talk some more, I'd be happy to listen."

"That's okay," Jack said, and hurried back to work. But early in the afternoon, he sought out Ammon and asked, "So, if I understand this right, it's important for me to be certain I did everything I possibly could to save the marriage. Then, if it doesn't work out, I can at least have peace."

"That's how I interpret it," Ammon said. "It makes sense to me."

"Yeah, I think it does."

With renewed determination, Jack committed himself to doing everything in his power to develop a better relationship with Lorie. He reminded himself to have patience and to be sensitive to her needs. But five months later, not long after Christmas, he sat down one day and realized that he'd given so much to her, he had nothing left to draw on. He tried to tally what she'd given him, and it basically amounted to some clothes and music that he didn't even like. She hadn't given him anything, and she'd taken *everything*. She'd taken his name, his identity, his personality. He'd changed nearly everything about himself, just trying to accommodate her and make her happy. But finally, he faced one harsh reality: *Nothing* he could do would make her happy.

Jack groaned at the thought. He'd saved himself for marriage, then put his heart and soul into it. He'd come into this relationship willing to give everything, expecting it to last forever. But he knew now that it wouldn't last forever. And he doubted it would even last until next month, if something didn't change.

He prayed for understanding and thought the situation through very carefully. As he thought about her family, he realized that there was actually a great deal of evidence that they were dysfunctional. Of course, his own mother was an alcoholic. But Jack knew in his heart that he had been raised with integrity—and that was one thing his wife didn't have.

Attempting to know exactly where Lorie's head was, he took her out to dinner and attempted to discuss the future. He expressed concerns for her apparent obsession with her career, and reminded her that they had decided they would start having a family after a year of marriage. Jack hoped that, if nothing else, motherhood, or the desire for it, might mellow her. But she told him she wasn't certain if she wanted children after all. Jack knew before the conversation ended that their marriage wouldn't make it, and he'd be torturing them both to persist any further. But it took him several days to draw up the courage to do what he knew in his heart had to be done. Unlike when he'd made the decision to marry Lorie, Jack fasted and prayed. He went to the temple one evening and sat for more than an hour in the celestial room, pleading for peace and understanding. He came away feeling peace, but not necessarily any more enlightened on why it had all turned out this way.

He was actually glad that Lorie was out of the house when he returned. After changing his clothes, he sat down to study the scriptures, hoping to find an answer. He read until he dozed off, then awoke when he heard Lorie. "Hi," she said, coming into the bedroom and tossing her purse onto a chair. "I thought you'd be asleep by now."

"I dozed off, but . . ." He couldn't think of anything more to say. She appeared so chipper, as if nothing in the world was wrong. He thought of the seemingly countless times he had pleaded with her to compromise and work on their relationship. He felt helpless, but more sad than angry.

While Lorie was in the bathroom getting ready for bed, Jack picked up the Book of Mormon and continued to read where he'd left off. At least when he was reading, he wasn't thinking about the present state of his life. He had barely begun when a phrase seemed to jump right into his heart. He suddenly felt out of breath, cold and warm at the same time. The sensation only increased as he read the passage again, and a perfect understanding settled into his mind.

Jack read it still again, attempting to relate the scriptural phrase to what the Spirit had just taught him. Alma chapter fourteen, verse eleven: . . . *and the blood of the innocent shall stand as a witness against them.* . . . The concept was symbolic, of course. But Jack understood now that his marriage to Lorie had been, at least in part, an opportunity for Lorie to overcome her lack of integrity and personal struggles and straighten out her life. And she'd made the choice to deny herself those opportunities. Even if Jack had not been in the most ideal state of mind when he'd fallen in love with her, the Lord understood and knew the desires of his heart. Jack knew in that moment that marrying Lorie *had* been the right thing to do. He'd given her more than a fair opportunity to grow and get beyond her struggles. And now, the right thing to do was to let her go.

"You okay?" she asked, startling him.

Jack looked up to see her standing at the edge of the bed. "Not really," he said. "How about you?"

"I'm great. What's wrong?"

Jack just shook his head. He needed more time to digest this and figure out how to approach it. She turned out the light and crawled into bed, snuggling up close to him. Jack couldn't even force himself to put his arms around her. In his heart, they were as good as divorced. He eased carefully out of the bed. "I'm a little restless," he said. "I think I'll hang out on the couch." He hurried from the room before she could question him further.

His night was restless, but he faced morning with the confidence to do what had to be done. Hearing that Lorie was up and getting ready for work, he quickly got dressed and folded up his bedding. When she came into the kitchen to grab a piece of toast, obviously in a hurry, Jack knew this was as good a time as any. If she didn't have time to argue with him, that would be all the better.

"Lorie," he said, "there's something I need to say."

"Okay."

"Seeing the way things are going, I'm . . . well, I'm moving out."

"What?" she laughed bitterly. "You've got to be joking, right?"

"It's obvious that you don't want to be a wife to me, Lorie. I'm not going to hang around and make us both miserable any longer."

"I never said I didn't want to be your wife, Jon. And I never said I was miserable."

"You didn't have to. You're practically never home, and when you are, you're like some old schoolmistress with a yardstick, waiting for a chance to smack me."

"I am not!" she snarled, obviously appalled by the analogy.

"Well, that's a matter of opinion. I'm just telling you how I feel." He didn't know whether she was startled by his honesty or just plain speechless, but he took the opportunity to say some things he knew needed to be said. "You know, Lorie, this is not what I thought marriage was supposed to be. I can't talk to you about *anything*. We don't do anything together except argue. I'm having a rough time coming up with something good between us to hold on to."

He expected her to throw anger back at him. Instead she gave him a teasing smirk, as if she could appeal to something base inside him. "I thought things were pretty good between us."

He knew what she meant, and it made him want to physically throw her out the door. He swallowed his anger and just said what he felt. "Oh, you mean in bed." Her eyes told him he had it right. "Well, I'm glad you've enjoyed it, my dear. But for me, that's the worst of it." Her expression hovered between astonishment and fury as he finished. "I feel like I'm sleeping with some prostitute. It feels sordid and cheap. And I *hate* it!"

Again Jack expected her to hurl angry, hateful things at him. But she just stood there with her mouth open. He hurried to say, "It really doesn't matter whose fault it is. It's over, Lorie, plain and simple. There is nothing more I can do for you."

Her eyes widened. "You're serious."

"Yes, I am."

"What are you saying? Divorce?"

"Annulment, if we're real lucky. I want my name back."

"I can't believe this."

"Neither can I. I would have expected that when a man gives his heart and soul to a woman, it might last longer than a heartbeat." She glared at him with so much shock, he feared he'd either scream at her or start to cry. "You'd better hurry," he said, "or you'll be late."

She seemed startled back to the moment. "We can talk later."

"No, we can't. I'll be gone when you get home."

"Jon, you can't really mean that—"

"My name is Jack," he said firmly. "Good-bye, Lorie."

She glanced at her watch and seemed suddenly flustered, but still speechless. "We'll talk later," she said more to herself, then she hurried out the door.

Jack listened to her car driving away, then a horrible, dark silence filled the room. He sank to the couch, feeling suddenly weak, and his thoughts rumbled as he lost track of the time. He realized that he really wasn't going to miss her; she'd stopped being the woman he'd fallen in love with a long time ago. And he would be glad to not have to deal with the drama she brought into his life. He asked himself if he loved her, and the answer was no. He'd fallen in love with her, but he'd quickly fallen out. Still, Jack hung his head and cried. A deep, indescribable pain oozed from the deepest part of him, hurling itself into the open air in heaving spurts. It wasn't for the loss of Lorie that he cried. It was for the pieces of his heart and soul he'd put into this marriage that could never be replaced. He cried for the broken dreams and empty promises, for the reality that life was hard, and sometimes the people you cared for most hurt you the worst. His mother came to mind, right along with Lorie. And the whole thing just made him sick.

When Jack finally calmed down, he called Ammon's cell phone to tell him he wouldn't be coming in today.

"What's up?" Ammon asked. "You sick?"

"Not physically."

"Is it Lorie?"

"Yeah, I'm packing. I just need some time."

"Is it over, then?"

"Yeah, it's over."

"I'm really sorry, Jack."

"Yeah, me too. But . . . I know it's the right thing to do. I'll be okay."

"I'm sure you will. Is there anything I can do?"

"No, I don't think so. There isn't much here that's mine. Most of the furniture was hers or given to us by her relatives. It won't take too long. I just need some time."

"Okay. Do you have a place to stay?"

Jack sighed. "I'm ashamed to say I haven't thought that far. If nothing else, I can drive an hour and stay in Mt. Pleasant."

"Now that's kind of dumb, when you're always welcome at my house. I mean it, Jack. You can put your things in the garage and stay with us for a few days until you can find a place."

Jack felt so grateful the tears threatened again. He choked them back and thanked Ammon, then got busy packing. It didn't take him long to scour the apartment for his belongings and put them in the back of his truck. He walked slowly through the apartment, checking drawers and closets to be certain he had everything. He didn't want to come back, and he didn't want to have to fight her for anything. As he saw it, their lives had remained separate enough that this would be easy. He wanted nothing more than what he'd come with. He even left behind most of the gifts she'd given him—things he'd never really liked that much, anyway. Then he locked the door and left without taking a key.

While Jack expected some kind of protest from Lorie, he was prepared to stand firm on his decision. But it only added to his heartbreak when she offered no resistance to having their marriage annulled. For weeks afterward, Jack struggled to come to terms with it. He had his own apartment and had settled in comfortably, but the peace he'd felt initially was difficult to hold on to when questions continued to assault him. In his heart he knew he'd done the best he could, but he still felt like a failure somehow.

Jack was feeling particularly low one evening when the phone rang just as he was getting out of the shower. He hurried to throw on a robe and answer it, but he was too late. The caller ID said *Peter Smith*, and he felt suddenly uneasy, wondering if something was wrong. Jack quickly dialed back. "So, what's up?" Jack asked after he'd explained to Hilary's father how he had known the identity of the caller.

"Well," Pete said, "your . . . uh, wife . . . told us to call you at this number, and—"

"Yes, well," Jack hurried to explain, "she's not my wife anymore." He gave a three-minute explanation and graciously accepted Pete's expression of concern.

"Are ya doin' okay?" Pete asked.

"Oh, it's been tough, but I'm hanging in there." Pete said nothing more and Jack added, "You still haven't told me why you called."

"Well, we just wanted to let ya know that Hilary's flyin' in day after tomorrow."

Jack had to sit down. He was startled to realize how he'd lost track of the time—and of Hilary, aside from sending his monthly contribution to her mission. He didn't even dare hope that her feelings for him might have changed. But he did know that she was the best friend he'd ever had. And if he'd ever needed a friend, it was now.

"Are ya there, Jack?"

"Yeah," he said, "I'm here." He cleared his throat. "The day after tomorrow, eh?"

"Yeah . . . and, well, the thing is . . . I just hate drivin' in Salt Lake, and all the other kids live the opposite direction from there. We were wonderin', if we drove to your place in Provo, if you'd mind drivin' us to the airport."

"When exactly . . . is she coming in?" he asked, hating the way his heart quickened at the thought of seeing Hilary again. Pete told him the time her plane would be arriving, and Jack said he'd be happy to drive them to the airport. But he insisted on coming to Mt. Pleasant to get them.

Long after he hung up the phone, Jack sat where he was, as if he'd turned to stone. He contemplated all that had happened in the year and a half Hilary had been gone, and all the heartache associated with it. Then he pondered what he'd learned. He'd jumped into marriage with Lorie by allowing his heart to rule his head—and he'd spent a good portion of his life feeling hopelessly in love with Hilary Smith for the same reason. If he looked at his feelings honestly, he couldn't deny that his love for Hilary was still there. If anything, his marriage to Lorie had made him love Hilary more. He loved her strong spirit and her deep integrity. But he also knew that a long time ago, she had been honest enough to make it clear where she stood. And he'd be a fool to expect anything more of her than what they'd shared in the past.

By the time Jack picked up Hilary's parents to go to the airport, he had geared himself up to accept Hilary's friendship for what it was, and to be grateful for it. And he was determined to keep his life in balance and not let his emotions rule him. If such a thing was possible.

CHAPTER SEVEN

*H*ilary practically pressed her face to the plane window as the pilot announced their approach to Salt Lake City. She quelled a sudden rush of butterflies at the thought of being home and seeing her loved ones again. Her mission had been successful, and it was difficult to leave behind the people and culture she had grown to care for; but she was glad to be home. Her only true sadness came with thoughts of Jack. She'd heard practically nothing from him since his marriage, and she could only hope things were going well. But she couldn't deny her disappointment in wishing he would be here to welcome her home, the way he'd been here to send her off.

Hilary finally stepped off the plane and was assaulted with hugs from her parents, her siblings, their spouses and children. She laughed and cried until they all began to disperse, and she realized Jack was standing alone and to one side, wearing a long coat, his hands behind his back. For a minute she thought it was her imagination. But their eyes locked, and just seeing him filled her with something indescribably warm. Her heart quickened with excitement. Then, in the split second it took for her to fully absorb the reality of his presence, her stomach tightened almost painfully. He wasn't the same man she'd left behind. He had the same thick, curly hair. The same penetrating eyes. The same strong stance. But his countenance plainly stated that he was hurting. But why? A thousand questions stormed through her mind as she moved toward him. She hugged him tightly, feeling an unspoken desperation in his embrace. He drew back slightly and looked into her eyes, then he pressed his forehead to hers, holding her arms in his hands, just as he'd done the night before she'd been set apart as a missionary.

"I guess you're wondering why I'm here," he said with a hoarse voice.

"You drove my parents?" she guessed with a little laugh, knowing how they hated to make the drive to Salt Lake.

"Yes, but . . . ," he began, then nothing more came out. He didn't know how to tell her, and it was evident that she didn't know how to ask.

"Is it Lorie?" she asked in a whisper, spurred on by the reality that her family was close by and they might not have another chance to talk for hours.

Jack nodded and forced it out in as few words as possible. "It's over, Hil. I left her."

Hilary took in a sharp breath. She was so stunned she couldn't even respond. She felt guilty for having the thought that she was *glad* they weren't together, especially when his pain was so evident. She couldn't hold back the tears, and she meant it when she said, "Oh, Jack, I'm so sorry."

"Yeah," he sighed, "so am I, but . . ." He nodded toward her family. "We'll talk later, okay?"

Jack remained on the sidelines as the family escorted Hilary to get her luggage, then decided on a place to meet for lunch. He helped carry her bags out of the airport, and Hilary wasn't surprised to find that Jack had driven her parents here in their car. She was surprised by the car, however, since she'd never seen it before. Her mother had written that they'd been able to get a new car, but Hilary had honestly forgotten.

The entire family met at a buffet restaurant. Hilary sat next to Jack and across from her parents, but he said little and she longed to be alone with him to talk. The food tasted good, but she was more enthralled with the reality of being reunited with her family. She especially felt an appreciation for her parents that she'd never felt before, and she marveled at how blessed she was.

After the meal, most of the family stayed and visited for over an hour. Then they shared embraces again and went their separate ways. Hilary's parents got into the backseat of the car, leaving her to sit in the front with Jack, who was driving.

"So," she said, once they were on the road, "the car is nice. I think it's great . . . the way you were able to get it."

"Yes," Millie agreed, "it's been a real blessing."

The small talk continued, while Hilary ached to talk about the *real* happenings in her absence. Instead they discussed the community of

Mt. Pleasant: who had died, who had bought this or that, who had been in accidents, who had married and divorced—but even then, Jack's situation didn't come up. In fact, Pete and Millie skirted around it so carefully that Hilary wondered just how bad it had been.

Hilary actually felt jittery with excitement when the scenery became familiar and she knew they were almost home. The fields were green with spring, and Sanpete County had never looked more beautiful to her. She put a hand to her heart and drew a deep, sustaining breath when the old farmhouse came into view.

Jack helped carry her luggage into the house, and he hung around while Hilary unpacked enough to bring out some of her keepsakes and talk about them. They all eagerly soaked in every word she said, but she was becoming steadily more impatient to hear what Jack had to say. She had thought he was comfortable enough with her parents to talk about it in their presence, but when he didn't, she wasn't certain how to find time alone with him.

The stake president stopped by the house on his way home from work to officially release Hilary from her mission. He visited for a short while, and a few minutes after he left, Jack stood up to leave as well. "I'm sure you're tired," he said. "I should get home and let you rest so you can—"

"Oh, I'm fine," she said. "I was hoping you'd drive me around the farm so I can see it again."

Hilary had never been so grateful for her mother's meddling as when Millie added, "Oh, that's a great idea. The two of you should have some time to talk."

"Are you sure you're up to it?" Jack asked.

"I am if you are," Hilary said. "The jet lag hasn't hit me yet."

Jack helped Hilary into his truck and started down the lane without a word. He drove slowly up and down the dirt roads that framed her family's land.

"I'm very grateful to you, Jack," Hilary said, breaking the silence.

"For what?" He seemed surprised.

"For looking after my parents the way you do."

"I haven't done much, quite honestly."

"According to Mother's letters, they know they can call on you whenever they need you. And that means a lot."

"I'm glad to help, Hilary. They're more family to me than my own family."

There was a subtle bite to his comment that prompted her to ask, "Things aren't going well there, I take it?"

"Let's just say my mother is full of a lot of *I-told-you-so's* and criticism, and my brothers just don't care about anyone or anything but themselves. Nothing's changed, really."

"Except perhaps that you've given your mother some fuel to work with?" Hilary guessed.

Jack first looked surprised, then something close to despair filled his countenance.

"Which brings us to later," she added.

"What?" He looked baffled.

"At the airport, you said we could talk later. It's later." He looked hesitant, but she knew they had to get all of this in the open. "Why don't you pull over somewhere and let's talk, okay?"

Jack nodded, and a minute later he drove the truck through a gate and parked it near her father's tractor. Switching off the engine, he turned to lean his back against the door. Hilary turned toward him and laid an arm across the back of the seat. Jack didn't know where to start, but since the subject of his mother had come up, he figured that was a less sensitive avenue.

"Well," he began, "my mother wasn't terribly thrilled with my getting married in the first place; it's as if she somehow wants to be the only woman to have any control over my life, and at the same time she wants nothing to do with me. I just don't get it. Anyway, when I told her I was getting married in the temple and she couldn't be there, she was full of all her usual anti-Mormon speeches. And then . . ." Jack looked away as he drew close to the core of his pain. "Well . . . when it became evident the marriage wasn't going well, my mother took full advantage of it. I haven't talked to her for weeks now. I don't see any point in it, really. Maybe on the other side of the veil, I'll understand why my mother is such a difficult woman. In the meantime, I can't handle her." He glanced at Hilary, then down at his hands as he rubbed his fingers together. "I can't even handle my own life right now."

Hilary watched Jack squeeze his eyes shut, and she ached at the evidence of his suffering. Taking his hand, she asked gently, "What happened, Jack?"

"I would wager that you could probably guess," he said. "It would seem you knew Lorie a lot better than I did."

Hilary swallowed hard. "I could only guess that she didn't turn out to be the woman she made you believe she was."

Jack sighed. "That about covers it." He looked at Hilary with hard eyes and added, "I wish you'd just say it and get it over with."

"Say what?"

"That you told me so. You told me not to marry her, and—"

"Jack," she interrupted firmly, "I'm not going to say *I told you so*. I'm not going to pass any judgments or criticize whatever happened or didn't happen. I just want you to know that I'm here for you—the way you've always been there for me." Hilary touched his face. "Talk to me, Jack," she urged.

Once Jack got started, the whole story just spilled into Hilary's lap, from beginning to end. And with it came spurts of emotion. He cried as he expressed all he'd lost. They talked about the things he'd learned, and about the fact that he knew marrying her had been the right thing to do. But it was easy for Hilary to understand why he was hurting in spite of his understanding. She was more relieved than she dared admit when he told her he really didn't love Lorie. But she did say to him, "You know, Jack, when I do give you up to the woman you marry, she's got to treat you every bit as well as I know you'll treat her."

Jack smiled when she said it, not willing to even consider the possibility that Hilary might be that woman. She saw the intensity in Jack's eyes and had to turn away. She knew that look well, and she cleared her throat tensely as she absorbed the reality that his feelings for her hadn't changed. She was relieved when he began talking again.

When the conversation finally ran down, Jack hugged Hilary tightly. "I love you, Hilary," he said. "I'm so glad to have you back."

"Yeah, me too," she replied. Hilary wanted to tell him that she loved him, too. She *did* love him—but not in the way that she knew he wanted her to. She couldn't say it and risk having him misunderstand.

Jack smiled and said, "It is *so good* to have you back." He took her hand. "You've changed."

"Is that good?"

"Yeah, it is. It's as if . . . everything good about you is just more defined."

Hilary felt warmed by the compliment, but she felt compelled to say, "You've changed too, Jack. I haven't once heard you whistle all day. And you're not chewing on a toothpick. And I haven't heard one redneck word come out of your mouth—like *bull-pucky,* or *criminantly.* Where exactly does one come up with words like criminantly?"

He chuckled. "I have no idea."

"And you haven't said *whoa, girl,* either."

In a voice far too severe for the conversation, he said, "Maybe it's for the better."

Hilary knew in her heart why he'd changed. Hoping he would eventually be able to fully find his own identity again, she said, "And maybe it's not."

Jack couldn't help the cynicism as he said, "You never liked those things about me, anyway."

Hilary didn't even blink before she said, "I like you for who you are, Jack."

A genuine smile accompanied the tears that rose in his eyes. "You can't comprehend what that means to me."

"Maybe I can," she said, and he nodded.

"Hey," he said, changing the subject, "whatever happened to that gypsy you had a crush on?"

She laughed softly. "Like most crushes, it faded with time. He's married now, I believe."

Hilary was disappointed when Jack had to go back to Provo the following day. She enjoyed being home and spending time with her parents, but she quickly became restless. She was accustomed to being very busy with a structured schedule. Now she felt at odds, and she knew she had to get involved in something as soon as possible or she'd go insane.

She was delighted to find that her teaching position at the studio was open. The woman who had taken her place would be finished with school soon and moving away. It worked out so well that Hilary couldn't question God's hand in her life. She also found out that Kim and Becky were still sharing an apartment, and they were thrilled to have her move back in with them. Hilary first made certain that Lorie wasn't living anywhere nearby. She quickly got back to work and enrolled in school. And since she'd sold her car before her mission, she was glad to be able to get another one.

In a matter of weeks, Hilary almost felt as if she'd never been gone. Except that she was a different person now. Her mission had given her a sense of purpose and serenity that she'd never dreamed possible. Her testimony was deep and sound. And she had to admit that her life was good.

Hilary saw Jack regularly, just as she had before. And again, it felt as if nothing had changed—except for the solemnity about him that made it difficult to forget the heartache he'd endured. Hilary frequently had to force thoughts of Lorie out of her head; they only spurred a deep anger on Jack's behalf. She knew she had to forgive Lorie and put it away, just as Jack was struggling to do. She was making some progress in that respect until Jack called her late one evening, simply asking her if she'd come to his apartment.

"What's up? You sound upset."

"Yeah, I'm upset," he said. "I can't talk about it over the phone."

"I'll be right over," she said, and hurried to grab her purse and sweater. She opened the door to leave—only to see Lorie standing there.

They both stood in stunned silence for a full minute while Hilary attempted to digest the fact that this woman had been Jack's *wife*. The full reality of that made her a little nauseous.

"You're back, I see," Lorie finally said.

"Yes, I'm back." Hilary fought hard to steady her expression and keep her voice even. Unable to find any words to say that were civil, she felt anxious to turn Lorie over to her sister. "Kim's in her bedroom," she said, motioning her inside. Then she hurried out to her car, grateful that she didn't have to remain in the same vicinity.

She arrived at Jack's apartment to see that he was as upset as he had sounded on the phone. "What happened?" she asked as soon as she was inside.

"Lorie was here," he said.

Hilary sat down, but remained at the edge of her seat while Jack paced the room. Had Lorie gone directly to see her sister after leaving here? "And?" she pressed.

Jack stopped pacing. He sighed and pressed his hands through his hair. Then he just said it. "She's pregnant."

Hilary took a moment to absorb this. "I assume from your mood that it's your baby."

"Of course it's my baby!"

"Okay, okay. But you've been separated for quite some time. Why is she telling you now?"

Jack sat down and put his head into his hands. "She's about four months along. She said she didn't want to tell me because we were already separated before she found out."

Hilary felt something uneasy beginning to stir inside her. While she was trying to figure out where her thoughts were headed, Jack startled her. "What are you thinking, Hil?"

"Nothing, really." She turned her focus to him. "So, what are you going to do? I hope you're not considering trying to work things out with her."

"No, of course not," he insisted, much to her relief. "I told her I'd support her through the pregnancy. I'll support the child. I want to be involved in its life. I'm its father, for crying out loud, but . . ." He sighed heavily. "I just didn't want it to be this way. I didn't want any connection to her at all. I don't want *my* child caught in the middle of all this. I don't want it raised with her attitudes and . . . oh, help. It just makes me sick to think about it. How could I be so stupid? I don't know why I ever married her to begin with."

"You told me that you knew marrying her was the right thing; that there was a purpose for it."

"I know, but . . . would God want a child caught in the middle of this? It just . . . it just seems so . . ."

Jack leaned back on the couch and closed his eyes. Hilary watched him while her thoughts continued to churn. She considered Lorie's personality, and the patterns of her behavior. She felt compelled to ask, "Jack, did Lorie . . . want the two of you to get back together? I mean, what's her attitude about all of this?"

"That's basically it. She said it was a mistake to end the marriage. I already told you what I said to her. She left pretty upset."

"I saw her just as I was leaving my apartment. She didn't look upset to me. She tends to be pretty dramatic; if she was upset, I would think she'd show it."

"Maybe. Maybe not."

Hilary shrugged. "Okay, but let me say something that's bugging me. I'm having trouble with someone like Lorie waiting four months to tell you something that would upset you and hold some control over your life. I'm not claiming to know her perfectly, and I've been gone a long time, but . . . it just doesn't seem like her."

Jack held his breath a moment as he began to grasp Hilary's implication. "Okay," he said, "I'm listening."

"I always had the impression that Lorie was the kind of woman who enjoyed drama and challenge. Once she conquered something, she moved on. She always wanted what she couldn't have. And she always wanted to be the center of attention. Am I being accurate so far?"

Jack thought about it a minute, startled by how accurately Hilary had just described his relationship with Lorie. Once she'd conquered him, she'd become bored. And most of their arguments had been full of drama, as if she'd been some kind of actress, playing out her life in a soap opera.

"So, let's just say that suddenly she's bored with whatever was keeping her busy when you left her, and now she's realized that you don't want her anymore."

"Are you saying what I think you're saying?" he asked cautiously.

"I don't know. What do you think I'm saying?"

"That this pregnancy is a hoax?"

"I don't know, Jack; I could be wrong. But I think if I were you, I'd want some proof before I started upsetting my life over it. And maybe I'm being really unfair, but if she *is* pregnant, I'd want some blood tests after it's born—just to be sure."

Hilary allowed Jack several minutes of silence to think about it. Then he looked up, saying, "Thank you, Hilary."

"For what?"

"For being levelheaded enough to help me see things clearly. I meant what I told her. Baby or no baby, I'm not wasting another day of my life on Lorie. But you're right; I need to know for sure. If she's pregnant, I'll take care of my responsibilities through legal channels. Maybe Colin can help me out there. And if she's not, well . . . that will certainly wrap her character up in a neat little package."

Hilary nodded.

"So, how do I get proof that she's pregnant?"

"Do you know who her doctor is?"

"Yeah. She went to see him regularly; every stupid little thing that came up, she was always going in for an office call. She told me several times what a great doctor he was, and she refused to see anyone else."

"He's probably the only doctor in town who would humor her," Hilary commented. "So, call his office. That shouldn't be too difficult."

Even though everything Hilary had said made sense to Jack, he still believed Lorie was pregnant. In spite of everything she'd done to him, he had difficulty imagining she could lie outright to him like that. But her doctor's office had no record of any pregnancy; they had seen her a few weeks earlier for a minor virus.

The minute Jack got off the phone, he called Lorie at work. "How are you feeling?" he asked.

"Oh, a little nauseous here and there," she said, "but I'm doing okay."

"Is that normal? I mean . . . I assume you've talked to Dr. Burlinson about all this."

"Oh, of course. He assures me everything's fine."

Jack wanted to ask her if they were talking about the same doctor, but he was so stunned that he didn't ask her anything. He knew he could call her on the lie, but it would only start an argument, and he just didn't have the energy to get into it.

"Are you still there?" she asked.

"Yeah. I . . . uh, well . . . listen, Lorie, you let me know when the baby's born, okay? Then we can take it from there."

Jack quickly got off the phone and went to his classes. But a week later he was still stunned at the thought of how horribly deceptive she was. If nothing else, the incident validated his reasons for leaving her. Nine days after her announcement that she was pregnant, Lorie called to tell him she'd miscarried. Just to reassure himself, Jack called her doctor again. Then he called Hilary and thanked her for being there for him, and for having the insight to get him through this as painlessly as possible. He wondered how he could ever get by without her.

* * * * *

In spite of being somewhat out of shape, Hilary was delighted to start teaching dance again. She'd forgotten how much she'd missed it until late one evening after lessons were over, and she turned the lights out. The only illumination in the room came from the lights outside. Hilary dug her favorite tape out and put it into the stereo, turning the volume up intolerably loud—just the way she liked it. As the once-familiar music began to play, she closed her eyes and inhaled deeply. *She'd come home.*

She quickly got back into the habit of dancing alone with the lights out. Spring merged into summer, with life going on much as it had before. On a hot night in June, Hilary was grateful for the good air conditioning in the studio as she turned the music up and began her deeply loved ritual. She responded to the bass pounding through the floor, and her feet began to move, as if by their own will. The music consumed her, and she felt her entire body become a part of it. She actually laughed aloud as the lyrics perfectly echoed her feelings: *Come alive! You can dance right through your life. In a flash it takes hold of my heart . . . I am music now! I am rhythm now!*

The next song on the tape was slower, and she moved easily into the music, like a liquid extension of the song.

Jack was grateful for his impulse to come here when he moved stealthily into the studio and found Hilary dancing. Oblivious to his presence, she moved to the music like some kind of angel, flowing weightlessly through the heavens. The familiarity of the song became suddenly poignant as he recalled dancing with her to this once before.

As Hilary's steps slowed, she seemed to dance with some invisible partner. Aching to hold her, Jack stepped behind her and took her outstretched arms. She gasped and turned, then laughed when she saw him. He briefly touched a finger to her lips to quiet her, not wanting to break this magical spell. Then he took her into his arms and danced with her, wishing his whole life could be this way.

Hilary was glad to see Jack. He'd kept track of her in the months since her mission, but he'd been more distant and guarded. She'd gradually seen him become more confident in getting over his hurt associated with Lorie, but she still sensed a solemnness about him that hadn't been there before. And her heart ached for him.

Watching Jack closely, Hilary wished she could read his mind. She felt suddenly breathless as he looked into her eyes, conveying an unspoken message that she knew well. *He still loved her.* But unlike in the past, she felt a tingling erupt somewhere inside at the thought. Suddenly uncomfortable, Hilary put her face to his shoulder, if only to avoid his gaze. His arm tightened around her, and she couldn't deny the security she felt in his embrace. Everything about him was so strong and protective, so thoroughly masculine. It was tempting to just allow herself to get caught up in the moment, and indulge in romantic thoughts. But that wouldn't be fair to either of them; they just weren't suited for each other, and she knew it. Or did she?

Hilary forced her thoughts elsewhere, trying to think of something logical and friend-like that she could discuss with Jack. But that tingling returned, increasing until it nearly consumed her. Trying to make sense of her feelings, she drew away to look into Jack's eyes, certain that reality would put everything back into perspective. But as they continued to dance, the music combined with his presence seemed to hold her powerless.

Is it fate or is it luck that brings us back? Or is it just a common point of view? I'll be here where the heart is, where the dreams that we've been after all come true. I'll wait for you.

As Jack's expression seemed to echo the lyrics they were listening to, Hilary's breathing suddenly sharpened. "Are you okay?" he asked softly, his brow furrowing.

"Yes," she chuckled tensely. "I mean . . . no. I mean . . . I guess I'm just out of breath. I was dancing pretty hard before you came in. I'm okay."

The song ended, and another began—a fast song with a hard beat that Hilary used for exercising vigorously. They stopped dancing, but Jack kept his arm around her, looking into her eyes as if searching for something. Then he smiled as if he'd found it. Hilary felt helpless to move or resist as he bent to kiss her. She closed her eyes, allowing her memory to wander to the kiss he'd given her before she'd left on her mission. Then, just as now, she couldn't deny enjoying it, but she felt certain it was simply something physical and primal. She felt somehow wicked for enjoying it. Reminding herself that she and Jack weren't right for each other, that she couldn't lead him on this way, she stepped back abruptly, trying not to appear as shocked as she felt. She touched her lips as if to convince herself that they were still tingling.

Seeing her alarm, Jack immediately regretted his impulse to kiss her. "I'm sorry," he insisted. "I don't know what came over me. I just . . . I mean . . . I know we're just friends, and I . . . know that's the way you want it, and I respect that . . . I'm so sorry, Hilary." He reached for her hand, relieved when she didn't pull away. How could he possibly explain the compulsion he felt to be close to her? *He loved her so much.* He'd tried to keep his distance from her, when being with her left him feeling so torn. But he could never stay away for long. And tonight he'd come here feeling especially lonely and down.

Hilary took a deep breath to steady her emotions. "It's okay." She laughed softly. "No big deal."

Again Jack looked into her eyes, but she turned away. "Hey, I'm starving. Could we go get something to eat?"

Jack hesitated, wishing he didn't feel so uneasy. "Sure."

"I'll just go change, and . . ."

She whisked out of the room, leaving Jack alone with the music and his aching heart. He sighed and glanced heavenward, silently uttering the same old prayer. If he and Hilary weren't meant to be together, why did he have to be plagued with these feelings? He just didn't understand.

Hilary offered to take her car. Driving somehow made her feel more in control. They ate burgers and fries, sharing small talk the way they always had. But Hilary felt anxious without understanding why. She was relieved when they finally returned to the studio where Jack had left his truck.

"Hey," he said as he got out, "I just remembered the reason I stopped by tonight. Nicholas Bennett's getting married. Remember him?"

Hilary nodded. He'd grown up in Mt. Pleasant, though she'd hardly known him.

"The reception is tomorrow evening. He's marrying a girl from Pleasant Grove, so it's not far. Would you go with me? I really want to go, but . . ." He wanted to tell her that after being married and divorced, going to something like this without someone to lean on would be terribly difficult. "I just don't want to go alone," he said. She smiled and nodded, and he knew she understood.

"What time?" she asked.

"I'll pick you up about six. Maybe we could hit a movie after . . . if you want. It's up to you."

Hilary took a deep breath. With the way she felt right now, she wasn't certain she could endure it. She simply said, "Let's just see how it goes."

"Okay, thanks. I'll see you tomorrow."

Jack got out of the car, and Hilary waited until he had started the truck before she drove away.

She had difficulty sleeping that night. In spite of physical exhaustion, her thoughts tumbled with rationalizations. Over and over she recounted what had happened inside her while she and Jack were dancing. Of course, she had just been caught up in the moment. He *was* a good dancer. He treated her well. He made her feel secure and comfortable. But the attraction just wasn't there. Or was it?

"Oh, help," she muttered and rolled her face into the pillow. Could she actually be falling for Jack Hayden? She didn't even have to question if he was good husband material; she knew him almost better than she knew herself. But the romantic interest had just never been there for her. He just wasn't her type.

As the night wore on, Hilary kept hearing echoes in her head of a hypothetical argument between her and Jack. He was telling her all the reasons they could be happy together. They shared the same values, the same religion. They could talk and laugh together. And cry together.

Then Hilary heard all of her own arguments hurtling back at him. Their goals and careers were completely different. They didn't like the same music, or the same . . . "Oh, garbage!" she said into her pillow. She knew in her heart those things didn't matter. The bottom line was simply that she'd never felt attracted to Jack. He just wasn't her type. She finally went to sleep, chanting it over and over in her mind. *He's just not my type. He's just not my type.*

Hilary kept busy the next day, keeping herself occupied every minute with the hope of keeping her head clear. But when Jack picked her up for the wedding reception, all her efforts had obviously been wasted. Her heart quickened at the sight of him. And while they drove to Pleasant Grove, where the reception was being held, Hilary found it difficult to even keep up a minimal conversation.

"Is something bothering you?" he asked, helping her out of the truck.

"No, why?" She smiled guiltily, feeling like she'd been caught stealing.

"You just seem . . . preoccupied."

"Well, maybe I am," she admitted. "Nothing to worry about."

Before they reached the door, Jack stopped abruptly. "What?" she asked.

He let out a deep breath. "I hate these things."

Hilary took his hand, grateful for an opportunity to do so. "One of these days, you're going to have to stop letting Lorie torment you."

He sighed. "I know."

"Hey," she touched his chin quickly, "we don't have to stay long, then we can hit a movie or something. Okay?"

Jack smiled as they went inside. "Okay."

He put his arm around her, and Hilary had to fight to keep a straight face when her heart raced all over again. The reception was nice, but she felt as if she were seeing it all from a distance. Her thoughts were completely consumed with Jack. She could hardly take her eyes off him. She'd never been afraid to admit he was handsome, but she'd never dreamed that just looking at a man could affect her this way. She found it difficult to believe this was the same man she'd been friends with for so long. Had he changed so much? Or had she just been blind? Jack Hayden was no backward farm boy. He was a refined, dignified man who had a deep love and respect for the land. He was not pretentious or prideful—things she knew she had struggled with herself in the past. He was selfless, honest, and hardworking. He loved his religion and he lived it. He was *all* man; an incredibly wonderful, handsome man. She *had* been blind. She'd been a blind fool!

While Hilary found it difficult not to just blurt out, "I love you, Jack," she felt she should be absolutely certain he was the one for her. He'd been so good to her, so committed. She couldn't lead him on now and hurt him if it wasn't meant to be.

As Hilary observed Jack in a whole new light, she nearly felt as if her heart would burst from the love she felt. He caught her eye once and smiled. His expression was familiar; the love in his eyes was as evident as it had always been. But the thought struck Hilary with a new heartache that she had never really understood before. She had known of Jack's feelings for years, but it wasn't until now that she even began to comprehend how difficult it must have been for him to feel something that wasn't being reciprocated. Hilary couldn't imagine loving Jack for even a day without knowing that he shared that love.

A tangible heartache consumed her on his behalf, and she gained a new respect for his continual patience with her—not to mention his commitment to being her friend all this time. *She loved him so much.*

Hilary thoroughly enjoyed the remainder of the evening. The two of them had gone out many times, but never had it been so pleasant for her. It was difficult to say good night, and again she couldn't sleep—but for different reasons. She was so consumed with happiness and excitement that she could hardly hold still. But tomorrow was Saturday, so she just enjoyed the feelings, knowing she could sleep in.

She fasted all day Saturday, praying in her heart for the spiritual validation of her thoughts and feelings. By the following morning, she knew beyond any doubt that she and Jack were meant to be together. There were no thunderbolts, no visions. Only an undeniable peace that filled her entire being. She lay in bed as long as she could get away with, just trying to absorb the reality. She found it difficult to keep from laughing out loud as the happiness consumed her. She could hardly believe it! All these years—all they had shared—and she never would have dreamed it would come to this. But she felt no hesitation or concern; only an excitement beyond description at the thought of being with Jack Hayden forever. The only problem was letting him know her feelings had changed without making a complete fool of herself.

Hilary finally got out of bed and slid to her knees in prayer. She thanked her Father in Heaven for giving her the answer to her prayers, and for sending her Jack. He'd been a friend to her through these years, and now he would be everything to her. Hilary prayed that Jack's heart would be softened toward her past stubbornness, and that she would be able to share her feelings with him in a way that would not make either of them uncomfortable. As she prayed, she began to wonder why she'd never felt right about marrying Jack before, yet she felt it now with such conviction. Why had this attraction never been there until a few days ago? Had she just been stubborn and blind? Perhaps that was part of it. But as Hilary ended her prayer and went about getting ready for church, the thought occurred to her that the time just hadn't been right before now. She momentarily froze in the hallway as the idea settled in deeper, with an accompanying warmth that let her know beyond any doubt that it was inspiration. She had needed these years to learn what would strengthen her for the future, and Jack had needed the same. Her mission, and the experiences they'd both had, were necessary parts of their spiritual development—including Jack's marriage to Lorie. That thought alone gave Hilary great comfort. In that moment, she could clearly see that God did indeed have his hand in the lives of his children. Even with all her shortcomings, Hilary knew that God was mindful of her and leading her down the right paths. And she felt certain the same applied to Jack. In spite of the difficulties he'd experienced with Lorie, Hilary knew they had been necessary to his progression.

Hilary felt the Spirit near as she went to church, occasionally being assaulted by butterflies at the thought of seeing Jack later. The minute she got home, she changed her clothes and drove to his apartment, knowing he would have just come from church himself. She was disappointed to arrive and find him gone. She knocked at the door even though his truck wasn't there, perhaps hoping someone had borrowed it. But she finally had to admit he wasn't home, and she headed back to her car, consumed with disappointment. She was putting the key in the ignition when Jack pulled up behind her. She saw him wave in her rearview mirror, and she put a hand to her middle, hoping to suppress a swarm of butterflies. "Hi," she said nonchalantly when she got out of the car and he walked toward her.

"Hi. What are you up to?"

"I was just . . . looking for you."

"Then I got here just in time. I was . . . held up at church a few minutes, talking to somebody who . . . well, it doesn't matter." He leaned against her car and folded his arms across his chest. "What can I do for you?"

"I . . . uh . . ." Hilary felt suddenly nervous. She could hardly look at him. "I . . . just needed to talk to you."

Jack sensed a severity in her tone that made him feel tense. If that didn't, her obvious nervousness did. "Did you want to go somewhere or—"

"That would be great," she interrupted.

"Okay. I'll just hurry and change."

Hilary nodded, and Jack went inside. He returned quickly wearing jeans with boots, and a denim shirt. Hilary wondered if he'd always looked this adorable and she just hadn't bothered noticing.

"Do you want me to drive or—"

"That would be great," she said, and he opened the passenger door of the truck for her.

"Where to?" he asked, pulling out onto the road.

Hilary nearly panicked. She hadn't even considered an appropriate location to talk to him. The reality of what she was approaching heightened her panic, and she could hardly breathe, let alone speak.

"Hilary?" Jack asked, fighting the urge to just demand knowing what was up. She looked practically terrified. Whatever she wanted to talk to him about was serious, and he knew it. He briefly contemplated his worst fear. Had she found someone else? "Hilary?" he asked louder.

"I'm sorry," she said, then blurted, "How about the temple lawn?"

Jack looked surprised, but complied without question. When they were sitting on the lawn, Hilary felt dumbstruck once again.

"You're making me nervous, Hil," Jack admitted.

Hilary chuckled tensely and forced herself to say what was in her heart. "Jack, there's something I need to tell you, but it's not easy. So, be patient with me."

Jack's nerves increased tenfold, but he only nodded.

"You know, Jack, I've been thinking a lot about the last few years— since Jeffrey died—and I realize I've been very immature and . . . probably unfair to you in many respects." Jack opened his mouth to protest, but she put up a hand to stop him. "Please . . . just hear me out. Our friendship has meant more to me than I could ever put into words. I can't comprehend what I ever would have done without you. And I've probably taken you for granted much of the time. But . . . well, it can't go on this way, Jack. We're both getting too old to be playing games. It's time we both got on with our lives."

To fill in the silence, Jack said, "I already tried that once."

"What?" she asked, too consumed with her own thoughts to grasp his implication.

"Getting on with my life. I tried that already, and it was a disaster."

"Well," Hilary sighed loudly, "I guess we all need some hard knocks to learn what we have to learn."

When she said nothing more, Jack thought his nerves would explode. "You were saying?" he pressed.

Hilary forced a smile and barely looked at him. Jack could almost feel where this was headed. His heart began to pound, but he kept quiet, fearing he'd erupt and make a fool of himself.

Hilary looked away and continued. "Jack, I'm only assuming that your feelings for me haven't changed. It's been a long time since we've talked about it, but . . ."

Jack couldn't bear it another minute. "Hilary, are you trying to tell me that you've fallen for someone?"

Hilary was surprised by the question, but she erupted with secret delight and forced herself to keep a straight face as she nodded her head.

Jack tried to tell himself that a part of him had believed this was inevitable. But the pain, already setting in, made it evident that he was poorly prepared. When Hilary said nothing more, he came right out and asked, "Are you in love with him?"

Hilary nodded again. Jack squeezed his eyes shut. A gasp of disbelief erupted from his lips. Hilary was so touched by his emotion that she could hardly speak. When he pressed his head into his hands, she knew she couldn't drag this out much longer. "Jack," she touched his arm, "please . . . hear me out. It's important for you to know that . . . well . . . I know beyond any doubt that this man is the right one for me, but . . . I'm afraid he doesn't know how I feel, and I don't know how to tell him."

Jack kept his head down, fighting back his emotion. He could fall apart later—in private. Right now, he was her friend, and he needed to be man enough to act like it. He forced himself to look up, and noticed that her nervousness had ceased. In fact, she was practically glowing. Whatever she had discovered, it was obviously right for her. He could see it in her countenance. He told himself he could go a long way on knowing she was happy.

While he was searching for something appropriate to say, Hilary asked, "Do you think I should just ask him to marry me, or something? Is that too forward—even in this day and age?"

"It wouldn't bother me," he managed to say, "but I can only speak for myself."

Hilary smiled, and he wanted to be angry with her for being so happy. But how could he? He felt inclined to ask, "Does he love you, Hilary?"

"I believe he does, but . . ." Hilary looked into his eyes, and the anguish she saw there forced all pretenses away. Tears brimmed in her eyes as she touched his face, saying with a cracked voice, "Will you marry me, Jack?"

Jack felt himself turn to stone. For a moment he thought she was joking, but her expression overruled that possibility. He wondered if he'd misunderstood somehow, but he didn't know how to clarify it. She smiled. Then she pressed her hand to one side of his face, and a kiss to the other. Her touch shocked him to reality. He pressed his hand over hers, holding it against his face, as if her touch alone might verify the truth of what she'd just said. His memory recounted her words in relation to himself. *I know beyond any doubt that this man is the right one for me, but I'm afraid he doesn't know how I feel . . .* A noise erupted from his lips, a laugh mingled with a sob. Their eyes met and she whispered, "I love you, Jack. And I want to be with you forever."

Jack heard what she said—very clearly. But it was as if a cloud had settled over his mind, keeping him from comprehending it. Had he convinced himself so completely that this would never happen, that he just couldn't believe it? He couldn't speak; couldn't even move. *He just couldn't believe it.*

"Jack? Are you okay?"

Her voice startled him and he turned away, as if not looking at her would make his brain start working again.

"Jack?" She touched his face again.

He shook his head and closed his eyes. "I . . . I don't understand, Hilary. I thought . . . you didn't . . ." He couldn't quite put it to words, and was grateful when she took over.

"I thought so, too, Jack. I mean . . . all these years . . . I don't know if I was just blind, or stupid . . . or both." She laughed softly. "Or maybe the time just wasn't right. In fact, I asked the Lord about it just this morning. He let me know beyond any doubt that you and I had needed this time to learn what we needed to learn . . . for whatever the future might bring."

Jack turned abruptly to look at her, and she could almost read his mind. With confidence she said, "Yes, even your marrying Lorie was important—for all of us. I don't claim to fully understand it, but I know it had to happen." Hilary fought the emotion rising in her throat as she attempted to share feelings that were difficult to describe. "I know it's impossible to explain or comprehend all the spiritual ramifications of our temporal lives. All I can say is that I know in my heart you and I are where we're supposed to be now, and all we've learned will help us through whatever may lie ahead."

Jack's heart began to pound in a way that made him wonder if it had temporarily stopped beating. Her words echoed through his mind, and reality descended over him in a tangible warmth, starting at the top of his head and slowly moving over his entire body. He took hold of Hilary's arms and pressed his forehead to hers. His voice trembled as he said, "I love you, Hilary. I love you more than life."

Hilary laughed through a sudden rush of tears and pressed herself into his arms. She could hear his laughter near her ear, and felt his breath against her throat. He kissed the side of her face, then her brow, then her eyes. And finally, her lips. He had kissed her before, and it had certainly left an impression. But in her present state of mind, Hilary felt as if heaven itself had opened up to rain happiness down upon her.

Jack kissed Hilary long and hard, then he took her face into his hands and just looked at her. He had often wondered what it might be like to hear confessions of love from her. He'd believed it would change the entire perspective of his life. Still, a part of him had never really believed it would happen. But it had! And the gratitude he felt was beyond description.

Hilary laughed and hugged him. "Hey," she said, "do you think we should tell my parents?"

Jack grinned. "Yeah, but we should tell them face to face, don't you think?"

"Yes."

"Okay. When?"

"How about right now?" she asked, and he laughed as he took her hand and dragged her toward the truck.

For the first time ever, Hilary sat right next to Jack as they drove toward Mt. Pleasant. They speculated about the future, talking and laughing. Jack felt as if he was dreaming. Everything was perfect. He put his arm around her shoulders, keeping one hand on the wheel. "I love you, Hilary," he said softly.

Hilary looked up at him, feeling warm from the inside out as she replied, "I love you too, Jack."

He laughed and let out a whoop. "Do you have any idea how good it feels to hear you say that, and to know you mean it?"

"Yes, actually, I do."

Hilary felt like a child on Christmas morning as Jack parked the truck in front of her parents' home.

"Okay," he said before they got out, "let's make this memorable."

Hilary nodded, and they walked into the house. Pete and Millie were delightfully surprised to see them. But once the usual greetings were exchanged, Millie asked, "What's wrong?"

"Oh, nothing," Jack insisted quickly, doing his best to appear glum.

Hilary sat on the opposite side of the room from him, trying to act nervous and concerned.

"Somethin' must be up," Pete insisted.

"Well, actually," Jack drawled, "Hilary has something she needs to tell you, and . . . even though I'm still having trouble believing it, I felt like I should be the one to bring her down and . . ." He feigned emotion and nodded toward Hilary, indicating that she should take over.

Hilary sighed loudly, fighting hard not to laugh. She thought briefly how Jack might feel if she was here to tell her parents that she was marrying someone else. The heartache she might have felt made it easier to keep her mood somber.

"What is it, Hilary?" Millie asked with concern.

"Well," Hilary cleared her throat tensely, "you know that Jack and I have been friends for a long time, and . . . well . . ." She tried to remember how she had put it to Jack earlier. "Well, eventually things just have to change. It's time we both got on with our lives, and, well . . ."

With a bitter edge to his voice, Jack said, "She's trying to tell you she's fallen in love with some idiot she intends to marry."

Hilary couldn't help chuckling, but she quickly slapped a hand over her mouth until she gained her composure. Pete and Millie both looked mildly upset, and Hilary quickly said, "I know the two of you have always had hopes that Jack and I would get together—even if you've never admitted it out loud. But . . . well . . . the thing is . . . that's exactly why you should be the first to know that . . ."

"What, Hilary, what?" Pete asked impatiently.

Hilary laughed. "Jack and I are getting married."

Pete and Millie were obviously stunned. Neither of them seemed to know how to respond until Hilary crossed the room and sat close beside Jack. He took her hand and kissed it. Pete laughed. Millie cried. Jack and Hilary just looked into each other's eyes, too in awe of their feelings to know what else to say.

When the reality finally settled in, Millie exclaimed, "This is the most wonderful news I've ever heard."

"Amen to that!" Pete added.

Over dinner, they filled Hilary's parents in on all the details. Jack watched Hilary as if he'd never seen her before. He felt so happy that he had to wonder if it was too good to be true. Then Hilary took his hand and smiled at him, and he couldn't doubt that it was real. So he just silently thanked God for leading him down the paths that had brought them to this day.

"So, have you set a date?" Millie asked while they were clearing the table.

"Sometime this summer," Jack said. "The sooner the better, as far as I'm concerned."

"Amen to that," Hilary said, mimicking her father.

The following day when Jack arrived at the job site, Ammon was quick to say, "What happened to you? Did you win a lottery or something?" He looked right into Jack's face and laughed. "What is this? Perma-grin? I don't think I could wipe that smile off your face with a sledgehammer."

"It's that obvious, huh?"

"Yeah, what's up?"

Jack laughed and shook his head, still unable to believe it. "You know Hilary."

"Well, I've never met her, but I know who you're talking about."

"We're getting married."

Ammon laughed. "She finally came to her senses."

"I don't know," Jack took a deep breath. "Whatever happened, I'm thoroughly enjoying it. I'd say life is just too good to be true."

"Well, I'm glad you feel that way. Because we should have had this hole dug last week."

"I'm on it," Jack said, pulling on his gloves and climbing into the backhoe.

Hilary felt almost lost without Jack on Monday morning, and decided that surprising him with lunch would be a good way to remedy that. He'd driven her past the subdivision where they were working a couple of weeks earlier, so it wasn't hard to find him. She pulled up behind his truck and got out of the car. She saw a few men looking her way, but Jack wasn't among them. One of them approached her as she came closer. By his distinctive appearance, she wondered if this was Ammon.

"Can I help you?" he asked loudly to be heard above the dull roar of a nearby backhoe.

"I'm looking for Jack Hayden."

He grinned. "You must be Hilary."

"That's right. And you are . . ."

"Ammon Mitchell." He removed a glove to shake her hand. "It's a pleasure to meet you at last. I hear there are congratulations in order."

Hilary nearly blushed. "News travels fast. Is Jack—"

"He's right over there." Ammon pointed toward the backhoe.

"Oh, my," Hilary said when she realized Jack was operating the thing. She knew he did construction, but she'd not imagined him doing *that*.

"I'll get him," Ammon said, and she wondered if he'd sensed her hesitance in trying to get his attention—from a safe distance.

Ammon jumped right up on the side of the cab and said something to Jack, then he pointed toward Hilary. Jack grinned and jumped down. Ammon took his place and continued to dig.

"Well, look at you," Jack said, pulling off his gloves. He brushed off his clothes, then greeted her with a firm hug and a long kiss.

"Mmmmm," Hilary said, looking into his eyes, "I'm going to have to make a habit of this."

"Of what?"

"Hunting you down to take you to lunch. Is that possible?"

"Sure. I'm not very presentable, but . . ."

"You look like a construction worker. I can live with it." Hilary didn't add that his thoroughly rugged attire only enhanced his masculinity, spurring that tingling sensation that had become common in his presence. She loved him with all her heart, and looked forward to a bright future as Mrs. Jack Hayden.

"So, when do you want to get married?" Hilary asked while they were waiting for the sandwiches they'd ordered.

Jack laughed and shook his head. "Maybe you should just pinch me good and hard so I won't think I'm dreaming."

Hilary leaned over the table, took hold of his cheek, and pinched it with a good deal of drama. "Is that convincing enough?"

"No," he grabbed her hand and leaned back over the table to kiss her, "but that is."

"Now, seriously, Jack," she said. "We need to set a date."

"I only have one opinion on that. As soon as possible. I want you to have a nice wedding without stressing you or your parents. So, you set a date that will give you enough time to do that." He took her hand and pressed it to his lips. With serious eyes and a hushed voice, he added, "We've been close too long, Hilary. We're too comfortable with each other to wait."

Hilary turned away and nearly melted into her chair at the implication. She felt herself turn warm and heard Jack chuckle. She turned back to look into his eyes. It was difficult for her to believe that she could be so happy.

After consulting with Hilary's parents, they set a date in August. Then they set to work planning the wedding, doing their best to stay busy.

In the meantime, Hilary thoroughly enjoyed life as Jack Hayden's fiancée. She'd never had so much fun; never dreamed life could be so good. In spite of the friendship they had shared, Hilary learned something new about him every day. His love of the gospel ran deep, as did his love of life. He had a way of looking at the world that somehow filled Hilary with joy and expectation.

Together they went hiking and on picnics. He even took her mountain climbing and taught her to rappel down a cliff. She knew it was something he and Jeffrey had done together some as teenagers, but she'd never imagined doing something so daring herself.

On a Saturday in late June, Jack borrowed a motorcycle and a couple of helmets from a friend, and they rode up around the Alpine Loop. When they stopped at the top to hike a little and eat some sandwiches, he told her that what he liked best about driving a motorcycle through a canyon was the way he could feel the air cool when they passed a body of water, even if he couldn't see it through the trees. Through the remainder of their ride, Hilary paid attention to the feel of the air and was able to see what he meant.

That evening, they barbecued at Jack's apartment with a hibachi that he kept out on the little deck overlooking the lawn below. The children of his downstairs neighbors were playing in the yard, and Hilary enjoyed listening to their laughter while Jack cooked their steaks.

"I didn't realize you were so adventurous," Hilary said with a little laugh.

"I didn't realize *you* were so adventurous," he replied, lifting his brows comically.

"Am I?"

"You're going to marry me, aren't you?"

"Yes, I am!"

"There you have it. Your life is destined to be one adventure after another."

"What are you trying to tell me? Are we going skydiving next?"

"If you want to," he laughed, "but I just meant that living with me could be an adventure."

Hilary took his hand. "I'm looking forward to every minute of it."

"Yeah, me too." Kissing her quickly, he went inside for a minute and came back with a plate to put the steaks on, then he sat next to Hilary. He motioned toward the children playing on the lawn. "Now, there's an adventure I look forward to," he said.

Hilary turned to look at Jack, attempting to absorb the reality that he would be the father of her children. A tingling erupted inside her that only increased when he turned to find her watching him. Their eyes locked with such intensity that Hilary had to wonder if they had loved each other in another time and place. "I don't know how I could have been so stupid all these years," she said.

"What do you mean by that?" he asked with a chuckle.

"If I'd had any brains, I'd have gotten a crush on *you* in high school."

Jack chuckled again, then his expression sobered. "It's like you said; the time wasn't right. Now that we are where we are, I'm glad it turned out the way it did. I'm glad you went on a mission, and I'm even glad for the experiences I've had. If nothing else, having a bad marriage will sure make me appreciate having a good one."

"We don't have to invite her to the wedding, do we?"

"Not a chance." He laughed and took the steaks off the grill. They went inside to eat, but left the sliding door open. During a quiet moment, the children's laughter erupted nearby and Jack chuckled.

"So, how many children do you think we should have?" Hilary asked.

"One at a time," he replied. "I think we'll know what's right for us when the time comes."

Hilary nodded and took his hand across the table. "I love you, Jack Hayden."

Jack grinned. "You just keep telling me that, and maybe one day I won't have to wonder if I'm dreaming."

As the summer progressed, Hilary found the perfect wedding gown and made arrangements for the wedding with her mother's help and some input from Jack. And while Jack continued broadening her horizons with new experiences, she lured him regularly to the dance studio after all her students had gone home, and they sometimes danced until midnight.

On a hot night in July, Hilary dismissed her last class, turned out the lights, and turned the music up. But after a few minutes she felt too exhausted to dance, so she opted for the next best thing and lay down in the center of the floor, where she could feel the pulse of the bass notes beneath her.

"What are you doing?" Jack shouted, and she looked up to see him standing above her.

"You scared me to death," she shouted back.

He looked her up and down. "You look like you're still alive to me."

Hilary laughed and held out a hand. He took it and tried to pull her up, but instead she tugged back, and he had no choice but to go to his knees beside her.

"What are you doing?" he repeated.

"Lie down right here," she urged, patting the floor beside her.

"Okay," he said once he had.

"Do you feel the bass in the floor?"

"Yes," he drawled.

"That's what I'm doing. I'm *feeling* the music."

They lay side by side for several minutes before Jack said, "Now, this is what I call an adventure."

Hilary laughed and slugged him playfully on the shoulder. "You're making fun of me."

"No, I'm not," he insisted. "It never would have occurred to me to *feel* music, but I have to admit it's intriguing."

"I look at it this way," she said. "Dance is like music personified. If a deaf person can see the dance, then he can hear the music—in essence."

Jack turned on his side to look at her. "Show me the music, Hilary," he said in a voice that she could barely hear.

Hilary turned to face him. "Kiss me first."

"You don't have to ask me twice," he said and pressed his lips to hers in a kiss that was as meek as it was memorable. Hilary felt warmed from the inside out as Jack took her hand into his, threading their fingers together. This experience, so familiar to her, now took on a whole new perspective with Jack's hand in hers, knowing they would be together forever. It was doubly wonderful, since they had shared friendship for so long.

"Now dance for me," he beckoned with a sensuous voice.

"You want me to dance alone?"

"I want to see the music." She looked hesitant and he added, "Do you have any idea how I felt the first time I came in here and saw you dance? If I hadn't loved you before, I would have fallen in love with you then." His voice lowered further. "It moves me. It's almost . . . spiritual."

Hilary sighed and jumped to her feet. "I feel awfully conspicuous."

"Just pretend I'm not here."

"You're lying in the middle of the floor."

He laughed. "That's what makes it an adventure."

Hilary changed the tape and reminded herself that this man was going to be her husband; her eternal companion. Surely she could do what she did best in front of him and not feel self-conscious. She started out by clowning around a little, but gradually she worked herself into the music and it was easy to pretend he wasn't there. She danced the perimeter of the room, going around Jack several times, only vaguely aware that he was watching her. With a heartfelt laugh she took a flying leap over the top of him. He laughed, and she did it again. The song ended and she stood beside him, out of breath. "How was that?" she asked in barely a whisper.

"Better than standing at the foot of the Eiffel Tower."

She laughed and sat beside him. "Have you ever seen the Eiffel Tower?"

"No, I don't have to. I've seen you dance."

While Hilary was trying to come up with a clever comeback, Jack touched her face, his expression so intent that she was nearly moved to tears. She'd never imagined that one man's love could make her feel so full, so complete—so absolutely good about herself.

That night, just as every night, before going to bed, Hilary got down on her knees and thanked her Father in Heaven for saving such a wonderful man for *her*. Everything in her life seemed so perfect that she almost felt guilty for being so happy.

The following evening, since Hilary didn't have to teach, she went to Jack's apartment and had dinner waiting for him when he got home from work. They'd both taken the summer off from classes. Occasionally they went to Mt. Pleasant to help out on the farm on weekends, but Jack was being kept very busy in the construction business. It was nice to see him come through the door after a long day and imagine how it would be after they were married.

Jack took a quick shower before they sat down to eat, then they washed the dishes together. "Can I tell you something I've had on my mind?" he asked, slowly drying a plate with a checkered dishtowel.

"Of course."

"You know, Hilary, after things fell apart with Lorie, I really began to wonder if I simply had no idea how to hear the answer to a prayer; to interpret my feelings and be able to trust them. I mean, I've always loved you. A part of me always believed we should be together, but . . . it never seemed quite right."

Hilary took the towel out of Jack's hand and urged him to sit at the table with her as he continued.

"And now, I realize my feelings were valid. I felt that way for a reason. And I look back and realize that I didn't feel completely comfortable about marrying Lorie, but logically, everything seemed so perfect. I told myself I was just hanging on to my feelings for you and letting them get in the way. She was so convincing, so persuasive— almost like the devil leading me into a perfectly appealing trap. And I fell for it, because I ignored my deepest feelings, my gut instincts."

Jack turned to look into Hilary's eyes and touched her face. "Now that we are where we are, I've learned something about trusting my feelings. They were right all along. The timing was just off. And I'm so grateful, but . . ."

Jack looked away, and Hilary sensed something that contradicted what he'd just said. "But?" she pressed.

"Well, this is probably really stupid." He chuckled tensely. "But . . . for a long time I've had this feeling that . . . well, it's hard to define, really. And it's kind of disturbing. I have to admit that when I believed my feelings didn't count for anything, I was able to just put this away and discredit it. But since I've acknowledged that my feelings about you were right, and my feelings about Lorie were right, then I have to wonder if . . ."

Hilary felt a cold chill. Maybe it was his expression, or the tone of his voice. Or perhaps she somehow sensed the feelings that were obviously causing him so much concern.

"You know," he went on, "the things Jeffrey wrote in his journal, how he felt like his life wasn't going to be what he'd expected; that it was difficult for him to comprehend any future beyond next month?"

Hilary didn't like how this was sounding, but she clarified, "He also said that he felt a great deal of peace."

"Yes, that's right," he said, then he didn't say anything else.

"What, Jack?" she asked, wondering if she wanted to know.

He cleared his throat and took a deep breath. He didn't want to verbalize it, as if silence might keep anything from happening.

"Jack, what is it?" Hilary persisted.

He gathered his courage and just said it. "Every once in a while, I have this feeling that . . . I'm not going to be around to do the things I've always wanted to do."

Hilary's heart began to pound before she fully perceived the implication. "What are you saying, Jack? Are you trying to tell me that you think you're going to die young or something?"

"I don't know. I mean . . . it feels that way sometimes . . . but not really."

"Well, what exactly do you feel?"

"I can't explain it. It's not like I've had a vision or anything. It's very vague. I just . . . feel like my future isn't going to be what I expect it to be . . . or maybe I'm just not going to be around to enjoy it." He shook his head in frustration. "That's all. I can't explain it any better than that." He looked into her eyes, and she could feel his inner torment. Then he chuckled and looked away, as if to disregard everything he'd said. "It's probably just some stupid paranoia. After what Lorie did to me, maybe I just have trouble believing I'm entitled to enjoy my life." He looked at Hilary again. "Maybe it's nothing."

"And maybe it's something," Hilary countered.

"And what do we do about it?" Jack asked severely.

Hilary thought about that for a minute. "We change absolutely nothing. We're going to get married and live life to its fullest, and enjoy every day together."

She hugged him tightly, and Jack had to admit he felt better. He knew that no matter what happened, he had Hilary now. And with Hilary, he believed he could face anything.

CHAPTER EIGHT

The following Wednesday, Claire, the owner of the dance studio, called Hilary and asked her to come in a little early so they could talk. "What's up?" Hilary asked when she arrived.

"Well, something's come up, and I'm not sure what to do."

"Is everything all right?" Hilary asked.

"Oh, yes . . . it's just that my husband has been given a job offer in Oklahoma. It's exactly what he's been working toward for years—a dream come true, really, and we both feel good about it. But . . . well, he's starting in less than two weeks, and I've got to either find someone to take over the studio or close it down. I'll be staying long enough to sell the house, but once it's sold . . . well, you get the idea."

"Wow." Hilary blew out a long breath. "So, I guess I'll either be getting a new boss, or looking for a new job."

"Hilary," Claire said firmly, "I'm trying to ask you if you would take it over."

"Me?" Hilary squeaked.

"You'd do great. You're perfectly capable of teaching all the classes. You've helped me with nearly every aspect of the business. The girls love you. It would break my heart to have to close it down when some of them are doing so well. They're comfortable with you, and—"

"Now, wait a minute, Claire. I may do okay with teaching, but I'm no businesswoman. I know practically nothing about that end of it, and—"

"Oh, you know more than you think you do. And we'd go over it all. You learn quickly."

Hilary shook her head. "Wow. I don't know what to say."

"Well, you don't have to decide right now. Think about it, and let me know. If you decide you want to do it, I'll take care of all the legalities. It would be *your* studio, Hilary."

"You mean, my lease on the building, my bills to pay."

Claire smiled. "Yes, and it would also be your fulfillment, your profit. It's a well-established business. It actually makes pretty good money, you know."

"Yes, I know. I'll think about it . . . and talk to Jack."

Hilary thought about it a great deal. And she prayed about it. But she didn't tell Jack. In her heart she knew that he wanted to settle in Mt. Pleasant when he finished school, which wouldn't be much longer. And having her tied to a business commitment wouldn't make the transition very easy. After a few days, she told Claire that she appreciated the offer, but she just didn't feel like it was the right thing for her. Claire's disappointment was obvious, and it was more difficult than Hilary thought it would be to let such an opportunity go. But even when time began running out for Claire, and she didn't know what she was going to do, Hilary knew in her heart that she was doing the right thing.

On a Thursday evening, less than a month before the wedding, Hilary called her parents from Jack's apartment to go over their plans. She had Jack get on the extension so they could both talk to her parents. After the conversation ran down, Jack asked Pete how things were going on the farm—as he always did. Hilary said good-bye to her mother and got off the extension to give the men time to talk about things that bored her terribly. She was sitting on the front room floor, stretching her leg muscles, when Jack emerged from his bedroom.

"You look really cute when you do that."

Hilary rolled her eyes. "What's wrong?" she asked.

"What makes you think something's wrong?"

"I know that look. What's wrong?"

"Well, your dad didn't come right out and admit it, but I think he's having some troubles on the farm."

"Why didn't he come right out and admit it?"

"Because he knows I'll go help him if I think he needs help."

"Well, he's right about that."

"Yes, he is," Jack drawled.

"So, what's the problem?"

"His tractor's not running. He's having someone work on it, but they're waiting for a part to be shipped—and in the meantime, he's borrowed a tractor from Eugene."

"Well, that's good, isn't it?"

"Yes, except that your dad's tractor has a fork on it. Eugene's has a bucket, which is not real conducive to hauling those round bales."

Hilary stopped stretching. "Can you even *do* that with a bucket?"

"Yeah, but it's tricky, and it's very time-consuming. The bales have already been sitting out there too long, and your dad's concerned—even if he wouldn't admit it."

Jack picked up the phone and dialed a number. "What are you doing?" she asked.

He held up his finger and spoke into the phone. "Hello. Is Ammon there? This is Jack. I'm good, Allison. How are you? Oh yeah, the wedding day is getting closer." He winked at Hilary. "Ammon," he said a minute later, "how's it going? Good. Hey, since we're kind of on hold until we get that inspection, do you think you could manage without me for a few days? I'd like to go to Mt. Pleasant and help out my father-in-law." Hilary smiled. Jack chuckled. "I know it's not official yet, but it's close enough. Anyway, I think Pete needs some help. Can you do without me until Monday, or maybe Tuesday?"

Jack listened and made a few noises, then he said, "Okay, that's great. I appreciate it. I'll see you Tuesday."

"So, you're going to Mt. Pleasant tomorrow?" Hilary asked.

"Yeah. Can you come? You don't have to teach, do you?"

"I could probably manage." She gave him a mischievous smile. "If you're not around, I don't see much point in staying here."

"Amen to that," he whispered and kissed her quickly. Their eyes met, and she could almost literally see his passion battling with his self-control. Her heart quickened when he kissed her again. Then again. Slowly, meekly, he seemed to savor every moment, poignantly expressing the message that she was everything to him. Hilary had never dreamed that a man could feel such intense affection for her. Yet even when the kiss went on and on, there was nothing that made her feel morally threatened or compromised. Jack proved to her more

and more that he was a perfect gentleman—a real man in the truest
sense. And she loved him, heart and soul.

He finally drew back with a long sigh, and slowly opened his eyes.
"I think I'd better take you home."

The desire in his eyes was evident, and it provoked a fresh tingling
in her that forced her to echo his suggestion. "Yeah, I think you'd
better take me home."

The following morning, they left early for Mt. Pleasant. Jack had
Hilary drop him off out on the farm where they found Pete working,
then she went to the house and found her mother bottling apricots.
Hilary enjoyed visiting with her mother as they worked together; she
found a sense of peace in imagining living close to her parents one day,
and in helping Jack run the farm while they raised a family together.

Jack and Pete came in for lunch. While they washed up, Hilary
helped her mother put out the makings for sandwiches, as well as a
jar of apricots that hadn't sealed. When Jack came out of the bathroom, he held his arms open toward Hilary. "Come and give me a big
hug, Hillie."

"Not on your life." She backed away and he laughed.

"Ah, come on. Just one hug."

"I'll have hives for a week."

"Chicken," he said with a smirk, and sat down at the table.

"So, how's it going?" Millie asked after the blessing had been said.

"Much faster with Jack here," Pete said. "He's better at balancing
those bales on the bucket than I am."

"I don't know," Jack laughed. "I nearly lost one. I was nervous
there for a minute."

"Nervous, why?" Hilary asked.

"Well, if that thing rolled backward, it could turn me into
peanut butter."

Jack laughed, but Hilary glared at him. "Jack! Those bales weigh
half a ton."

"Closer to a ton, I think," Pete said.

"Well, they need to be hauled," Jack interjected, "and I don't know
how else to do it."

"Isn't there any other way? Can't you borrow a tractor with a fork,
or put the fork on this one, or—"

"Not without a whole lot more trouble than just doing it with what we've got." Jack smiled at Hilary. "Relax; it'll all be done in a day or two. Before it needs to be hauled again, the tractor will be fixed."

"I hope so," Pete said. "I'd swear they were sendin' that part by Pony Express. The tractor's not *that* old."

When lunch was finished and the men were headed back out to the fields, Hilary kissed Jack quickly, saying, "You be careful now."

"I will," he said and kissed her again. "I promise." Then he smirked. "Can't I have a hug?"

Hilary laughed and pushed him out the door. "Get out of here. I'll hug you later, after you've showered and changed your clothes."

That evening, Jack and Hilary took her parents to the drive-in theater to see a movie. Jack stayed the night at their house, as he usually did, wanting to avoid his mother as much as possible. She'd been terribly cynical about his plans to marry Hilary, and he couldn't think of one good reason to even go see her.

Pete and Jack left for the fields long before Hilary even got out of bed on Saturday morning. She spent the day helping her mother make apricot jam. Millie made up a quick batch of bread later in the morning, and they all had hot bread and fresh jam for lunch.

On Sunday, they went to church together and shared a relaxing day. When dinner was over and cleaned up, Jack and Hilary went out to the back lawn and sat in the shade of the huge oak tree. Hilary looked up at it and thought of Jeffrey.

"What are you thinking?" Jack asked, pushing a stray lock of hair back off her face.

"Jeffrey used to climb this tree and throw pebbles at my window, just to annoy me."

A few minutes later Jack said, "Do you think he would be pleased . . . about you and me?"

Hilary smiled. "I know he's pleased. And who knows? Maybe he's helping us along from the other side."

"That's a nice thought."

Hilary leaned back against the tree trunk and Jack settled his head in her lap and closed his eyes. She was beginning to wonder if he was asleep when he said, "Hilary, I'm thinking of taking over my father's land when the lease option runs out. I miss it." He paused and opened his eyes. "Do you think we could be happy here? Do you think we could make it work?"

Taking note of the caution in his voice, she looked at him deeply. "Why wouldn't it work?"

"There was a time when you wanted nothing but to get out of this town. And if you can't be happy here, then we'll work toward settling elsewhere. I tried to make Lorie happy here, but she wouldn't have it. I want you to be honest right up front, Hil. If you don't want to be here, I can do something else. I can make a good living working with Ammon. And when I finish school, there will be other options, but . . ."

"Jack, listen to me." He sat up, and she took his hand. "You should know that I've come a long way since the days when I hated being here. I know now that I was only running from myself, and feelings and memories I didn't want to face. I mean it from the bottom of my heart when I say that if this is something you feel strongly about, I don't have a problem with it. We can discuss our options, pray about it, and do what we feel is best." She smiled and touched his face. "If I'm with you, I believe I could be happy anywhere." She glanced around and added, "This is a beautiful place to raise a family. We have so much here."

"Yes, we do," he agreed firmly. "But what about your dancing, Hil? I don't want you to give up something you love so much."

"Well," she tipped her head, "I do enjoy teaching, but what I *really* need is just a place to dance. We could build a house with a family room big enough to move around in. I could manage. And hey, who knows? Maybe I could even open my own dance studio here."

"That would be great." Jack's eyes sparkled, and she felt indescribable peace at the thought of living out her life here with him.

"What about your allergies?" he asked.

Hilary laughed softly. "I'll be fine as long as I have you . . . and plenty of antihistamines."

"And I stay away from you when I've been in the hay."

"That, too," she agreed.

"Maybe you could even see an allergist and get some help. The insurance I have through my job is pretty good, and once we're married, you'll be covered, too."

"Hmmm, that's a nice thought."

"What? Living without allergies?"

"Being married."

"Amen to that," Jack said as he settled his head into her lap again.

The remainder of the day was pleasant. But as evening approached, Hilary found herself dreading tomorrow. She needed to go back to Provo and get some things taken care of before her dance classes began in the afternoon. Jack was going to stay and finish up the last of the hay, and she would be driving back to get him late in the evening.

"Maybe I should just call in sick and miss work tomorrow," she said, her head leaning on Jack's shoulder where they sat close together on the couch. It was nearly ten o'clock, and she hated to have the day end.

"Why?" Jack asked.

"Because I don't want to be without you."

He chuckled and pressed a kiss into her hair. "Even when we're married, we'll still have to work."

"I know, but . . ." She didn't finish her sentence, but Jack hugged her as if to say that he knew how she felt.

"You know, Jack," Pete said, "you don't have to stay tomorrow. There isn't much work left; I can finish it up."

"You have a doctor's appointment tomorrow," Jack said. "And according to the weather report, it might rain on Tuesday. I can finish it up, while you do what you have to do up north. It's no big deal. Ammon's not expecting me back to work until Tuesday."

"Well," Pete shook his head, "I hate to have you out there workin' alone. You're too good to us, son."

Jack chuckled. "It's the other way around . . . *Dad.*"

Pete laughed. "I like the sound of that."

"Me, too," Hilary murmured through a yawn.

"Okay," Jack said, pulling Hilary to her feet, "it's time you went to bed, young lady."

She laughed when he lifted her onto his back and carried her up the stairs and to the door of her bedroom. He bounced her up and down to make her laugh and scream at the same time. Then he allowed her to slide off his back. "I hate this part," she said as he turned to face her.

"Yeah, me too. But we'll be married soon." He smiled. "It's about time to get those announcements addressed, isn't it?"

"Yeah, I guess we'll be doing a lot of that next week." She yawned again.

"Good night, the future Mrs. Hayden."

Hilary grinned. "Good night."

Jack kissed her quickly and went back downstairs to brush his teeth.

In spite of being exhausted, Hilary found it difficult to sleep that night, for reasons that eluded her. Looking at her future she couldn't help but be happy—so happy that tingling and butterflies threatened to overwhelm her. Still, an elusive cloud seemed to hover nearby. Maybe she was just dreading tomorrow with so much time driving alone, and having to be without Jack. Perhaps it was simply the time left before the wedding; it seemed like forever. But at least they had a date now . . . at least she could see the light at the end of the tunnel. And with that thought, she finally drifted off to sleep.

The following morning, Hilary woke up late. She found a note saying that her parents had already left for their appointment in Provo, and Jack had gone out to the farm early. While she hurried to get on her way, everything seemed to go wrong. Being alone, she was left to answer several phone calls and search for three different things she couldn't find. It was past eleven when she finally got out of the house, then she had to stop to buy gas and check the oil in her car. She'd told Jack she would come and find him out in the fields to say good-bye, but if it hadn't been for her intense desire to see him, she likely would have just headed straight out of town and called him later. She nearly talked herself out of stopping, certain he would understand. But she stopped anyway, reasoning that she had no deadline to meet that couldn't be adjusted. There was nothing in life she enjoyed more than being with Jack.

* * * * *

Jack was in the fields early, anxious to get the hay up and moved so the huge bales wouldn't impede the growth of the next crop. The impending weather report motivated him further. Working with the bucket on the tractor, as opposed to a fork, made the work much slower; and working alone, without another man to help guide the bale onto the bucket, it was especially tedious. He had to basically roll the bale until he could push it against something to give him the leverage to lift it onto the bucket, then he had to perform a balancing act to get it moved to the wagon and unload it.

As the morning wore on, Jack began to feel impatient for Hilary to come by on her way to Provo. He ached to see her, as always. And he longed for a break. But time dragged by and she didn't come. He frequently glanced at his watch, wondering if she'd forgotten, or worse, if she'd run into some kind of trouble. Scanning the field he was working in, he figured he'd move a couple more bales, then break for an early lunch and find out if she'd left yet.

For some reason, Jack had a particularly difficult time getting the next bale onto the bucket. As he lifted the hay, it teetered slightly and he held his breath. Then he sighed as it seemed to settle into place. But the moment he moved the tractor toward the wagon, the bale teetered again. Then it happened in an instant. The bale rolled backward. Jack saw it coming and jumped in an attempt to dodge it, but the huge bundle of hay bounced off his body, momentarily sandwiching him between its weight and the tractor seat before it hit the ground. Jack fell on his back with a hard thud, which knocked the air out of his lungs. It took him a minute to catch his breath, while he felt his heart racing. A number of times he had imagined such a thing happening, and he realized now that it had really scared him. Knowing he could have been seriously injured, he uttered a silent prayer of gratitude that he wasn't hurt. Then the pain settled in, and with it came a reality too horrifying to even consider. All he could do was pray.

* * * * *

It didn't take long for Hilary to find the tractor as she drove the dirt lanes surrounding the long stretches of farm land. But she couldn't see Jack. She'd seen his truck parked near the haystack, and she knew he would drive the tractor back there when he was finished. She parked the car and got out, scanning the area in search of his familiar tall frame. She could hear the tractor idling and knew he couldn't be too far, so she walked toward it and called his name. With the tractor running, she doubted she could hear his response anyway. She climbed up on it to get a better view, wondering where he might have walked to. Perhaps he'd seen some cattle or sheep where they didn't belong, and he'd gone to help another farmer.

"Jack!" she called, then she nearly fell off when his voice startled her.

"I'm right here!" he shouted, but Hilary could barely understand him over the dull roar of the engine. In the second it took her to turn off the tractor and jump down, the subtle uneasiness she'd felt since she got out of the car blew into full-fledged panic. He seemed stunned and a little disoriented. His expression made it clear that he wasn't just taking a little nap in the field. He was in pain.

"What happened?" she demanded, falling to her knees beside him, oblivious to her allergies. "What's wrong?"

Jack took her hand and squeezed it, smiling slightly. "You're late," he said. "I was worried about you."

"I just had a hard time getting away." She looked down the length of his body, certain he'd been hurt, but not knowing how to ask. She couldn't see any blood, but his pain was evident. "Maybe it's a good thing I was late."

Jack nodded, and his chin almost quivered before he pulled her close, hugging her tightly. "I was praying you would come," he said close to her ear at the same time she felt him tremble.

"Jack." She eased back and looked into his face. He was avoiding something, and she knew it. "What happened?" she demanded again.

Jack glanced toward the bale of hay several yards away. "It fell on me," he said. "I tried to jump off when I saw it coming, but . . . I didn't quite make it, and . . ."

"Jack!" she squeaked. "It *fell* on you?" He nodded. "Oh, good heavens!" She began to breathe so hard she feared she would hyperventilate. "Is anything broken? Are you hurt? You must be hurt. It's a wonder you're not dead. That thing weighs a ton."

"I know," he said so tonelessly that it sent a shiver through her.

While Hilary silently thanked God that she had been delayed long enough to be here for him, thoughts of Jeffrey's death hurled through her mind. Trying to remain focused on the moment, she took a deep breath and declared, "I'm going to get some help. I don't think you should move until we find out if you're hurt. Are you in much pain?"

"Yes, my back, but . . ."

"Well, don't move. I'm going to call for help, but it will take a few minutes and—"

"Hilary, wait." He grabbed her arm. "Don't leave me."

"Jack, I have to get help. Try not to move and . . ." Hilary stopped when the look in his eyes chilled her. While the image of a ton of hay falling against him hovered in her mind, a part of her was convinced that by some miracle he'd escaped any serious injury. But . . . there was that look in his eyes—like a character in a horror movie encountering some unspeakable evil. He was scared. He was *terrified*.

"What is it, Jack? Are you—"

"I can't . . ." He hesitated saying it, as if remaining silent might keep it from being a reality. He gripped Hilary's hand, and his shaking increased. "Hilary, I . . . I can't move . . . I can't . . . oh, heaven help me, Hilary. I can't feel my legs."

For a moment, Hilary couldn't breathe. Then she had to consciously will herself to stay calm. She touched his face frantically. "Everything's going to be all right, Jack." Tears burned into her eyes. "Do you hear me? I'm going for help, and . . . everything's going to be okay."

Jack nodded stoically and reluctantly let go of her. He attempted to relax, gazing up at the cloudless sky. The high sun hurt his eyes and he closed them, willing himself to move, but half of his body felt dead, and above that point the pain bordered on unbearable. He'd never hurt so much in his life.

Hilary scrambled frantically back across the field, fighting back her emotions. She could cry later. Right now, Jack needed her. Launching herself into the car, she turned it around and raced up the dirt lane to the first house. She knew these people vaguely, and prayed they would be home. It seemed forever before the door was answered, but they eagerly allowed her to use the phone. Knowing help was on the way, she hurried back to where she'd left Jack.

She sprinted back across the field and sank to her knees beside him, and his eyes came languidly open. "They'll be here any minute," she assured him, touching his face. "Are you all right?"

Jack shook his head slowly, realizing he'd been unconscious. "I'm scared, Hilary."

"So am I," she admitted, pressing her face to his shoulder.

She could hear sirens approaching in the distance and held to him tightly, as if she might never have the chance again. His arms came around her, and she could feel his fear in the desperation of his embrace.

Jack joked with the paramedics while they helped him, but there was no hiding the pain he was in. When the ambulance finally drove away, Hilary got in her car and forced herself to breathe deeply. Before she put the car into gear, she realized she was itching and looked down to see her arms covered with hives. She felt angry at the need to return home to change clothes and take a quick shower, but she knew if she didn't she would be too sick by the end of the day to be any good to anyone.

Going mechanically through the motions of getting cleaned up, Hilary prayed continually in her mind that Jack would be all right. She took an antihistamine for her allergies, grateful to have one that didn't make her sleepy. Then she rubbed some cream on her arms where the hives were the worst and hurried toward Provo, still praying constantly, driving as fast as she could without breaking the law. Fear and anguish hovered somewhere between her head and her throat as she tried to comprehend what might be happening. The pressure became intense and she *wanted* to cry, certain it would ease this torrent of emotions. But tears wouldn't come; or perhaps she feared allowing them to get started.

Hilary fought to keep from trembling visibly as she walked into the emergency room of Utah Valley Regional Medical Center, where she was told to wait. To pass the time, she tried to call home from a pay phone but got no answer. Of course, her parents always did errands and shopping when they went up north to their doctor's appointments. She had no idea where to find them, and it could be hours before they got home. She called Claire to tell her she wouldn't be able to teach today. Then she waited. Then she tried home again. Then waited.

A nurse finally came out and called her name. "You're here with Jack Hayden?"

"That's right."

"Are you family?"

"I'm his fiancée. He has no family that's available right now."

"Okay," she said, "we're sending him to Intensive Care on the second floor. The doctor will talk to you there."

Hilary wanted answers, but she didn't know what questions to ask. Methodically she went to ICU, where she was again told to wait. She shot to her feet when a doctor finally entered the little room where she'd been left on the second floor. He smiled and urged her back to her seat, sitting beside her. But there was a gravity about his countenance that chilled her through. It was difficult to digest every aspect of his detailed explanations, but certain words stuck in her mind. Broken vertebrae. Damaged spinal cord. *Paralyzed.* Irreparable. Lifestyle adjustments. Depression. Counseling. Surgery. Rehabilitation. Physical therapy. The positive note came when she was told that he'd miraculously escaped any internal injuries that would have complicated the problem immensely.

It took every ounce of Hilary's strength to keep from crying as the doctor told her that one in a thousand victims of spinal cord injuries might have some degree of recovery. He talked briefly of the emotional struggles encountered through such an ordeal—for herself as well as for Jack. He spoke of patients becoming suicidal, of the difficulties involved in recovering and restructuring their lives. He emphasized the importance of support and encouragement from loved ones. And he told her how he had seen many people go through this and go on to become happy and successful.

He asked if she had any questions. While Hilary's head was spinning with everything he'd said, it was difficult to come up with an intelligent question. But one thought stood out prominently. He was talking about Jack. And she loved him. No matter what the future entailed, no matter what had changed, they were meant to be together and she knew it. She simply shook her head and asked, "Can I see him?" He told her that would be fine, and in the few minutes before a nurse came to get her, she prayed fervently for courage. She found it ironic that the memory came to mind of the moment she'd known beyond any doubt that she and Jack were meant to be together. She'd asked the Lord then why she'd never felt anything romantic for Jack before that time. And the answer had been plain and simple: she'd needed these years and experiences to prepare her. Was this what she'd needed to be prepared for?

Hilary pressed a trembling hand over the knot in her stomach as she was led down the long hall in ICU. The nurse kindly introduced herself, which alleviated Hilary's tension momentarily. Then she stepped into the room, consciously willing herself not to shake. *Be brave. Don't cry.* She repeated the words over and over in her mind. *Be brave. Don't cry.* The room was dimly lit, and she briefly felt as if she'd been transported to another time and place.

In a calm, quiet voice, the nurse briefly explained the purpose of everything attached to Jack, while Hilary found herself trying not to look at him. Instead, she perused the monitors for his heart and blood pressure, and the IV dripping methodically. She was told that Jack would be groggy, since he'd been given something for the pain. Before Hilary could voice her question, the nurse answered it: Although he could feel nothing below a certain point, he was experiencing quite a bit of pain above the injury. Then the nurse left her, saying that she was welcome to stay as long as she liked for the time being.

Hilary's shaking increased when she realized she was alone with Jack. She stepped slowly toward him, wondering if he was asleep. He looked all right, and for a moment she nearly forgot about the doctor's report. *Be brave. Don't cry,* she told herself again as tears threatened. Feeling a little weak, she quietly slid a chair closer to the bed and sat down.

"Is that you, Hilarious?" Jack asked in a voice slurred by medication.

She chuckled, but with a crack in her voice that easily gave away the fact that she was trying not to cry. She took his hand and squeezed it. "Yes, it's me."

Jack slowly turned his head and opened his eyes. A smile touched his lips. "I'm so glad you came."

"I don't want to be anywhere but with you, Jack."

He smiled again, and she struggled to find something to say.

"You should be at work," he said, closing his eyes.

"It's okay," she murmured. "I made arrangements. I'll stay as long as they'll let me. I mean . . . I have to go to work tomorrow, but . . . I'll be here every minute I can, Jack, and . . ."

Hilary had to stop when the tears threatened again. Jack looked at her as if to question her silence. She forced a smile and squeezed his hand. He closed his eyes again and muttered, "They tell me it's pretty bad. I—"

A nurse came into the room, and while she was looking over the monitors, two others entered, one a man. They talked among themselves and joked a little with Jack while they efficiently shifted his entire body to one side and propped it with pillows. They explained the need to shift his weight every couple of hours to avoid pressure sores. Hilary wanted to ask more about that, but she couldn't find her voice without tempting her emotions. While she watched them, it occurred to her that there was a great deal she needed to learn. *Their lives would never be the same.*

CHAPTER NINE

After the nurses left, Hilary asked, "Are you okay?"

Jack grunted. "I think you'd better clarify that question."

"Are you in pain?"

"Not as much as I'd like to be."

It took Hilary a moment to grasp his implication, then she had to look away. She wanted to ask him a thousand questions. She wanted to assure him that nothing had changed between them. But there was nothing she could say that wouldn't bring up the reality, and she just wasn't ready to talk about it. She turned back to find him staring at her with eyes that seemed to beg for something. But what? Hope? Assurance?

Not knowing how to ask, she simply took his hand. Then she touched his face. "I love you, Jack," she murmured, and tears rushed forward so fast she pressed her face to his shoulder to hide them. She managed to choke them back long enough to draw back and say, "I need to try and call my parents. I'll be back, okay?"

He nodded and she hurried from the room, feeling as if a dam was about to burst in her head. She rushed down the hall, through the waiting area, and into the ladies' room. She was grateful to find a regular bathroom where she could lock the door, rather than an open room with several stalls. The fan was noisy and the walls were thick. She gasped as if she could finally breathe, then she pressed her face into the corner as the first sob erupted. Then another, and another, forging a painful route out of her into the open air. She turned and pressed her back into the corner, sliding down the wall until she sat on the floor and wrapped her arms up over her head, sobbing in torrents. When the deluge of tears finally subsided, she took a deep breath and reminded herself that she was a woman capable of accomplishing anything she set her mind and heart to. As if to confirm that it was true, she felt a tangible warmth encircle her. Tears threatened again at the evidence that God was with her in this. She was where she was supposed to be. And she knew it.

Now that she'd had a good cry, Hilary went to the sink and washed her face. Relieved of a degree of the tension that had been building ever since she'd found Jack on the ground, she forced herself to breathe deeply and face whatever lay on the other side of that door. She attempted to call home again, but still there was no answer.

She returned to Jack's room and approached the bed warily. *Don't cry. Be brave.* "Are you asleep?" she whispered.

"Nah," he groaned, but he said nothing more. Hilary just sat and held his hand while he slipped in and out of sleep. The nurses came in again to turn him to the other side, then he dozed off again. Hilary observed the process and began to contemplate the reality of being married to a paralyzed man. Wheelchairs and handicapped parking spaces began to take on a whole new meaning as she tried to imagine what day-to-day life might be like for them now. She could foresee the potential struggling and suffering ahead for Jack, and wondered if she had the strength to carry him through. Then she recalled the warmth she'd felt earlier. She knew beyond any doubt that her place was with Jack, and God would see them through this—together.

While the threatened changes in their future were downright terrifying, Hilary couldn't comprehend what Jack might be feeling. What thoughts were going through his mind? She wanted to ask him, to talk to him. But she didn't know where to begin, and wondered if giving him some time to adjust might be better.

She was startled by Jack's voice. "You're still here."

"Of course." She smiled and took his hand.

"You look exhausted."

"Oh, I'm okay," she lied.

"What time is it?" he asked.

"A little after nine, I believe," she said, thinking she should try again to call her parents.

"Hey," he said, seeming a little more coherent than he had been, "will you make a call for me?"

"Sure." She sat forward a little.

"Will you call Ammon? His number's in the phone book. I don't think I'll be going to work tomorrow."

Or ever, Hilary thought.

She was grateful for an excuse to leave the room for a few minutes. Ammon's number was easy to find, but her heart began to pound as she heard it ringing on the other end. This wasn't going to be easy.

"Hello," a woman answered.

"Uh . . . hello . . . I hope I'm not calling too late, but . . . is Ammon at home? This is Hilary Smith. I'm calling for Jack Hayden."

"Oh, it's not late," she replied. "I'll get him." She paused and added, "You must be the bride-to-be."

"That's right," Hilary said, wondering how long it would be now before they could marry. She forced her thoughts elsewhere as Ammon's wife continued.

"Well, I've heard so much about you. I'm looking forward to meeting you."

"Yes, me too," Hilary said quickly.

"I'll get Ammon."

"Hello," Ammon said into the phone.

"Hi. Uh . . . this is Hilary. Jack's fiancée."

"Of course. What can I do for you?"

"Well . . . Jack asked me to call you. He's . . ." Hilary couldn't say it. Ammon's voice betrayed his concern. "Is something wrong?"

"Yes. Uh . . . he's in the hospital. ICU, actually."

"Good heavens. What's happened?"

Hilary swallowed hard, finding it difficult to say aloud. "He's uh . . . well, he broke his back, Ammon. He's . . . paralyzed."

A gasp on the other end of the line was followed by silence. Finally, Ammon said, "I . . . I don't know what to say."

"That makes three of us. I mean . . . Jack's not talking much, either."

"Is it . . . permanent?" he asked.

"I . . . uh . . . believe so. But . . . I guess it takes time to be certain. I don't know."

He asked what had happened, and she tried to explain the best she could from what Jack had told her. He made her promise to let him know if she needed anything, and said he'd be in touch. Hilary felt proud of herself for staying emotionless through the conversation, until she hung up the phone and realized that she felt numb. She almost wanted to cry, ached to release some of the pressure that continued to gather in her head. But even securely locked in the ladies' room, she couldn't make the tears come. Convinced that it was just as well, she went out to the waiting room, surprised to find her parents just stepping off the elevator. "What are you doing here?" she gasped, gratefully accepting their embraces. But even then she couldn't cry.

"We got home late from shopping," Millie explained. "We had trouble finding everything we needed. Mick next door was watching for us, I guess. He ran right over and told us what happened. We got right back in the car and got here as fast as we could."

Millie and Pete each squeezed one of Hilary's hands, while silence preceded Pete's question. "How is he doin'? Is he . . ."

Hilary mechanically told them all that had happened from her perspective, along with the doctor's prognosis. They both cried, but Hilary felt detached. Perhaps she was simply exhausted.

Jack brightened up when Pete and Millie entered the room. He smiled and laughed as they joked with him, and told them with confidence that everything was going to be all right. While Hilary wanted to admire his positive attitude, she had a nagging suspicion that he was putting up a front to keep them from getting upset.

She walked her parents back to the lobby, where Pete nearly collapsed on one of the couches, tears streaming down his face. "Dad? What is it?" Hilary asked, taking his hand.

"He shouldn't have even been out there. It should have been me. I shouldn't have let him do it alone. I should have—"

"Now, listen," Hilary insisted while silent tears rolled down Millie's cheeks. "You told Jack he didn't need to do it. It was his choice to go out there. It was just an accident. Accidents happen." As she said it, Jeffrey's death came to mind. She exchanged a quick glance with both her parents that made it clear they were sharing her thoughts.

"At least he's alive," Hilary added. She swallowed the knot in her throat and added, "It could be so much worse."

Pete and Millie assured Hilary of their love for Jack, and their commitment to see this through—whatever it entailed. "He's as good as family," Pete said, "and that's got nothin' to do with you marryin' him."

"I know." Hilary smiled sadly and looked down.

"And how are *you* feeling about all of this?" Millie asked.

"It changes nothing, if that's what you're wondering." She drew back her shoulders and took a deep breath. "Jack and I are supposed to be together. I know that with all my heart and soul."

Pete hugged Hilary, saying with a cracked voice, "That's my girl. We're with you all the way."

Pete and Millie left for Mt. Pleasant after midnight, once they saw Hilary safely back to her apartment to get some sleep. The insomnia she had feared never came as she slipped into a fitful sleep, awaking soon after dawn. For a minute, she wondered if the occurrences of the day before had been nothing more than a bad dream. But the reality quickly settled in, and she hurried to get a shower so she could get to the hospital and be with Jack.

Hilary arrived to the news that Jack was going in for surgery that afternoon. The broken vertebrae would be fused to stabilize them, and to prevent any further injury to the spinal cord. Hilary sensed Jack's solemnity even more today, but still, she didn't know how to deal with it. While the nurse was doing the usual routine, she slipped from the room, forcing herself to do something she'd dreaded ever since they'd arrived at the hospital. She dialed the number and forced a steady voice when Judy Hayden answered the phone.

"Hello, this is Hilary."

"Yeah," Judy said.

"I have some bad news. Are you sitting down?"

"Is Jack . . . ," she began, but nothing more came.

"He's been in an accident, Judy. He's in ICU at the hospital in Provo."

"Is he . . ." Again Judy didn't finish her question.

"He's going to be all right. . . in a manner of speaking."

"What do you mean?" Judy asked, and Hilary realized it was the first time she'd heard the woman's voice sound soft and sincere.

"He's paralyzed, Judy." Hilary's voice trembled as she said it, then she took a deep breath and willed back the first hint of emotion she'd felt since yesterday.

No sound came from the other end of the phone.

"Are you with me?" Hilary asked.

There was only a little noise to indicate that they'd not been disconnected.

Hilary cleared her throat and continued. "He's going in for surgery later today to have the vertebrae in his back fused together, to avoid any more damage to the spinal cord." She almost said she'd keep Judy posted, but instead she stated, "I'm sure the hospital can keep you updated on his progress if you call. Or I can be found somewhere around here most of the time." She swallowed and added, "I'm sure he'd love to see you. He's in room 202."

While Hilary was trying to find words to get off the phone, Judy asked with that bitter edge she was famous for, "So, are you still going to marry him, or—"

"Yes, Judy," she interrupted firmly, "I'm still going to marry him." With that she quickly ended the call.

Hilary returned to Jack's room to find Ammon Mitchell sitting by the bed, talking and laughing as if nothing in the world was wrong. "Hello," he said, standing to shake her hand.

"Hello," she replied. "Thanks for coming."

"Oh, I've got to keep Jack in line," Ammon said. "They told me that only family was supposed to come in, but well . . ." He laughed. "I told them I was his brother."

Jack laughed at this, and Hilary couldn't help but chuckle. Ammon Mitchell was far too dark to even remotely pass for a blood relative of Jack Hayden.

After Ammon left, Jack held out his hand toward Hilary. "You spend too much time here," he said. "Don't you have a life?"

Hilary forced a steady voice. "Not without you in it." Smiling, she added, "I do have to leave for work . . . probably while you're in surgery. But I'll be back as soon as I'm finished."

Jack nodded and urged her closer. While she was doing her best to hug him, he whispered, "I'm scared, Hil."

Hilary pressed her face to his and closed her eyes. "So am I," she admitted. "But we're going to make it through this together." She drew back and looked into his eyes, saying firmly, "You're still you, Jack, no matter what. And I love you." Moisture brimmed in his eyes, and she hugged him again.

Hilary had a hard time leaving the hospital to go to work,

knowing Jack was in surgery, and there was no one to be there for him when he came out. Resigning herself to the fact that she had no choice, she hurried to the studio, thinking perhaps it would be better for her to keep busy than to sit and wonder how the surgery was going. But by the time she reached her final class, she was so uptight that she wondered if she'd taught anything effective at all. While she'd gone through the motions of her lessons, her heart and mind were with Jack. The whole thing still had a feeling of being somehow dreamlike. Since her initial outburst in the hospital bathroom, she'd hardly been able to shed a tear. She'd felt frustrated by her numb emotions, but at the same time she dreaded being exposed to the reality of her feelings.

She was nearly finished with her final class when Janna slipped quietly into the classroom. Hilary exhaled as if she'd been holding her breath for hours, wondering how Janna always seemed to know when she needed a friend. They'd not talked since Hilary had called to tell her she was going to marry Jack.

Hilary dismissed her students five minutes early and hurried to embrace Janna without explanation. "Are you okay?" Janna asked, looking into her eyes.

Hilary shook her head. "How did you know?"

"I don't *know* anything. I've just had this feeling you needed me. I've been calling your apartment for two days. Your roommates haven't seen you at all." Janna gave her a penetrating stare and asked, "So, what is it? What's wrong?"

Hilary took a deep breath. "Jack's been in an accident. He's in the hospital."

Janna's concern was evident as she ushered Hilary to a bench at one side of the room. The last few students left as their rides arrived, and the two women were left alone.

"Is he okay?" Janna asked.

"Well . . . he's going to live. I keep telling myself I'm grateful for that, but . . ."

"But?"

"He's paralyzed."

Hilary heard Janna take in a sharp breath. She leaned back and pressed a hand over her chest. "I can't believe it."

"That seems to be the consensus. I *still* can't believe it."

"Is it permanent, then?"

"It seems that way. Little of what they tell me makes sense. You would probably know more of such things than I would." A new light of gratitude dawned on Hilary as she remembered that Janna was a nurse. Still, she felt an urge to get back to the hospital. Glancing at her watch, she said, "There are a hundred questions I want to ask you, but . . . Jack had surgery and . . . I need to get to the hospital. Can we . . ."

"How about if I follow you over . . . only if you want me to, of course."

"Want you to?" Hilary forced a little laugh, hugging Janna again. "I haven't needed a friend this much since Jeffrey died."

Janna picked up her purse. "That's what friends are for."

Hilary arrived at the hospital to a good report. Everything was going as well as could be expected. She talked to Jack for a few minutes, but he was especially groggy. She left him to sleep and sat in the waiting room with Janna.

"So, how are you feeling?" Janna asked.

"Numb. I feel absolutely numb. But then, it's just as well. I don't want to cry in front of Jack, and—"

"Why not?"

The question took Hilary off guard, and all she could say was, "I don't know. I just . . ."

"Maybe he needs to see you cry, Hilary. If you feel like crying, for heaven's sake, cry." Hilary nodded and Janna added, "How do you think Jack is feeling . . . emotionally?"

"I can only guess he feels the same way . . . numb, I mean. He hasn't said much of anything. I don't know, maybe he's crying when I'm not around."

"Or maybe he's not crying at all."

"Don't they call that denial?"

Janna chuckled. "I don't know that denial is always such a bad thing. Personally, I think it's somehow connected with that promise from God that we'll never be given more than we can handle. Do you think, if Jack could grasp the full spectrum of what's happened all at once, that he could bear it?"

"Probably not."

"So, it will come in layers, I'd guess—for both of you."

Hilary liked the way Janna's words settled comfortably inside her. "How did you get to be so wise, so strong?"

Janna's eyes turned briefly sad. "Just been through a lot, I suppose. I've learned quite a bit about human nature and struggles, and I've spent a lot of time with a good counselor. If I've learned something that can help you through this, I'm more than happy to share it."

Hilary squeezed Janna's hand. "Well, I'm certainly grateful to have you here now."

Hilary and Janna talked until nearly midnight. They covered the physical aspects of what had happened to Jack, and what his future might entail. Janna had cared for spinal cord patients before, and her ability to talk about it candidly helped immensely.

Concerning the emotional aspects of the situation, Janna said, "I've never dealt with anything like this directly, Hilary, but my guess is that the adjustment is going to be really difficult for Jack—much more so than if he was the kind of person who was accustomed to working behind a desk or a computer. I mean, most men take some pride in being physical, right? It's a very male thing to be stronger than a woman. Jack's a farmer, a builder. His identity is being threatened here, Hilary."

"What can I do?" she asked.

"I'm no professional, but I'd say you show him that your love is unconditional, and you just help him through one step at a time."

"It's that simple?"

"Simple, yes. But probably not very easy. I think you should take it one day at a time. I'm here as much as you need me. I mean that."

Hilary expressed her frustration concerning Jack's family. But Janna reminded her that he had Hilary's family, and she felt a little better.

"I guess I need to think about what we *do* have, not what we *don't* have," Hilary mused.

"Yes, and that's *exactly* what you're going to have to remind Jack of—every hour of his life, until he's strong enough to understand it himself."

The implication struck Hilary deeply, and it hovered with her through the night. The following morning she dragged herself out of bed, exhausted to the core. She headed to the kitchen in search of something to eat, but only made it to the front room, where she slumped onto the couch. A knock at the door startled her, but before she could even stand up, it flew open. Everything that was bad suddenly got worse when Lorie waltzed into the apartment and closed the door behind her.

"Kim?" she hollered, unaware of Hilary sitting there. "Are you here?" She disappeared into Kim's room and came out a few minutes later. When her eye caught Hilary, she smirked subtly as if she'd found something to play with. "What happened to you?" she said as if Hilary was covered with mud or something. "You and Jack aren't fighting, are you? He can be so awful at times."

Hilary exercised great self-control to keep from venting all her hurt and anger on Lorie. She silently counted to ten to calm her anger, then stated in measured tones, "Jack's been in an accident. I've spent most of the week at the hospital."

Lorie's expression could have won her an Academy Award. "Is he going to be all right?"

"It's hard to say," Hilary replied, then went to her room if only to avoid any further conversation. She felt no need or motivation to give any further explanation. Wanting only to be with Jack, she forced herself to take a shower and grab a piece of toast. She didn't give Lorie another thought.

* * * * *

Jack stared into nothing, forcing his thoughts into the dark void he'd created in his mind. Occasionally his thoughts would slip into the memory of the accident. Over and over he could see that bale rolling toward him; then he relived the helplessness of lying on the ground, unable to feel anything, unable to move. And he was still helpless. If he wasn't thinking about the accident, he became absorbed with the reality of the present. He'd never been in a hospital before, never even had an illness that had kept him down for more than a day or so. Never in his life had he even imagined such helplessness, such complete vulnerability. He couldn't get out of this bed if his life depended on it. He'd never felt so defenseless, so *useless*. And if the present wasn't bad enough, the prospect of the future was too frightening to even consider. The reality that his condition would likely be permanent was simply more than he could bear.

The only remotely positive thing that Jack could think about was Hilary. But thoughts of her reminded him that their plans for the future had been severely altered—all because of a moment of stupidity. He felt as if he'd betrayed her somehow; broken her heart. She'd promised him they'd get through this together, but he doubted she had any comprehension of what that meant. How could she, when he didn't?

Jack tried to pray. But all that he could think to say was a great big *why?* He felt betrayed and angry and completely alone. And even knowing that feeling this way wasn't right didn't change the way he felt. It was as simple as that.

Realizing there was nothing he could think about without opening himself to the despair that surrounded him, Jack simply forced his mind into a void. He could stare at nothing and think of nothing and feel nothing. And that made his mind as numb as the lower half of his body.

The only relief came when Jack had visitors. When someone was with him, distracting him with idle conversation, it was easier to avoid thinking of anything distasteful.

He glanced at the clock, wondering where Hilary was. When the door opened he felt certain it was her, but because of the way they had him situated on the bed, he could only guess. Everything inside of him bristled when he heard Lorie say, "Hello, Jon."

Forcing a steady voice, Jack stated, "You must have the wrong room. There's nobody here by that name."

He heard her sigh. "I'm sorry. Hello, Jack."

He didn't answer. She walked around the bed where he could see her. She was still beautiful. And he still hated her. He kept expecting her to say something, but she didn't. It was easy to discern the purpose of her visit. She loved drama; loved being in the middle of it. Her expression hovered somewhere between pity and misery, like some actress in a soap opera. He didn't know how she'd known he was here, but he wanted her to leave. She was the last person on earth that he wanted to see him like this.

When silence persisted, he finally said, "I was just lying here thinking that life could be no worse. It was good of you to come and remind me that it could be."

"That wasn't a very nice thing to say." Lorie folded her arms, and her expression hardened into a familiar scowl that he hated.

"I'm sorry. It was the best I could come up with." Wanting to get to the point, he added, "What are you doing here, anyway?"

"I came to see how you're doing."

"I should think it would be obvious."

"Well, what happened? I mean . . . I saw Hilary at the apartment. She just said you'd been in an accident, and you were here, and . . ." Jack was surprised that she didn't know any more than that. Then it occurred to him that if she did, she probably wouldn't be here. When he said nothing, she went on. "I was just so worried about you, and . . ." Her chin quivered before she rushed to his side and took his hand. "Oh, Jack, I wonder if we didn't make a mistake. I mean . . . maybe we should try again. I want to be there for you, Jack."

"I'm engaged, Lorie."

"Oh, I know, but . . ." The standard tears appeared. "I love you, Jack."

"I'm more prone to believe that you love what you can't have. And you love drama, too. That makes me a prime candidate on two counts at the moment." She looked alarmed, but she was listening. "So, what happens when the drama is over, and you have me back? Then what?"

"Well, we'd work things out. We'd start over." She touched his face, but his attempt to pull away was thwarted by the way they had him situated on the bed. "I want to help you through this, Jack. I want to be there for you."

Jack observed his ex-wife, marveling at how transparent she was. Her predictability nauseated him, if her syrupy attention didn't. "You know, Lorie, I can't think of one good reason to believe that what you're telling me is true. But I find it intriguing to think of you taking care of me for the rest of my life. It might actually teach you something—if such a thing is possible." She hid her distress well until he added, "I think you'd do well pushing around a wheelchair for the next fifty or sixty years, don't you?"

The question in her eyes was quickly replaced by an unmistakable fear. She'd backed herself into a corner, and she knew it. The thing that bothered Jack most was wondering how he might feel if he'd actually *wanted* her back. As it was, he only felt disgusted, and his voice deepened with anger. "Why don't you get your lying little carcass out of here, and leave me in peace."

"Jack, I . . ." She looked so stunned and distraught that he almost felt sorry for her. Almost, but not quite.

"You have no idea what love is, *Miss* Walker. It's lucky for you that we're already divorced; it'll save you the humiliation and scandal of having to leave a crippled husband. Heaven forbid that anyone might suspect you couldn't bear having your lifestyle cramped by something that really mattered. You would no more commit yourself to me, crippled or not, than you would jump in the sewer. You're a deceitful little witch, and we both know it."

Still she said nothing. Jack felt so angry he wanted to throw something. He wanted to scream at her and vent some of this horrible anger that had nowhere to go. The longer she stood there, the more angry he became. With the hope of avoiding a scene, he said through clenched teeth, "Now get the hell out of my room and my life before I really lose it."

Hilary had barely opened the door of Jack's room when she heard his angry words. She hesitated, listening discreetly while an unexpected rush of emotion overcame her. Following a moment of silence, Lorie rushed into the hallway, too absorbed in her thoughts to even give Hilary a glance.

Hilary took a deep breath and moved quietly into the room. Standing beside the bed, it was evident to her that Jack thought he was alone. His breathing was labored with anger, and tears leaked from beneath his closed eyelids. The numbness Hilary had felt completely dissipated, and she clamped a hand over her mouth to keep from sobbing aloud.

Jack's eyes flew open when he realized he wasn't alone. He didn't know why Hilary was crying, but he did know that just seeing her there, knowing that she shared his anguish, eased a degree of the heartache consuming him. She said nothing as she pushed her arms around him the best she could, crying into the pillow next to his face. Jack held her and cried, as if her display of emotion had given him permission to feel what he'd been afraid to feel. The contrast between Hilary and Lorie became stark. Hilary *did* know the meaning of love. Whether she chose to be a part of his future or not, she was here for him now. And that put a little light into an otherwise black existence.

Their tears gradually merged into a comfortable silence. Hilary sat close to the bed, leaning her chin close to Jack's face, toying idly with his hair. "Are you okay?" she finally asked.

"I'm better now," he admitted, touching her face. His voice cracked. "I'd never make it without you, Hilary. You're the only person in my life who . . ." He didn't finish, but Hilary knew what he meant. Neither of them had seen any sign of Jack's mother or brothers. And no matter what Jack might say, Hilary knew their indifference had to hurt. She pressed a kiss to his face, murmuring with conviction, "I will always be here for you, Jack—always. No matter what happens, you and I are forever."

Jack started to cry again. And even though nothing more was said, Hilary felt certain it had been good for him to get some of his emotion out.

Pete and Millie came to visit the following day, and Jack seemed better with them around. Hilary felt certain that their love and acceptance of him couldn't help but make up for what was lacking in his own family. Cards and letters began pouring in from people in Mt. Pleasant, many of whom Jack hardly knew. Even though he didn't say much, she knew it helped. Each day the wall of his room become more densely covered with get-well wishes as Hilary taped up the incoming mail after he read it.

Jack recovered well from his surgery, and Hilary was relieved when he was moved to the rehabilitation area of the hospital. Here he would work with therapists and begin adjusting to his new way of life. Hilary carefully moved every card and note to the wall in his new room, and put a framed copy of their engagement portrait on the bedside table.

Knowing there were changes ahead for her as well, Hilary prayed concerning the future and felt good about her decision to withdraw from school for the time being. Determined to learn everything she could, she borrowed Janna's medical books and studied areas that were pertinent to Jack's situation, and she asked questions of every doctor or nurse who would take the time to talk to her. She continued teaching, but spent every spare minute with Jack. She often brought him meals, since he quickly tired of hospital food. They played Scrabble and card games, and they talked and laughed.

While the routine became comfortable for both of them on a certain level, Hilary was keenly aware of the fact that they never talked about anything beyond trivialities. They discussed his medical condition and physical progress, but never about how it affected him emotionally. And the more time that passed, the more difficult it became for Hilary to know how to approach it.

Pete and Millie came regularly, as did Janna. Occasionally she brought Colin, and Jack seemed to enjoy his visits, even though they had little in common. Ammon came often, and brought his wife a time or two. Hilary was touched when he told Jack he would make sure his insurance benefits continued until other arrangements could be made.

Hilary admired Jack's faith and determination as he smiled at everyone who came to see him, assuring them he was doing great and the future looked good. But there was something about his attitude that made her uneasy. If only she knew how to talk to him about it! She knew he'd talked to counselors a number of times, since it was part of the standard rehabilitation program. But he always evaded her questions concerning what they talked about, and she didn't have the fortitude to press him.

As long as Hilary remained busy, she managed to keep from getting down. Whenever discouragement tempted her, she reminded herself to stay strong for Jack's sake. If he could keep smiling in spite of all he was going through, she certainly could. But a day came when she found it impossible to ward off the feelings she'd been trying to ignore far too long.

"What's wrong?" Jack asked, startling her from her thoughts. Hilary glanced toward him warily. "And don't say *nothing*," he added when she didn't answer.

Tears welled in her eyes, and she made no effort to hold them back. "We were supposed to get married tomorrow."

Jack looked away, sighing loudly. "I know."

Hilary forced out a laugh to avoid crying harder. "Maybe we should just break you out of here and elope."

Jack didn't even crack a smile. "You deserve better than that."

Hilary put a hand over her mouth and squeezed her eyes shut. Jack wheeled the chair closer and put his arms around her. As her face met his shoulder, the dam burst on all her pent-up emotion.

"I'm so sorry," he whispered.

"What are you apologizing for?"

"I made a stupid mistake, Hilary, and we're both paying a very high price."

Hilary looked into his eyes, attempting to perceive the full depth of his confession.

"It was an accident, Jack. Accidents happen all the time."

"It was *stupid!*"

"Okay, maybe it was stupid. But it happened. You were doing the best you could with what you had to work with. It's done. There's certainly no good in beating yourself up over it. What if it had been a car accident? What if I'd been driving, and it was my fault? Would you be putting me down and—"

"No, of course not."

"So, give it up." She sighed and added, "You were out there helping my father, Jack. Do you have any idea how hard he's taking this?"

Jack was surprised. "He hasn't said anything to *me.*"

"Well, what do you expect him to say? You haven't said anything to *him,* either." In a softer voice she said, "What is there to say?" She looked at him hard. "At least you're alive. Jeffrey was out there helping someone when he died, Jack. You cannot imagine how grateful I am that you're still here. I'm not sure I could live through that again. And I know my parents couldn't."

Jack sighed and tugged at the mass of curls at the back of his neck. "The whole thing is just so *stupid!*" he said again.

"Give it up," she repeated. "It's the future that matters now."

Hilary wondered what she had said when the muscles in his face tightened. "What?" she demanded when he said nothing. Now that they were talking, she wished they had done it a long time ago.

"The future?" His tone was cynical. "This changes everything between us, Hilary."

"As far as you and I are concerned, I don't see that it changes anything."

Jack looked at Hilary as if she'd just turned green. His astonishment frightened her. "Hilary," he said indignantly, "don't think for one minute that I would still expect you to go through with this."

Hilary couldn't believe what he was saying, but she forced herself to stay calm. "With what?"

"Do you really believe I would condemn you to life with half a man?"

Hilary's breathing became sharp. "What are you trying to say, Jack? Are you trying to tell me that you don't want to marry me?"

His eyes hardened. "I was prepared to give you up before for the sake of your happiness. I could learn to live with it."

It took Hilary a moment to find her voice, and when she did, it wasn't calm. "Well, *I* can't live with it! I *love* you, Jack. I know now as much as I ever have that you and I are meant to be together. I consider this nothing but a temporary setback."

"Temporary?" he bellowed. "I can't walk, Hilary. That's permanent!"

"Not in the eternal perspective, it's not!"

"Well, a lifetime is a long time to have to live with half a man."

"Half a man?" she echoed. "Have you lost half of your brain? Your heart? Your spirit? I didn't learn to love you because you had legs, Jack. Now, why don't you stop being so selfish and think about *me* for a minute? This threw a curve ball into *my* life too, you know. But I am *not* prepared to live without you. We will adjust, and we can have a good life together—provided you can stop being too proud to accept the fact that changes happen."

She leaned close to him. "You're the one who told *me* that you believed love could overcome *any* earthly struggle. Now, did you mean it or not?"

Jack's eyes softened before he turned away. "I don't know, Hilary. I don't know anything anymore."

"Do you love me, or don't you?"

Jack looked surprised. "Of course I love you, Hilary, but . . . that's exactly why I wonder if it would be better to let you go."

A familiar vulnerability rose in his eyes. Hilary knew the look well. She'd first recognized it that day at the cemetery when he had first confessed his love to her. She swallowed her anger and attempted to absorb the full meaning of what he was telling her.

"Oh, Jack," she touched his face, "let me tell you something." She looked directly into his eyes. "I know beyond any doubt that you and I are meant to be together. I haven't questioned that for a moment, although I have wondered if I have what it takes to get you through this. But my Father in Heaven has made it repeatedly clear to me that this is where he wants me to be."

Jack drew a deep breath and urged Hilary closer, holding her tightly. He tried to comprehend that in spite of everything, he had Hilary. It broke his heart to think of the struggles this would bring into her life, but he loved her too desperately to argue.

Hilary eased back and penetrated his eyes with hers. "We have so much to be grateful for, Jack. It could be *so* much worse."

"I know, Hilary, I know." His head hung forward. He closed his eyes. "An hour doesn't go by when I don't think about some of the other people in here and all they . . ." His voice cracked. "By heaven and earth, Hilary, I will never take the use of my hands for granted." He hugged her close to him again. "And I have you. I thank God about every five minutes for having you in my life, but . . ."

"But?"

"I don't want to be a burden to you, Hilary. I don't want to be a burden to *anybody,* but especially not you. I want to take care of myself, and—"

"With time, you will, Jack. With time, everything will be okay."

Jack swallowed hard and told himself he should believe her. But at this point, he just couldn't comprehend the possibility of everything ever being okay again.

CHAPTER TEN

*L*ate in the evening, Hilary slipped out of Jack's room, leaving him asleep. "Meg," she said quietly to one of the many nurses she had come to know well, "can I talk to you a minute?"

"Sure." Meg stepped away from the nurse's station and gave Hilary her attention.

"Are you on this same shift tomorrow?"

"Yes, I am, actually. Did you need something?"

"Well, yes . . . but I'm not exactly sure what. You see . . . tomorrow was supposed to be . . ." Hilary hadn't wanted to cry, but the tears wouldn't be held back. ". . .Our wedding day."

Meg gave her an empathetic smile and a quick hug, then handed her a clean tissue from her pocket. Hilary blew her nose and composed herself. "Anyway, I'm not sure what to do, but I want to make the day special somehow. I'd like to surprise Jack with something, but I don't want to break any hospital rules or anything, and . . ."

"Well, I'm sure we can figure out something," Meg said. "Why don't we just go have a little chat and see what we can come up with?"

Hilary left the hospital that night full of excitement, instead of consumed with the reality of what should have been. The following day, she called Jack and told him she had some things to do and she'd see him later. "I'll bring some dinner in, okay?"

"That sounds great," he said, but she could hear sadness in his voice.

She spent the remainder of the day busy with phone calls and errands, wishing she had thought of this earlier and been more prepared. She got to the hospital early evening and called Meg at the nurse's station from the lobby. "It's clear," she said, and Hilary hurried to Jack's room. Since Meg had arranged for Jack to be elsewhere doing physical therapy, Hilary had a chance to make everything perfect.

"You've got about half an hour," Meg said as another nurse helped her bring a small table into the room. Hilary quickly covered it with a lace cloth and put candles on it, even though they wouldn't be able to light them. She made certain the room looked presentable, then she changed clothes in the rest room and Meg helped pin on a corsage. The steak dinners she'd picked up at a nearby restaurant were transferred to Hilary's best dishes—the ones she'd set aside for her home— and ready to be heated in the microwave at the nurse's station when the time was right.

"Does everything look all right?" Hilary asked Meg, quickly glancing around the room.

"Everything's perfect . . . you especially."

"And the food's ready?"

"As ready as it can be." Meg chuckled. "Relax. We'll take care of everything."

Hilary hugged her quickly. "Thank you, Meg. You don't know how much this means to me."

"Well, I see a lot of heartache here. It's nice to be able to help put a little cheer into somebody's life once in a while."

When everything was ready, Hilary realized she was nervous. She knew this evening could never make up for what should have happened today. But at least she would make it memorable.

* * * * *

Jack was about to head back to his room when Meg stopped him at the doorway. "You can't go anywhere until you change your shirt," she insisted.

"What's wrong with my shirt?" he demanded.

Meg tossed him a shirt and jacket he recognized.

"Where did you get these?"

"Out of your closet, I assume. Not me personally, of course, but . . ."

Jack gave her a sidelong glance. "Did Hilary put you up to this?"

"Maybe she did. All I'm going to tell you is that if you don't change your shirt and put on that jacket, you're not going anywhere."

"What are you going to do? Beat me up?" Jack asked lightly.

"Oh, you don't want to know what I'd do," Meg retorted in a comically dramatic tone.

"Okay, okay," Jack said, and proceeded to replace his sweatshirt with the cream-colored collarless shirt that he hadn't worn in a very long time. Meg took the sweatshirt and handed him the tweed jacket.

"How do I look?" he asked, and Meg dramatically pulled a hand mirror from behind her back, along with a comb. Jack smirked and combed his hair back off his face. "Good thing I shaved this morning, eh? But maybe I could use a haircut."

"No time for that, but then, I think Hilary likes it that way."

"How do you know?"

"Who wouldn't?" Meg said, taking the mirror and comb. "Okay, you can go now."

The nurse who had taken Jack down to therapy followed him back to his room. He refused to let anyone push the chair, but she did hold the door open for him. He hesitated until the nurse gently nudged him to his senses.

Jack entered the dimly lit room and took a deep breath. He knew how he was *supposed* to respond, but it took enormous willpower to push away thoughts of what should have been in order to enjoy the moment. "Wow," he said, absorbing the elegant table set for two, and Hilary standing beside it. He'd never seen that dress before. She'd never looked more beautiful. *If only he could just stand up and take her in his arms!*

Not wanting to ruin their time together before it had begun, Jack forced his negative thoughts away and held out a hand to her. He could feel her love for him in the gentle squeeze of her fingers, and his heart quickened when she bent to kiss him.

As Hilary set out the meal, she realized she was nervous. She wanted this to somehow compensate for the setback in their lives, yet in her heart she knew it never could. Jack was obviously pleased with her efforts, but he said practically nothing beyond an occasional compliment.

When the meal was finished, Hilary's nerves increased. Their eyes met across the table, exchanging a silent *Now what?* She wondered if it would have been better to just stay away today; to just let this day pass as if it were any other day. But it was too late for that now. She only prayed they could get past this awkwardness and find some enjoyment together.

"The meal was wonderful, Hilary. Thank you."

"You're welcome," she said quickly, "but . . . well, let's just say it's a good thing I didn't have to cook it myself. It might not have been so pleasant."

"You're a very good cook, Hilary."

"Well," she glanced down, "I can manage, but I certainly hope you're not expecting me to compete with my mother. You'd be sorely disappointed." Hilary sighed, thinking this was a ridiculous conversation. But she didn't know how to get beyond it.

"The reasons I love you have nothing to do with your abilities in the kitchen, Hilary."

"I know," she admitted, wishing she could read his mind. She knew that neither of them were saying what they were thinking, and she wondered which frightened her more: hearing their thoughts voiced or keeping them restrained in silence.

Jack watched Hilary closely, trying to concentrate on how beautiful she was, how much he loved her—rather than the obvious sadness in her eyes. Even when she smiled, there was no disguising her heartache. He struggled for something to say—anything to draw attention away from the reality. But there was nothing. Nothing beyond the weather and a handful of trivialities they'd run through in the first ten minutes of their meal. While he feared bringing it up, he was becoming more afraid of what might happen if he tried to hold it inside much longer. Still, he did his best to force the anger down, and his voice was soft when he said, "We should be dancing."

Hilary looked mildly alarmed before she turned away. The quiver in her voice was barely discernible. "You never really liked dancing much, anyway."

"I liked dancing with you." He took a deep breath and hoped he wouldn't regret adding his next thought. "You should have a man who can dance, Hilary."

Hilary turned abruptly to face him, startled by his implication. She firmly stated, "The reasons I love you have nothing to do with your ability to dance."

He chuckled with a bitter edge. "It's a good thing." His eyes turned hard. "But what about my ability to walk, Hilary?"

Hilary's heartbeat quickened. Her relief to be talking about things that were bubbling inside was tempered by an indescribable fear. Did she really want to know how he felt, what he was thinking? Could she really say what she felt without hurting him?

Jack's voice broke the deafening silence. "I asked you a question. What about my ability to walk?"

Her voice was as firm as her gaze. "It doesn't matter, Jack."

Jack found it increasingly difficult to keep his anger from showing. In a strained voice he replied, "Yes, it matters."

Hilary didn't know if it was the look in his eyes or the tone of his voice that forced her to turn away. Or maybe it was the reality of having to face up to what he was saying. She sensed his anger, and she knew its source. She'd been expecting to see it erupt long before now, but she still felt poorly prepared to face it.

When she said nothing, Jack leaned toward her and his voice lowered. "Don't sit there and lie to me—or to yourself. It matters, and you know it."

Hilary shook her head vehemently, but there was so much emotion in her throat that she couldn't even force a sound out without sobbing.

Jack's voice became husky with emotion. "Are you trying to tell me that everything I've lost makes no difference; that it changes nothing? Are you trying to say that we can just pick up where we left off, as if nothing happened?"

While Hilary was struggling to find voice enough to clarify what she meant, he snarled, "It matters, Hilary! Admit it, dammit! It *matters!*"

Hilary gave up trying to keep her emotion out of it. She was crying and he knew it. "It doesn't change who you are," she insisted. "And it doesn't change how I feel about you."

"Well, maybe it should. The man you agreed to marry was someone who could provide a living for you; someone who could protect you and take care of you. That man doesn't exist anymore, and you and I are both going to have to face up to that. We can pretend all we want, but it isn't going to take away the reality. This is all very nice," he motioned to the table where the remnants of their meal lay like some monument to a discarded fantasy. He clenched his fists and then his teeth. "But it's not what should have been!"

Hilary's emotion rushed into the open like an exploding geyser as he echoed her feelings. He glanced at the clock as if to verify the time of day in relation to the time they'd had printed on a deep stack of now-useless wedding announcements. "You should be dressed like a queen, and I should be waltzing you around the cultural hall, Hilary. We should be cutting wedding cake, and posing for pictures that we'd show our children someday." His voice grew hoarse with emotion as the over-lying anger dissipated. "We should have reservations at a nice hotel, Hilary." He whispered fiercely, "I should be making love to you." The anger slipped back in. "This should be our wedding night! Do you have any idea how long I have dreamed of sharing such things with you? But it will never happen—not the way I wanted it to; not the way it should. That's the bottom line, Hilary. I will never be able to dance with you again. I will never be the kind of husband you deserve. And it *hurts*. No matter how positive I try to tell myself I should be, there is no way around that bottom line. And it hurts. Admit it, Hilary. It hurts!"

Hilary was crying so hard she couldn't admit anything. Jack watched her and felt his heart breaking. As horrible as the reality was for him, the true hurt came when he thought about how all of this affected Hilary. He'd loved her as long as he could remember. He'd wanted nothing for years but to take care of her and make her happy. He felt like he'd cheated her out of the life she deserved. He couldn't question that she loved him, and he couldn't deny his gratitude for her commitment to him in spite of what had happened—because he couldn't comprehend getting through this without her. But he ached for her, and he had to wonder in his heart if being with him was the best thing for *her.*

Hilary continued to cry, while Jack felt helpless to do anything about it. Then it occurred to him that in spite of all he'd lost, there were some things he could still give her.

"Hey." He moved close to her and lifted her chin with his finger, silently thanking God for his ability to at least wipe away her tears. Some of his newly acquired friends here at the hospital couldn't even do that. As bad as this was, he didn't have to think very hard to realize that it could have been worse.

Jack watched Hilary's eyes, wishing there was something he could say to somehow compensate for everything else he'd already said. But everything he'd told her was true, and nothing could change it. Still, one fact remained strong, and he knew in his heart that it *did* make a difference. "I love you, Hilary," he said, and tears slid down his face. He took her hand and urged her onto his lap, where she clung to him as if he was her air to breathe. He couldn't deny what that meant to him, knowing he would be completely lost without her. He'd wondered occasionally if she was the only thing that kept him from becoming suicidal. Without her, he couldn't think of much to live for.

Hilary welcomed the security of Jack's closeness. She felt wrapped in the warmth of his spirit even before he put his arms around her, and she gladly took advantage of having his shoulder to cry against. And cry she did. She cried long and hard, comforted by the evidence that he was crying, too. She thought how tragic it was that this evening would end up this way. Then it occurred to her that the best and most appropriate thing for them to do together today was exactly what they were doing. They shared the same heartache, and it seemed right that they should cry together.

Hilary lost track of the time as she cried herself into a numb silence, then she just relaxed her head against his shoulder, absorbing his silent comfort like a balm to her soul. While she was searching for conversation, Meg knocked lightly at the door and entered timidly. "I'm so sorry to interrupt, but it's time for—"

"I know the drill," Jack said, albeit lightly.

Hilary slipped reluctantly away from him. Their eyes met, and she felt an increase of her love for him. She knew in her heart that all they shared would make them stronger, and their relationship more meaningful.

While Jack was assisted with his usual evening routine, Hilary changed back into her jeans and cleaned away all evidence of their *romantic* evening. She took everything out to her car and returned to his room to find him lying on his side, with the head of the bed elevated. She wanted to be close to him, but didn't know how to do it without being forward or presumptuous. She felt as if he'd read her mind when he held out his hand for her, saying, "Come here, Hilarious. It's not exactly king-sized, but there's plenty of room for a skinny little thing like you."

Hilary sat on the bed beside him, putting her head against his shoulder. She felt him press a kiss into her hair, and it was easy to relax. The silence was not uncomfortable, but she felt the need to speak her hopes for the future; to remind him that they had much ahead to look forward to, even if it wasn't going to turn out exactly as they had expected. "We can get married soon, Jack," she whispered. "Everyone says your recovery has been remarkable. You're doing great, and it won't be long before—"

"Hilary," he interrupted, but his voice was gentle, "I don't get through an hour here without significant help from somebody. And I'm not getting married until I can take care of myself."

Hilary bit her tongue to keep from protesting as she wondered exactly how long that would be—if ever. She'd learned a great deal about his condition, but there was much she *didn't* know. And she had no idea whether he would ever be able to *completely* care for himself.

She moved her head just enough to see his eyes. "Is it so wrong for me to help you, Jack? It's okay to admit that you can't do everything alone, isn't it? Better me than someone else."

"That's a matter of opinion, I suppose." He didn't want to admit how difficult it would be for him to be dependent on her for his physical needs. Perhaps it was determination; perhaps it was pride. Whatever his motivations, he would not spend the rest of his life feeling like a burden to Hilary.

"What do you mean by that?" she asked, determined not to let their communication close up again.

"I mean that you are the woman I love; you're not a nurse, not a caregiver. No matter how we feel about each other, life has changed for both of us, and we need some time to reevaluate—to be absolutely certain we're doing the right thing."

Hilary lifted her chin. "I know with all my heart and soul that being with you is the right thing for me."

"Well, I appreciate your confidence, Hilary. I really do. But *I* have to know it for myself, and I'm not ready to cross that bridge yet. So you're just going to have to be patient with me. I have to come to terms with the changes in myself before I can be any good to you—if such a thing is even possible anymore."

Hilary wanted to ask him to clarify that. But his expression told her he was drained emotionally, and she had to admit that she was, too. She laid her head against his shoulder again and sighed. "I've got forever, Jack. I love you. I'll always love you."

"I love you too, Hilary," he whispered and pressed a kiss to her brow.

Hilary had nearly drifted off to sleep when Jack had a muscle spasm in his leg that startled her. The first time it had happened, she'd thought he was regaining something. But she'd quickly learned that it was simply a spontaneous reaction that he couldn't feel and had no control over.

She reluctantly slipped away after giving Jack a lingering kiss. He languidly opened his eyes, gave her a wan smile, then drifted back to sleep.

During her brief drive home, Hilary reflected on the evening. It hadn't been entirely pleasant, but she felt they had made some progress. And now that this day had passed—a day they'd dreaded ever since the accident—they could move forward and work toward the goal of recreating their life together and making the most of it.

Hilary's thoughts were as positive as she could possibly make them, but she still cried herself to sleep. And she felt relatively certain that when Jack awakened in the night as he said he often did, he would cry, too.

The following week, Hilary was faced with some stark difficulties. Prior to Jack's accident, she had given official notice that she would be moving out of her apartment. Consequently, someone had been found to take her place, and she had no choice but to go elsewhere. But where? She wanted to talk to Jack about it, but she felt it was best that she lay out a plan and ask his opinion, rather than burdening him with problems that he was helpless to solve. Taking her problem to the Lord, she worked through a possible solution. She felt good about it, but it was difficult to bring it up to Jack. Still, she knew it had to be done, and prayed that it wouldn't contribute to the discouragement he was continually battling.

Hilary went to the hospital and read the *Ensign* while she waited for Jack to return from one of his many therapy sessions. If nothing else, they were keeping him terribly busy these days. His face brightened when he entered the room. She noticed how he had learned to open the door and enter without any assistance. Every inch of progress gave her hope for a bright future.

"What are you doing here?" he asked as they exchanged a quick kiss.

"Just waiting for you," she said, setting aside the magazine. "How's it going?"

"Good . . . or so they tell me." He looked at her closer and asked, "What's wrong?"

"Nothing's wrong . . . really. I just need to talk to you about some things."

"Okay," he said, disguising a rush of nerves, "let's talk."

Hilary took a deep breath. "Well, I think I've got everything sorted out. But I didn't want to follow through on anything without talking to you first, and . . ."

"Okay," he said when she hesitated.

"Well, first of all . . . ," she just hurried to say it, "since I was supposed to be married by now, I had committed to move out of my apartment. And now someone else is scheduled to move in. So . . ."

"So, you have nowhere to go," he said without seeming too upset.

"That's right, but . . . I was thinking, since your apartment is sitting empty, and I was going to move in there anyway, maybe I should just . . . well . . ."

"It sounds like an obvious solution to me."

"What?" she asked tensely.

"You moving into my apartment. That is what you're getting to, isn't it?"

"Yes, but . . . are you sure? I mean, the lease isn't up for a couple more months, I think. So that would be better than—"

"Hilary, I have a good idea. Why don't you move into my apartment. It's fine. Why are you so nervous?"

She took a deep breath, embarrassed by the evidence of how easily he could see through her. "It's just . . . not easy to talk about, but . . ."

"It's okay." He took her hand. "I'm just wondering how you're going to pay the rent. I know it's a lot more than the percentage you're paying for your place. And then there are the utilities."

"Well . . . it'll be tight, but . . . I think I can manage if I . . . well, that brings me to the other thing I wanted to talk to you about."

"Okay." Jack seemed relaxed and attentive, so she hurried to continue.

"I have to go back a little. A while back, Claire . . . you know who Claire is."

"The woman you work for. I know."

"Claire's husband got a job in Oklahoma. He's been back there for a few weeks now, while Claire's been trying to sell the house and figure out what to do with the studio. When it first came up, she offered me the option of taking it over."

"What do you mean by 'taking it over'?" he asked.

"I mean . . . it would be *my* business. She said she would have it all done legally. It easily brings in enough to pay all the expenses, plus the wages she's been giving me, and profit above that. I already do most of the teaching, and she does the business end of it, but . . ."

"But?"

"I told her no."

Jack looked alarmed. "Why?"

"Well, when she first asked me, we had made the decision to move to Mt. Pleasant as soon as you finished school. I prayed about it, and I just felt like it wasn't right to tie myself down to something that would interfere with our goals for the future."

Jack sighed and briefly rubbed a hand over his face. An undefinable emotion rose in his throat as he couldn't help thinking of Lorie and her determination to follow her career, no matter what it did to her marriage. He sensed where this was leading, but he didn't know how to ask. When the silence persisted, she went on.

"All these weeks, Claire has been stewing and fretting over what to do. Nothing else was working out. She didn't want to just dissolve the business, because it would leave all those students with nowhere to go. And now . . . well, under the circumstances, I feel like it would be a good thing for me to take on the studio. I would have to put more time into it, but it would increase my income enough to help get us through until . . ."

Jack's focus shifted abruptly to her. "Until?" he asked firmly.

Hilary felt the answer on the tip of her tongue, but she also felt a strong prompting that this was not the time to discuss their long-range goals. In a soft voice she said, "I don't know, Jack. The future is uncertain; I realize that. But I feel like this is the right thing for me to do—not only now, but for my future. This is something I could do for the rest of my life and be happy."

Jack nodded. "Well, then, it sounds good to me. I think it's great." He was silent for a moment then added, "If it's something that could keep you happy for the rest of your life, then why were you willing to give it up?"

Hilary glanced away. "I would think the answer is obvious."

"If it was obvious, I wouldn't be asking."

Hilary looked directly at him. "I would give up almost anything to have you in my life, Jack. It's as simple as that. Of course, I try to make my decisions according to the Spirit. At the time, I knew it was right. And if things had gone according to our original plans, I would have gladly gone back to Mt. Pleasant with you. And like I told you, perhaps I would have worked toward opening my own studio there."

"And in the meantime, you were willing to go out and drive a tractor through alfalfa fields—which you are allergic to—because it was what I wanted to do."

"That's right. Have you got a problem with that?"

Jack's eyes softened. "No. I just want you to know that it means something to me."

"Even though it will never happen?"

She could tell that her comment struck him hard, but she was glad she'd said it. He didn't seem upset as he said, "Maybe *especially* because it will never happen." He sighed. "I'm glad you're taking the job, Hil. It would seem the Lord is looking out for us—me especially."

"He wants us to be together, Jack."

"I know." He glanced away. "Let's just give it some time, okay?" Hilary nodded. Jack cleared his throat and asked, "Will you be able to manage going to school along with all the extra responsibility at the studio?"

Hilary sucked in her breath. She'd obviously overlooked telling him something. "Uh . . . I'm not going to school."

"Why not?" he demanded.

"Well, you're not," she said lightly, but he didn't seem amused. She said more seriously, "I withdrew when I went in to withdraw you. I put your tuition refund in the bank when I deposited your last paycheck . . . you already knew that. But I did the same with mine. It gives us something to fall back on if . . . things get tight."

"And I'm sure they will when the medical bills start pouring in."

"Your insurance is really good."

"I know. but . . . there are still percentages to pay. And eventually I've got to pay Ammon back for the premiums."

"Don't worry about that right now."

"How can I? There's obviously nothing I can do about it."

"What's wrong?" she asked, noting that his expression had turned somber.

Jack tried to discern what was bothering him most. "I didn't want you to drop out of school. I feel like you're sacrificing too much for my sake."

"I prayed about it, Jack. I have enough education to make a living. I have a good job. Besides," she laughed softly, "I've been reading medical manuals. I'm still getting an education . . . of sorts."

"I love you, Hilary," he said with so much sincerity that she was nearly moved to tears.

"I love you too, Jack."

"Yes, that is readily evident."

Their eyes met in a time-stopping moment. She was about to ask what he was thinking when he said, "Is there anything else we need to discuss?"

"Uh . . ." Hilary thought quickly. There were other things that would have to be dealt with eventually, but she didn't want to overwhelm him with too much at once. "I don't think so."

"Well, I asked your father to sell my truck."

Hilary bit back her impulse to scream and get angry. He loved that truck, and she knew it. Just like he loved the land his father had worked. It was all so horribly unfair. But there was nothing to say, so she just held his hand and listened.

"He told me he might have found a buyer, so he'll send you the money when he gets it."

"Okay," she said. "I'll . . . uh . . . do my best to spend your money wisely."

"I'm not worried about that."

"I've been getting your mail, and all of your bills are paid up to date."

Jack chuckled and said, "Look at us, talking as if we're an old married couple."

"We're as good as married, in my opinion," she said.

He just smiled. And Hilary felt some hope. They were making progress.

While Jack was busy with more therapy, Hilary felt restless. It was too early to go to the studio, and she really had nowhere to go and nothing to do. Wandering down the hallway, she noticed a few wheelchairs lined up along the wall. Impulsively, she sat in one. Then she started wheeling it down the hall. She went up in the elevator, then down in the elevator, exploring the hallways in between. She noticed things she'd never noticed before. Everything looked a little different from this perspective. She felt a little too short to get the best view out the windows, or to see the pictures on the walls. The drinking fountain felt awkward. She wheeled into the snack bar, where she had become a regular customer. "Hey," the girl who worked the day shift said to her, "what are you doing in that thing?"

"I'm gaining empathy," she said. "And since it's so exhausting, I need a chocolate malt."

While her malt was being prepared, Hilary noticed how high the counter seemed. And she wondered how it might feel to know she couldn't get out and sit on one of the barstools. She was going to take the malt with her, then realized that she couldn't hold it and turn the wheels on the chair. So she sat at one of the tables to drink it, thinking very hard about how her feelings might compare if the word *permanent* had been attached to them.

When Hilary had finished her malt, she wheeled around the hospital a little more, this time watching the faces of people she passed. It was usually subtle, but she sensed something different in the way people regarded her. It was difficult to pinpoint, and yet she considered the likelihood that people would probably be much more open-minded about wheelchairs in a hospital. She wondered what kind of silent responses she might get if she were out in public.

By the time she returned to Jack's room, her arms were aching and her hands sore from turning the wheels. She understood now why Jack was developing new callouses on his hands that were different from those he had from doing farm work and construction.

"What on earth are you doing?" Jack asked as she struggled to get through the door, even though it had been left partly open.

"You make this look so easy," she said, pulling her chair up to face his. Then she showed him her reddened hands, and he took them into his.

"What is this?" he asked.

"Empathy."

Jack looked into her eyes as he grasped the implication, then he kissed the palms of her hands and pressed them to his face, silently thanking God for sending him a woman like Hilary.

He continued to hold her hands while she told him what she had learned on her little excursion. Then she reluctantly had to leave for work.

Hilary was delighted to be able to tell Claire that she would take over the studio. It all worked out so well for both of them that she couldn't question God's hand in it. She wondered over the reasons for not having felt right about it before, and realized that even though this seemed meant to be, it was important for Jack to know that she had been willing to make the sacrifice. Hilary also wondered, if her taking over the studio was meant to be, what that meant about Jack's accident. Then, out of nowhere, she recalled the feelings Jack had shared with her not long after they'd become engaged. What had he said? He'd told her he felt like something would happen to him; that his future would not be what he'd expected. Was all of this meant to be? The thought was so chilling she almost didn't want to think it. But she couldn't get it out of her head.

The next time she was at Jack's apartment, she felt compelled to read his patriarchal blessing. He'd shared it with her before, but she wondered if the present circumstances might shed some new light. As she read, she recalled Jeffrey's journal entries and how they had given her peace about his death. And now, a new understanding came to her mind concerning Jack's situation. She couldn't claim to fully comprehend all that had happened and why, but she found peace in the evidence that God was mindful of Jack, and this was all part of a much bigger plan. She wondered if she should share with Jack what she had discovered, but she felt strongly that the time wasn't right. Perhaps a part of him already knew, or maybe he just wasn't ready to digest it. Hilary only hoped that with time, they would be able to understand the full perspective of all that had happened.

Hilary's parents came up from Mt. Pleasant and spent a weekend helping her move. Since she had very little furniture, it wasn't too big a job. Ammon was happy to come and help move the few heavy things. Pete and Millie spent a lot of time with Jack at the hospital while they were in town. Hilary enjoyed seeing them together; Jack always seemed more like himself when he was around her father.

Hilary had spent a great deal of time at Jack's apartment before the accident, and she had been in and out several times since to take care of things for him. But it felt almost eerie for her to be here now,

mingling her things with his, as if they were married. She found it
ironic to be living among his belongings, while his absence was so
pronounced. She contemplated how it might feel to lose a spouse to
death and be surrounded by the loved one's possessions. The thought
gave her a new level of empathy for the struggles of others, and also a
new gratitude as she reminded herself that Jack was alive, and they
still had a future together.

Settling into running the dance studio was easier than she had
expected. She spent time with Jack every day, amazed at the progress
he was making. Occasionally she even sneaked him out of the
hospital to get some drive-thru food, and once they went to a drive-in
movie. The first time she tried to help him transfer from the wheelchair to the car, it was nearly a disaster. He ended up making it by the
skin of his teeth, while they laughed so hard they were crying. The
next time they did better, and she loved being with him outside of the
hospital, which gave her a taste of the future—which gave her hope.

Hilary kept closely in touch with Janna, who was always full of
encouragement and support. Her friend was there to listen as Hilary
vented thoughts and emotions that were too sensitive to share with
Jack at this point. And Janna always had sound advice that eventually
proved invaluable. Whenever Jack showed signs of anger or belliger-
ence, Janna reminded Hilary, "I think he wants proof that you truly
love him in spite of the changes. You can tell he's testing it by the
things he says. He'll probably continue to test it for quite some time.
You just have to love him unconditionally and see the test through."

Along with everything else, Hilary searched diligently for an apartment to rent that was wheelchair accessible. The one she lived in now
was on a second floor, among other problems. Hilary quickly learned
that her quest would not be easy. She still had some time before the
lease was up, but she was more concerned about where Jack would go
when he got out of the hospital. All she could do was keep looking
and pray that something would open up before they needed it.

While Hilary greatly anticipated Jack's release from the hospital, as it
drew near they were confronted with a whole new dilemma. Though it
had never come up between them, Hilary had wondered and worried
about where Jack would go. If they were already married, the answer
would be obvious—if he could get into the apartment where she was

living. But they weren't married, and it wouldn't be appropriate for them to be living together under the same roof until they were. Jack had come a long way toward taking care of himself, but he still couldn't be left on his own twenty-four hours a day. Hilary knew they needed to discuss it, but she dreaded bringing it up, knowing it would be a difficult topic.

The point was forced into the open when Judy showed up at the hospital one afternoon. Hilary was sitting on the bed, going over her bills. Jack was sitting in his chair, reading.

At the knock on the door, Jack hollered, "Yeah," without looking up, obviously thinking it was a nurse. Hilary realized who it was before Jack did, but she didn't know what to say. When he looked up to question the silence, his back straightened and the tension in his eyes was immediately evident. "Hello, Mother," he said tonelessly. "What brings you all the way up here?"

Judy cleared her throat. "I, uh . . . came to see you."

Jack wished with everything inside of him that he could bridge the gap that existed between himself and his mother. But he knew in his heart that if it had been possible, he'd have done it years ago. He felt certain that his present condition would only widen the chasm. It was difficult to find the motivation to be amiable, and it took discipline not to be terse. He settled on indifferent. "What's the occasion?" he asked.

"I . . . uh," she laughed uncomfortably, "heard you were getting out of the hospital soon, and . . . well, I just wondered what your plans are."

Jack exchanged a brief glance with Hilary that she understood well. Judy had not been the least bit concerned with his *plans* for years.

"I don't know, Mother," he said with light sarcasm, "I thought I'd become a quarterback or something." She didn't seem amused, so he added more seriously, "I haven't thought too much about it, to be honest." He finished with a skeptical, "Why?"

Judy cleared her throat again as she pulled an envelope out of her purse and handed it to Jack. He turned it over but didn't quite dare open it. Instead he asked, "What is it?"

"Well, you know, your father left me well cared for. He was always putting money away in bonds and such things. And his life insurance was good." Her voice cracked just enough that Jack knew she'd not come to terms with her husband's death. "Anyway," she said more steadily, "I know your expenses must be horrible with all the time you've been here, and I . . . I just wanted to help out a little. Perhaps it, uh . . . makes up a little for . . . well . . ." She looked suddenly as if she wanted to disappear.

"For what, Mother?" Jack asked, wondering what she was *really* getting at.

She drew back her shoulders, but she wouldn't look at him. "For not . . . being able to help you any other way."

Jack understood now what she was trying to tell him. It wasn't a surprise, but he had to wonder why it hurt. Quickly reasoning that he wouldn't want her to help him anyway, he just said, "Thank you, Mother. We appreciate your thoughtfulness."

He almost expected her to make some attempt at casual conversation, but she took hold of the door, saying, "Let me know when you reschedule the wedding."

When Jack made no response, Hilary said, "We will. And thank you."

Judy rushed from the room as if she'd just been released from prison. Hilary's heart ached for Jack as he turned to look at her. He sighed, then slowly opened the envelope. His expression didn't change as he took out the check and looked at it. "Why do I feel like I've just been sold?" he asked.

Hilary could easily guess, but she reminded herself that Jack needed to talk more, so she just said, "I don't know, why?"

"Is it just me, or do you get the impression this is guilt money? It's obvious she doesn't want me coming back home and becoming a burden to her. Not that I'd go live under her roof under these circumstances—not in a million years. But still . . ."

"I hear what you're saying," Hilary said. "And you're probably right, but . . . it could be worse."

"And how is that?" he asked with an edge of bitterness that she well understood.

"At least she gave you some money. She didn't have to do it. And the fact is, we need every penny we can get our hands on."

"Well," he said, tossing the check onto the bed on top of her bank statement, "these pennies ought to help."

Hilary gasped and resisted the urge to jump off the bed and dance right then and there. "Jack, this is ten thousand dollars. Do you realize how much this will help?"

"Yes, it will help," he said. But in spite of his smile, Hilary knew the money represented something difficult for him.

"I'm sorry," she said. "I can understand why this is hard. If you don't want me to cash it, or—"

"Hilary, I want you to put it to good use. You're the financial wizard. I won't deny it's a blessing, and I'm grateful. But I still feel like I've been sold."

Hilary knew they could get into a deep, analytical conversation about his mother and what he was feeling right now. But she knew there was nothing to say that hadn't been said before. Instead, she scooted close to Jack and took his hand, kissing him on the nose. "Well, you know what? She can't sell you, because you're mine. And I'm not going to let you go—ever."

Jack looked into her eyes, wishing he could find words to express what that meant to him—especially under the circumstances. Which brought to mind a point that he knew couldn't be avoided any longer. "Hilary, I don't know where to go when I get out of here."

"If I had my way, you'd just move in with me. It's your apartment, anyway."

"You've been paying the rent," he stated. "But I don't think that's a very appropriate option—under the circumstances."

"I know, but . . ." Hilary didn't know how to tell him that she desperately wished they were already married, which would alleviate this problem altogether.

"Besides," he went on, "that apartment isn't even remotely wheelchair accessible."

"I know," she admitted, "but . . . I've been looking for a place that is, and when we're married, we can—"

"And in the meantime?" he asked.

"Maybe we should just hurry and get married," she suggested, and Jack was surprised to realize she was serious.

"Listen, Hilary," he said, "I've told you before, I want a wife, not a nurse. And I'm not getting married until I can get through the course of a day without any help from you."

His defensiveness disturbed Hilary, but she only said, "And in the meantime?"

Jack looked away, and his face muscles tightened. "I don't know, Hilary. I just don't know."

Hilary changed the subject, but she left the hospital feeling scared and uncertain. During her classes, her mind became so preoccupied with Jack's dilemma that she went home that evening actually feeling angry toward the circumstances that had kept them from being married sooner. Why hadn't she fallen for him long ago? If she hadn't been so dense, they could have been married and settled long before the accident. And if she was his wife, she could take him home with her and be there for him, even if he was too proud to let her help him with his personal needs.

She had only been home a short time when Janna called to see how she was doing. As always, it was easy for Hilary to unload her burdens on her friend. They talked for nearly an hour, and Janna reminded her to have faith and remain prayerful. Hilary knew her friend's advice was sound, but it all seemed so abstract and difficult. Exhausted, she fell asleep quickly after praying that everything would turn out all right, and that by using whatever means were necessary to get through this, Jack would be able to keep his dignity and learn to feel good about himself again.

* * * * *

The nurse had barely left after helping Jack with his morning routine when Colin Trevor came to his hospital room. He was wearing a shirt and tie, just as Jack would expect an attorney to dress on a work day. But he couldn't help wondering why he would come *here*. Jack couldn't recall ever seeing Colin without his wife; and even though the two of them had come to the hospital several times, he'd always felt like it was more to support Hilary than for him personally. And that was fine. But as soon as greetings were exchanged, Jack had to ask, "So, what brings you here?"

"May I sit down?" Colin asked.

"Sure," Jack motioned to the chair, "make yourself at home. The room's a little too cozy for my taste, but the service is good."

Colin chuckled and seemed slightly nervous. "I'll get right to the point, Jack."

"I wish you would. I hate suspense."

"You know, of course, that Janna and Hilary have become very close. I know Hilary's friendship means a great deal to Janna. It's one of those things where you could almost believe they'd been friends in another life."

"Yeah," Jack said, "I know what you mean." He wanted to ask what that had to do with the point, but he didn't.

"Anyway, Janna talked to Hilary on the phone for a long time last night. And the only reason I'm telling you this is so you'll understand why we are aware of what's going on with you. Janna's been concerned for both you and Hilary right from the start, and I share Janna's concern."

"I'm with you," Jack said, beginning to feel nervous himself.

"Jack," Colin looked into his eyes, "did you know that Janna is an LPN?"

"A what?"

"A licensed practical nurse."

Jack absorbed this information, wondering where it would lead. "No," he admitted, "I didn't know that. Or maybe I did, but I forgot."

He briefly considered a few reasons for Colin's visit that might be related to his wife's being a nurse. But he was completely taken off guard when Colin said, "Jack, what I'm trying to say is . . . well, we want you to come and stay with us."

"Did Hilary put you up to this?" he asked once he recovered from the surprise.

"No," Colin chuckled, "not at all. She poured her heart out to Janna—the way she always does. Then Janna poured her heart out to me—the way she always does. This is my idea. Of course, Janna was delighted. She puts a lot of effort into helping other people, Jack. It's kind of become a hobby of hers. She's struggled through so much herself that I think she's got this incredible gift of empathy. I don't know. Whatever it is, she was thrilled with the idea of having you in our home—just until you can adjust enough to get on with your life. I know you and Hilary will get married as soon as possible. But in the meantime, we'd love to have you come. Janna's got the experience to help you with whatever you need. We have an extra room, and it would take very little to make the house accessible for your needs."

Colin stopped talking, as if to allow Jack the time to consider his offer. Jack was too stunned to speak. "So, what do you think?" Colin finally asked when the silence grew too long.

"I don't know what to think," Jack admitted. "I mean . . . I'm grateful for the offer, but . . ."

"If you need time to think about it, that's fine," Colin said. "I know this is a big adjustment for you. The last thing we want is to make you feel obligated or uncomfortable. Of course, you'd have to put up with our kids, but . . . well, it would be our pleasure."

While Jack's pride battled with his lack of choices, he finally said, "Thank you, Colin. I would like to think about it. I'll talk to Hilary, and . . . we'll be in touch."

Colin nodded, then asked Jack how he was doing. He stayed for nearly an hour, talking about sports, the weather, and a couple of things he'd heard on the morning news. Jack had never related very well to white-collar people, but he had to admit that Colin Trevor was a decent guy.

* * * * *

Hilary was later than usual arriving at the hospital, since she'd had some errands to run. She stepped off the elevator and came face to face with Colin Trevor. "Hello," she said. "What are you doing here?"

"Oh, I just had a little visit with Jack; figured he could use some company."

"That's nice." Hilary smiled.

"Well, I'll be on my way," Colin said, getting on the elevator. "I've got to get back to work."

"Thank you," she called as the doors closed between them.

Hilary hurried to Jack's room to find him sitting at the window, staring outside. "Hello," she said, kissing him quickly. "How are you?"

Jack didn't even look at her. "How am I supposed to be?"

Hilary discounted his terseness. "I didn't ask how you're supposed to be. I asked how you are."

"The same as I was yesterday."

"Jack," she said, "maybe we should talk."

"I don't want to talk, Hilary. I want to get out of here. I want to have a life again."

"Okay, but . . ." She quickly considered their options and spoke up on the one she thought was most feasible. "Jack, maybe we really should just get married . . . soon. We could arrange it quickly. We have our temple recommends. We could just—"

"Hilary," Jack said in a voice more firm than gentle, "I don't want to marry you until I can take care of myself. And I can't do that yet. The last thing I want is to become a burden to you."

Hilary sighed. "Oh, Jack, you could never be a burden to me. Never." She touched his face. "No matter what, Jack, you're still my hero."

Hilary regretted saying it when his eyes hardened further. With deep sarcasm he said, "Yes, your hero, your knight in shining armor, your protector—who can't even walk. Some hero."

Hilary counted to ten, as she had trained herself to do in dealing with his bad moods. While she was counting she asked herself, as she often did, *What would Janna tell me to do?* "I get the impression you're upset about something," she said.

"I'm upset about *everything.*"

"I know this is difficult, Jack, but I'm not going to let you take it out on me. You can cry or scream or throw things if you have to, but don't take it out on me."

"I'm sorry," he said, taking her hand. Not liking the direction of their conversation, he changed it. "Colin was here."

"Oh, yes. I saw him when I got off the elevator. I must say I was surprised to see him here alone. Did he—"

"He invited me to come and stay with them." If Jack had any question about Hilary's being involved in this, it was answered immediately by her dumbstruck surprise. She was obviously at a loss for words, so Jack went on. "He told me Janna's a nurse, and she would be there to help me."

"Wow," Hilary finally said, "I never dreamed . . . I mean, they're wonderful people. It's just that . . . such an idea never even occurred to me."

"Colin said it was his idea."

Hilary tried to gauge Jack's feelings about this. When she couldn't, she just asked, "So, what do you think?"

"I don't know what to think. They're little more than strangers, Hilary. I've barely visited with them a few times."

"They're good people who are giving you an option. Would you prefer staying in a care center where—"

"No!" he shouted. "I would prefer taking care of myself!"

Hilary swallowed and counted to ten. She'd become accustomed to occasional outbursts of anger, but they still upset her. Drawing on her self-discipline, she replied in a quiet, firm voice, "Eventually, you will be able to take care of yourself for the most part. But it will take time. If we were already married, I could take care of you. But we're not, and it wouldn't be appropriate. When we get married, then—"

"Is that why you want to marry me, Hilary? To take care of me?"

Hilary swallowed and counted to ten—again. "My reasons for marrying you are the same as they've always been. I love you—even when you shout at me."

Jack sighed guiltily and took her hand. "I'm sorry, Hilary. You just told me not to take it out on you, and here I am—doing it again."

"Maybe if we talked more about how you feel, you wouldn't have so much anger inside." He said nothing and she pleaded, "Talk to me, Jack. We can work this through."

"I just need some time, Hilary."

She nodded, trying to convince herself that she could believe him. But she had a feeling things were going to get a lot worse between them before they ever started getting better. Changing the subject, she asked, "So what did you tell Colin?"

"I told him I needed to think about it."

"And what are you *going* to tell him?"

Jack blew out a long breath. "I don't know that I have any other options. I hate the thought of being dependent on *anyone* like that, but . . . what else can I do?"

"They're wonderful people, Jack."

"I know."

"And we'll be married soon." She kissed him and pressed her forehead to his.

"I love you, Hilary. I really do."

"I know," she whispered and kissed him again.

Colin and Janna came to the hospital together that evening while Hilary was teaching dance classes. Their eagerness and excitement at Jack's acceptance of their offer made him feel a little better. But he still hated this. He hated everything about it.

Before Jack was released from the hospital, Hilary took the majority of his clothes and personal items over to Janna's house. She was moved to tears as Janna showed her the wood ramp they had built from the driveway to the back porch, and the way they'd had the bathroom door widened. "Ammon Mitchell did it," Janna reported.

"Jack's boss?"

"That's right. We met him at the hospital one evening. We knew he'd get it done quickly and do it with some care. As you can see, he did a good job. I've made arrangements to rent some of the equipment we'll need, and the insurance should cover most of the cost. I think we're about ready for him."

Janna led her to the room Jack would be using. Again Hilary felt emotional. She knew he would be comfortable and well cared for here, and her gratitude to Janna and Colin was more than she could express. She only hoped that Jack would feel the same way.

CHAPTER ELEVEN

*J*ack couldn't help feeling good about finally leaving the hospital. The weeks he'd spent there had been long and difficult, and he knew he had to be grateful to have a place to go. But he felt a little bit like an unwanted child going to a foster home as Hilary drove him to Colin and Janna's house. He recalled coming here once before, prior to Hilary's mission, but his memories were vague. He felt down-right nervous as Hilary pulled the car to the end of the long driveway, and he noticed the newly built ramp that led to the back porch.

"Ammon built the ramp," Hilary said as if she'd read his mind.

"Really?" He added facetiously, "I didn't know he could do that sort of thing."

Hilary got out of the car and opened the hatchback. She'd had the car since she'd returned from her mission, but she had since learned that a hatchback was ideal for carting around a wheelchair. It was much easier than getting it in and out of a trunk. The chair was lightweight and much easier to handle than the standard hospital wheelchair Jack had used before he got his own. This one had no handles, no armrests, and a low back that made it easier for him to maneuver. The chair encouraged independence, which was especially appealing to Jack.

Hilary opened the car door and put the chair at his side. It took him some time to transfer from the car seat, but he did it without help, and Hilary marveled at how far he'd come. She felt certain that his upper body strength played greatly in his favor. "Oooh, that was impressive," she teased, while a little tingle of excitement skittered over her shoulders. The changes in his life had in no way decreased her attraction to him.

"Just wait till you see me pop a wheelie."

"Can you do that?" she asked as he moved up the ramp.

"No, but it's something to aspire to."

"Just be careful you don't break your neck, too."

"I think I'd rather not, to be truthful." His tone remained light, but Hilary knew he meant it when he said, "What I've been through is a piece of cake compared to that."

"Amen," Hilary murmured just as Janna opened the back door with a cheerful greeting.

Hilary and Janna exchanged an embrace, then Janna turned and took Jack's hand into both of hers. "It's so good to have you here, Jack. Come in and make yourself at home."

"Thank you," he said and moved through a sliding glass door into a large dining area.

"The children are in school," Janna told them, "except the baby, of course. He's sleeping. So enjoy the peace and quiet while it lasts."

She took them on a brief tour of the main floor, which was comprised of a small front room, where a staircase went up to the second floor. A larger family room was just off the dining area. Jack followed Janna, and had no trouble maneuvering everywhere he needed to go. While they were in the kitchen, Janna said, "Now, we want you to make yourself at home. We have pretty basic household rules. You can eat whatever you can find, as long as you clean up after yourself. Sometimes we have to schedule hot water so we don't run out, but this bathroom is pretty much yours, since we have two upstairs."

Jack wheeled into the bathroom, noting the shower chair and handrails. He wondered how much work they had gone to in preparation for his stay. "It's very nice," he said, thinking it sounded trite. But he didn't know what else to say.

"And here is your room," Janna announced, going into a large bedroom off the family room. "It was supposed to be the den," she said as Jack went to the center of the room and looked around. "But we never actually *did* anything in here. It was more like a place to temporarily store everything we didn't want to put away. So, we put everything away, and . . . voilá! The guest room."

"It's really very nice, Janna," Jack said. "I don't know what to say."

"You don't have to say anything." Janna shrugged. "I'm glad we're here." A baby's cry could be heard in the distance. "Oh, I'll be right back," she said and hurried up the stairs.

Jack took closer inventory of the room and realized that his own belongings were already in place. In addition to a bed, a dresser, and a recliner, there was a TV, a VCR, a portable stereo, a telephone, and an alarm clock.

"It's nice, isn't it?" Hilary remarked.

"Yeah," Jack said. "I feel almost guilty for being treated so well."

"You deserve to be treated well," she said. "Just don't get too comfortable. After we get married, I'm not sure you'll have it so cozy."

"I'll have you," he said in a voice that warmed her.

Janna returned with the baby and a notebook, suggesting that they discuss a tentative routine. She said to Hilary, "Do you want to write or feed Jake his bottle?"

Hilary impulsively said, "I'll feed the baby . . . if he'll let me."

"Oh, he likes anyone who gives him attention."

While Janna asked Jack questions and made notes, he was more preoccupied with watching Hilary feed the baby. His thoughts began to wander to the reality that he was no longer a man capable of having children. The reality hurt so much that he had to force himself not to look at her.

Hilary had to leave for work in mid-afternoon, and Jack found it difficult to see her go. Again he felt like a child being left somewhere strange and unfamiliar. He knew everything would be all right, but he felt out of place. A short while later, the children began arriving home from school. Matthew was the first to come in. As Janna introduced him, Jack was amazed at how much he looked like Colin. Almost sixteen, Matthew had obviously hit puberty early. He towered over his mother, and even though Colin wasn't here, Jack wagered that he even had an inch or two over on his father. In spite of a typically guarded teenage demeanor, Matthew was polite, and even made a little conversation with Jack.

About an hour later, the two little girls came in from first and second grade. Caitlin was the older of the two, with blonde hair and features that didn't strongly favor either of her parents. Mallory had dark hair and strongly resembled her mother.

"Your children are adorable," Jack commented to Janna while she was starting dinner. "I noticed they all have curly hair."

Janna smiled. "That makes you fit right in."

Jack laughed. "You're not old enough to be my mother."

"No, but maybe your big sister."

"Now, that's something I've never had."

"Well, if you did have a big sister, she probably would have tormented you endlessly. I'll try to be more tolerable than that."

Wanting to feel useful, Jack asked if he could help. Janna seemed pleased with the offer and set him to work cutting vegetables at the table. While he was chopping celery, Mallory appeared and stared at him. "Hello," he said.

"Hello," she repeated.

"What are you doing?" he asked.

"Nothin'."

"Mallory, run along and play," Janna said. "Don't bother Jack."

"Oh, she's all right," Jack insisted.

Mallory continued to watch him. "How come your legs don't work?" she asked.

Jack heard Janna sigh as she glanced over her shoulder. But he looked back at her as if to say it was okay. "I broke my back," he explained to Mallory. After a moment, her face scrunched up as if she was trying to grasp the connection and couldn't.

Janna rescued him by sitting down and pulling Mallory onto her lap. She touched a place on the child's back and explained, "Inside of the bones that go down your back, there is something called the spinal cord. It goes all the way from your brain down your back, then it spreads out all over your body. It's like electricity going from your brain that makes everything in your body work. When Jack hurt his back, the spinal cord was damaged. So now he can't feel or use his legs."

Mallory looked thoughtful and Janna asked, "Do you understand?"

The little girl nodded, and Janna went back to her cooking. Mallory continued staring at Jack, then asked, "Does it hurt when you stub your toe?"

Jack chuckled. "No, I can't feel my toes."

This seemed to bother the child, but she soon disappeared.

"Sorry," Janna said. "The innocence of children can make life interesting."

"It's fine," Jack insisted. "If I can learn to talk about it with Mallory, maybe it will make talking to everybody else easier."

"Can't hurt."

Mallory returned a few minutes later. She watched Jack for a minute then asked, "Can you still go to the potty?"

"Mallory!" Janna scolded.

"It's okay," Jack said. "Yes, Mallory. I can still go to the potty." He added more quietly after she left, "Sort of."

"It's awful when your children embarrass you like that."

"I wasn't embarrassed," he said. "Now, if Hilary had asked me that . . ." He chuckled and shook his head.

Janna turned and pointed a fork at him. "If you're going to marry her, you'll have to get over that."

Jack shrugged. "Yeah, I guess I will."

A few minutes later Mallory returned again, holding a stuffed penguin. She said to Jack, "When I was five years old, I got really sick. I had a sore throat and I had to take icky medicine, and I had to stay in bed lots of days. My daddy brought me Baxter to make me feel better."

"Did Baxter make you feel better?" Jack asked.

"Yes. But I don't need Baxter anymore, because I'm six years old and I'm not sick." She seemed momentarily at a loss for words, but certainly not shy. "Would you like to hold Baxter? Maybe he will make you feel better, too."

Jack glanced at Janna. Motherly pride glistened in her eyes as she observed her little daughter. "Thank you, Mallory," he said. "I would like very much to hold Baxter as soon as I finish what I'm doing. I don't want to get him dirty."

Janna suggested, "Why don't you go put Baxter on Jack's bed, and he can wait there for Jack."

"Okay," Mallory said. She started to leave, then turned back to ask, "Will you hold Baxter while you're sleeping, Jack?"

"Yes," he smiled, "I'll take very good care of Baxter. Thank you."

Mallory skipped off to Jack's room, then returned only long enough to say, "I put him on your bed, Jack."

"Thank you," he said again, and Mallory finally went off to play.

"I hope my children don't plague you too much," Janna said.

"I love children," Jack said, then he wished he hadn't. He could almost feel Janna wanting to ask how he was coping with the fact that he would never have any of his own.

Jack made no further comment, and he was relieved when Janna took the vegetables he'd finished cutting. "Thank you," she said. "We might actually eat on time tonight, if Jake cooperates. He can be a very demanding baby."

"Glad to help," Jack said, then went to the family room where Matthew was watching TV. The evening went relatively well, and Jack found that he felt a lot more comfortable than he had anticipated after being there only a matter of hours. Within a few days, he felt almost as much at home as he'd come to feel during his weeks at the hospital. Colin and Janna both had a way of making even the uncomfortable seem easy. Through some trial and error they developed a workable routine, where Colin actually did more for Jack than Janna did. She was most helpful to Jack by being there to answer his questions and give him suggestions on how to do certain things. He enjoyed being around the children, even if they mostly kept their distance.

"You've worked with paraplegics before, I take it," he said one morning to Janna.

"No. But I've worked with two different quadriplegics." She went on to talk a little about the differences, which reminded Jack to be grateful for what he had.

"Boy, I really lucked out there, didn't I."

"Yes, actually," Janna said. "The challenges are so much more intense with little or no use of your hands."

"How do you suppose they cope?" Jack asked.

"Well, the woman I worked with wasn't coping. She was very angry and bitter, even though it had been years. The gentleman I worked with, however, did very well. He was continually trying to become more independent, and his focus was always on what he *did* have, and what he *could* do. Not the other way around."

Jack became lost in thought until Janna startled him. "I would guess that's easier said than done."

"Yeah, I guess it is," Jack said.

He felt suddenly uncomfortable with the way Janna was watching him, as if she could see right through to his soul. "You know, Jack," she said, "you don't have to talk to me. And if I get too nosy, just say so. But we're here to help you adjust, and we all know the emotional adjustments have to be a lot tougher than the physical ones. I'm no counselor, but I've had my share of struggles. And I've learned a thing or two along the way."

Jack recalled Hilary telling him that Janna had been through some rough times, but to watch her now he found it difficult to believe. He doubted that she could have any comprehension of what he might be feeling. But she'd aroused his curiosity enough to make him ask, "Like what?"

"What have I learned? Or what have I struggled with?"

"Both."

"That's a pretty big question to answer."

"You don't have to answer it," Jack said. "I've got all the time in the world, but I know you're a very busy woman, and—"

"Oh, I'm in no hurry, but . . ."

"But?" Jack pressed.

"I'm not sure you'd want to hear it."

"If you don't want to talk about it, I understand. I just—"

"No, it's not that. I don't mind talking about it; at least not anymore. There was a time when I couldn't. It's just that most people don't want to hear about it; such things make them uncomfortable. The only time I really talked about it was when I did some volunteer work at a crisis center. *Those* people understand."

"What people?"

"People in crisis."

"Would I qualify as someone in crisis?" Jack asked.

"You seem to be handling things pretty well, but we reach new layers of hurt and healing all the time."

"So tell me," he said. Not only was his curiosity piqued, but he was finding that he actually felt comfortable talking with her. It occurred to him that she actually would make a good counselor; perhaps that was part of her gift in being a good nurse.

"Okay. Where do I start?"

"At the beginning."

"Well," she said, "I could give you the nutshell version."

"Okay."

"My father abandoned my mother and me when I was a baby. He came back when I was thirteen and sexually abused me."

Jack took a deep breath. Already he was a little stunned.

"I met Colin when I was fifteen. When I was eighteen, my mother died. Amidst the trauma of the whole thing, Matthew was conceived. But instead of telling Colin the truth, I left the state. I married a man who would regularly beat me into unconsciousness. I had some miscarriages because of the abuse. He's in prison now, which makes life better for all of us."

"Wow." Jack was amazed. "And you obviously got back together with Colin."

"Yes, but even that hasn't been easy. After Mallory was born, we were separated for about a year and a half—long enough for me to have a nervous breakdown and finally come to terms with everything."

"How *did* you come to terms with it?"

"One step at a time. I was blessed with a man who loved me enough to carry me through. I was blessed with good friends—like Hilary. I had a good counselor. And most important, I had the gospel. It took time to understand everything that had happened, but in the end I knew beyond any doubt that my Father in Heaven understood, and my suffering had been atoned for."

Jack quickly pressed a hand over his mouth as her words struck something in him. But he almost felt afraid to think too hard about it. While a part of him wanted to talk, a bigger part simply wanted his feelings left alone. He wondered if Janna somehow sensed this when she concluded their conversation with a smile and went to the basement to put in some laundry.

Hilary came by a few minutes later. Her daily visits were the bright spots in his life, even though he found it difficult to think of bridging the gaps that still remained between them.

"Want to go to the store?" she asked.

"The store?"

"Groceries, silly. I have to go shopping, and I don't want to go alone."

"I'm game," he said. "I think I could fit it in between my facial and my pedicure."

Hilary laughed, but she didn't miss the subtle bite in his words. She knew he needed to get on with his life and find something constructive to do with his time.

"Oh, hello, Hilary," Janna said, emerging from the basement stairs with a basket of laundry.

"Hi. We're going for groceries. Need anything?"

"Actually, yes. That would be great." Janna hurried to look in the fridge, calling over her shoulder, "A pound of margarine, a gallon of two percent milk, and a couple of tomatoes." She closed the fridge. "That should get me by until tomorrow."

Jack enjoyed his outing with Hilary. First they went to lunch, but she insisted they weren't driving through this time. "If you want to eat, you're going to have to get out of the car."

"Yes, ma'am," he drawled with an exaggerated accent, which made her laugh.

After lunch they went to the store, then she pulled the car up in front of the apartment and hurried to take her two bags of groceries inside. When she returned to the car, Jack said, "I'd almost forgotten what this place looked like."

Hilary took his hand. "It's not the same without you there." When Jack just looked out the window, Hilary added brightly, "Which reminds me . . . before I take you home, there's something I want to show you."

"Okay."

"What is this?" Jack asked when they drove into an apartment complex that seemed to go on for blocks.

She pulled into the third parking section and said, "Okay, let's go."

"Where are we going?" he asked, feeling nervous for reasons he didn't understand.

"Just get out."

"What about Janna's groceries?"

"It's cold outside. They'll be fine for a little while."

Hilary got the chair for Jack, and he transferred to it with little trouble. "Lead the way," he said. She ambled up the walk and around the corner, where she turned a key in a door.

"You first," she said, motioning with her arm.

"What is this?" he asked, hesitating at the door.

"This is what I've been searching and praying for for weeks."

Jack glanced at her skeptically and went inside. Hilary closed the door and leaned against it while Jack glanced around the empty apartment.

"I talked to the landlord here when I first started looking. He told me everything was full, and there were no leases ending on anything wheelchair accessible until spring. I'd practically given up on finding anything. Then, a few days ago, I felt prompted to call this guy back. He told me an apartment had opened up." Hilary walked into the kitchen and motioned for Jack to follow her. "It's not Buckingham Palace, but I think it's adequate."

Jack said nothing as they went back through the front room and down the hall to look in the two good-sized bedrooms, and the bathroom that had original fixtures suitable for Jack's needs. The apartment had not been modified; it had obviously been built to be wheelchair accessible.

"So, what do you think?"

While Jack attempted to deal with the turmoil of emotions going on inside of him, the silence grew too long. "Jack?" she asked.

"Why is it suddenly available?" His curiosity was a good means to avoid her question.

Hilary looked uncomfortable. "Does it matter?"

"Maybe."

Hilary sighed. "A paraplegic woman lived here. She died a couple of weeks ago."

"She died *here?*" he asked.

"I don't know what bearing this has on anything."

"I just want to know if the place is haunted," he asked with a smirk, but Hilary wasn't amused.

"No, she didn't die *here.* She drank too much. Apparently she left late at night and was hit by a car." She sighed and added, "You still haven't told me what you think."

"It's nice," he said. Then he smiled. "Where are you going to live?"

Hilary couldn't tell if he was just teasing her, or if his flippancy was an attempt to cover some other emotion. "I've already put down the deposits in my name, Jack Hayden. You want to live here, you're going to have to live with me."

"Sounds feasible," he said, and went back to the front room.

Hilary found him heading toward the door and bolted in front of him to block his way. "Could you say something that actually makes sense before you leave?"

"Like what?"

"Do you like the apartment?"

"Yes, Hilary, it's great."

"Okay, so it must be the prospect of living with me that you're having trouble with."

Jack turned away, and his face tightened. "What makes you think I'm having trouble with anything?"

"What makes you think I'm stupid?"

"I have never said you were stupid."

"You didn't have to. You sit there and expect me to believe nothing's wrong, when it's more than obvious that something is." At his defensive glare she softened her voice. "Just talk to me, Jack. If something about this makes you uncomfortable, you've got to speak up."

Jack blew out a long breath. "I'm sorry, Hilary. The apartment's great. It's perfect. I just . . . wish that . . ."

"What?"

"Oh, the list is too long to even start."

"Maybe we should make a list of what we *do* have, and not think so much about what we *don't* have." He said nothing, and she went on. "Okay, the apartment's great. So, what's wrong?"

"How are you going to move everything?"

"I've got plenty of help. Ammon. Mom and Dad. Colin, Matthew, and—"

"Okay. I get the idea."

"So, what else is bothering you?"

"I just need some time, Hilary," he admitted.

"Yes, you've told me you need time—time to be able to take care of yourself. You're doing good. We ought to be able to at least set a date and . . ." She stopped at his obvious change of expression. "What?" she demanded. He said nothing and she guessed, "Oh, I see. *Time* has nothing to do with being physically capable."

"Yes, it does," he insisted.

"But that's not all."

"No," he admitted, "that's not all."

"Then what is it?"

"Listen, Hil, I really don't want to talk about this right now."

"Why not?"

"Because I'm not ready to," he shouted. "If it doesn't make sense to me, how am I supposed to tell you and have it make sense?"

Hilary turned away and closed her eyes. Tears seeped through her lashes.

"Why are you crying?" he demanded as if she'd done something wrong.

"I hate it when you shout at me," she said, opening the door to go outside. He followed her out, and she locked the door.

When they were in the car he said, "You're still crying."

"I'm sorry," she snapped. "I can't hold it inside as skillfully as you do."

"That's not fair," he snarled.

"Fair?" Hilary slammed on the brakes and swerved the car over to the curb. "Let me tell you about *fair*. Life is not *fair*, Jack."

"You think I don't know that?" He turned away. "Why don't you take me home."

"No, I'm not going to take you home. You want to go home? Then you're going to have to wrestle me for the keys and drive home yourself."

Jack was angry, and she knew it. But that's what she wanted. "Now you're really being unfair," he snapped.

"You'd better believe it. But I've got your attention, now, haven't I? As I was saying: Life is not fair. Sometimes it cheats. That accident has already cheated you and me out of a great deal. But you know what? I can live with that. You know why? Because accidents *happen*. And that's life. But we have choices. We can choose how we respond to what happens. Now *you're* the one who's not playing fair. The cards are in your hands, and you're *cheating*, Jack. You're cheating me out of what I have rightfully earned in this arrangement. When life cheats, we have no choice but to buck up and face it. But if *you're* going to start cheating, I have a choice. I don't have to put up with it."

Jack glared at her as she gave him the perfect opening for telling her exactly what was bothering him. "Well, maybe it's really not a good idea for us to get married after all," he growled.

"Not if you can't have a civil conversation with me, it's not," Hilary insisted.

"Look who's talking about civil conversation."

"Better this than no conversation at all. I have a right to know what's going on inside of you, Jack. This is my life, too. And I have a right to know where my future is headed, one way or another. If you're not willing to commit yourself to me, then at least have the decency to let me know."

"It's not that, Hilary," he said. His tone was quieter, more humble.

Hilary softened her voice to match his. At least he was talking now. "Then what is it?"

"I just . . . don't know if I'm . . . right for you."

Hilary had to count to *twenty* to keep from erupting again. "That's *my* decision to make, Jack. It's *my* life."

"Well, maybe you're not seeing the full picture."

"Then help me see the full picture, Jack. If there's something I'm not getting, you're going to have to help me understand. Because I'm not giving up that easy."

Jack sighed and pushed a hand into his hair. After a length of torturous silence, he finally found the words to say, "Hilary, I know we need to make some decisions. And I know I don't make this easy. Just . . . give me a few days . . . to sort out my thoughts. Then we'll talk, okay?"

"A few days? Could we make an appointment?"

"Yes, if it would make you feel better."

"It would. How about Sunday at three?"

"Okay."

"Okay," she echoed. Then nothing more was said.

"Will you take me home now . . . please?" he asked.

"Well, at least you're being polite."

Jack smiled, hoping it would ease her anxiety. But she didn't smile back.

"There's one more thing I have to say right now," she said.

"Okay. You're not going to yell at me, are you?"

Hilary shook her head. Tears glistened in her eyes. "I love you, Jack. I want to be with you forever."

"I love you too, Hilary."

She wanted to scream, *Then marry me so we can get on with our lives*. But she only nodded and drove toward Janna's house.

Hilary was putting the groceries in the fridge when Janna came downstairs with the baby. "Where's Jack?" she asked.

"He's playing Nintendo with Matthew," Hilary said.

Janna looked at her closely. "You've been crying."

"It's that obvious?"

"Yes. Do you want to talk?"

"No, but I probably should."

Janna led the way upstairs to her bedroom, where there was no chance of Jack overhearing them. They sat together on the edge of the bed, and Hilary poured out the full burden of her concerns and frustrations. Janna listened, not saying anything until Hilary had run down. "Do you remember what I told you soon after the accident . . . about Jack's behavior?"

Hilary had to think for a minute. "You said he would try to make me prove that I really loved him in spite of everything."

"That's basically it."

"Do you really think that's what he's doing?"

"I would guess that on a conscious level, he's thinking you would be better off without him. And subconsciously, he wants validation that your love for him is real and unconditional."

As Hilary thought about Janna's theory, it made so much sense that she had to ask, "How do you figure out such things?"

Janna smiled. "I felt exactly the same way once. I was terribly unfair with Colin, for those very reasons."

"How did you get beyond it?"

"Well, after some hard knocks and some big mistakes, we finally learned what was really going on, and how to fix it. Of course, in our situation, it was Colin in your position. You can ask him, but I can tell you what he'd say."

"Tell me."

"Well, Colin would say," Janna lowered her voice to imitate her husband, "Draw your boundaries, then love him unconditionally."

"You really think Colin would say that?" Hilary asked.

"Say what?" Colin appeared in the doorway, removing his tie.

Janna stood and greeted him with a kiss. She gave him a quick overview of their conversation, then said, "So, tell Hilary what you think she should do."

"Well," Colin gave a little shrug, "I'd say you should draw firm boundaries. No matter how much he's hurting, you can't allow him to pass it on to you and treat you badly."

Hilary exchanged a knowing glance with Janna and said, "Okay. I think I'm doing that. And?"

"Then you love him unconditionally. It's the love that really gets you through."

The women exchanged another glance and Colin asked, "What?"

"Nothing," Hilary said. "I think it's good advice. Thank you." She headed toward the door and asked, "Anything else?"

"Yeah," Colin said. "Pray."

"I'm doing that, too," Hilary said, then she hurried down the stairs.

A short while later, when Hilary was about to leave, Janna said to her and Jack, "I was wondering if . . . well, a couple of times a month we like to have some friends over for dinner and to play Uno or something. We usually send the kids over to Grandma's for the night—except Jake, of course. Anyway, we were planning on doing something this Friday evening, and we'd love for the two of you to join us. In fact, we were talking about inviting Ammon and his wife over, as well."

"That sounds nice," Hilary said. "I have Fridays off. That's perfect for me."

"Jack?" Janna looked right at him.

"Sure. It sounds great. It's your home. Whatever you want to do."

"Okay." Janna turned to her husband. "I'll take care of the food. You have to call the guests."

"I think I can handle that," Colin said, winking at his wife.

Hilary left for work, and Jack kept to his room most of the evening, while fragments of his conversation with Hilary kept flashing through his mind. He'd told her they could talk on Sunday. And he knew she was right; she deserved to know where they stood one way or the other. For her sake, it was time he sorted out his feelings and got to the heart of the problem. He slept little that night, and the following day he felt distracted and confused.

On Friday morning, he came into the kitchen to find a degree of chaos. Janna was doing something at the counter with the baby in one arm, Caitlin was reading aloud to her mother between bites of cereal, and Mallory was whining for someone to pour her some milk. "Just a minute," Janna insisted. "I can only do three things at a time—or so you seem to think," she added under her breath.

"I've got it," Jack said.

Janna turned, appearing briefly startled as he poured Mallory's milk. "Oh, thank you, Jack." Then to Mallory, "What do you say to Jack?"

"Thank you, Jack," Mallory said, then she gave Jack a toothless smile that made him laugh.

"You're welcome, Mallory."

Janna set the baby on the floor, saying to him, "You're just going to have to manage for a few minutes while I finish packing these lunches."

The baby immediately started to cry and Jack said, "Will he let me hold him?"

"Of course," Janna said, quickly lifting the baby onto his lap. He almost wished he hadn't offered when his desire for children of his own rose up to taunt him. But in his heart, he knew he had to face the things that were eating at him. He had to be prepared to tell Hilary exactly why he didn't want her burdened by what he could—and couldn't—bring into her life.

When Friday evening came, Jack was hoping Hilary would arrive first so he wouldn't be left to socialize without her. But his hopes were dashed when an unfamiliar couple arrived. Jack was drying a couple of pans that Janna had just washed when he heard Colin answer the door, then he heard joking and laughing. This couple followed Colin into the kitchen as he said, "Jack, I want you to meet some very good friends of ours. This is Dr. Sean O'Hara and his wife, Tara. Sean, Tara—this is Jack Hayden. He's temporarily part of the family."

"It's a pleasure to meet you, Jack," Sean O'Hara said with a hearty handshake.

"And you," Jack said.

"Hello," Tara said, and Jack returned the greeting. If Hilary wasn't going to arrive soon, he hoped that at least Ammon would. Jack wasn't much for socializing with people he didn't know. He followed Colin and Sean to the family room, thinking he could at least listen to them visit and not have to actively participate. Then Janna hollered, "Colin, I need you for a minute."

"Be right back," he said and hurried away.

Sean was quick to say, "This temporary family thing is great. I had one myself once . . . well, actually, they still seem like family. We've kept in close touch."

"That's nice," Jack said when the silence indicated he needed to say *something*. "They treat me well. I can't complain." More silence prompted Jack to ask, "So, what kind of doctor are you? I'm afraid I've dealt with quite a few lately."

Sean chuckled. "I'm a psychologist, actually."

"Oh," Jack drawled, "I've dealt with a few of those, too."

"Ooh," Sean said facetiously, "some of us can be pretty scary."

"Some are scarier than others."

Colin returned just as the doorbell rang, and Jack was relieved to see Hilary, who came in without waiting for an answer. "Hello, Hilary," Janna called from the kitchen.

"Sorry, I'm late," she said to Jack, bending over to kiss him. Before Colin was finished introducing Hilary to Sean and Tara, the doorbell rang again. Janna answered it and led Ammon and his wife, Allison, back to the family room.

Janna had just begun introductions when Allison squealed, "What are *you* doing here?"

Sean got up and crossed the room, laughing as he said to her, "I was about to ask you the same thing."

They laughed and hugged tightly while Janna said, "I take it the two of you know each other."

"Yeah, you could say that," Sean said, then he laughed and hugged Allison again.

Over dinner, Sean O'Hara told the story of how he'd come to Utah after joining the Church and being disowned by his family because of it. He explained how Allison's family had taken him in and helped him through some tough challenges. They'd been like a second family to him ever since. "Allison's as good as my sister," Sean said.

"Well, it certainly is a small world," Colin commented.

"It certainly is," Allison added.

"And isn't it amazing how we've each had our own struggles?" Janna said.

Jack briefly caught the exchange of glances around the table. He felt certain that every one of these people knew the meaning of adversity, yet each of them seemed so confident and strong at the moment. He wondered if he could ever feel that way about himself again. Of course, no matter how he adjusted to his circumstances, Jack knew that his trial was permanent. He could never get beyond it. He only prayed that he could learn to cope.

CHAPTER TWELVE

Saturday was a long day for Jack. While he knew that Colin, Matthew, and Ammon were busy moving all of Hilary's belongings—and his—into the new apartment, he helped watch Janna's children while she prepared a meal that she could take over later.

About four o'clock, Janna said, "I'm going over there with the food. Want to come along and see how it's going?"

"Sure," he said, wondering if it would be better if he just stayed out of everyone's way.

They arrived at the apartment to find Colin and Ammon taking the couch out of the back of Ammon's truck. "It's about time you showed up!" Ammon hollered lightly as Janna went inside with a pan of lasagna. "We could use some help here."

"What do you want me to do?" Jack hollered back. "Supervise?"

"Exactly!"

"Looks like you're doing fine to me." Just as Jack said it, Ammon nearly dropped his end of the couch. "Well, on second thought . . ." They all laughed and he added, "That's okay. It's an ugly couch anyway."

Jack followed the couch into the apartment, surprised to find it looking relatively livable. Allison was sitting on the kitchen floor, putting pots and pans into a cupboard. Janna was setting paper plates and cups out on the table. And he found Hilary in the bathroom, scrubbing the bathtub. "Hello, beautiful," he said.

Hilary looked up and grinned. "Welcome home."

Jack glanced around. He wasn't going to say anything about that one way or the other until they had a chance to talk tomorrow. "Everything looks great."

"I've had good help. It's all gone pretty smoothly. The other apartment is all emptied out; I just have to go back Monday and finish up some cleaning. And I think I'll be settled in here enough to cope before bedtime."

"Good." He cleared his throat. "I don't suppose there's anything I can do."

"Sure there is." With no hesitation, she handed him a rag and a can of cleanser. "You can give that sink a good scrubbing while I help Janna put dinner out."

"That takes a lot of muscle," he said with light sarcasm. "I don't know if I'm up to it."

Hilary kissed him quickly and smiled. "I'm sure you'll manage."

When Jack was finished with the job, he went to the front room, where they were about to bless the food. "Jack?" Hilary said.

"What?"

"This is your home—in essence. You should ask someone to say the blessing."

Jack was momentarily caught off guard. He glanced around, then felt compelled to offer the prayer himself. In it he expressed gratitude for all they had been blessed with, most especially good friends.

The meal was a big hit, but while everyone was sitting on the floor to eat, Ammon pointed at Jack and said, "How come *he* doesn't have to sit on the floor?"

"'Cause I'm the only one who brought my own chair," Jack retorted like a snotty schoolboy.

"The other chairs are in the back of the truck, if anyone wants one," Colin said.

"I like this," Jack said. "It's the first time in months that I've felt taller than everybody else in the room."

They all laughed, but Hilary wondered if anyone else could see the truth behind Jack's humor. He'd been joking and laughing ever since the accident, but she felt certain there was a great deal going on inside of him that wasn't funny at all. Recalling that he'd agreed to talk to her tomorrow afternoon, she felt a sudden chill. She only prayed they could get beyond whatever was holding them back and get on with their lives. She knew in her heart she was supposed to be Jack Hayden's wife, and she would not rest easy until she was. She felt as if everything else was in limbo until that happened.

While everyone pitched in to finish unloading the trucks and put things in order as much as possible, Jack put books on the bookshelf and folded the linens that the dishes had been packed in. When everyone was getting ready to leave, Hilary offered to take Jack home later. But he insisted that she was tired and didn't need to go out again tonight, so he'd ride home with Janna. He didn't tell her that until they cleared the air between them, he wasn't completely comfortable alone with her. The thought saddened him, but he didn't know what to do about it.

"I'll pick you up at three tomorrow," Hilary said to Jack as he headed out the door.

"I'll be ready," he said, and they exchanged a brief kiss.

The following morning, Jack went to church with the Trevor family. He'd declined their earlier offers to take him, which made this his first time at church since the accident. It was even more difficult than he had anticipated. People were kind and friendly, but he recognized the same subtle glances he'd received on his few little jaunts into the outside world with Hilary. Some glances were full of pity; some held a subtle disdain, as though his very existence reminded people of things they didn't want to look at or think about. Only a few individuals were completely genuine with him, and those were the greetings he truly appreciated.

On a spiritual level, Jack found sitting through the meetings difficult. He'd never had trouble trusting God, and he certainly wasn't foolish enough to blame God for what had happened to him. But he had too many unanswered questions to even consider being at peace with himself. And if he couldn't be at peace with himself, he certainly wasn't going to find any peace with God. So he felt just plain uncomfortable. But then, that about wrapped up his whole life now: he just felt uncomfortable. It only took a glance at his lower body to remind him that it wasn't what it was supposed to be. It was like wearing something stiff and restrictive, and wondering if he'd ever be able to break it in enough to be comfortable.

After church and dinner with the family, Matthew washed the mixing bowls and pans that wouldn't fit in the dishwasher, and Jack dried them. He found Matthew to be unusually mature for his age, and they actually got along fairly well. Jack wondered, as he watched the boy now, if there was something in the past his mother had described earlier that had made Matthew more sensitive and somber than the average teenager.

Jack had barely put the dishes away in a lower cupboard when Hilary came to get him. He felt poorly prepared and more than a little nervous. As they drove she said, "It's pretty cold out. Do you mind if we go back to the apartment?"

"No, that's fine," was all he said.

"You worked some more last night," he said as he entered the front room to find it looking very much like the front room of the apartment he'd lived in before the accident.

"Yes," Hilary sat on the couch, "I wanted to be able to relax today, and I knew I couldn't if my surroundings were too horrible."

Following an awkward silence, Hilary said, "I assume you want me to start."

"You *are* the talkative one."

"That's funny, I always thought *you* were the talkative one. When you used to drive me back and forth to Provo, you talked nonstop, telling me how I needed to get my life in order and get on with it." Hilary felt the irony as she added, "Funny how things change."

"They certainly do."

"Okay," she said with determination, "if you want me to start, I will. I just need to know where we stand, Jack. We've spent a lot of weeks just taking it one day at a time because we had no choice. Well, our choices are opening up here. I need something to hold on to; a goal. Is that too much to ask?"

He said nothing, and she went on. "You know, this apartment is more yours than mine, Jack. If things aren't going to work out, I can certainly move elsewhere. I'm sure you could manage. You can get some disability compensation; get a grant; go back to school. You'd do fine, I'm sure, but . . ."

"But?" He sounded angry. Hilary shrugged her shoulders and he said, "What are you trying to say?"

"I'm trying to tell you that there are always options. You don't need me to survive, Jack. And I can certainly find another place to live when you're ready to be independent. Whatever we decide to do can't be based on such things. I just want to know where we stand so we can set some goals. But we can't do that if you don't tell me how you feel."

"Okay, but . . . maybe we need to define *goal* here. My goals lately have had a pretty narrow focus. I never would have imagined having to set a goal to get from my bed into a chair without falling on my face. Or to put my own pants on without any help. Most people don't have to set a goal to get into the car in less than fifteen minutes."

Hilary was taken aback. She'd certainly been as aware of his struggles as anyone. But the reality made her stop and remember to remain empathetic through this conversation.

"Okay," she said, "and now that you're doing so much better with those things, what do you see in the future—for you?"

"For me?" He laughed with a bitter edge. "I honestly don't know, Hilary. I know I should say that I'll buckle down and go back to school, and try to learn something I can do to make a living. But I can't even comprehend what I could possibly do without going insane. I haven't thought that far yet. I know I've got to face it, and I will. I have no intention of being your charity case for the rest of my life, so—"

"You are hardly that."

"Then who exactly is supporting me?"

"If it were the other way around, you would support me and you know it."

"Yes, I would. But it's different."

"And how is that?"

"I'm a man. I'm *supposed* to be the provider."

"Oh, so the problem is pride," she said with an edge to her voice.

"Pride?" He laughed. "I don't have any pride left, Hilary."

"The hell you don't," she replied so fast and so firm that he was stunned. "You *reek* of pride, Jack Hayden. And if it's not pride that's keeping you from marrying me, then exactly what is it?"

Still Jack said nothing.

"That is what we need to talk about most, isn't it? It's evident to me that you are avoiding anything to do with the commitment we made before the accident. From my perspective, I can only guess it's difficult for you to realize that our marriage will not be conventional."

"That's an understatement," he growled. "I have nothing to give you, Hilary. *Nothing!*"

"Define nothing."

"I can't provide a living, for one thing."

"That's only temporary. I'm not the first wife who has worked to support her husband through college. You can cross that one off the list."

"I can't do any of the things around the house that a man should be able to do."

"So, we'll hire somebody to do those things. That's pride talking if I ever heard it. Some men just don't know how to do those things, and some men just don't want to. Now, why don't you tell me the *real* reason."

Jack turned to look elsewhere, and she knew she was hitting close to a nerve—a nerve that he'd been steering her away from for weeks. In an attempt to lighten the mood, she added, "The only difference I can see that matters is that you're shorter than me now."

"Is that supposed to be funny?" he asked.

"Yes, actually."

"Well, I don't think it's funny. And if that's pride, so be it. But everything I've always been, everything I wanted to be for you, is gone."

"No, Jack. Everything you have been for me is right here." She pressed a hand to his chest. "All those times you were there for me, letting me cry, listening to my hurts, soothing away my fears, teaching me to believe in myself. Those are the things that make me love you, Jack. And those have nothing to do with your spinal cord. I love you, Jack, for who and what you are. How many times do I have to say it to make you believe me?"

"I don't know, Hilary. Maybe there's a part of me that just can't quite believe you'd really stick it out with me . . . the way I am now."

"Why? If it were the other way around, would you abandon me?"

"No."

"So, why would you credit me with having so little character that I would back out on you because you can't walk?"

"It's more complicated than that, Hil. Not walking is only part of the problem."

"It's irrelevant to a good relationship."

"Not necessarily."

Hilary began to feel confused and went back to her question. "Why, Jack? Why would you even think I would desert you in this?"

Hilary leaned close to him and took his hand. He had no choice but to look inside himself and come up with an honest answer. It came quickly to his tongue, but it refused to be voiced without accompanying emotion. Moisture burned into his eyes as he said, "Maybe because the only other women I've loved have done exactly that."

Hilary felt a new level of understanding fall into place. Why had she never seen it before? His mother had abandoned him emotionally when he'd turned his life to values she didn't share. And Lorie had left so many broken promises in his life that they were impossible to count. "Oh, Jack," she said, pressing a hand to his face, "I mean it when I say I want to be with you forever. And I would do everything in my power to make it work."

"I know, Hilary. I really do. But . . ." He gathered his courage and moved toward the point that he knew had to be reached. "I wonder if you really comprehend the sacrifices you'd be making. If I can't give you what you need to be happy, I don't want to hurt either of us by pretending I can."

Hilary was about to jump in again with reminders of all that he *could* give her, but his expression was so severe that she knew he was getting to the heart of what was troubling him. She waited patiently while he pushed a hand through his hair and rubbed nervous fingers over his thigh. "This is really hard for me," he admitted with a quiver in his voice that made her heart ache.

"It's okay," she said, taking his hand.

Jack drew back his shoulders and just said it. "I can't be a husband to you, Hilary. Not like I should be."

"And what if we had already been married?"

"I thank heaven we weren't."

She knew he was getting to a point, but she felt compelled to say, "I considered my commitment to you eternal the moment I told you I would be your wife."

Jack sighed. He really hated this. "Hilary, don't you understand?"

"Not if you don't help me understand."

"I can't be a *husband* to you."

"You already said that."

"I know, but . . ." He looked frustrated. "You're certainly not making this any easier."

"I'm sorry, Jack, but I'm lost here."

"Okay," he said, "you want the bottom line? I'll give you the bottom line." He leaned close to her and lowered his voice. "We cannot be physically intimate, Hilary."

Hilary was so stunned that it took her a full minute to absorb the implication. She had to use great self-control to keep from laughing. *He was serious.* "What are you trying to say, Jack? Are your lips paralyzed?"

"Hilary," his voice lowered further, as if he feared being overheard, "we cannot have a sexual relationship."

He expected her to somehow be shocked or upset. But she matter-of-factly asked, "Who told you that?"

"I don't have to be a rocket scientist to figure out the obvious." He repeated it as if she was a child and he was trying to be patient. "We cannot have a sexual relationship, Hilary."

Hilary's eyes didn't even flicker as she retorted firmly, "Oh, yes we can. Marry me, and I'll prove it."

Jack looked so surprised that Hilary couldn't hold back a little laugh. "What?" she questioned. "Did you think it had never crossed my mind?"

"Maybe I did."

"Well, it's not only crossed my mind, but I've been doing my research. I mean . . . I understand that intimacy should be as much emotional as physical, but I also understand that the physical aspect is an important part of a good marriage. Now, if . . ." She stopped as she realized what she was about to say. Jack already looked stunned. She felt she had to ask, "May I speak candidly here? At the risk of embarrassing myself, there are some things I believe should be clarified."

Jack motioned with his hand for her to continue.

"I know you are not capable of feeling anything below the waist, Jack, but your body is still capable of functioning."

Hilary hoped he could read between the lines and understand what she meant. She had no desire to spell it out in black and white. His expression was so completely incredulous that she had to clarify, "You didn't know?"

Jack couldn't answer. He was too busy attempting to absorb this revelation. His heart quickened as he leaned forward. "Are you telling me that . . . we can . . ."

Hilary nodded firmly, sparing him from having to say it. Jack leaned back and pressed a hand over his mouth as emotion rushed to his throat. Hilary took his other hand, and he gripped it tightly. "No one ever told *me* that," he muttered.

"Maybe you never asked."

Jack chuckled to avoid crying. "Apparently you did."

"Yes, I did. And next time you talk to the doctor, I think you should ask. He can explain it better than I can—without getting embarrassed."

Jack nodded, but she sensed he was too emotional to speak. "I take it this makes a difference," she said calmly.

"Yes," his voice cracked, "it makes a difference. I didn't want you to go your whole life without ever experiencing such things."

"And what about you, Jack?"

"I can go a long way on just holding you close, Hilary. I just want your life to be full and complete."

"You really do love me, don't you, Jack."

"Of course I love you. That's why it's so difficult to bring such a burden into your life."

Hilary searched between the lines and realized that while she was concentrating on the emotional and spiritual aspects of their relationship, Jack had been measuring everything in physical increments.

"Listen to me, Jack. I need to make something perfectly clear. Even if you had *nothing* left—if you had broken your neck and severed your spinal cord and there was nothing physical left at all, I would still love you. I went to the Lord a long time ago and asked him if it was right for me to stay with you, because I didn't want to lead you on or promise something I wasn't capable of giving. I understand that some things will be more of a challenge for us. But I also understand the eternal perspective, Jack. When forever comes, you will be whole and strong, and we will be together. Do you comprehend what that means?"

"Yes, I do, Hilary. But we have a lifetime to get through first. And I want you to be happy."

"Then marry me, Jack. Being a part of your life is what I need to make me happy. I want *you*, Jack, and I don't consider it a burden." She knelt beside him and took his hands into hers. "I would consider it a privilege to die for you, Jack. Let me *live* for you. Let me be there for you—to help you through this."

While Jack felt immensely grateful for the evidence of her love and commitment, he felt he had to say, "Hilary . . ." He urged her onto his lap, and she laid her head against his shoulder. "Sometimes I just feel . . . dead inside. It's like . . . even if I'm physically capable of something, can I make you happy if I . . ."

"What?" she urged gently.

"It's so hard to explain. It's just that . . . I always felt such a passion for life; such a desire to experience things, and feel things, and . . . now it's like that part of me is dead."

Hilary looked into his eyes. "Everything's still there, Jack. It may take time to find it all again. But there's no connection between your spinal cord and your spirit. And it has nothing to do with your passion for life. It's still there. I know it is."

Jack had to ask, "And what about my passion for you?"

"What about it?"

"What if . . ."

Before he could finish, Hilary pressed her mouth over his and pushed a hand into his hair. She kissed him like she'd never dared kiss him before, if only to prove her point. She felt his response even more quickly than she'd expected. His breathing quickened as he pressed his hands to her back, urging her closer. It wasn't difficult for her to find the pulse in his neck, and she pressed her fingers against the evidence of his quickened heart rate. She drew back just far enough to look into his eyes as they opened with a dreamy glaze.

"You seem pretty alive to me," she said.

Jack barely managed to nod as he absorbed what he was feeling. He hadn't felt this alive since the last time he'd been able to stand and hold Hilary in his arms.

She sighed and touched the side of his forehead. "Maybe there's more to passion up here than you realize."

"Maybe there is," he said, his voice husky.

"I rest my case."

Jack sighed and hugged her tightly, wishing he'd been smart enough to talk to her about all of this a long time ago.

"And you know what else, Jack?"

"What?"

"If you can function sexually, you can father children."

Jack looked into her eyes, hardly daring to believe it. "You're serious."

"That's what the doctor said. He told me it might be a challenge, and it could take some time and extra effort. But he said there is no reason why you couldn't have a family." Hilary smiled. "So, unless there's something wrong with me, I think we'll have children."

Jack looked into her eyes, unable to find words to express his joy. He hugged her tightly, murmuring close to her ear, "I just assumed . . . it wasn't possible."

Hilary looked into his eyes, clarifying what she felt was an important point. "Jack, even if we couldn't have our own children, I would still want to be your wife. I believe there are always options."

She snuggled close to him, wanting to stay in his arms forever. She felt him kiss the side of her face and urge her closer still before he said, "There's one more thing I have to ask you, Hilary."

"I'm listening."

"Will you marry me?"

Hilary couldn't even answer before emotion overcame her. His proposal was the marking of a great milestone. She was so happy that all she could do was hold him and cry.

"Hey," he lifted her chin to look at her, "you didn't answer my question."

"How about tomorrow?"

Jack laughed. "The temple is closed on Mondays."

"Okay, Tuesday," she said, and they laughed together.

"No, seriously," Jack said, "let's talk about this."

"Okay, but first I have to blow my nose."

Hilary went into the bathroom and came back to find Jack sitting on the couch. "You know, this is a really ugly couch," he said.

"Yes, but . . . it works. Where did you get it, anyway?"

"It was handed down from an aunt. She's very sweet, but her taste in furniture is somewhat lacking."

Hilary snuggled up next to Jack and said, "We were talking about getting married."

He smiled so naturally that he seemed more like himself than he had in a very long time. "So we were. How long would it take to pull a wedding together . . . realistically? I mean, we had it all planned once, right?"

"Well, the important thing is scheduling the temple and the cultural hall, and getting the announcements printed and mailed. The printer told me they'd keep our announcement on file; they can just change the date. I think everything else can be thrown together pretty quickly."

"Okay, so how long?"

"Let's see . . . announcements should be sent out two weeks before the wedding, and—"

"Hilary, how long?"

"I don't know exactly, but . . ."

"What I want to know is . . . can we be married before Christmas?"

She smiled. "I don't see why not. It's not even Thanksgiving yet."

"Good, because I want to spend Christmas here . . . with you."

Hilary laughed and hugged him tightly. They spent the remainder of the day making plans, and set the date tentatively for December sixteenth—a weekday, when there would more likely be time available at the temple on such short notice.

When Hilary took Jack home, Colin and Janna were thrilled to hear the good news. "I'm sure going to miss all the work you do around here," Janna said.

"And the kids are going to miss you, too," Colin added. "We're leaving that ramp there as long as the house stands." He pointed a finger at Jack. "We expect you to come and visit frequently."

"Hey, if you feed us, we'll come anytime," Jack said, and Hilary laughed. She felt as if she truly had him back; and if not completely, at least they'd made a lot of progress.

That evening Hilary made some phone calls, then she called Jack to tell him they were spending Thanksgiving with her parents. "That's a nice thought, Hilary," he said, "but—"

"It's all taken care of, Jack. Ammon's going down Tuesday to help Dad build a ramp. He said business is slow anyway. Dad's had the materials for weeks. Do you think my parents could live without you ever coming to visit? They love you."

"I know they do. Sometimes I just feel like people are too good to me."

"You know, Jack, in the long run I believe people get out of life what they put into it. Do you know how many times I've heard my father say that he almost felt guilty for everything you've done to help him all these years? If people treat you well, Jack, it's because you deserve it, and you've earned it. So let's just keep thanking God for all we've got, and we'll get through just fine."

"Okay. And tell your parents I'm really looking forward to Thanksgiving."

"Yeah, I will. I'm looking forward to it, too."

By Tuesday, Hilary had most of their wedding plans in motion. The announcements had been ordered, and arrangements had been made with the Manti Temple and the church building in Mt. Pleasant where they would have the reception. The address labels had never been put on the old announcements, and were waiting in a box along with the postage stamps. A few phone calls was all it took to reactivate orders that Hilary had made months ago.

Jack felt a mixture of emotions as they made the drive to Mt. Pleasant for Thanksgiving, knowing the last time he'd traversed these roads had been in an ambulance. Difficult memories assaulted him as they passed the field where the accident happened, but the house soon came into view and he shifted his attention to being *home* again. This place was truly more like home to him than his own home had ever been, and he reminded Hilary of that as they pulled up beside the house. The ramp was easily accessible, and Jack commented as he broke it in, "That Ammon is a clever boy."

"It never hurts to have friends in high places."

Before they got to the door, Pete and Millie came out in a flurry of excitement. Jack actually felt emotional at the evidence of their love and support, but he managed to keep from crying—unlike Millie, who was so happy to see him that her eyes leaked for ten minutes.

Jack thoroughly enjoyed being here, where he'd always felt so comfortable. Once or twice he thought of his mother and brothers and wondered what they were doing; then it occurred to him that he really didn't care. He just uttered a silent prayer of thanks for being given so much to compensate for all he had lost.

Jack insisted that he wasn't eating if he didn't earn his keep. He was put to work at the table peeling yams and potatoes, while other members of Hilary's family slowly filtered in from out of town. They all greeted him enthusiastically, and expressed genuine pleasure at the announcement of their newly scheduled wedding date. Hilary's little nieces and nephews showed varying degrees of curiosity about Jack's condition, but little Mallory had given him a great deal of experience and he was able to answer their questions easily.

While Pete offered the blessing over their Thanksgiving meal, Jack held Hilary's hand beneath the table and felt the warmth of the Spirit surrounding him. He truly did have much to be thankful for.

After dinner, Jack was given the assignment of entertaining the children. He lay on the front room floor and read stories aloud, while the kids took turns sitting in his chair. "How are you going to get back in the chair?" one of the children asked.

"I was wonderin' that myself," Pete piped up from where he was sitting in his favorite armchair.

"They taught us a few tricks before he left the hospital," Hilary said. Rather than explaining, she just helped Jack into the chair.

By using Hilary for leverage, he could make the maneuver without putting much weight on her. It was a little awkward, but Jack laughed and said, "We're getting better at this."

"We make a good team," she said and kissed his nose.

"What if you were alone?" one of the children asked.

"I don't know," Jack chuckled. "I've never gotten on the floor when I was alone. It could be scary."

By evening, everyone had gone home except for Jack and Hilary. Pete dozed off on the couch while Jack sat close by, reading a magazine. Hilary sat in the kitchen with her mother, going over wedding details. Millie seemed pleased with the plans, and there was no question about her love and acceptance of Jack, although she admitted quietly, "I know this is the right thing for you, honey, and there is no man on earth as good for you as Jack. I only hope your life together won't be too difficult."

"Everybody has struggles, Mother. People get married all the time with no idea that their spouse is going to contract some disease or get in an accident. Children are born with problems. I don't think of this as taking on something difficult. I look at it more as keeping life from getting . . . dull." She laughed softly when she said it, feeling a little tingle inside at the thought of being married to Jack.

"I don't question your ability to take care of Jack," Millie said. "You're a strong girl with a strong will, and you can do anything you—"

"I'm not going to take care of Jack, Mother. Not any more than he's going to take care of me, at least. Jack is going to take care of himself."

"Is that possible?" Millie seemed astonished.

"Of course it is. We've gotten to know many people, with injuries far more severe, who do very well at taking care of themselves. Of course, it will take some time for him to completely adjust, but he's doing well."

Millie gave a pleasant sigh. "That's wonderful. I guess there's a lot about such things that I don't know."

"Well, I would prefer that you ask so we can talk about it, rather than assuming."

"I don't want to make Jack uncomfortable—or you. If—"

Jack appeared in the kitchen doorway. "*Jack,*" he said facetiously, "would prefer that you talk about it as opposed to pretending that everything is the same." Millie blushed as he pointed a finger at her, smirking adorably. "I heard you talking about me. Shame on you."

Millie stammered quickly, "Oh, Jack . . . I . . . I . . ."

Jack moved close to her and gave her a hug. "I'm teasing you, Millie. You can say anything you want about me . . . as long as it's true. You can ask me anything you want, too." He moved around her and opened the fridge. "Is there any of that pie left? I can hear it calling me."

"Oh, there's plenty. I'll just—"

"I can get it." He pulled out the pie and handed it to Hilary, who was sitting at arm's length. "Where's the cream?"

"It's up on the—"

"Oh, I see it." Jack barely managed to reach it, then he turned to the table where dessert plates had been left. While he served himself a piece of pie, Pete came into the kitchen.

"Did I hear somethin' about pie?" he asked.

Pete dished himself a piece of pie. Hilary said she didn't want any, then she ate half of Jack's and he scowled at her as he got himself another piece and smothered it with whipped cream. They talked about the wedding plans and told Pete and Millie about their new apartment. "I wish we could have made it up to help you move," Pete said.

"Oh, that's okay," Jack said lightly, "Hilary did a great job."

"Yes," she said, "I'm great at rounding up cheap labor. All they wanted was food, and Janna took care of that."

"You have good friends," Millie said.

"We certainly do," Jack agreed. Then he nodded toward her. "And good family."

"Ammon certainly seems like a nice young man," Millie said. "When he came to build the ramp, he also fixed that cupboard door. And he wouldn't let us pay him a dime."

"He's like that," Jack said.

"Reminds me of someone else I know," Pete said, glaring comically at Jack.

Jack smirked. "I was just storing up brownie points for now, with the hope that I could keep eating Millie's pie."

"Well, he won't be getting any pie from me," Hilary said. "I never was much good at baking."

"Maybe *I* should start baking," Jack said.

"It's the only way you'll get anything home-baked without coming to Mt. Pleasant," Hilary said.

"I'll give you lessons," Millie added.

"I might take you up on that," Jack said.

"It would be a pleasure." Millie practically beamed.

"I know," Jack's eyes widened with exaggerated enlightenment, "I could be Mr. Mom and take care of the kids while you go to work, Hilary."

She caught a typical undertone in his voice that she was beginning to understand well. In spite of her parents' presence, she called him on it. "You could never be happy with that, and I know it. Your jokes might fool everybody else, but they don't fool me."

Jack leaned back, his expression so severe that it was tempting for Hilary to regret what she'd said. But she didn't.

"Hilary," Millie said, "maybe this isn't a good time for the two of you to—"

"It's a perfectly good time," she said gently. Then to Jack, "They're as good as your own parents—better, in fact. You've admitted so yourself. But if you would rather discuss this later, just say so."

"It's fine," Jack said. "And you're right. I don't think I could be content at home, taking care of the kids all the time. And I certainly don't want you supporting me for the rest of my life. But the idea of sitting behind a desk or a computer for the rest of my life seems worse."

Hilary's parents seemed slightly uncomfortable, but she was glad it had been brought up when Millie said, "This is much harder for you than you let on, isn't it, Jack."

Jack looked at her intently. "Yes, I suppose it is."

"But you're doin' good, Jack," Pete said. "So much better than I thought you would."

"Yes," Jack said, "but . . ." He thought of a whole string of things he could say; things that were rolling around in his head continually. But he settled for, "It's just hard."

Hilary took his hand across the table and squeezed it.

Pete cleared his throat and said, "There's somethin' I've wondered about . . . and I did hear you say we could ask you anything."

"Go for it," Jack said.

"Well," Pete said, "when you were talkin' about stayin' at home with kids, I . . . well, does that mean you'll try to adopt, or . . ."

After weeks of believing differently, it warmed Jack to be able to say, "I lucked out on that one, Pete. Apparently it's still possible for me to father children."

"Really?" Millie erupted with a little giggle.

"Really," Hilary said.

"I talked to the doctor about it a couple of days ago," Jack said. "He told me that injuries can vary a great deal, and the nervous system is a tricky thing. But he believes everything is in order in that respect."

Pete smiled. "Well, that certainly is a blessing."

"Yes, it is," Jack agreed. Then he turned to Hilary. "We have much to be grateful for."

It was difficult to leave Mt. Pleasant that night, but Jack assured Pete and Millie that when he got just a little more independent, he and Hilary would be able to come and spend the night.

The remainder of the weekend was more fun than either of them had had in months. On Friday, they helped Janna and Colin put up their Christmas tree and make fruitcakes. Then they all went to the latest Disney movie and out for hamburgers. On Saturday they went shopping and bought a little tree for their apartment and some minimal decorations. When the apartment was decorated, they watched a movie and fixed a spaghetti dinner together.

On Sunday they went to church together in their new ward. Again Jack felt a variety of attitudes directed subtly toward him. But there were many kind greetings, and the bishop was warm and friendly. He seemed pleased that they were getting married—especially when they told him it would be in the temple.

On Monday Hilary ran some errands, then stopped at Janna's house to see Jack. Her first surprise was to find the door locked. She rang the bell and got no answer. It was rare that Jack went anywhere with Janna or Colin, but he obviously had. Wondering what to do, she decided to at least try the back door. It too was locked, but she found a note taped there. Her nerves reacted before she even read the hurriedly scribbled message: *Hilary, We tried to call. We're at the hospital. Janna.*

"Oh, help," Hilary muttered and ran back to the car. She nearly started to cry when she couldn't find a parking place at the hospital, wondering what on earth had gone wrong. Running the long distance from where she'd parked to the main lobby, she considered the possibility that perhaps this had nothing to do with Jack. She wasn't even sure what to say once she finally made it to the information counter, completely out of breath. She sputtered an uncertain, "Was a Jack Hayden admitted today?"

Praying she would be told *no*, Hilary's heart fell as she heard, "Yes, he's in room 717."

"Thank you," Hilary said, and found herself trembling before she even got to the elevator. *Please, not now,* she muttered to herself. *Not when we're finally so close to getting married. Please, don't let something happen now.* Hurrying down a long hall on the seventh floor, she was assailed by thoughts of all the possible complications she'd learned about that were associated with paralysis.

She found Janna sitting in a chair reading, just outside room 717. "What happened?" Hilary insisted in a shaky voice.

Janna looked up, startled. Then she smiled. "You must have found my note."

"Yes, I found your note. What happened?"

Janna stood and took hold of Hilary's shoulders. "Now, calm down. It's not that serious."

"Is he . . ." She motioned toward the door.

"There's a nurse with him. You can see him in a few minutes. Just calm down."

Hilary forced herself to breathe slowly. "Okay. Tell me."

"He's got an infection. He might not have even needed to be hospitalized, but the doctor wanted to get some antibiotics going through an IV and get on top of it quickly, so it wouldn't get out of hand . . . especially since he's supposed to get married soon. That's exactly what the doctor said. Everything's going to be okay."

Hilary sighed and nearly collapsed in the chair Janna had been sitting in. "Oh my gosh, Janna, if anything happens to keep this wedding from taking place again, I think I'll lose my mind. He deserves to be healthy and enjoy his life."

"And he will," Janna insisted. "Colin and Ammon are coming in after work to give him a priesthood blessing. He's going to be just fine."

Now that her worst fears had been assuaged, Hilary asked, "What kind of infection?"

Janna sat beside her. "You learned about pressure sores."

"Yes, but remind me."

"If the body weight isn't shifted regularly, pressure develops in a certain area and the skin and tissue start to break down. Jack's been mostly taking care of himself the last few days, so we don't know when it started. But last night . . . well, apparently the catheter had some leakage, and complicated the problem, which is on his hip. He woke up this morning with a fever, and he's going to have to pretty much stay down until it heals. It *can* be very serious, Hilary. But we're getting it under control, and he's going to be fine."

"He's not in any pain?"

"No. If he could feel it, he would have sensed discomfort long before it got out of hand. But he's going to need to learn to shift his weight more frequently to keep it from happening again. It's a habit he's going to have to develop. I think this will give him some motivation."

The nurse came out of Jack's room, and Hilary shot to her feet as she asked, "Is he okay?"

"Oh, yeah." The nurse smiled kindly. "You must be Hilary."

"That's right."

"He told me I'd better take good care of him, because he had a date with Hilary that he wasn't going to miss." The nurse smiled again. "Must be a pretty important date."

"Yes," Hilary said, fighting back a sudden rush of emotion.

"A wedding date," Janna provided. "On the sixteenth."

"Ooh," the nurse said. "Well, I'm sure he'll be there. He's pretty determined." She motioned toward the door. "You can go on in."

"Hey," Janna stopped Hilary with a hand on her arm, "I've got to get back and pick up Jake."

"Thank you." Hilary hugged Janna tightly. "I don't know what we would ever do without you."

"I'm glad I'm here," Janna said, then she urged Hilary into the room.

Jack looked up from where he lay on his side to see Hilary standing near the bed, looking as if she was either going to burst into tears or hit him.

"What?" he asked, and she burst into tears. She quickly found her way to his shoulder, and he just held her while she cried. When she didn't stop, he couldn't help chuckling.

"This is not funny!" she insisted and hit him, albeit lightly. "I was scared to death!"

"Well, I was a little scared myself, but I'm going to be fine—honest. I am going to be at that wedding if it kills me."

"A lot of good that would do me," she said.

"I'll be there," he repeated and kissed her.

CHAPTER THIRTEEN

*J*ack was released from the hospital a few days later with strict instructions, some powerful antibiotics, and a strong determination to never let it happen again. He knew that by forming good, strong habits of doing regular weight shifts, the problem could be avoided. And he never wanted to feel this sick again. As restricted as he felt in a wheelchair, being confined to bed made the chair awfully appealing.

Jack recuperated well, and found that he was greatly anticipating his wedding day. He'd come to terms with the feelings that had held him back, and he knew in his heart this was right—for both of them. But he found he was nervous concerning certain aspects of his marriage that would be unique. He mentioned it to Colin, hoping that another man might be able to help.

Colin was easy to talk to, and Jack didn't feel the least bit uncomfortable, even when Janna joined their conversation. From the perspective of her medical training, she encouraged him to just talk to Hilary about his concerns. She suggested that open communication could prevent either of them from having distorted expectations. "Your situation is unique," she said, "but certainly workable."

"Personally," Colin said, taking his wife's hand, "I think physical intimacy that is void of anything emotional or spiritual, really isn't worth much."

Jack thought of his relationship with Lorie and uttered a silent *amen*.

"Just like everything else you deal with," Colin went on, "I would think if you focus on making the most of what you have, and concentrating on the emotional aspects, you can't go wrong."

Jack agreed, and he did feel better. But he still felt apprehensive. Talking to Hilary wasn't as embarrassing as he thought it would be, and she reminded him that the consummation of a marriage was something sacred—a wonderful gift from God. It was certainly nothing to be treated lightly, and she was glad for his willingness to talk about it so they could both be realistically prepared to handle a unique situation.

The Sunday before the wedding, Jack had recovered completely from his infection, and Janna invited Hilary over for dinner. When the meal was finished and the children had dispersed, they discussed the final preparations for the wedding. Hilary had canceled her dance lessons for the entire week, giving them time for a brief honeymoon.

Everything was under control, but Hilary felt nervous, as any bride-to-be would. Still, she had only to look at Jack and catch the anticipation in his eyes to know beyond any doubt that this was her destiny. As long as they exchanged those vows over the altar, anything else that might go wrong just didn't matter.

Their wedding day dawned with clear skies and slightly warmer temperatures. Hilary spent the night with her parents and didn't see Jack until he arrived at the temple with Colin and Janna. Everything moved along smoothly as it usually did in the temple, but Hilary felt almost numb until she was standing in the bride's room, with Janna and her mother fussing over the details of her dress. A rush of nerves assaulted her, but even then it was tempered with an undeniable peace.

Jack was hardly aware of being disabled once he entered the temple. He was treated with such kindness and respect, and every inconvenience was dealt with efficiently and cheerfully. Everything fell into perfect perspective when he entered the sealing room with Hilary, where the warmth of love from family and friends surrounded them. Every adult in Hilary's family was present, and he felt certain that Jeffrey was among them. Colin and Janna were there, as were Ammon and Allison. And their new bishop and his wife had driven all the way from Provo to lend their support.

The temple president himself was there to marry them, and prior to the ceremony he took a few minutes to talk to Jack and Hilary. He briefly explained the wonders of eternal marriage, and gave several points of good advice, maintaining a mood that was enjoyable and pleasant as well as sacred. But the point that struck Jack the deepest was related to commitment. With a deep, soul-searching gaze that went slowly back and forth between Jack and Hilary, this man told them in a strong, hushed voice, "Commitment is the key to a lasting marriage. The two of you are going into this with some unique challenges. But every marriage has challenges; perhaps yours are only more tangible than some. No matter what might lie around the corner, it will be your commitment to each other, to God, and to the marriage that will carry you through. True commitment requires selflessness, and as long as you both remain selfless in the solving of problems, turning to your Father in Heaven for answers, you can't go wrong.

"Now," the president said more lightly, "let's get on with this. The angels are waiting. And there are angels here. I can testify to that."

Jack turned to look at Hilary and knew by the tears in her eyes that she shared his thoughts. He realized then that in essence, it had been Jeffrey who had brought them together. And they both felt him close at this moment.

"Now," the president continued with a pleasant lilt in his voice, "the wonderful thing about being in the care of a loving Father in Heaven is that he will always provide the means to compensate for anything beyond doing the best we can do." He smiled warmly at Jack. "So that means you can marry this lovely young lady without actually kneeling at the altar, and—"

"Oh, but I *am* going to kneel at the altar," Jack said, much to Hilary's surprise.

"We've got this covered," Ammon interjected. "We even practiced."

"All right, then," the president said. "Let's get married."

With little effort, Colin and Ammon each took one of Jack's arms and helped him kneel at the altar. When they were situated and Jack took Hilary's hand into his, the president said lightly to Hilary, "Now, there may be three men on the other side of the altar, but you only get to marry the one who is holding your hand."

Hilary laughed softly. "What a relief."

Through the ceremony, Hilary felt so overcome with emotion, so completely filled with the Spirit, that she knew this moment could carry her through many difficulties. At the same moment she spoke her vows, moisture rose in Jack's eyes, and she silently thanked God for giving her so much.

The remainder of the day sailed through without a glitch. Even the absence of Jack's mother didn't bother him for more than a minute. In fact, it was something of a relief not to have to deal with her and wonder how she might embarrass herself. She had declared to Jack that if he was going to be married where she couldn't attend the ceremony, then she wouldn't attend the reception. But she had attended the reception when he'd married Lorie in the temple, which made him relatively certain that her declaration had more than a little to do with his disability. She'd felt uncomfortable with his religious convictions for years, and now she was doubly uncomfortable.

Jack's brothers did come to the reception and expressed sincere congratulations. But it was apparent that they, too, were uncomfortable with his new way of life.

The reception was enjoyable and everything went well, but Jack was relieved to have it over and get out of his tuxedo. Hilary was full of laughter as they left the reception and headed toward Provo. During the drive they recounted the success of the day's events; then silence settled around them. Jack briefly became preoccupied with thoughts of how it should have been. An intense heartache began to settle in, but he forced his negative thoughts away, concentrating instead on the reality that Hilary Smith was now his wife. Praying for the ability to concentrate on the good and not allow anything to mar their time together, Jack was able to smile genuinely at Hilary as she pulled up in front of the hotel and announced, "We're here."

At the door to their room, Jack uttered his first thought. "I should be carrying you over the threshold." Hilary touched his face and smiled. Then she unlocked the door and plopped herself onto his lap. Jack laughed as he wheeled the chair into the room and the door closed behind them.

Jack was only slightly nervous as he sat in bed reading a small book he'd found on the bedside table, *Things To Do in Provo*, while Hilary spent an enormous amount of time in the bathroom. "What are you doing in there?" he finally hollered.

"I want to look perfect," she hollered back. "And I'm trying to teach you patience."

"It's working!"

He could hear her laugh before she called, "What are you doing out there?"

"I'm learning patience . . . and I'm learning about all the things there are to do in Provo. I've lived here for years, and I didn't realize it was such a hot spot."

"Well, that's nice . . . since we can't afford to spend our honeymoon anywhere else." She opened the bathroom door as she added, "Is it okay to spend your honeymoon in the same city you live in?"

Jack glanced up and audibly caught his breath. He tossed the brochure on the bedside table. "I don't think we'll need this." He wondered if her heart was beating as fast as his when he said, "It worked."

"What worked?" she asked.

"All that time in the bathroom. You look perfect."

Hilary sat beside him on the bed, and a memory popped into his mind of the first time he'd really taken notice of her. She'd been little more than a child, with a long braid hanging down her back, teasing Jeffrey about some girl who kept calling him on the phone. The memory was so clear that he could almost hear her laughter. And now, here she was, *his bride.* It was a dream come true for him, and the reality was almost too incredible to grasp. A rush of indescribable happiness surged through him, erupting in a burst of laughter.

"Is something funny?" Hilary asked in alarm.

Jack shook his head and tried to explain. Then the moment suddenly became funny, and he couldn't stop laughing. She became caught up in his laughter, even though she was obviously baffled, and he couldn't resist the urge to just hug her. "I love you," he finally managed to say.

"I love you, too . . . but what's so funny?"

"Nothing is funny . . . except you sitting there wondering what was funny." Knowing that made no sense, he just mopped his eyes and hurried to explain. "I just . . . can't believe it. I'd pinch myself if I could feel it. I mean . . . little Hilary Smith, the girl who used to make me laugh; the young woman who declared she would never marry somebody like me—*Hilary Smith* is sitting on my bed in a hotel room," he took her hand, "wearing my ring on her finger."

Hilary smiled. "And that makes me Hilary Hayden. And that means I have every right to be where I am now."

Jack pulled her closer and kissed her the way he'd always wanted to. He was grateful for the time they had spent talking and preparing for this moment. He felt completely at ease and comfortable with Hilary, and her obvious love and acceptance warmed him through. He was pleasantly surprised at his own passion, and the way he felt so complete as he held her in his arms and felt her drifting contentedly off to sleep.

Their "home-town honeymoon," as Hilary called it, proved to be the most enjoyable three days Jack had ever lived. They spent most of their time at the apartment, basking in each other's company as if they were staying at the finest hotel.

On Sunday afternoon, they had a gift-opening party at their apartment with Colin and Janna, Allison and Ammon, and Hilary's parents. Colin and Janna were the last to leave. While Janna was helping Hilary rearrange some things in the kitchen, she asked, "So, how was the honeymoon?"

Hilary gave a contented sigh and couldn't help smiling. "It was incredible. I just . . . love him so much."

Janna smiled. "That's great. Although I must say we miss him. I almost feel like he's become part of the family."

"Well," Hilary said, "we're glad to have *family* like you. I'm sure we'll see each other often."

"Of course."

In the front room, Colin leaned back on the couch and said to Jack, "So, how was the honeymoon?"

Jack just smiled and said, "There's nothing wrong with Hilary's nervous system."

Christmas was the best that Jack ever remembered. He'd never felt such purpose and belonging. There was no extra money to buy each other gifts, so they decided instead to write letters to each other, expressing all they felt at this time. On Christmas Eve they shared a candlelight dinner, then lay on the floor by their little Christmas tree and read their letters aloud.

On Christmas Day they went to Mt. Pleasant, arriving in time for brunch with Hilary's family. They spent the night, and the sense of belonging deepened for Jack. He'd practically lived in this home for brief periods of time in the past, and Pete and Millie had always taken him in with full acceptance. But now he was truly a part of the family, and it meant more to him than it might have if his life had not been altered so drastically.

Getting into a routine after the new year wasn't terribly difficult. But as the routine began to settle, Jack began to feel an indescribable helplessness. He felt restless and uptight, but he didn't quite know what to do about it. Hilary suggested that he take some steps toward getting back into school. She told him she knew he would qualify for a grant and some benefits that would help, and she brought home all the necessary papers. But he just couldn't bring himself to do anything about it. He told her he just needed some time; and even though he sensed her frustration, she was patient with him and gave him the space he needed to adjust.

Hilary was asked to serve as a Primary teacher in their ward, and she willingly accepted the calling. Jack was asked to be the secretary in the elders quorum, and he turned it down. When Hilary asked why, he simply told her he couldn't do it. Her attempts to clarify were met with anger, so she dropped it, rationalizing that he needed time.

A blessing came in the form of some good home teachers, but Hilary doubted it could be coincidence that one of them had a wife in a wheelchair. Bill Spencer not only showed a great deal of genuine empathy toward Jack, but he also had a van with a hydraulic wheelchair lift. Since Bill worked at home and his hours were flexible, he offered himself as a taxi driver to Jack anytime he needed to go anywhere. Each month when the home teachers came, Bill practically turned cartwheels to find some avenue of giving them service. Hilary appreciated his attitude when she was able to call and ask if he'd take Jack to a doctor's appointment when she had to work. Bill's eagerness made her hope that eventually he could reach something inside Jack and help him cope with whatever was troubling him. But Jack was so upbeat and cheerful when the home teachers came that Hilary doubted they would ever suspect that everything wasn't perfect.

Tension deepened as the finances became even tighter when medical bills began coming in for the percentages the insurance wouldn't pay. Ammon had faithfully paid the insurance premium as if Jack was still one of his employees, and he insisted he would continue to do so as long as Jack had no other options. Even though the worst of Jack's medical needs were behind him, Ammon said that life was too precarious for him to be uninsured. Recalling his brief hospital stay for a silly infection, Jack knew Ammon was right. Even so, he hated feeling so dependent.

Hilary took on a second job to help cover the financial situation, working weekdays as an office assistant at an elementary school. The hours worked out nicely, since she could leave in time to get to the studio and teach her afternoon dance classes. But she was gone from home a great deal, which contributed to Jack's restlessness. He did his best to help around the house, but he felt terribly inadequate at even the simplest household chores, and he spent more and more time just watching TV to kill the long hours with nothing to do. Hilary gently suggested that he set some goals and move forward with making some changes in his life. He knew she was right, but he couldn't get up the motivation to do it. She took him out of the house as frequently as possible, and she brought him books from the library to give his mind "something positive to absorb," as she often said. But they usually went back unread.

While Jack sensed Hilary's growing frustration, he felt himself spiraling into a downward cycle that he didn't know how to break. Hilary remained patient, and she always went out of her way to help him when she was around. But a day came in June when his discouragement became too intense to ignore.

They were sitting at the table, eating a late dinner she had hurriedly thrown together after returning from dance classes. The kitchen where they sat was in moderate disarray, and he knew Hilary was exhausted. He wanted to apologize for being such a burden to her, but he knew it would open a conversation he didn't want to have. "Do we have any ketchup?" he asked tonelessly.

"I'll get it," she said and slid her chair back.

"I can get it," he insisted, moving toward the fridge. But she didn't seem to hear him. "I said I could get it," he repeated, wishing it hadn't sounded so harsh.

"Fine," she said, but she remained standing, staring at him as if he'd turned into some kind of a monster. Maybe he had.

"I'm sorry," he said, but his tone of voice was no kinder. "You do too much for me. That's all."

He got the ketchup out of the fridge, well aware that it took him three times longer than it would have taken Hilary. She sat motionless until he returned to the table, then she stood up and grabbed something out of a high cupboard, slamming it onto the table. He didn't realize it was a box of toothpicks until she took one out and stuck it in his mouth. "Chew on that," she said. "Chew it to shreds." He looked baffled and she clarified, "You were far more pleasant to be around when you used to always have a stupid toothpick in your mouth. So chew on it. Take the box. Use them all. I don't know why you ever stopped."

"Lorie hated it," he said with absolutely no emotion. "She wouldn't put up with it, so I stopped."

"Well, you should start again. If she'd had any brains, she would have realized how adorable you looked with a stupid toothpick sticking out of your mouth."

Hilary watched Jack's dumbstruck expression and realized how absolutely ridiculous this conversation sounded. A little chuckle erupted before she could hold it back. Jack just stared at her. "Shut up and eat your ketchup," she said.

"I didn't say anything."

"Eat your ketchup anyway."

Hilary hoped the tension had been alleviated. But the following morning—while Jack was chewing on a toothpick—he dropped the remote control. Passing by him on her way from the kitchen to the bathroom, Hilary bent down to pick it up. "I can get it!" he snapped so harshly it startled her.

"You can't reach it. I was just trying to help."

"Well, don't! Okay? Just leave me alone and let me take care of myself!"

"Fine," she snarled back. But instead of hurrying on to the bathroom, she folded her arms and waited for him to get it. He had a tool she'd given him for getting things he couldn't reach, but it was in the kitchen, and she knew he wouldn't take the time to go get it while she was standing there. Attempting to be casual, he strained as far as he could to reach the remote. In the process, he fell from his chair and cursed under his breath. He glared at Hilary as if this was her fault, but she simply said, "Your pride is going to kill you one day, Jack Hayden. And I'll probably be at work when it happens."

Hilary left for work with Jack still lying on the front room floor, looking angry. She knew he could get back in the chair without her help, but it would take considerable time and effort. And if he was so determined to get by on his own, she was determined to let him do it.

She went straight from the school to the studio, and didn't leave there until after eight o'clock. Weary to the bone, she wished she had the money to stop and buy a couple of hamburgers so she wouldn't have to cook. But she didn't. Still, having to go home and cook didn't dismay her as much as having to face Jack. All day her thoughts had been with him, and her heart went out to him. But she felt helpless to do anything more than she'd already done. Perhaps that was the problem; maybe she was just doing too much. Hadn't he said himself that she did too much for him? Was that the problem?

Almost without realizing it, Hilary found herself headed to Janna's neighborhood instead of going home. She sat in Janna's driveway for ten minutes, telling herself that she should be home. Finally she went to the front door, praying Janna would be home. She always had a way of helping Hilary put things in perspective.

Matthew answered the door with his typical teenage lack of enthusiasm. "Hi. Mom's in the kitchen," he said as she stepped inside.

"Thanks, Matt," she said.

Janna was loading the dishwasher. "Hilary," she said with pleasure. "What a nice surprise." Her smiled faded when she paused to take a good look at Hilary. "Ooh, I would guess you need to talk."

"It's that obvious?"

"I'm afraid so."

"Mind if I use your phone?"

"Go ahead."

Hilary called the apartment, fighting a rush of nerves as Jack answered.

"Hi," she said.

"Hi."

"Is everything okay?"

"As okay as it always is," he said blandly.

Hilary counted to ten. "Have you had anything to eat?"

"I got a sandwich a while ago. I'm fine."

"Good, because I really don't feel like cooking."

"I didn't figure you would."

Again Hilary counted to ten, wondering if the subtly critical tone behind his statement was her imagination.

"I'm at Janna's. I'm not sure when I'll be home."

Silence.

"Are you there, Jack?"

"Yes. Is everything okay?"

"As okay as it always is," she said.

Silence.

"I'll see you later." Hilary hurried to get off the phone, hating the turmoil she felt when she tried to talk to him.

While Janna finished cleaning up her kitchen, Hilary expressed her frustrations. When she fell silent, Janna sat down at the table and looked into her eyes. "The only thing I can tell you," she said, "is what I've always told you. Firm boundaries. Unconditional love."

"I thought I was doing that."

"What are your boundaries?" Janna asked.

"Well, I don't let him get away with being angry or belligerent with me, and . . ."

"And?"

"I don't know."

"When you took on the second job, didn't he agree to help around the house more?"

"Yes."

"Has he done that?"

"No."

"Okay," Janna said, "so perhaps you should simply express your frustrations to him, and together you can write down the division of household responsibilities. Then it's not so abstract."

"But I don't think he'll do it."

"Make the list, or do the work?" Janna asked.

"Neither."

Janna laughed softly. "He sounds like a teenager."

"Okay, so what do you do with a teenager?"

"Well, Matthew is expected to do certain things, and when he doesn't, there are consequences."

"How do you enforce consequences with a grown man?"

Janna became thoughtful. Hilary leaned back and folded her arms, certain that solving these problems could not be as simple as Janna seemed to think.

"I have an idea. It might be a place to start, at least."

"I'm listening," Hilary said, only slightly cynical.

"He claims he doesn't want you to do anything for him. So *don't* do anything for him."

"Isn't that a bit extreme? I mean, maybe I shouldn't do so much for him, but to do *nothing* . . ."

"Maybe it is a little extreme, but it might make your point. Then eventually, the two of you will be able to balance things out."

"Okay, so I do nothing for him. Is that going to get him motivated to set some goals and do something worthwhile?"

"I don't know," Janna said. "But it might get his attention."

"And how does that solve the problem of him doing his part around the house?"

"You want my opinion?" Janna asked.

"That's what I'm doing here, isn't it?"

"Okay. I say you do nothing at all. You're working two jobs. He's capable of working in the kitchen, doing a little laundry, keeping things picked up around the house. Right?"

"Right."

"So, turn the whole thing over to him. You're the breadwinner. Let him be the homemaker."

Hilary didn't know how to explain how uncomfortable that made her.

"What's wrong?" Janna asked.

"It just seems so . . . so . . ."

"What?"

"That's a real sore point for him, Janna. I wonder if it would do more harm than good."

"If he doesn't like housekeeping, then he needs to get an education and get a job."

Janna said it so strongly that Hilary was taken aback. "I'm surprised to hear you talk that way," she admitted. "I thought you cared very much for Jack, and—"

"That's just it," Janna interrupted firmly. "Don't you get it, Hil? If you love him, you'll stop being codependent and force him to face up to the reality of his life. That's the only way he'll ever come to terms with it.

And he'll never be happy if he doesn't come to terms with it. He's not going to feel good about himself until he can do something with his life. And he won't, as long as you let him sit around and do nothing. The changes may not happen overnight, Hilary, but if you set those boundaries and keep them clear and defined, eventually he'll get the picture."

Hilary watched her friend closely, attempting to digest everything she'd said. "Are you trying to tell me I'm codependent?"

"You are preventing him from progressing by taking responsibility for his inappropriate behavior."

Hilary sighed and pressed a hand over her eyes, as if it might push the concept into her brain. "I think this is making sense," she finally said. "But where do I start? I don't want to just go home and get angry and—"

"You don't have to get angry, Hilary. That's where a lot of people go wrong. If you get angry when you put up your fence lines, then that unconditional love is absent—or at least it will appear that way to Jack. You simply state your case."

"For instance?"

"Okay, I'm you," Janna said. "I go home and say, 'Jack, there's something I need to say. I'm feeling terribly overwhelmed and stressed out. If I'm going to keep working two jobs, I will need you to . . .' You fill in the blank. Tell him specifically what you expect of him. Tell him you simply cannot do it all."

"What if he argues with me?"

"Just stay calm and reflect what he says, so you can get to the heart of what's bothering him. And then," Janna held up a finger, "no matter what, don't you renege on that boundary. If you can't hold that line, then you'd better set the line somewhere else to begin with." She then suggested an idea to get the ball rolling in the right direction, and promised to come over Saturday and help it along.

Hilary drove home feeling more enlightened and more prepared—which was typical following one of Janna's pep talks. But she also felt nervous, and prayed she would have the strength to handle this appropriately.

Hilary entered the apartment to find that the dishes had been washed, but everything else looked worse than when she had left. And Jack had gone to bed. He was asleep when she crawled between the sheets, but she thought it was just as well.

On Saturday morning, Colin came to pick up Jack and take him out for the day. Janna stayed at the apartment and helped Hilary give it a good cleaning. "Shouldn't you be home with your children?" Hilary asked.

"Matthew is watching them. He needs to earn money, and it's good for him. I told him to call here if there's a problem."

By the time Jack and Colin returned, the apartment looked better than it had in weeks. Janna and Colin had only been gone a few minutes when Jack said, "Wow. It looks great. You've been working hard."

"Well, Janna helped, but . . ." Hilary prayed for guidance and strength, and it was easier than she'd expected. She stated her case to him exactly as Janna had suggested, and was surprised when he made no protest. She told him that since everything was in order, she would like him to keep it that way; that she would pick up after herself, and asked that he do the same. She agreed to cook on the days she didn't teach, and figured they could get by on sandwiches and prepared foods the other days. She wanted to suggest that he could cook two or three times a week, but she didn't want to push for too much at once.

For a few days, everything went better. Jack seemed more relaxed than he had in quite some time, and they spent some quality time together. She teased him that chewing on those toothpicks had sure helped, since he'd quickly taken up the habit again. But she felt certain it had more to do with letting him know exactly where he stood.

A week beyond her declarations, however, Hilary noticed that the apartment wasn't looking very good. As it got progressively worse, she called on Janna for a suggestion. "If he's not keeping his part of the bargain," she said, "You don't have to keep yours."

To Hilary this felt like game-playing, but she trusted Janna and simply stopped cooking. She really didn't mind getting by on frozen burritos, canned soup, and sandwiches. She washed her clothes, but not his, and picked up after herself, but never touched anything that belonged to him. And no matter how uncomfortable a situation might be, she allowed him to do every little thing for himself.

While she was hoping and praying he would get the idea and start doing something, instead he became progressively more lazy. And the more lazy he became, the more difficult he was to live with. He avoided being outright belligerent or disrespectful to Hilary, because he knew she wouldn't put up with it. But everything that came out of his mouth was negative or cynical; and more often than not, he reacted coldly to any attempt at warmth or affection from Hilary. If she tried to talk to him, he responded with bitter statements that made it clear he was beyond negotiating. If she suggested counseling, he retorted with, "Can a counselor make me walk again?" If she suggested that he had much to be thankful for and a lot of life left to live, he responded with, "Maybe it would have been better if I'd just been killed."

When Hilary called Janna, practically hysterical with frustration, Janna calmly asked, "What are your choices?"

"I have no choices. You tell me I can't renege. But I can't live like this."

"Then don't."

"What are you suggesting, Janna?"

Janna was quiet for a long moment. "Hilary, do you remember the circumstances I was in when we met?"

"Yes."

"Well, to this day, Colin swears that a great deal of heartache could have been prevented if he'd had the courage to just leave."

"Leave?" Hilary practically shrieked.

"Calm down and let me finish. I was having trouble dealing with my unresolved baggage. That applies to Jack, don't you think?"

"Yes. Go on."

"I refused to do anything about it, and I was letting it come between me and Colin. Does that apply to Jack?"

"Yes."

"Colin had done everything he possibly could, and it made no difference."

"I'm with you."

"The counselor suggested he get a separation, to let me know that he wouldn't put up with it. Colin didn't do it. The results were a nightmare."

Hilary said nothing.

"If you have any doubts, Hilary," Janna said gently, "take it to the Lord. He knows what's best. Sometimes commitment takes the form of being committed to what's best for the person you're committed to."

"But Jack won't see it that way."

"If he's worth having, Hilary, he won't let you go—not permanently, anyway."

Hilary was more disturbed by Janna's suggestion than she dared admit. But after several more days of living in the dark void that Jack had created around himself, she knew what she had to do.

CHAPTER FOURTEEN

*Y*ou know what, Jack?" Hilary opened a drawer and started pulling out clothes and tossing them on the bed. "I'm damned if I do, and I'm damned if I don't."

She'd had every intention of handling this without getting angry, but his apparent indifference as she'd attempted once more to discuss her concerns had finally sent her over the edge. "I tried to be helpful, and you resented it," she said grimly. "I tried to leave you to take care of yourself, and you don't." She started stuffing her clothes into a bag. "I thought we could talk things through, work it out, find a balance. But apparently that's out of the question."

Jack couldn't remember the last time he'd felt anything besides depressed or angry. But he felt downright panicked when he considered Hilary's speech in light of the fact that she was packing her clothes. "What are you doing, Hilary?"

"I'm leaving, Jack." She pushed past him into the bathroom and starting pulling things haphazardly out of the drawers and cabinets, throwing them into her bag. "I don't know where I'm going. I don't know what I'm going to do. I only know that I'm getting out of here."

"You can't just walk out on me, Hilary." His voice clearly expressed his distress. "Not after all we've been through. You can't possibly—"

"You know what?" she interrupted. "I've stayed this long on the premise of *all we've been through*. But that just isn't enough anymore. I get nothing positive from you whatsoever. You are *not* the man I fell in love with." She stopped what she was doing and faced him. "The Jack Hayden I loved *died* when that bale of hay fell on him, and some jerk showed up in his place."

Jack opened his mouth to speak, but she wouldn't let him. She knew what he was going to say, and she had no desire to hear it. "Don't give me your *maybe I should have died* crap. This isn't about breaking your back, or losing the use of your legs. This is about losing your heart and soul. They're *gone,* Jack. And I'm not going to live like this anymore. I'm *not!*"

Jack was so stunned he couldn't bring himself to speak. He felt a million miles away as he watched Hilary finish packing. "And that's it?" he finally said when she walked toward the door.

Hilary counted to ten and looked over her shoulder with her hand on the knob. "I've done everything I can, Jack. If you come up with something I've missed, let me know. In the meantime, I've got a life."

Jack sat where he was until the sun had gone down and the house became dark. He kept waiting for her to come back or call. He wanted to hear her say she'd been angry, and she wanted to try again. He finally got something to eat and went to bed, certain she'd show up any minute. But he drifted off to sleep and woke up the next morning with no sign of Hilary. His first thought was that something had happened to her, but in his heart he knew she was physically fine. She'd just left him. She'd really done it. He was tempted to feel angry, but it only took a few minutes to know that eventually he would have to get past the anger and admit to the truth. She was right; everything she'd said was true. But how could he explain to her this complete helplessness he felt? It was like a dark cloud surrounding him, and he couldn't break out of it.

He went through the motions of washing some dishes and doing a little laundry, thinking perhaps Hilary would show up and notice that he was trying to be helpful. But the sun went down again without a word from her. And bit by bit, his understanding began to dawn. Their problems really had nothing to do with his lack of help around the house, at least not directly. No, it was deeper than that—and he didn't know how to fix it. But he wasn't so stupid that he couldn't see one thing for certain: he couldn't fix *anything* without Hilary in his life.

He'd kept a prayer in his heart since the moment she'd walked out the door; but now he bowed his head and prayed fervently, with all his heart and soul, to know what steps to take. He wondered where she was, what she was doing. Where would he find her? He could start making calls, but . . . he glanced at the clock. She was at the dance studio, teaching classes, and she would be finished in less than an hour. His first thought was the impossibility of getting there, but just as quickly an idea popped into his head. Bill Spencer had insisted a dozen times that he'd give him a ride anywhere, anytime. Jack hurried to the phone, praying that Bill was available.

"Sure," Bill bellowed through the phone, "I'll be right over. No problem."

Jack had barely changed his shirt and freshened up when Bill came to the door. He was friendly and talkative, and didn't ask any questions about why Jack wanted to surprise his wife at work. He simply seemed pleased that Jack would call on him. Jack only prayed that Hilary would be willing to listen to what he had to say.

* * * * *

Hilary spent the night at Janna's house, grateful that she had a place to go where she didn't have to justify her reasons for not being at home. They sat up until two in the morning, talking through every aspect of the situation, while Hilary occasionally cried. A little before midnight, Colin came to say good night to his wife, and sat for a few minutes to talk. "How do you feel about harboring runaways?" Hilary asked him.

Colin smiled and took Janna's hand. "You know, Hilary, sometimes leaving is the only thing you can do to get someone's attention. I know Jack loves you, but you're the only one who loves him enough to make him face up. If you've done everything you can, then maybe your absence will force him to think about some things. If it doesn't, there's nothing you can do."

Hilary nodded as his words validated everything she was feeling—including her fear that Jack would choose to harden himself against what had happened to him, rather than softening his heart and learning to believe in himself again. But knowing what Colin and Janna had been through to make their marriage work gave her the confidence to believe she could get through this.

While Hilary lay awake in the bedroom where Jack had once stayed for several weeks, she contemplated how blessed she was to have such good friends. She thought back to when she'd first met Janna. At the time, Hilary had believed her own life would fall neatly into place without complications. But obviously the Lord had foreseen the need for a friend like Janna in her future. And she was grateful.

Hilary slept late and had to hurry to work at the school, then went straight to the studio to teach. When classes were over, she changed into a skirt and blouse and turned out the lights. However, being temporarily homeless, she didn't feel the motivation to leave. She ached to just go home and hold Jack in her arms; but she knew from experience that being with him would not necessarily ease her loneliness. There were chasms between them that she didn't know how to bridge. *And she missed him.*

She didn't even bother to turn on any music as she sat down in the center of the dance floor, hugging her knees to her chest. She felt lost and helpless. And alone. By habit she turned her mind to prayer, knowing that nothing except divine intervention could get them past this.

"You're not dancing." Jack's voice startled her, and she looked up. Her heart quickened just to be in the same room with him. In spite of all that had come between them, he still evoked feelings in her that made her wonder how she could ever live without him.

"I don't feel like dancing," she said. He moved toward her and she asked, "How did you get here?"

"I jogged," he said, attempting to lighten the mood. But Hilary didn't even crack a smile. More seriously he said, "Bill gave me a ride. That's a pretty cool van he's got. We should get one, don't you think?"

"That would be great," she said in a toneless voice that covered her fear. She didn't want to open up a whole new argument, but she couldn't go back to him unless something changed. She just *couldn't.*

Hilary sensed his nervousness, but she didn't quite dare look at him. She squeezed her eyes shut and prayed with every ounce of strength that he would say what she needed to hear. She was beginning to wonder how long the silence would go on when Jack slid from his chair and lay on his side next to her, leaning up on one elbow.

He cleared his throat and began in a timid voice. "There's something I need to say to you, Hilary." Her heart began to pound, fearing he might be in a state of mind where he thought she would be better off without him. At this point, she wasn't sure if she could handle it.

"Hilary," he touched her chin and turned her face toward him.

"I'm listening," she said, wishing her voice hadn't quivered.

"You know, when everything fell apart with Lorie, one of the hardest things for me to swallow was the way she could let go so easily. Then I realized I felt the same way. I really could live without her. And I wondered why I had married her to begin with if I actually felt that way. The point I'm getting to, Hilary, is that I *can't* live without you."

Hilary clamped her eyes shut as if it might hold back the tears. But they crept out anyway, and she felt Jack wipe them away before he continued. "I know I've been a fool, Hilary. I know I haven't been fair to you. It sounds pathetically stupid to say I'm sorry, but I am. I'm sorry, Hilary. And I will do everything within my power to keep you in my life." His voice broke with emotion. "Please, Hilary. Talk to me. Help me through this."

Hilary tried to swallow the knot in her throat. He'd certainly said what she'd needed to hear. Still, she had to ask, "How do I know you're not just saying whatever it takes to get me to come home?"

Jack wondered briefly where she had learned to be so spunky. Then he recalled that *he* was the one who had encouraged her to believe in herself and stand up for what she believed. It took him a minute to come up with an appropriate answer, but he said it with conviction, knowing it was true. "I know, Hilary, because I know you won't put up with empty promises." He touched her face again. "You may save me from myself yet."

Hilary resisted the urge to throw herself into his arms. Forcing a steady voice, she asked, "So, what exactly are you promising?"

Jack sighed. She certainly wasn't making this easy, but then, he was to blame for her behavior and he knew it. She'd told him he was proud and stubborn, and maybe she was right. But nothing made him more humble than the prospect of losing Hilary. Not even losing half of himself could compare; he knew that now. And if there was any man left in him at all, he would give her what she deserved.

"I can't promise I'll be perfect overnight, Hilary, but—"

"I can live with going one step at a time, Jack," she interrupted, "as long as we keep moving forward and don't get bogged down."

"Okay," he relaxed a little, "then how about this step? I will do my fair share, Hilary. I know I haven't kept my end of the bargain, and I will. Heck, I'll even cook a couple of times a week."

"This is sounding good," she admitted, her voice lightening a little.

"And I will treat you with the respect you deserve," he continued. "I know it's not right for me to take out my bad moods on you."

Hilary looked into his eyes, as if she could gauge the depth of his promises. He was right when he said he couldn't be perfect overnight, and she couldn't expect him to be. But if he could do as he'd promised, even most of the time, she knew she would feel a whole lot better about their marriage.

"I love you, Hilary," he said with so much conviction that she tingled inside.

That did it. There was no resisting him now. She only hesitated a moment before she pushed her arms around him, holding him close as she whispered, "I love you, too, Jack."

He laughed and held her tighter, then he kissed her in a way that he hadn't in weeks. He kissed her and kissed her, then he whispered tentatively, "Turn on the music, Hilary. I want to feel the music in the floor."

Hilary did as he asked, and they lay side by side, holding hands, as one song played, then another. Jack held her and kissed her, then he asked her to dance. Hilary felt uneasy at his request. She'd not danced in his presence since he'd lost the ability to dance. She knew he sensed her apprehension, but she didn't know how to explain it.

"Hilary," he said, pressing a hand over the side of her face and into her hair, "dance for me. Let me see the music."

Hilary recalled the night he had lain in the center of the floor and she had danced for him. It had been before the accident; before either of them had comprehended the reality of how life could be altered in an instant. Seeing the sincerity in his eyes, she got up and gradually worked herself into the music. She leapt over the top of him and he laughed. So she did it again. She danced until exhaustion consumed her, then she lay down beside him to feel the music in the floor. The tape ended and clicked off, leaving a hollow silence in place of the music. But Hilary felt completely content in her husband's arms. She knew there were rocky roads still ahead, but she had hope. And she had Jack's love. Finally, she felt at peace.

It was nearly midnight before they decided they should go home. But with the slick wood floor and no other furniture in the room, getting Jack back into his chair proved a definite challenge. Three times they ended up rolling onto the floor in a tangled heap, then laughing until it hurt. But the laughter released a great deal of tension, and they arrived home feeling like newlyweds again.

Jack did as he'd promised and became fairly efficient at keeping the apartment tidy and the laundry done, and when Hilary came home from teaching, he usually had something for her to eat. He never ventured beyond cans and boxed mixes, but Hilary felt his love in the effort he made. And she couldn't deny the decrease in her stress level.

Jack's temperament also remained more even, as he'd promised. He rarely said anything unkind, even though his moods were often less than ideal. And when he did, he was quick to apologize. Hilary had to admit gratitude for his efforts, but in her heart she knew his change of behavior was little more than going through motions for the sake of keeping her happy. *Jack* wasn't happy, and she knew it. Four months after she'd spent that one night at Janna's, he'd still not made a single phone call to make inquiries about getting on with his life. He'd made no effort to fill out the forms that Hilary kept close at hand. And through all of his efforts to make civil conversation and keep a light mood around her, he never even hinted at discussing anything related to the future. It had been more than a year since the accident, and even though he'd come remarkably far in a physical sense, she wondered if he had progressed at all in coping with it emotionally.

Janna was always there to keep Hilary holding on to all that was good, and helping her try to understand what Jack might be feeling. Hilary felt Janna was right in suggesting that when Jack had married Lorie he had lost much of his emotional identity. And even though Hilary had buoyed him up and he'd mostly recovered from the experience, there were undoubtedly emotional scars left behind. His mother's attitude had also likely contributed to the problem. And now he had lost his physical identity—a part of him that had always been strong and secure, inextricably connected to his sense of purpose and belonging. Hilary understood all of that, and she tried to talk with Jack about it. He listened and agreed, but he didn't seem to come any closer to finding peace with himself or having any hope for the future.

As usual, when Hilary found herself at the end of her rope, she found herself at Janna's house. Janna answered the door looking frazzled and worn out. "What's wrong with you?" Hilary asked right off.

"I'm supposed to ask you that," Janna retorted lightly, motioning her inside.

They went back to the family room, where Janna collapsed onto one of the couches. Caitlin was lying on the other one, wrapped in a blanket, and Jake was playing on the floor. The house looked worse than Hilary had ever seen it. "What's wrong?" Hilary repeated.

"Oh, everything," Janna replied. "I mean . . . not really. I'm just having a bad day. Or maybe it's a bad week." She laughed slightly. "Or maybe it's a bad nine months."

"Janna?" Hilary gasped. "You're pregnant?"

"Yes," Janna admitted, "and it seems I just get sicker every time. I feel *awful*. As you can see." She motioned to her surroundings.

"I'm sick," Caitlin announced to Hilary with an obvious plea for sympathy.

"I'm sorry, Caitlin," Hilary said. "What's wrong?"

"I'm just sick," the child responded.

Janna motioned Hilary into the kitchen, saying softly, "She's just got a little fever. Nothing serious. Just enough to make her *cranky*." Janna growled as she said the last word. "Why don't you talk to me while I clean my kitchen. It will motivate me."

"Why don't I help you clean your kitchen?"

While they visited and worked together, Hilary said nothing about her own problems. She knew in her heart what Janna would say, and there was no need to burden her with it all over again. Hilary knew how to solve her problems—at least as far as she was able. She just had to gather some courage and do something about it. And she didn't need Janna to remind her of that—again.

While they were working, Jake began to scream. Janna hurried to the other room and Hilary followed, observing as Janna questioned her daughter. "What happened?"

"He was bothering me."

"Bothering you, how? Did he hurt you?"

Caitlin didn't answer, but as little Jake pushed a story book close to Janna, it became evident that he had simply wanted his sister to read him a story.

"Did you hit him?" Janna asked Caitlin. Only her guilty eyes answered. "He wanted you to read him a story, and you *hit* him?"

Caitlin started to cry.

"Now, listen, young lady," Janna said. "Just because you're sick doesn't give you the right to treat others badly. If you can't get along with the people you live with, then go to your room and stay there."

Caitlin dragged toward the stairs, crying as if her world had ended. Janna comforted Jake and distracted him with something else. When they returned to the kitchen and Caitlin's wails could be heard from above, Janna chuckled and said, "She'll get over it. She just wants some attention and sympathy."

Hilary helped Janna finish cleaning up her kitchen, then she made Janna sit down while she picked up the toys in the family room, did a quick cleanup of the bathrooms, and put a load of dirty towels in the washer. "Oh, thank you," Janna said when Hilary returned to the family room. "Your timing's good. I really needed a friend."

"Well," Hilary admitted, "maybe I needed to give some service. I feel better myself." She chuckled wryly. "It's too bad Jack couldn't get out and do something for somebody once in a while."

"Maybe he should."

"That's easier said than done. He's turned down three church jobs since we got married. He won't even do his home teaching."

"Things are not getting any better, I take it."

"No."

"Want to talk about it?"

"No. I just think it's time to put up a new fence line."

Hilary left Janna's house feeling better. But she was nearly home before she recalled clearly the brief scenario she'd observed with Janna and her children. With the memory a light came on inside her mind, as if to tell her she'd gotten some good advice after all. She could see herself saying to Jack, just as Janna had said to Caitlin, *Just because you're sick doesn't give you the right to treat others badly. If you can't get along with the people you live with, then go to your room and stay there.* Of course, Hilary couldn't send Jack to his room, but she *could* make it clear that he wasn't going to live this way; not in *her* home. Knowing that she needed to approach him in an effort to move things forward another step, she fasted and prayed for help and guidance.

On Saturday, when she didn't have to work, she made up her mind that this was as good a time as any. "Jack," she said, sitting near him in the front room, "we need to talk."

"Okay," he said, turning down the volume on the TV—just a little. "What do you want to talk about? Menus? Laundry soap? Or how about—"

"Please, Jack," she interrupted, "don't be flippant."

Jack sighed and turned his eyes back to the television. "I don't know how else to be."

Hilary grabbed the remote and turned the set off. Jack's glare was subtle but unmistakable.

"Something's got to give here, Jack. We can't go on like this indefinitely."

He looked stunned. "Haven't I done what I said I would do? Haven't I—"

"Technically, yes. Technically you have done what you said you would after I left in June. But you're only going through motions, Jack. Your heart isn't into it. Your heart isn't into *anything*. Deep inside, I know you're sitting there wishing you had died in that accident, whether you admit it or not. And it's affecting everything around you—most especially me. This is not the way we agreed to live when we got married. This is not what I bargained for."

Jack's entire demeanor turned hard. "Yes, Hilary, this is what you bargained for. You married a crippled man. And this is what you get. If that's not good enough for you, then—"

"That is the stupidest thing I've ever heard. Don't you dare try to convince me that you came into this marriage with no plan beyond doing housework and sitting in front of the television. You have done absolutely nothing to improve yourself since we got married. *Nothing*. We agreed to have a family, Jack, but I can't be having babies if I'm working sixty hours a week to pay the rent. I'd say you've had more than ample time to adjust."

Jack's eyes told her he knew she was right, but a familiar layer of pride made them as hard as his voice when he asked, "So what are you going to do? Leave me?"

Hilary had fasted and prayed in preparation for this, and she sought the help of the Spirit now. Before she had hardly absorbed the idea, it flew out of her mouth. "No, Jack, I'm not leaving. Do you know why? Because I'm *committed* to this marriage. I'm committed to making it work, whatever it takes. And if you're not going to live up to that commitment, then *you* can leave."

Jack stared at her incredulously. "You're serious."

"You'd better believe I'm serious. I really thought you loved me, Jack. You used to tell me you loved me more than life. Well, apparently you were lying."

Spurred by his deep sense of honesty, Jack responded defensively. "I *do* love you, Hilary. I would gladly die for you."

"I'm certain you would. But then, that would have been easy in comparison, wouldn't it? You'd die for me, but you're not willing to live for me. How dare you sit there, wishing you were dead, when I thank God every day of my life that you survived that accident. I thought my prayers had been answered, but I guess I have to accept the fact that you're a free agent, and I can't make your choices for you. You told me you love me more than life, but you don't love me enough to live for me."

"I'm alive, aren't I?" he practically snarled.

"You call this living?" She motioned to his surroundings for emphasis. "You might as well have died, for all the benefit you're getting out of being alive."

"My thoughts exactly."

"You see!" She threw her hands in the air. "You're a liar, Jack Hayden. You don't love me more than life. You loved your ability to walk more than life—more than *me.*"

Jack bristled at the accusation, but he bit his tongue. He couldn't possibly counter what she'd just said, but there was a point he had to make. "Maybe you're right, Hilary. Maybe you *would* be better off without me. Maybe I should just leave and—"

Anger filled her countenance so quickly that for a moment he thought she was going to slap him. Instead, she pushed her face only inches from his and snarled, "You just don't get it, do you! How many times do I have to say it? I didn't fall in love with you because you have legs, Jack. I love your heart, your mind, your spirit. And you're *choosing* to let those things die. Your body will be made whole again in eternity, Jack, and that's what I'm working toward. But if you don't start living again, you're not going to have anything *but* your body in eternity—and I'm certainly not going to be around. Because I'm not going to settle for less than I bargained for when I agreed to be your wife. I can make the sacrifices to spend my life with your physical condition, whatever it may be, and whatever difficulty it might entail. But I will *not* spend the rest of my life living in this emotional and spiritual abyss you've created for yourself. *I will not!"*

Following her tirade, Jack became eerily silent. Hoping she hadn't pushed him too hard and too fast, she felt like this would be a good time to just back off and let it drop. In a softer voice she said, "What you do with your life from here on is your choice, Jack. But I'm not going to stand by and let you waste it away at my expense."

Hilary left the house long enough to calm down, then she went back and fixed dinner. They ate together in silence. She cleaned up the kitchen, did some laundry, then went to the bedroom with a book while he watched television until long after she'd gone to sleep. He slept in late the next morning and didn't go to church. In fact, he rarely did these days.

Hilary sat alone through sacrament meeting, aching for her husband, praying in her heart that the things she'd said would leave an impression and get him moving. Then she went to Primary and tried not to think about it.

On Monday, Hilary came home from work to find that Jack had obviously done nothing; and on Tuesday the house looked worse than it had in a long time. Fearing that her little talk with him on Saturday had only plunged him into deeper depression, Hilary prayed fervently for help.

By the time she got to the studio, Hilary was feeling depressed herself. But then, she usually did these days. She felt out of control of her life, and she hated it. She taught the first two classes, then got ready to leave so she could make it to a meeting that evening. Occasionally she had one of her older, very talented students teach a few classes to trade the payment of her dance lessons. This gave her the chance to be free when other things came up.

With everything under control, she left in time to go home, grab something to eat, and get to her meeting. But she didn't want to go home, and prayed for the courage to face whatever she might find there. She was only a few blocks from home when a thought occurred to her with such strength that she knew it was the Spirit prompting her. *You do have control,* it said. A sweet warmth filled her at the thought.

Hilary felt strong and confident when she walked into the apartment, and she wasn't surprised to find Jack watching television, surrounded by total disarray. Without even a greeting, she found a pair of wire cutters, went outside, and cut the television cable.

Jack was obviously upset and baffled when she went into the front room to find him frantically pushing buttons on the remote control. He didn't say *hello* or *how are you*. He just said, "Something's wrong with the cable. Call them and—"

Hilary tossed the wire cutters on the floor in front of him. "No need for that," she said coolly.

Jack stared at her incredulously. "You've got to be joking. You cut the cable? That's my only connection to the world, and you—"

"I guess you're going to have to find another connection to the world."

"I'll call the cable company myself and have them fix it, and—"

"And I'll cut it again if I have to. So, you can either climb up the back of the apartment building and fix it yourself, or you can find yourself a wife who will put up with your vegetating in front of the TV and doing absolutely nothing with your life."

Jack shook his head in disbelief. "I never thought *you,* of all people, would be so insensitive."

"Well, maybe I am. But I don't know what else to do."

"And what am I supposed to do while you're gone all day?"

"Washing a few dishes wouldn't hurt. And then you could fill out those forms to apply for a grant so you can go back to school. I've brought home updated ones three times. And I'm *not* going to do it for you. Checking out the want ads for a job might kill a little time, too."

"A job?" He laughed bitterly. "Doing what?"

"I don't know, Jack. You've got hands. You've got a brain. *You* figure it out."

Hilary could tell that Jack was angry, but at the moment she just didn't have the energy to deal with it any further. "I've got a meeting," she announced.

"What kind of meeting?" he growled.

"It's a stake leadership meeting for Primary," she said, and went in the bedroom to change her clothes.

Hilary arrived at the church twenty minutes early, and sat quietly contemplating her frustrations. She hoped she had done the right thing, and prayed that Jack would find something inside himself to build on.

When the meeting was over, she stopped the stake Primary president a moment to ask her a question. They ended up talking for nearly an hour. It turned out that this woman had a child who had been born severely disabled. Hilary went home feeling immensely grateful that her own circumstances were not nearly as bad as they could be. She felt rejuvenated from the evening, and hopeful that they could get beyond this slump. But when she walked in the door to see no improvement, exhaustion descended upon her. Jack was sitting in the front room, still looking angry. But he asked in a civil tone, "How was your meeting?"

"Good."

When nothing more was said, she added, "I'm going to bed."

Hilary had just climbed between the sheets when Jack appeared in the bedroom doorway. "Maybe we should talk," he said.

Hilary sighed. "Maybe we should, but I'm exhausted, Jack. Can it wait?"

He said nothing for a full minute, and she nearly drifted off to sleep.

"Did you get some supper?" he asked.

"No, but I'm too tired to eat." What she really meant was that she was too tired to clean up the kitchen enough to even find room to fix a sandwich. Knowing she always cleaned up after herself for the most part only added to her frustration.

Jack said nothing more before Hilary fell asleep. She left for work the next morning while he was still sleeping. He woke up to the alarm, then lay in bed for a long while, trying to talk himself into getting up. But motivation eluded him as his thoughts hovered with Hilary. The anger he'd felt yesterday was gone.

Feeling helpless and frustrated, Jack attempted to turn his mind to prayer. But even that was difficult. As he stopped to ask himself why, he realized that he'd become spiritually apathetic as well. He'd just stopped caring; it was as simple as that. But now, with nowhere else to turn, he closed his eyes and immersed himself in prayer. He spent most of the morning in bed, just thinking and praying, trying to make sense of what was holding him back and wondering how to get beyond it.

A knock at the door caught him by surprise. He knew he could never get into the chair and get there in time to answer it. And the people they knew well were aware of a hidden key so they could come in if Jack couldn't get to the door. He was just hoping the visitor had left when he heard the door open, and a deep male voice hollered, "Jack? Are you here?" It was Ammon.

"I'm here," Jack called back, "but you're taking your life into your hands coming in here. It's a war zone."

Ammon appeared in the bedroom doorway and put his hands on his hips. "Having a bad week, I take it." He glanced subtly at the messy bedroom.

"More so than usual," Jack retorted. "What are you doing here?"

"Work's at a standstill. Thought I'd just see how you're doing. It's been a while."

"So why today?" Jack asked, feeling too skeptical to believe that Ammon might be the answer to his prayer.

"I don't know. I just . . . felt like you could use some company." He looked sad as he added, "I miss you."

Jack said. "Yeah, well . . . according to Hilary, you won't find me here."

"How is that?" Ammon chuckled.

"She says that Jack Hayden died in that accident and some jerk showed up in his place."

Ammon laughed so hard that Jack wanted to hit him. "Is it that funny?" he asked.

"Actually, yes. I think Hilary's the best thing that ever happened to you."

"I won't argue with that, but . . . well, I don't think my wife is very happy with me. And I can't say that I blame her." Ammon looked hesitant to ask for specifics, but his curiosity was evident. Jack motioned to the surrounding mess and added, "Would you be happy coming home to this after working two jobs to keep your husband fed?"

Ammon simply asked, "So, what are you going to do about it?"

"What *can* I do about it?"

"Are you asking me?"

"I did, didn't I?"

"Yes, but do you *really* want me to answer it, or—"

"Just answer the question, Ammon." Jack's terseness surprised even himself.

"Oh, come on, Jack. Look at yourself. After a year of this, are you still trying to convince yourself that your only value was in your ability to do manual labor? I'd bet that Hilary's not upset because the house is a mess. Could I venture to guess that she would like to be home to clean it?"

Jack sighed and pressed his lips together, almost wanting to tell Ammon to shut up and leave him alone. But Ammon stared him down. Then he smiled, saying easily, "Why don't I just help you get started a little, all right? I'm not so bad at housework myself. Then we can talk . . . in more productive surroundings."

Two hours later, Ammon and Jack sat at the table to eat a sandwich. Jack said, "Look at us. I feel like we should be sharing recipes and comparing cleaning products."

Ammon laughed. "What's wrong with that? I'm not ashamed to admit that what Allison does in the home has a lot more value than what I do to go out and make a dollar."

"At least you can go out and make a dollar."

"And you can't?" Jack didn't answer, but Ammon went on to say, "Do you think all of the work you've done in the past took no brains? Sure, you need to make some adjustments, but I get the impression you haven't even tried to think of something you can do. And I'd bet a month's wages you haven't asked your Father in Heaven to help you find a job."

Jack shook his head, wondering if this guy could read his mind. Or if the Spirit was somehow involved in this. He knew the truth in his heart; Ammon's visit was a testimony that his Father in Heaven loved him. Now it was up to him to act on it and get out of this rut he'd dug for himself.

"You know, Ammon, I probably owe you at least a month's wages for insurance premiums."

"You don't owe me anything, Jack. It was all absorbed into business costs, and it wasn't that big a deal." He paused and added, "Are you trying to tell me that you *have* prayed to find a job? If I made that bet, would I lose?"

Jack nodded. "I prayed for help." He glanced at the clock. "About six hours ago."

They laughed together and talked for another hour. Ammon shifted the conversation from Jack's problems to his own frustrations on the job. When he finally left, Jack just sat there for a few minutes. The apartment looked considerably better, but it still needed some serious help. And he was tempted to just go back to bed. But to do what? His habit of watching TV was no longer an option. Then he thought of Hilary. He couldn't blame her for being discouraged. And when it came right down to it, he was capable of doing something about it.

Hilary called from the school. Her voice was sweet as she asked how he was doing.

"I'm okay. How are you?"

"I'm fine," she insisted. "Do you need me to bring home anything?"

"I think we need milk. I don't know of anything else."

There was a long pause. "I love you, Jack," Hilary said with emotion.

"I love you, too, Hil. Don't work too hard, okay?"

"I should be home around seven," she said. "Lisa's going to teach the last class tonight. I'll see you then."

Jack felt extra motivation as he hung up the phone. He straightened things up a little more and did three loads of laundry. Then he sat by the bed and folded the clothes, leaving very little for Hilary to put away. He even vacuumed and rather enjoyed it. He couldn't do much about the bathtub, but he did clean the basin and toilet with little trouble.

When Jack couldn't see anything else that obviously needed doing, he looked at the clock. It wasn't even five yet. The hours until Hilary got home seemed long. He tried to imagine how she might react to coming home to a relatively clean apartment. Then the image expanded, and he wondered if he could actually manage to cook some dinner—not something out of a box or a can, but some *real* food. He looked around to tally the available ingredients, then he called Janna to ask for some pointers.

While he cooked, Jack heard echoes of all that Hilary had recently said to him storming through his head. He felt good about what he'd done today, but he knew that was only a small part of the problem. As difficult as it was, he knew it was time to take another step—figuratively speaking. He laughed at the thought.

* * * * *

Hilary had spent her day with a lingering heartache. She wondered if Jack was still angry with her for cutting the TV cable. She wasn't sorry she'd done it; she only hoped it would help the problem and not make it worse. Driving home, she prayed that she could face whatever was waiting for her with fortitude, and that she could show Jack her love for him without allowing him to waste his life away. She sat in the driveway for a few minutes, steeling herself to enter the house with a good attitude.

CHAPTER FIFTEEN

*H*ilary came in the door and caught her breath. The front room was dark, but obviously clean. A light shone from the kitchen, illuminating the table set for two—with candles, no less. She closed the door behind her and took off her coat. Jack emerged from the kitchen looking somewhat sheepish, like a schoolboy with a bouquet of dandelions behind his back. "Hi," he said, as if it was the most eloquent greeting he could come up with.

"I, uh . . . wonder if I'm in the wrong apartment," she said lightly.

"You're married to Jack Hayden, aren't you?" he asked.

"Yes."

"Well, this is the place. That jerk who was impersonating him is gone—hopefully for good."

Hilary didn't know whether to laugh or cry. She felt renewed already from the evidence of his love. He really cared about her, and she knew it. She only hoped this would not just be one more temporary effort that would merge into a new stage of denial.

When Hilary said nothing, Jack motioned toward the table. "Shall we eat?"

"Yes, of course. It smells wonderful."

Jack flipped off the kitchen light, and they sat across from each other at the candle-lit table.

"It's not macaroni and cheese," she commented after the blessing.

"No."

"I thought you said you couldn't cook."

"Well, Janna kind of talked me through it. She said spaghetti wasn't too difficult."

"It's very good. You and Janna make a good team."

"She told me she might consider opening a new business: a hotline for idiots in the kitchen. Although I think she's got her hands full at the moment." Hilary nodded and he said, "She's pregnant, you know."

"Yes, I know."

"But you didn't tell me."

Hilary shook her head but said nothing. Jack could easily guess her reasons for avoiding the subject. She wanted children of her own, and the prospect of that happening under the present circumstances was uncertain at best. Which brought Jack to the point he knew he needed to make. "Hilary," he said gently, "we need to talk."

She looked up. The obvious emotion in her eyes compelled him to say, "I don't know why you put up with me, Hilary."

"You're everything to me, Jack. I love you."

"Yes, that's apparent," he said, then they finished their meal in silence. Together they cleared the table, while Hilary wondered if it would be up to her to take the initiative in getting back to their conversation. She was relieved when Jack said, "I'll wash the dishes tomorrow. Let's talk."

Jack moved from his chair onto the couch and motioned for her to sit beside him. He put his arm around her and pressed a kiss into her hair, then he cleared his throat and began, "When I called Janna today, we talked about more than cooking."

Hilary pulled back to look into his eyes. "Really?"

"She's a very wise woman. And maybe knowing that she's faced her own unspeakable struggles makes it easier to believe her when she tells me I can get beyond this."

Hilary sensed a multitude of thoughts churning inside him, and she waited patiently, allowing him the space to express them.

"We talked about a lot of things, Hilary, but she said one thing in particular that really hit me hard."

"And what is that?" she asked gently.

"She told me it's not my inability to walk that's holding me back." Jack swallowed hard, finding it difficult to say. "She said it's fear that's crippling me. And . . . I think she's right."

Hilary was so in awe of hearing such things come from his mouth that she couldn't speak. The silence dragged on until he finally said,

"She told me there are many disabilities that people struggle with: abuse, dysfunction . . . the list goes on and on. In fact, she told me about some people she's worked with at the crisis center that helped put my troubles into perspective."

Again there was silence. Jack pulled Hilary closer, as if she was suddenly his air to breathe. She could feel him crying, and just held him tighter, while silent tears trickled down her own face. "Oh, Hilary," he murmured, "I want to get past this. I want to *live* again, to feel alive again. And I . . . I believe it's possible . . . at least with you here to help me, but . . . I don't know where to start. I don't know what to do. I feel so helpless."

Hilary gave him a few minutes to calm down before she asked, "Did Janna have any suggestions on where to start?"

"Well, she said I should just pick something I'm afraid of, and do it." He shook his head. "But I'm lost on that. Everything just feels so overwhelming, and . . ."

When he said nothing more, Hilary urged, "Just talk to me, Jack. Tell me what bothers you most. What's hardest for you? We'll work on it together."

Jack thought about it for a few minutes before he said, "I always felt like I could make a difference before. When I worked construction, I could work long and hard and make things happen. Ammon always told me how much he appreciated that, and how I eased stress for him because he could count on me to accomplish a lot. And it was the same when I helped your parents; I could go out there and work hard and make life easier for them. What can I do for them now?"

Hilary was momentarily astonished to realize that he honestly couldn't see anything beyond his ability to work. She took his hand and looked into his eyes. "Jack, I know my parents really appreciated the work you did for them—on the farm, and around the house—but that's not why they love you. That's not the *real* difference you made in their lives."

Jack's eyes became skeptical, as if he suspected she might lie to him to make him feel better. But she gave him a penetrating stare and said, "You made a difference to them because you filled the emptiness in their lives. You made up for Jeffrey's absence in a way that nobody else ever could have. You make them laugh. You lift their spirits."

Hilary took his hand. "You did the same for me, Jack. That's why we were best friends for so long. That's why I turned to *you* when I needed a shoulder to cry on and some good advice. The important things have *nothing* to do with your physical ability to do anything.

"You *can* make a difference in people's lives, Jack. But you have to get outside yourself to do it. If you're sitting here in front of the television, you don't have the chance to lift someone's spirits. Who's to say that just by sitting in church with a smile on your face, you might not be encouraging someone who's feeling overwhelmed by *their* struggles? What you're dealing with is tough, Jack. No one is questioning that. But in your heart I think you know it was supposed to happen; that this is what *you* need in order to accomplish what God wants you to do in this life."

Jack looked so dumbstruck that Hilary almost regretted what she'd said. But a quick search of her feelings assured her that it needed to be said.

Jack suddenly lost his ability to breathe as he attempted to absorb what Hilary had just said. The more he tried to comprehend it, the more constricted his chest became. "What are you saying?" he finally managed.

As Hilary observed his reaction, she realized that all these months, while he'd been struggling, she had taken it for granted that he knew and understood things that he obviously hadn't. "Jack," she said gently, "you told me how you often felt that your life wasn't going to be what you'd expected; that something was going to happen. Surely you remember that you—"

"Yes, I know that, but . . ." His heart was pounding so hard that he couldn't find words to finish.

Hilary uttered a quick prayer for guidance in helping Jack understand what the Spirit had helped her understand a long time ago. Then she recalled that reading his patriarchal blessing had helped her. She went to the bookcase and pulled out his journal—the one he hadn't written in for more than a year. Tucked inside the cover was a well-worn copy of his patriarchal blessing. She sat beside him again and scanned to find the right paragraph.

Jack felt something tremble in the deepest part of him as he took the paper from Hilary and attempted to focus enough to read.

The afflictions in your life were chosen before you left your heavenly home to give you the strength in mind and spirit to assist those who are sent to you. By depending on the Spirit to guide and carry you, your example and testimony will be a strength to others who will reset their feet along paths that will bring them to exaltation. And even though you knew that your personal struggles would be great, you enthusiastically accepted the opportunity to be an instrument in the Father's hands, to accomplish his will.

Jack had read his patriarchal blessing a thousand times, although he'd not looked at it since the accident. But the words before him had never made sense until now. It wasn't the words themselves as much as the indescribable warmth that filled him. In an instant, his entire perspective changed. This was not some curse or punishment. This was something that had been woven into the pattern of his life a very long time ago; something that *he* had agreed to, knowing it would be better for him—and for those around him.

As he finished reading and looked into Hilary's eyes, he couldn't possibly find the words to tell her that everything had changed. *Everything.* He knew the adjustments ahead in his life would not be easy, and there were many obstacles and fears yet to be overcome. But he knew in his heart that God was mindful of him, and there was a plan for his life. He knew, too, that he *could* make a difference in this world. To his wife. To his friends. Perhaps to people he'd not yet encountered. And Hilary was right; he couldn't make a difference if he just sat at home feeling sorry for himself.

Jack and Hilary talked until far past midnight, sharing feelings and hopes that neither of them had dared express before now. The following day, Jack made some phone calls and filled out several forms to apply for a grant. With any luck, he would be able to start classes in January.

On Sunday, Jack went to church for the first time in a long while. And for the first time since the accident, he felt grateful to be there. He absorbed the spirit of the meeting, and felt privileged to take the sacrament. When the bishop shook his hand and greeted him with enthusiasm, Jack apologized for not being willing to serve in the ward, and told him he would like to be considered for a church calling. A week later Jack was called to be the gospel doctrine teacher.

He felt tempted to tell the bishop he wasn't sure if he was up to something that took so much knowledge and study. But, reminding himself to have faith, he accepted. Within a few weeks he found he could actually feel quite comfortable in front of his class, and he really enjoyed teaching. Beyond that, he grew to rely on the time he had to study at home in order to teach his lessons effectively.

Six weeks after Hilary had cut the television cable, Jack wondered what had been possessing him. Even since the cable had been repaired, he rarely turned on the TV. Realizing that Hilary *never* watched TV, he called the cable company and had it disconnected. He was much too busy to watch TV anyway, and he figured they could manage with the basic channels. While he was doing the majority of the housework and laundry, and half of the cooking, he was also spending a specified amount of time each day on the phone, trying to find a job. He met with little success, and he began to feel the harsh repercussions of being disabled. But he could always talk to Hilary about it at the end of the day, and she helped him see the perspective.

Jack spent time every day studying for his Sunday School lessons, and he and Hilary seemed to find more time to spend together. They started going out once a week, often with Janna and Colin or Ammon and Allison. His friends as well as his wife helped him keep perspective when he wondered sometimes if he would *ever* find work he could enjoy and be good at. Even when the approval came through for him to go to school, he felt frustrated in wondering what he could study that would actually mean something to him. It was hearing Ammon complain about the problems he often found in house plans that gave Jack the idea to look into drafting and architecture. The idea gave him some real excitement when he was actually able to register for classes in that area.

Jack liked the improvement he could see in his life, and he sensed a serenity in Hilary that hadn't been there in a long time. But he still hated having her work two jobs, and he prayed he could find a way to make things easier for her. Then, on a morning in November when it was snowing hard and he was finding it difficult to concentrate, Ammon called to see how he was doing. Through the course of their conversation, as Ammon complained a little about the usual frustrations of his work, he happened to mention that he'd been down to the building supply store, where they were short-handed and everything was in chaos. It wasn't until Jack got off the phone that the thought struck him as an opportunity. He'd been in that particular store to get supplies dozens of times. He knew who the manager was, and with any luck, the manager would remember him.

When Hilary got home from work, Jack said, "Don't take your coat off. We're going out to eat."

"We are? But—"

"Don't argue with me. Let's go."

"Okay," she said, following him outside. They were sitting over soup and sandwiches before she said, "So, is this a special occasion or—"

"Yes, it is, actually."

"What?" she demanded. "I can tell you've got something up your sleeve. I can't stand the suspense any longer."

Jack smiled and leaned toward her, whispering dramatically, "I've got a job. I start tomorrow."

Hilary gasped. Then she laughed. "Tomorrow? Really?"

Jack nodded, then hurried to explain before she exploded with questions. "The thing is," he summarized, "they need someone who not only knows where to find everything, but someone who can answer questions and make sure that customers get what they *really* need for the job. I *know* all of that."

Hilary just smiled. "Of course you do." She laughed again.

"Is something funny?"

"No, I'm just happy."

"Happy that you don't have to work two jobs indefinitely?"

"Well, that will be nice, but . . ." She took his hand. "I'm so glad to see you finding a life again. I know you'll do well in whatever you set your mind to."

Jack sighed. "I only wish I had done this a year ago."

"Well, maybe the time just wasn't right. You've become a lot more capable physically in the last several months, and well . . . maybe you just needed to work some things through. The important thing is, you're doing it now."

Jack kissed Hilary's hand. "I love you," he said. "Thank you for not giving up on me."

"You didn't give up on me," she countered, and he smiled.

Hilary looked suddenly concerned and he asked, "What's wrong?"

"How are you going to get there? I mean, I can take you some, but—"

"I've already got that covered," he assured her. "I've checked bus schedules, and that's an option—one I'm not terribly excited about, but it's temporary. Besides, Bill said he'd be happy to take me whenever I needed a ride. Once I start bringing some money in, I'd like to look into getting a car I can drive; then it won't be a problem. I don't want to have to depend on anybody else."

Hilary leaned across the table and kissed him quickly. "Just don't get too independent, okay? I'd like to feel needed a little."

Jack kissed her again. "I *do* need you, Hilary. But not for taxi or maid service. I need *you.*"

"I need you, too," she said, and Jack felt some peace in knowing he could actually give her what she needed. He could be there for her, be her friend, her lover, her helpmeet. And with time, he believed he could actually provide a living for her.

Suddenly, time that had dragged for Jack through the last several months began to fly. Now that he was employed, he and Hilary reworked the household schedule. And when Jack started classes, they knew it had to be reevaluated again. Looking carefully at their finances, they found that the medical debt was manageable, and Hilary's car was now paid for. They found that they could get a loan for another car, consolidate it with their little remaining debt, and have a monthly payment less than Hilary's car payment had been. For Jack, having a car with hand controls, that he could get in and out of without assistance, gave him a whole new sense of independence. Since Jack was making more money than Hilary had been making at the school, she was able to leave that job and be at home more, which made it possible for Jack to work and go to school.

By spring, Hilary felt in control of her life enough that she could have a baby. She had seen Claire teach dance almost until her due date more than once, and she felt confident that she could do the same. She had several college-age students who could teach classes for her when necessary, so the studio could keep running even while she took maternity leave. After talking with Jack and praying about it, they decided it was the right thing to do. But six months later, Hilary was still not pregnant. And while it troubled her somewhat, she was more concerned about how Jack would perceive it. He'd come a long way, but there were elements related to his disability that still troubled him. Little was said between them, but as they regularly visited with Janna and Colin, seeing their happiness with the new baby, Hilary knew it disturbed Jack.

Even so, each day Hilary expressed gratitude to her Father in Heaven for all they *did* have, and she tried not to worry about it. Jack was doing beautifully in school. They'd been able to get a home computer, and he was thriving on his growing knowledge of interesting ways to use it.

Another blessing came when Ammon and his wife made a surprise visit on a Sunday afternoon. They'd left the children with Ammon's sister, and after the small talk ran down, it became evident that there was a purpose to their visit.

"Jack," Ammon said, "I want to build you a home."

Jack and Hilary exchanged a concerned glance before Jack said, "That would be great, but . . . I don't think we can qualify for a mortgage just yet. Maybe after I finish school and get a job that pays—"

"Hear me out," Ammon interrupted. "Do you remember how you had me put a percentage of your wages away for the purpose of building a home?"

Jack had to admit, "I'd honestly forgotten."

"Well, it's been earning interest."

"It should go to pay for those insurance premiums."

"I've told you a dozen times, Jack, they were absorbed by the business. It was no big deal. Let it go."

Hilary gave him a cautious glance and a gentle nudge with her elbow. She might as well have screamed, *Be gracious, not prideful.*

"Okay," Jack said. "I'm listening."

"Anyway," Ammon went on, seeming a little nervous, "I can give you my cost on all the materials. I'm in a position where I can donate my labor if I work on it along with some other projects going up in that new subdivision. I've already got several lots; you can take your pick."

Jack blew out a long breath. "This is sounding good, Ammon, but . . . well, first of all, I'm glad you like me and all, but donating your labor on an entire home is . . . well . . ."

"I'm not going to criticize you for being proud, Jack," he said, "because I think if I were in your position I'd feel the same way. But . . . I *want* to do this; I feel like it's the right thing to do. And I wonder if you realize how much you do for me."

Jack chuckled. "What on earth do I do for you?"

"Well, I'll tell you—if you promise not to get uptight."

"Okay, I'll listen. Then I'll beat you up."

Ammon chuckled. "You're on. The thing is, Jack, you know the business I'm in can be pretty stressful."

Jack nodded, knowing it was an understatement. Ammon was commonly caught between mortgage companies and people buying homes, with deadlines and expectations that were often impossible to meet.

"The thing is, you always listen to me complain, and you've dealt with it enough to know how I feel. Besides, whenever I start getting weighed down with my worries, all I have to do is think of you, and it's easy to pick up and keep going. You remind me—just by being there—that there isn't a problem that can't be overcome. You're an example to me, Jack, and I consider myself lucky to be your friend."

"And now you want to add more stress to your life by building *me* a home?"

"I want to do this, Jack. And I really think we can work out the loan. I know of a few strings I can pull; and if all else fails, I have an investor who will work with me unquestionably on this one. We can start out with payments equivalent to your rent, and build up to something that's workable for your income."

Jack knew it might not be entirely fair, but he had to say what he felt. "I'm not real keen on taking charity, Ammon."

Ammon's eyes flashed. "This is not charity, Jack. You're going to have to pay for your home like everybody else in the world. This is simply an opportunity to get into a home while the getting is good. We can cover the details more later. I just want to know if you're interested."

"Of course I'm interested," Jack admitted. "I want a home to raise my family in. But I don't want you putting your neck on the line for me."

"I won't be."

Ammon spoke with enough confidence that Jack had to ask, "Who is this investor?"

Ammon hesitated.

"Well?"

"It's my father-in-law. He lives in Australia, and he—"

"Your father's Australian?" Jack asked Allison.

"My stepfather, actually," she explained. "He's a wonderful man, Jack. He's been aware of your situation since the accident. He simply wants to finance your home in a way that will be workable for you. When you reach a point where it's possible, you can refinance the house and pay him off. That's all."

They talked through some of the possibilities of the situation, and Jack told Ammon that he and Hilary would discuss it and pray about it. A few days later they drove out to the building site where Ammon met them, and they picked out a lot. That evening, Ammon came over with some possible floor plans. "With a few minor adjustments, we can build the home to suit your needs," he said, pointing out where he would put a ramp in the garage, and how he could enlarge the master bathroom.

Jack asked if he could keep the plans and look them over. He and Hilary discussed their ideas, then Jack experimented with some ideas of his own. When he saw Ammon again, he showed him a new set of plans he'd done on the computer. Ammon listened as Jack pointed out certain advantages in space and traffic flow in the home. "This is amazing," Ammon said, studying the plans closely. "With just a few simple changes, you've made the entire floor plan more . . ."

"Productive?" Jack suggested.

"Yes." Ammon's eyes became intent as he said, "You have a gift here, Jack."

Jack leaned back and sighed. He knew Ammon meant it. And it gave him hope.

Through the following weeks, Ammon took advantage of the unusually dry winter weather to make considerable progress in building Jack and Hilary's home. And Jack was so busy he wondered how he'd ever had time to be discouraged. Between working and studying for his Sunday lessons, he put every minute into his schooling that he possibly could, feeling anxious to get it behind him.

Hilary was delighted to see Jack doing so well. But the more involved he became in achieving his goals, the more she longed to find her own fulfillment. Pregnancy continued to elude her; and while she felt compelled to get some medical intervention and do something about it, a part of her hesitated. Jack was doing so well, and she didn't want to throw another complication into his life. So she just tried to stay supportive of him and kept busy running her studio. She put on a big dance recital that consumed every spare moment, and in spite of Jack's busy schedule, he attended both performances. He even arranged for a dozen red roses to be presented to her onstage.

Three years after Jack's accident, Hilary was amazed to see how far he had come. He was so thoroughly independent that those who knew him couldn't help but be inspired. He put a great deal of effort into taking good care of himself, knowing that his body was particularly vulnerable to infections and other problems. He put his whole heart into his church calling, and no matter how busy he got, he was always there for Hilary, offering his love and support. They moved into their home and consequently received new callings; Hilary taught Primary, and Jack became an assistant ward clerk. They enjoyed their new ward and neighborhood. She had every reason to believe that life would only continue to get better—except for that one lingering disappointment that she hardly dared mention. And then they got the phone call.

It was Friday, and Hilary had no classes. Jack had just come in from work when the phone rang, and he answered it.

"Thank heaven you're home," Colin said with obvious anxiety. "Is Hilary there?"

"Yes. What's wrong?" Jack demanded.

"I'll tell you when you get here. Can you come over? Both of you?"

"Yes, of course we can. We'll be right there."

"Who was that?" Hilary asked, looking as alarmed as he felt.

"It was Colin. He wants us to come over. We'd better hurry."

Through the short drive across town, Jack and Hilary speculated on what might have gone wrong. But neither of them had come even close to guessing.

Colin answered the door, looking upset. His eyes were hard and angry. The house was unusually quiet.

"What's wrong?" Jack demanded as soon as they were in the door. "Is somebody sick, or hurt, or—"

"No. Everyone's fine—miraculously so. I took the children to my mother's. Matthew's in his room." Colin pushed a hand through his already mussed hair, and Hilary noticed he was shaking.

"Where's Janna?" she asked.

"She's upstairs. I think she could really use you right now."

Hilary didn't question that, but she wanted to have some idea of what was going on before she approached the situation. She was wondering how to ask when Colin said, "Russell was here."

"Who?" Jack asked. But Hilary already knew. And her heart dropped to the pit of her stomach.

"Her first husband," Colin snarled. "He has no purpose in life beyond his desire to kill Janna. Every time he gets out of prison, he's here like lightning." He became emotional as he added, "I think Janna could use a woman to talk to right now. And then I'd like Jack to help me give her a blessing. And Matthew, too. He's pretty shaken up."

Hilary hurried up the stairs, and Colin practically collapsed on the couch. "Looks like you're pretty shaken up, too," Jack said. "Want to talk about it?"

Colin *did* talk about it, but not before he put his head into his hands and cried for a good ten minutes. Jack just waited patiently, not liking the thoughts churning around in his own head.

Upstairs in the bedroom, Hilary found Janna curled up on the bed, staring at the wall. With her eyes puffy and red, it was easy to see that she'd reached the state of numbness that usually followed a good, long cry.

"Are you okay?" Hilary asked.

Janna's eyes shifted toward the doorway where she stood, then she reached out a hand. "I'm better now," she said as Hilary took it and sat on the edge of the bed.

"What happened?" Hilary asked.

Janna leaned up against the headboard and reached for a box of tissues on the bedside table when tears threatened again. "I . . . uh . . . I had just put the boys down for their naps, and . . . I walked into the hall and . . . there he was. I knew he was out on parole, but . . . I just didn't think he would really be stupid enough to try it again. I mean . . . he's spent more than ten years in prison. Wouldn't you think he'd get the idea? Of course, I've realized through the years, as I've studied psychological behaviors, that Russell must be psychotic, to say the least—

among other things." Janna took a moment to calm down and blow her nose. "Anyway, I just froze. I told myself I knew how to stand up to him, and I wasn't going to be afraid, but . . ."

Janna became so upset that she couldn't even talk for a few minutes. When she calmed down, she managed to say, "Then I realized he had a gun, and . . . I thought of my babies being so close, and . . . I knew how crazy Russell could be. And . . ." She paused again to get control of her emotion.

"But obviously you're all right," Hilary said. "What happened?"

"Matthew stayed home today. He said he just didn't feel well. I didn't even know he was awake . . . but all of a sudden he was there. He knocked the gun out of Russell's hand somehow, and . . ." Again Janna became emotional. She looked into Hilary's eyes, and her voice became soft with a helpless desperation. "I felt safe then. I knew that my Father in Heaven was looking out for me. But then . . . Matthew took the gun . . . and he put it to Russell's head, and . . . he cocked it, and . . ."

Hilary held her breath, praying this story wouldn't end with tragedy.

"I froze again," Janna said. "I didn't even dare move to go call the police. I could see Matthew's anger; I could *feel* it. He was just a child when all of the abuse was happening. No one knew more than Matthew how bad it had been. And there he stood, taller than Russell. I could feel his hatred. And here he is, so close to going on his mission. I could almost literally see the horrible repercussions that such a thing would bring into his life."

"Please don't tell me he did it," Hilary muttered, crying herself now.

Janna shook her head vehemently. "No, he didn't do it. But it took a lot of talking to get him to back off. He said some awful things to Russell; things that made me realize Matthew's memories must be horrid. And he hit Russell, hard, more than once. After the police took Russell away, Matthew just . . . he just crumbled, and . . . I realized that no matter how far we've come, there are some things inside that never go away. I regretted the choices I'd made all over again; choices that left my son exposed to such horrors."

Janna fervently expressed her gratitude for being protected. She knew that God was looking out for her and her family, and she knew from past experience that time would put this in perspective and she would be all right. But she was concerned for Matthew. "He's got a strong spirit," she said. "I know he'll be okay, but . . . I just pray he'll be able to deal with that anger before it comes back to hurt him."

Hilary just held Janna's hand as she talked out every concern and cried out all of her emotion. For years, she had leaned on Janna and been grateful to have a friendship that had carried her through so much. But now she saw their relationship in a new light, and was grateful to be here for Janna. She knew in her heart that there had been a divine hand in bringing them together initially, and she was awed to see how God answered prayers through the workings of a friend.

* * * * *

After Jack heard the whole story from Colin, he asked if he could talk to Matthew.

"He's in his room," Colin said.

"Well, I can't exactly go down to the basement and find him," Jack said.

"Good point." Colin went to the basement and returned a minute later. "I told him you wanted to talk to him. He'll be up in a minute."

Jack wondered if Matthew would be hesitant to open up. Jack had spent a lot of time in his home and with his family, but his relationship with Matthew had always been casual and light for the most part. It took little effort, however, to get Matthew to talk about what had happened and how it made him feel. With clenched teeth he admitted, "I wanted to kill him. I wanted with everything inside of me to just pull that trigger."

"Why didn't you?" Jack asked.

"My mother told me that if I did it, I would never find peace. She said I could probably get away with it legally, but I would never get away with it morally. And . . ." Matthew became emotional as he spoke. "When I asked her if she'd found peace with it, she told me she had. And I knew she meant it. I wanted so badly just to make sure he could never threaten or hurt her again, but . . . if she could find peace, after everything he's done to her, then . . . I knew maybe I could find peace with it, too." Matthew cleared his throat and added, "So I hit him instead."

Colin watched his son with empathy etched into his expression. He grasped Matthew's hand and said, "I'm proud of you, son. I'm not sure I would have had the will power to not pull that trigger."

"Well," Matthew said more lightly, "I didn't think shooting someone would look real good on my mission papers."

"No," Jack chuckled, "it probably wouldn't."

A few minutes later, Janna and Hilary came down the stairs. They talked together for quite a while, then Jack helped Colin give his wife and son priesthood blessings. They were promised comfort and peace, and they were also told that Russell would no longer be a problem.

Hilary came away feeling very humbled and grateful that everything had turned out as well as it had. Thoughts of it hovered with her for several days, and she called Janna often to see how she was doing. After a week, Janna reported that they were doing much better. Matthew had sent in his papers after having discussed the incident with the bishop, and with Sean O'Hara, who had been his counselor in the past. Janna reported that Matthew was handling it well, and she felt certain he would be able to serve his mission and progress into adulthood without severe scars from the abuse he'd witnessed in his childhood.

When Hilary reported to Jack what Janna had said, he seemed pleased; but she sensed that something was disturbing him. In fact, he'd been in a more somber mood since all of this had happened. She felt a need to talk to him, but old memories made it difficult to approach him. Janna had talked to her about the way healing comes in layers, and struggles could arise when they were least expected. Hilary only hoped that whatever was troubling Jack would not prove too difficult to deal with.

In the midst of all this, word came that Jack's mother had passed away very suddenly. Jack certainly wouldn't miss Judy; he'd not had a relationship with her for years, and the distance between them had not been his choice. He knew he'd done everything he could, so any regrets were quickly resolved. Still, the reality of her death added to his somber mood, deepening Hilary's concern. And Jack couldn't help but feel disconcerted as his father's land was sold and the assets divided among the three sons. How could he not think of how he'd dreamed of owning it himself, of working the land for the rest of his life?

Jack discussed his feelings with Hilary and resolved to concentrate on all that was good in his life. If nothing else, his inheritance made it possible for them to get completely out of debt except for the mortgage, and to refinance the house in a way that was workable.

Hilary could see that Jack's attitude was good, but there was no denying that something was troubling him—and it had nothing to do with his mother's death or his father's land. She prayed they could deal with whatever it was, and move ahead.

CHAPTER SIXTEEN

While Hilary was trying to get up the courage to ask Jack what was troubling him, she was given a heartening indication of how far they'd come. Jack opened the conversation himself one evening after dinner, making it clear that he would not let this problem, whatever it was, eat at him and come between them.

"I need to talk, Hilary. I don't know where to start or what to say. I only know there are thoughts in my head that won't go away; things that make me break out in a cold sweat, and . . ." He shrugged his shoulders. "I don't know, Hilary. I just don't know."

Hilary took his hand. "What kind of thoughts, Jack?"

By his expression, she knew he didn't want to voice them.

"It's okay," she assured him.

"Well," he said, "when I think back to all the time I spent just sitting around and avoiding the world, I know I was scared. There were things that frightened me, and things that just made me feel at a loss. When I started getting out more and accomplishing things, it helped me gain some confidence, but . . . I realize now that there are still some things I'm afraid of. And I don't know what to do about it."

"What are you afraid of, Jack?" she asked gently. "You can tell me."

"I know. It's just that . . . well, some of it's kind of abstract; hard to explain."

"And what about the rest of it?" she asked.

Jack looked into her eyes and wondered how she could read him so well. He sighed and looked down. "Ever since this thing happened with Janna's ex-husband, I . . ." He took a deep breath. "I just keep wondering what I would do if somebody broke into our home; if someone threatened you—or me. The concept of being so vulnerable never even occurred to me before the accident, Hilary. I've always been strong; I was always able to protect myself. No one ever bullied me, or even tried to hurt me. But now, I can't protect myself. And far worse, I couldn't protect you. I just don't know how to deal with that, Hilary."

Hilary thought about it and had to admit, "I don't know either, Jack. I don't have all the answers."

Jack chuckled. "That's funny, you always *seem* to have the answers."

Hilary shrugged her shoulders. "I just ask Janna. Her experiences have given her a lot of wisdom and insight." Hilary noted the interest in his eyes and suggested, "Maybe we should invite Colin and Janna over for dinner tomorrow—if they can come, of course."

"They haven't seen the house since we got settled in," Jack said. "Just warn them that we have ulterior motives."

Colin and Janna came to dinner the following evening. "The house looks great," Colin commented after they'd had a brief tour.

"Yeah," Jack said lightly, "this is the house that Jack didn't build. But I confess, we are extremely grateful to have it."

The four of them talked and laughed and had a good time. It wasn't until after dinner, when they were gathered in the front room to relax, that Janna said, "So, Jack, Hilary tells me there's something you want to talk about."

Jack appreciated the fact that he felt comfortable with these people and there was no need to be embarrassed about admitting that he needed some feedback. "Do you ever feel like a counselor?" he asked Janna.

She laughed softly. "I'm hardly qualified for that." She glanced at Colin. "I don't know how I should feel about admitting that I know a few things from personal experience. At least if I can pass something along, I can say it was worth it—well *maybe* it was worth it," she added lightly.

"You're a very wise woman," Jack said. "You've already helped me and Hilary through a great deal."

"Well," Janna glanced down humbly, "there's a price to be paid for wisdom. I'd venture to say that before your life is finished, you'll have a great deal of wisdom to pass on to others, too. We were blessed to have a wonderful counselor who taught us a lot, and—"

"May I say," Colin interrupted, "that he taught us a lot, but the things that left the deepest impression on me came from *his* life's experiences. He knew what it was like to struggle. If nothing else, trials give us empathy and compassion—or at least they should. Personally, I think it has something to do with the commitment we make at baptism to bear one another's burdens. We need to struggle in order to have empathy. And we need to reach out in order to make a difference."

Hilary commented, "Wisdom must run in the family."

Colin only smiled at Janna, as if they shared some wonderful secret.

It was easy for Jack to express his fears, then Janna took the conversation back to her experiences in getting away from her abusive first husband. She explained that when she allowed herself to be ruled by fear, she had problems. But when she learned to put her trust in the Lord, after doing all she could, he always looked out for her. "He compensates for our weaknesses, Jack, whatever they may be. All we have to do is apply the faith and do the best we can."

"It's as simple as that?" Jack asked.

"Well, look at it this way, Jack," Colin said. "I was at work when Russell came this time. That left me helpless. The biggest, strongest, fastest man in the world is helpless with a gun pointed at him. You are no more helpless than the rest of us, Jack, because circumstances and situations can vary. If we couldn't put our trust in the Lord, we would always be living in fear. My personal belief is that he will protect us as far as it coincides with his will, provided we're doing our best to live righteously. He is certainly not the instigator of accidents and wickedness, but there are times when he is bound by natural law to allow things to happen— because of our choices, and to give us the opportunity to grow."

Jack thought how this concept related to the accident that had paralyzed him, and he believed within himself that what Colin had said was true.

"In regard to dealing with fear," Janna said, "I've heard from more than one source that the best way to overcome fear is to face it head-on. In a way, I guess that's what I did with Russell. But to put it in simple terms, if you're afraid of being in a crowded elevator, for instance, then you just go out and spend a day getting into crowded elevators."

"I suppose that makes sense," Jack said.

"Of course, there are some things that can't be faced head-on, and that's where the spiritual aspect takes over."

"After I do all I can do, I put it into the Lord's hands," Jack clarified.

"That's the way I see it," Janna said.

For several days, Jack contemplated the things Janna had said as they related to him. Admittedly, he felt much better. Seeing that there were certain things he had no control over, he came to realize that he'd done all he could to protect himself, his home, and his wife. Then he told the Lord he was putting the problem into his hands. Beyond that, he figured faith had to take over—which for him meant putting forth the effort to replace negative thoughts with positive ones, and praying daily for protection and guidance.

In analyzing some of the other things he feared, Jack worked out a way that he could face them head-on. He told Hilary one morning, "I'm taking some time off work today."

"To do what?"

"I'm going to face my fears."

Hilary had to smile at his attitude. "Ooh, like the white knight going into the forest to slay the dragon."

"Something like that."

"So, what exactly does this entail?"

"If I tell you, you might get scared." He grinned. "Or I might get embarrassed. When the dragon is dead, I'll tell you about it."

"Be careful," she called as he headed for the garage.

Later that day, Jack left work and went straight to a government building that housed many different offices, and where he figured he would encounter a wide variety of people. Recognizing that one of his fears was not being able to get somewhere he needed to go, he had to admit that the only answer was in getting help from someone—which brought him to what he was *really* afraid of. He knew it might sound silly, but he actually got knots in his stomach at the thought of having to ask a perfect stranger for help. He didn't know if it was pride, or the fear that he might be taken advantage of. Whatever it might be, he was determined to get over it—once and for all.

Jack waited at the foot of five stairs that led to one of the building's entrances. He knew that if he went around the corner to another door, there was a ramp. But that would defeat his purpose. Watching people closely, Jack waited for an opportunity to ask for some help. Of course, he was accustomed to being independent, and he knew it would take two men to lift him up those stairs. He couldn't recall being lifted by anyone, anywhere, since he'd left the hospital, and the idea wasn't terribly comfortable. But then, that's why he was here. If it happened and he survived it, then he could stop dreading the possibility that it might happen.

While he sat there and thought through the situation, if only to avoid thinking of how much he hated it, Jack had to admit he'd come far. The uncomfortable glances he received from many who passed by were something he'd become accustomed to. He searched for glances that were open and friendly, but the only ones he met were from women. One in particular stopped to tell him there was a ramp around the corner. He thanked her, then persisted with his quest.

Jack became distracted with his thoughts when he looked up to see two of the biggest, meanest-looking guys he'd ever encountered. They looked like they'd just ridden their Harleys in from some gang hideout in Death Valley. Jack felt his blood pressure rise several notches when he realized they were coming straight at him. *Oh my gosh, they're going to hurt me,* was his only recognizable thought. A firm hand, wearing a fingerless black leather glove, settled on his shoulder as a gruff voice said, "How ya doin' there, buddy? Ya look like ya could use some hep."

By *hep,* Jack assumed he meant help. He nodded, and in less than twenty seconds he was at the top of the stairs, breathing so rapidly in his relief that he barely managed to utter, "Thank you."

"No problem," came the reply, and then they disappeared into the elevator.

Jack pondered the encounter for a moment, then he laughed and went out the other door, down the ramp, and around the building. He felt better, but he knew he'd only dealt with part of the fear. He hadn't had to *ask* for help. And he wasn't going home until he did. He knew the building wouldn't be open forever, so he had to get on with it. By the time the doors were locked at five o'clock, Jack had been carried up the stairs three times. One pair of helpers even stopped to visit for a while, which he actually enjoyed.

He was on his way out of the building to go home when he noticed a pair of LDS missionaries standing near the pay phone, looking mildly distressed. It wasn't difficult to approach them and ask, "You guys need anything?" They responded with a warm greeting, then admitted they had an appointment across town, and their ride had fallen through.

"Come on," he said, "I can give you a ride."

"Can you *do* that?" one of them asked.

"I certainly can. And I've got a prime parking spot not too far from the door."

They looked pleasantly surprised, but said nothing as they followed him outside. "I was a missionary once," Jack told them, which immediately made them relax and begin chatting. They waited patiently while Jack got into the car and removed the wheels from the chair to lift it over him.

"Hey, that's pretty cool," one of the elders commented.

Jack dropped them off at their appointment, then went home to tell his wife that he had conquered his dragon. She didn't think it was the least bit silly, and it felt good to tell her that he hoped the need to ask a stranger for help would never arise—but if it did, he could handle it. "And," he added, "I even had the chance to give some service today." He told her about the missionaries, and how good it felt to actually be able to do something to help somebody else—however minor it may have been.

Just after Christmas, Colin and Janna received word that her first husband, Russell, had been sent back to prison; and because he had broken parole three times by attempting to harm Janna, he had been put away for life. Their relief was indescribable. And the following week, Matthew left on his mission, which brought back memories for Hilary of her own mission. She was amazed to see how much her life had changed since then, and it was easy to admit that the three years she and Jack had been married had been the best of her life—in spite of the struggles.

Even so, the passing of time couldn't help but remind her that they were still without children. She knew that Jack was concerned, too, although she doubted he felt the absence of children as keenly as she did. It remained unspoken between them for the most part, although Hilary knew it needed to be dealt with eventually. If they weren't able to have their own children, then they needed to work toward adoption and be prepared for all it entailed. And while a part of Hilary felt impatient, she hesitated opening the whole thing up, knowing it would be difficult. Deciding it would be better to wait until Jack finished school and was settled into a career, she bided her time and counted down the months until he would graduate.

A few weeks after they went to the Missionary Training Center to see Matthew off, Jack and Hilary were called into the bishop's office. Jack teased Hilary about being asked to serve as the Relief Society president, which she knew was absurd. Still, she agreed that the call would probably be for her. They were both stunned into silence when Jack was asked to be president of the Young Men's organization.

When Jack finally came to his senses, he laughed. "You're joking, right? You've got to be joking. This is just to make me feel better when you *really* ask me to be the nursery leader." The bishop's somber expression prompted Jack to add fervently, "Please tell me you're joking."

"I'm quite serious, Brother Hayden. My counselors and I have all felt very strongly that you are supposed to have this calling. Of course, before you accept—or decline—I want you to take some time and pray about it. It's important that you have your own personal witness that it's right for you. That's the only way you can make it through the tough moments in a calling such as this—and there will be tough moments."

Jack felt his head spinning as the bishop talked briefly about the thirty-seven young men in their ward. He took hold of Hilary's hand and squeezed so hard that he feared he might hurt her. "Bishop," he said when he got a chance to break in, "you're talking about working with young men—scouting, right? I'm an Eagle Scout; I know what it takes to pass all those things off. Camping, and swimming, and sports, and—"

"That's right."

"Bishop?" Jack practically squeaked. "I can't lead thirty-seven young men in such things. I *can't.*"

"There are other men in the organization to assist you, Brother Hayden. You don't have to take the entire project on single-handedly. You are welcome to delegate whatever is necessary. It's a strong leader with a strong testimony that these boys need. Your physical capabilities have little to do with it."

"But, Bishop, I haven't even served in the organization. I don't know anything about it. I don't know these boys, or—"

"You're not the first person to be put into a position cold. You'll learn quickly, I'm sure."

"I can't believe it," Jack said every ten minutes after they left the bishop's office. Hilary said nothing. She just smiled at him as if she thought this was all very amusing.

"What's so funny?" he demanded while she brushed through her hair before going to bed.

"Nothing's funny, Jack—except the way you keep shaking your head and muttering to yourself."

"Well! I just can't believe it."

"I can believe it. I think you'd do wonderfully."

"You're serious."

"Yes, I'm serious."

"But Hilary, it's such a *physical* calling. How can they expect me to—"

"The calling is what you make of it, Jack. I think you might actually surprise yourself. The bottom line is that you need to pray about it and get your own answer. If you know the Lord wants you in that calling, then . . ."

"Then I'd better do it," he provided.

Hilary smiled. "You see, Jack, with that kind of faith, you can do anything."

He squeezed his eyes shut and shook his head. "I just can't believe it."

Three days later, Jack called to tell the bishop he would accept the calling. On Sunday, when he was sustained, Jack could almost feel the chapel rumble with shock. But no one raised their hand to oppose the calling. When he went into priesthood meeting with everyone knowing he was the new man in charge of all the boys ages twelve to eighteen, he decided it couldn't be any worse than asking strangers for help.

Jack learned a new definition of the word "busy" as he settled into working with the Young Men. He'd never attended so many meetings in his life, never had so many different things to keep track of—most specifically, thirty-seven boys, each with his own personality and struggles. He quickly found that the bishop had been right: there were a few things he couldn't do, but he was perfectly capable of carrying out the majority of his responsibilities. And the men who worked with him were more than willing to compensate for his incapacities. Jack stayed home when the boys went snow camping, and he sat at the edge of the pool when they worked on their swimming merit badges. He refereed when they played ball. And when they just messed around on the basketball court after nearly every activity, he joined them. He found that he was still pretty good at making long shots, and he could work up a pretty good sweat trying to keep the ball away from three or four deacons.

Jack got his degree in April. Hilary cried through the ceremony, and they celebrated with friends and family, looking forward to a bright future. But several weeks later, Jack still hadn't been able to get a better job. Hilary kept telling him he needed to be patient until the right opportunity opened up. "A lot of people struggle to find the right job when they finish school," she told him. "It doesn't necessarily have anything to do with your disability."

"Well, it certainly doesn't help any," Jack growled.

"You know, Jack, companies are required to hire so many minority employees. *You* are considered a minority. In some ways, you have it better in that respect than the average Caucasian male."

"Yeah," he grumbled, "I get better parking places."

"Lighten up," she said. "You'll find something. In the meantime, we're not starving."

"No, but we still have that ugly old couch." Jack couldn't help but laugh when he said it. "And quite honestly, I don't want to sell building supplies for the rest of my life."

"You won't. Be patient."

Hilary repeated the same advice silently to herself. She wanted to believe that with patience alone she would eventually get pregnant, but in her heart she knew it was going to take more than that. Jack kept so busy that it was easy to avoid talking about it, but one evening he returned from the church earlier than usual and found her curled up on the bed, crying. "What's wrong?" he asked from the bedroom doorway, startling her.

"What are you doing here?" she snapped and frantically wiped the tears from her face.

"I live here!" Jack moved close to the bed and noticed the heating pad she was lying on. He knew she was having cramps. While she was trying to ignore Jack's inquiry, he said, "I take it you're still not pregnant. Is that why you're crying?"

Hilary only had to look at him, and she knew her eyes gave away the truth. He was right. And by the way he put his arms around her and held her, she knew he was more sensitive to the problem than she'd given him credit for.

"I'm so sorry, Hilary," he murmured.

"What are you apologizing for?"

"Because you would be pregnant by now if I weren't—"

"And what makes you so sure the problem is you?" Hilary pulled back and looked at him hard.

"It's obvious, isn't it?"

"No, Jack, I don't think it's obvious. If the problem is with you, it's not because of your paralysis."

Jack wanted to argue with her, but he knew it wouldn't solve the problem. In a softer voice, he asked, "So what do we do? Try adoption?"

Hilary blew her nose and sniffled loudly. "I assume that first we go the medical route. I know there's a lot they can do these days, but . . ."

She started to cry again. Jack lifted her chin with his finger and wiped at her tears. "Hey," he said, "why haven't you brought this up before?"

"I just . . . didn't want to make things more complicated for you. I just . . ."

When she didn't finish, he guessed, "You didn't want me to get depressed again."

Hilary nodded, unable to deny that he was right.

"I'll admit it's been troubling me, even if I haven't said anything. It breaks my heart to think of you not being able to have children of your own because of *me*. I've overcome a lot of struggles, and I've learned I'm not as helpless as I once thought I was. But when it comes to this, I'm not sure there's anything I can do to change it." He took her hand and squeezed it. "I'm just grateful that you love me, in spite of the complications I've brought into your life."

"Of course I love you," Hilary insisted, while deep inside she instinctively believed this problem had more to do with her than him.

Hilary didn't tell Jack she was going in to have testing done. She figured if they found a problem with her, there would be no need for Jack to do anything at all. When all the data had been gathered and Hilary was given the results, she felt such a mixture of emotions that it was difficult to know how to respond. She found no motivation to do anything at all, and she was sitting in the dark when Jack came home from work.

"What are you doing?" he asked when he flipped on the light and found her there.

"Just . . . thinking," she said.

Noting her somber mood, Jack felt a deep concern that made his heart quicken. "About what?" he asked cautiously.

Hilary cleared her throat and tried to get to the point. "I had some tests done. I talked with the doctor today, and—"

"You don't have to feel badly about telling me the problem is mine, Hilary." He didn't bother adding that he was a little put out to know that she had gone through this testing without even telling him. "I don't blame you for not wanting to tell me, but it's time we faced the reality. I think I've known the truth all along, but I didn't want to admit it. It's already hard enough to feel like a real man. This is just one more thing that makes me wish I could be more for you, Hilary."

Hilary watched him as if there was suddenly a mist between them. His voice was not as angry as it was self-recriminating. But as his words came back to her, a new layer of hurt settled in.

Jack felt something horribly uneasy as he watched huge tears collect in Hilary's eyes, then fall down her face. Her lip quivered until she bit it, but her expression was firm with courage as she lifted her chin and said, "The problem is with me, Jack."

Jack's breathing stopped as if it had hit a brick wall. He turned away and grimaced in self-punishment. He struggled for something—anything—he could say to take back his thoughtless words. He could hear her breathing sharpen as she added, "I don't see any need to talk about it. You've already told me how you feel."

"Hilary," he protested, "you can't possibly believe that—"

"Don't say anything else!" She shot to her feet, barely maintaining her composure. "I've had all I can take for one day." She stared at him for a long, agonizing moment. Then as if she had suddenly been struck by something unbearable, she pressed a hand over her mouth that didn't even begin to hold back the sobbing as she hurried down the hall and slammed the bedroom door.

Three hours passed before Jack finally found the courage—and the words—to attempt to undo what he had done.

Hilary heard Jack come into the darkened room and her heart quickened. She'd lost track of the time as she'd wrestled with her thoughts and emotions. She'd managed to come to terms with some things, and she had developed a new understanding of others. But now she felt drained; completely devoid of any strength that might get her beyond this moment. All she wanted was Jack. She needed to know that his love for her was strong and unconditional. She needed the replenishment and rejuvenation he was capable of giving her.

Her relief deepened when he moved onto the bed and eased close to her back. Reaching an arm around her, he took hold of her left hand, fingering her wedding ring as he whispered in her ear, "I know you probably don't want to talk to me right now. But you have to. You know why? Because when I put this ring on your finger, you promised to talk to me, even when—or perhaps *especially* when—I act like an idiot and make a fool of myself."

Jack heard no response beyond some sniffling. But she wasn't recoiling, so he tightened his arms around her and kissed the side of her face. "I love you, Hilary," he murmured. "And you have to believe me when I tell you that I would never, *ever* have said those things to you."

Still no response beyond a sniffle.

"Hilary, are you listening to me?"

She nodded her head, and Jack figured if she wasn't ready to talk, at least he had the opportunity to say everything he needed to say.

"Hilary, I've been thinking—and praying. And I think I've learned some things in the last couple of hours. It's hard to put into words, but . . . I'm going to try. The first thing is that . . . well, when the accident happened, I found it difficult to believe you could still love me and want to be with me in spite of my physical disabilities. With time, I was able to see that your love for me was real, and you've taught me a great deal about what real love means—things I certainly never learned from my mother. But I think somewhere deep inside, to this day, I still couldn't comprehend that your love was complete. I guess I've always assumed that somewhere inside of you, you were wishing that I was different, that I was capable of being physically perfect. But while I was sitting in the other room, asking myself how

I *really* felt about what you just told me, something occurred to me that I'd never considered before. I know in my heart how much I love you, and I don't love you any less for whatever may be wrong with you physically. Any disappointment I might feel is nothing compared to my heartache on your behalf, knowing this is probably harder for you. And then I realized that in a small way, it helped me understand how you've felt about me all along. Let's just say that . . . I think I understand love a little better than I ever have before. And . . ." Jack took a moment to fight back the lump gathering in his throat before he went on. "And along with that, I also understand now that circumstances can't destroy my birthright. I can choose how I respond to my circumstances; I am in control of how I let them affect me. You taught me that, Hilary. And I want you to understand the same thing." Again he forced back his emotion to continue.

"And the other thing I learned is . . . well, I want children, Hilary. And I know you do, too. We'll work together to do whatever we have to do to have a family, but . . . I can see a new perspective here. Or maybe . . . I've been able to finally put the pieces together on something I've been learning a little along the way. What I'm trying to say is . . . well, you've told me this a hundred times, Hilary, but now I know it's true. It's not what we *don't* have that matters, it's making the most of what we *do* have. Not having children would be difficult, yes, but we would find a way to be happy in spite of it. And if we live for the blessings, everything will be restored to us perfectly in the next life."

A rush of emotion caught him off guard. But the tears were cleansing as he admitted, "I know in my heart, Hilary, that you and I will dance together again. And we will have children. And we will know joy beyond any earthly comprehension."

Jack took a moment to gather his emotions, well aware that Hilary was crying, too. "I don't know if I ever told you this," he continued, "but whenever I come up against something really difficult; whenever I start to feel angry with my circumstances, I close my eyes and imagine how it feels to hold you in my arms and waltz you around the room—except there are no walls, no floor. It's just you and me and heaven. I wonder sometimes if it's easier to keep an eternal perspective when eternity holds such tangible promises for me. But those promises mean nothing, Hilary, without you. I don't need money, or success, or children, or even the ability to walk to make me happy. I only need the gospel—and you. And that is why I would never want to do or say anything to hurt you."

When the silence grew long, Jack wondered if she had gone to sleep. Then she turned in his arms to face him, even though he couldn't quite make out her features in the darkness.

"I know, Jack." Her voice was hoarse from the time she'd spent crying. "I guess what hurts most is . . . I wonder why you can't believe in yourself the way you believe in me."

Jack sighed and pressed a kiss to her brow. In spite of the hurtful things he'd said—however unintentionally—she was more concerned about their implications for him. It was easy for him to admit, "I asked myself that question several times in the last few hours."

"And did you come up with an answer?"

"Actually, I think I did. I asked for some understanding, Hilary, and maybe it all ties in with everything else I've told you. Maybe this is just one more learning experience for me."

"For both of us," she corrected.

He kissed her quickly and explained, "I heard that scripture in my head: *Love thy neighbor as thyself.* It had never occurred to me before now that we have to love ourselves first, before we have anything to give. Some of us would do well to turn it around and remember to "love thyself as thy neighbor—or thy wife." I know all too well from experience that when I'm not feeling good about myself, I'm no good to you or to anybody else."

Knowing she had a new obstacle to face, Hilary said, "I think I would do well to remember that myself."

"It's going to be okay, Hilary. We'll adopt if we have to. I know it takes time, but . . . hey, we can borrow Colin and Janna's kids occasionally. I have thirty-seven boys to keep track of, and you have nine five-year-olds in your Primary class."

Hilary laughed softly. "Yes, we certainly have plenty to keep us busy." She nuzzled close to Jack and asked, "Do you want to hear what I learned while I was lying here thinking?"

"Of course. Let's hear it."

"As you said, it's kind of difficult to put into words, but . . . I think it has to do with empathy. Knowing that there is something physically wrong with me gave me just an inkling of how you must feel every day. And yet I have hope, and something to work toward."

"So do I," he murmured, and kissed her.

They held each other in contented silence until Hilary said, "Jack, the doctor prescribed something for me that he feels confident will solve the problem."

Jack pulled back enough to look at her, even though it was dark. "Really?"

"Yeah."

"Then maybe it's not so serious after all."

"Maybe; I guess time will tell. If this doesn't work, we'll just have to go on to the next step." She hugged him tightly. "As long as I have you and I know you love me, I can make it through anything. Just hold me like this when I have to cry and get it out of my system, and I'll be fine."

"I'll consider it a singular honor," he said with a touch of drama. Then he kissed her. And kissed her. And everything was perfect.

CHAPTER SEVENTEEN

*W*hile Hilary found it easier to relax and enjoy life, knowing that she was doing everything she could to have a baby, Jack became increasingly frustrated with not being able to find a job where he could use his degree effectively.

On a particularly low day, he found it difficult to ward off thoughts of what could have been. While Hilary worked in the kitchen, he was straightening up the bedroom a little, his mind wandering into territory that was better ignored. His feelings were similar to the moments when he'd feel the reality that his father was dead, and realize he would never have the chance to go to him for advice, or just be with him, until the next life. His father had been gone for years, but occasionally the heartache still crept in. He missed his father, and knew that he always would until they were reunited.

And now, Jack occasionally felt the same way about his disability. He'd come to terms with it as something he had to accept and live with—just as he had his father's death. For the most part, he'd found peace within himself over it. But there were moments when he simply missed the things he used to do, the dreams that would never be fulfilled in this life. The feelings weren't enough to catapult him into depression, but it was enough to remind him that he still felt a level of mourning for what he'd lost in that accident, the same way he continued to mourn the loss of his father. Only the promise of eternity made either of his losses bearable. But there were some days when eternity was simply more difficult to grasp . . . and today was one of those days.

It was Saturday, and he tried to keep busy by helping with some extra cleaning around the house. But while he was dusting the furniture in the bedroom, he noticed Hilary's dance shoes sitting on her cedar chest. He picked them up and blew the dust off them, realizing he'd never really taken notice of them before, although they'd been sitting out as long as he'd been married to her. They were too worn to wear anymore, but their tattered look was a testament to the time she'd spent dancing in them. In fact, he knew she had several pairs like this inside of the cedar chest, and she was determined to never part with them because they represented a great deal of hard work.

Jack turned the shoes over in his hands, fingering the worn leather soles and noticing the complete absence of pink satin over the toes where it had worn away. The ribbons that tied around her ankles were frayed and tattered. He didn't understand why holding Hilary's dancing shoes would make him cry, but it did. In his present mood, the shoes represented something she loved and had worked very hard at. And he couldn't help being painfully aware of his inability to participate in that aspect of her life. He closed his eyes and let the tears fall as his memories wandered through the times they'd danced, just the two of them, in the darkened studio. For a moment the memories felt so real he could almost taste them. He wanted more than anything to just walk in the other room, take her in his arms, and waltz her around the kitchen. But he couldn't. And there was no good to be found in thinking about such things.

He consciously tried to will the negative thoughts away, praying for help to ward off this melancholy mood. Then he conjured up the image he'd often indulged in, of dancing with Hilary in a heavenly setting, knowing that one day he would be made whole again. Jack thought of how deeply it touched him to know that Christ had atoned for his struggles. *I am the resurrection and the life,* he had promised. While Jack held Hilary's shoes, his sadness turned to joy; his heartache to peace. He would be with his father again, and he would be whole again. He knew it with every fiber of his being.

He was startled when Hilary came into the room. He saw her take in the fact that he was sitting there crying, holding her shoes in his hands. He was trying to gather the words to explain when she said, "It doesn't matter, Jack." He marveled at her perception; at how well she knew him. She knelt beside him and took the shoes from his hands, setting them back where they belonged. While he wondered how to tell her that his tears were now more from peace than heartache, she repeated, "It doesn't matter."

"I know."

"I love you, Jack."

"I know."

"And everything will be perfect, when forever comes."

"I know, Hilary. I do." He pulled her close to him and just held her, thanking God for all he'd been given.

Jack continued to feel frustrated at not being able to find a job, but he did his best to stay busy and keep looking. They remained close to Janna and Colin, socializing with them regularly. And they reported that Matthew was thriving on the work he was doing in Russia.

Jack also kept in close touch with Ammon. At times Ammon was so busy that they wouldn't talk for a few weeks, then they would catch up and always manage to encourage each other. On a day when Ammon had no work because of a holdup in funding from a mortgage company, he met Jack at work and they went out to lunch. Ammon made the comment, "Did I tell you we're building a home in your subdivision that's wheelchair accessible?"

"No," Jack drawled. "Do you know why?"

"I assume it's because someone who uses a wheelchair is going to live there."

"Very funny," Jack said, and Ammon laughed.

"I honestly don't know," Ammon said more seriously. "I know it's a family, relocating from somewhere in the Midwest, due to a job transfer, I believe. They're in an apartment waiting for the house to get finished, so I'm making it my top priority. I've only met the father; Scott Henderson is his name. I believe they're members of the Church. Either way, I'm certain you'll get to know them." Ammon grinned. "I just wanted to let you know you have something in common with one of your neighbors."

"I'll keep that in mind," Jack said, and the conversation turned to Ammon's frustrations with circumstances beyond his control and aggravating technicalities. Jack mentioned a few things he'd learned that might help him deal with the stress and handle it the best he could. But Ammon still seemed uptight when Jack went back to work.

A week later, Jack felt prompted to call Ammon. At the business office for Mitchell Construction, all he got was voice mail. Calling Ammon's cell phone, all he got was voice mail. Calling his home, all he got was Allison kindly telling him that she could never find him either. After more than a week of never connecting, Jack decided to take a day off work and act on the prompting that Ammon needed something he had to offer. He left home before sunrise and went to the construction company's business office, knowing it was the only time he was sure to catch Ammon there. He sat in his car in the parking lot for ten minutes before Ammon's truck pulled in. Jack tapped on the horn, and Ammon walked over to the car. "What are you doing here?" he asked with a laugh. "Don't you know it's practically the middle of the night?"

"I know this is the only way to find you."

"I'm sorry I haven't returned your calls," Ammon said. "I haven't been trying to avoid you, honestly. I just—"

"It's okay. I understand. Can I come in for a few minutes?"

"Sure. I'll be inside."

It took Jack a few minutes to get in his chair and get into the office, where he found Ammon sitting behind a desk that was absolute chaos. "So, what can I do for you?" Ammon asked, and Jack was amazed to realize he was serious.

"You're asking me?" Jack laughed. "With everything you have to worry about, you're willing to help *me?*"

"If I can."

"Well, you can't. I'm here to help you. Look at this mess! Now, why don't you hurry and tell me what's going on, and I'll see if I can clean this place up and cover the phone while you go out on the job. Just promise me you'll turn on the cell phone so I can ask you questions."

Ammon said nothing.

"What's the matter?" Jack asked. "Is your head paralyzed?"

"Maybe," Ammon admitted. Then he said, "You're serious."

"Of course I'm serious."

"Don't you have to go to work?"

"No, I have the day off. They owe me several vacation days. If I don't use them, I'll lose them. So, don't just sit there and stare at me. Tell me what's going on."

Ammon still looked dazed, and Jack leaned toward him, saying firmly, "I was gracious enough to let you build me a home. Now why don't you be gracious enough to let me find your desk and keep your sanity!"

Ammon chuckled and shook his head. "Okay, fine." He looked around as if he didn't know where to start. Jack asked him questions, which got his momentum going. While Ammon talked, Jack wrote a few things down. He asked Ammon for the phone numbers of his subcontractors and the people he was building homes for.

Jack and Ammon talked on the phone a few dozen times through the course of the day. But their communication paid off; Ammon returned to his office when his day was finished to find some semblance of order. Jack came back the next day, and this time he only had to call Ammon three times for progress reports so he could appease the people who were anxiously awaiting their new homes. He scheduled the painters, the electricians, and the cabinetmakers. And he managed to work around a stressed-out mortgage officer who was attempting to close on a home that wasn't quite ready for inspection.

On the third day, Jack actually felt in control, as if he'd been doing this forever. And he found that he was enjoying the work. At noon he left the office, picked up some lunch for himself and Ammon, then went out to the job site, where they discussed the status of all the current projects. An hour later, Jack returned to the office to work on some bids for upcoming jobs. He was still at it when Ammon returned early that evening.

"You're amazing, you know that." Ammon leaned back in a chair and put his feet up. "For the first time in I don't know how long, I actually feel like I'm on top of what I'm supposed to be doing. I can find the paperwork I need in less than thirty minutes, and I'm not avoiding angry phone calls."

"Glad I could help," Jack said nonchalantly.

"So, now that I can think straight, what was it you were trying to get hold of me for? Surely it wasn't to save me from drowning."

"Not initially," Jack said.

"Okay, then what?"

"I've been working on some house plans I want you to look at. You know some of the things I had you do on my house to utilize the space more efficiently? Well, I've been experimenting with some different variations on the same idea. I was thinking how you've grumbled about the available plans you've had to work with, and how some of the problems you've encountered could be made easier with a few modifications."

Ammon's eyes widened. "It sounds too good to be true. Where are these plans?"

"They're at home. I can bring them in tomorrow, or—"

"Tomorrow is Saturday, and I'm taking the day off to be with my family. It's the first time in weeks I've dared to do that. How about if I drop by tomorrow evening and take a look at them?"

"How about if you bring Allison, and we'll have dinner? I make a mean batch of spaghetti."

"It's a deal," Ammon said.

When Saturday evening came, Jack was pleased to note that Ammon was even more impressed with the house plans than he had hoped. They discussed the possibilities for most of the evening while Hilary and Allison slipped off to the bedroom to visit. Occasionally they could hear a burst of feminine laughter that eventually made them search out their wives and find out why they were having so much fun.

On Monday, Jack found it more difficult than usual to go to work at the building supply store. He found absolutely no fulfillment in what he was doing, and through the day he contemplated the seemingly endless job applications he'd submitted without success. He was glad he'd been able to help Ammon get on top of things, but after spending time doing something he actually enjoyed and found gratifying, the mediocrity of his work at the store seemed all the more grueling.

The week was long and difficult for Jack, and by Saturday he realized he was actually fighting to ward off depression. "Hey," Hilary said, startling him from his dreary thoughts, "how about if I finish up what I'm doing, then we can go do something?"

"Like what?" he asked.

"I don't know. Whatever you want to do. I need to get groceries, and it's always more fun if you come with me. Then, if nothing else, we could drive down to see Mom and Dad. It's been a while."

Jack didn't really feel like doing anything, but he knew she was trying to distract him from his bad mood. And he knew he should probably let her. "Okay," he said. But before she finished cleaning the bathroom, Ammon called and asked if he could come by. Hilary left for the grocery store just after he arrived.

"So," Ammon said, "how's the job search coming?"

"You're taking your life in your hands to even bring that up," Jack said lightly, but with an edge to his voice.

"That good, eh?" Ammon said with subtle sarcasm.

"Why?" Jack asked, wondering if he had heard of an opening somewhere.

"Because I'm sinking, Jack. In the week since you helped me, I've got everything right back to where it was—a mess! I can't believe how much of my stress you alleviated. How did you do it? I mean . . . you got people and problems off my back that have been there for weeks. I don't get it."

"It's simple," Jack said. "I've just learned what every other person with a disability has to learn eventually. If you can't do something, you find a way to get around it. There is no problem that can't be solved one way or another."

Ammon shook his head in disbelief. "You know, Jack, I've been asking myself why I didn't hire somebody a long time ago to cover the business end of the whole thing. And the reason is that I knew it had to be somebody I could trust completely. There's a lot of dishonesty that goes on in this business, and I think one of the reasons I've been able to succeed is that I maintain my integrity. Well, I can't have somebody mediating for me if I don't know beyond a doubt that they will honor that integrity—at all costs. And I have to have somebody who knows the business; someone who has been out there, who knows every practical aspect of what goes into the building of a house. Quite honestly, Jack, I wouldn't even consider offering this job to anyone but you."

Jack liked what he was hearing. In fact, he liked it so much that he actually felt butterflies swimming inside of him. But there were some things that needed to be clarified. He looked hard at Ammon and asked, "You're not just doing this because you feel sorry for me, are you?"

Ammon rolled his eyes and groaned. Then he gave a frustrated laugh. "You know, Jack, if I didn't like you so much, I'd give you a black eye. Why in heaven's name would I feel sorry for you? I'm certain you could eventually find a job and do very well at it, and I'm not so sure that working for me is going to be any more pleasant for you than selling two-by-fours. But I *need* you. Do you hear what I'm saying? Why don't you consider taking some pity on *me*? If it's not something you want to do, just say so. Or if you don't want it to be permanent, I'll take you while I can get you—at least until you find work doing what you want. But right now, I *need* you. Do you have any idea how much money you can save me just by problem-solving and overseeing the operation? And on top of that, if we can incorporate your expertise and be able to use our own house plans, we'll be sailing."

Jack said nothing for a few minutes while a host of thoughts mulled around in his head. After a while Ammon stood up and said, "Do you mind if I get something to drink?"

"No, go ahead. You know where everything is. Get me one while you're at it."

Ammon returned with two glasses of soda on ice. "So, what do you think?" he asked after taking a long swallow.

"I'm still thinking," Jack said.

Ammon waved his hand to indicate that he could take his time. Jack quickly considered all the obvious questions. He knew that long-term job security was not a problem; Ammon had been effectively running his construction business for several years, and his income was more than adequate. In spite of the fact that construction was a fluctuating business, Ammon always kept his head above water, and he'd kept a number of employees for several years. Ammon knew what he was doing, and Jack knew he would be fair. He wondered if he could really be content in the long run, and he truly believed he would. The job would have diversity and challenge, and he wouldn't necessarily be stuck in the office all the time. Of course, the future was always unpredictable, but no more for this job than for any other.

Ammon's voice broke into his thoughts. "You know, Jack, I don't need an answer this minute. Think about it. Talk to Hilary. I'll take you just as soon as you can give fair notice at your other job. I'll take you yesterday, in fact."

Jack chuckled, then he nearly stopped breathing when Ammon quoted him a starting wage that was more than double what he was currently making. "Can you afford that?" he questioned.

"As I see it, I can't afford *not* to hire you. Mistakes and poor communication cost money. When I'm stressed out and overwhelmed, those things happen a lot more. In the long run, I'll be able to accomplish a lot more work with a lot fewer complications. Not to mention that I can't count how many times I've been asked this week . . ." He raised his voice to mimic the people he worked with. ". . .Where's that guy you had in the office? I'd rather talk to him. He's not as ornery as you are."

"Yeah, right," Jack laughed.

"Well, they may not have said that exactly, but that's what they meant. You were only there three days, and everybody already misses you." Ammon sighed and took another drink. "I know you have to make your decision, Jack. But I really feel like you're the answer to my prayers—and Allison's, for that matter. So you think about it and let me know. Talk to Hilary, and—"

"Talk to Hilary about what?" she asked, coming through the family room with an armload of groceries.

Jack said, "Is it okay with you if I work for Ammon?"

Hilary glanced back and forth between the two men. "Sure. Go for it," she said and moved on to the kitchen.

Jack grinned and said to Ammon, "I guess that settles it. I'm yours."

Ammon looked stunned. "Don't you want to think about it, and talk to—"

"No," Jack said. "I don't need to think about it. There are some things that you just know are right. I haven't felt this good about something since Hilary asked me to marry her."

Ammon laughed. "She asked *you* to marry *her?*"

"Well, sort of."

"You're serious. You're really going to take the job."

"Yes. I'll give my notice Monday. I can still put some hours in for you in the meantime. They can pretty well manage without me these days. Maybe that's one of the things that bothers me most."

Ammon laughed again. "Well, if you need to feel needed, you've come to the right place." He laughed harder. "I can't believe it. Allison said you'd take the job, but I didn't think you'd feel sorry enough for me."

Ammon left while Hilary was putting away the groceries. Jack went to the kitchen to help her and she asked, "What was that all about?"

"Ammon offered me a job. I took it."

Hilary pulled her head out of the fridge to stare at him. "I thought you were kidding."

"No." He chuckled. "Do you have a problem with it?"

"Of course not," she said. "It's wonderful. I assume you'll be doing what you did while you were helping him last week."

"That about covers it."

"And you feel good about it?"

"I do," Jack said firmly. "I really do." He eased close to her and pulled her onto his lap. "And guess what?" he whispered. "He's going to pay me more than double what I'm making now."

"Really?" Hilary laughed and hugged him. "Oh, that's incredible. Then we can get you a better car, and—"

"Now, wait a minute. Let's get our priorities straight here. The first thing I'm going to do is buy a new couch." They laughed together, and he added, "And then I'm going to take you on a second honeymoon. And then," he drawled, "we're going to buy a crib and a stroller and a highchair and—"

"All in good time," she said softly.

"Yes," he hugged her tightly, "all in good time."

Jack enjoyed working with Ammon even more than he had expected. It all worked out so well for both of them that they had to agree there had been a divine hand involved. Jack knew that if Ammon could be content the rest of his life building houses, he could be content designing them and overseeing the business end of the process.

Jack also began to actually feel comfortable in his church calling. It was time-consuming and not always easy, but he found it fulfilling to see that he could actually make a difference in these young men's lives. He realized it was difficult for them to grumble to him about their petty complaints while he was sitting there in a wheelchair. His own experiences as a youth served him well in working with more than one of the boys, but especially a young man named Josh, who had been completely inactive until his grandmother's death.

Josh was almost seventeen and looked full-grown. He had no problem admitting to Jack that he smoked and drank and was intimately involved with a girl named Shawna. His parents didn't mind if he came to church and Mutual activities as long as he minded his own business about it, which was reminiscent of Jack's growing-up years. Josh's parents were both heavy smokers and drank casually, which Jack had also grown up with in varying degrees. Jack kept quiet about his own past for the time being, thinking it might serve him better to bring it up later on. But still, it gave him an empathy for Josh that made it easier for them to connect.

Josh had started coming to church when his grandmother, just before her death, had told him it saddened her to see that his parents had not raised him with the gospel. She had always wanted to see him bless and pass the sacrament. Josh's biggest problem lay in the realization that he couldn't do that without being worthy. He nearly left and never came back, but with some urging from Jack and the bishop's patience and kindness, he had committed to taking some steps to put his life in order. He'd come to church occasionally, but he never missed a Mutual activity. And Jack had high hopes that Josh would actually meet his goal—and perhaps even make it to a mission.

Jack developed a relationship with each of the young men he worked with, but in his heart he believed Josh was his special assignment. It was as if the Lord had matched them up. He felt certain if he could help Josh, serving in this calling would be worth it. And then David moved into the ward.

The bishop called Jack on a Sunday afternoon to tell him that a new family had just moved into his subdivision the previous day. Jack had noticed the moving truck go by, and the bishop had visited with the parents. Three of their four children were in Primary, but there was a thirteen-year-old boy who was having some struggles. "They tell me he's been especially belligerent lately," the bishop explained. "The move has been difficult for him. I was wondering if you would mind going with me to meet him this afternoon."

Jack eagerly agreed. He later picked the bishop up at his home, and they visited during the short drive. "I understand this home we're going to was built by the company you work with," the bishop observed.

"Most of this subdivision was," Jack said. "That's why I'm living here."

The man of the house answered the door and looked mildly surprised to see Jack. But Jack was used to it, and Brother Henderson seemed completely relaxed as the bishop introduced him. Jack recognized the name from helping indirectly with finishing the house, which was the perfect opening for their conversation. They'd been there a few minutes when Sister Henderson came into the room. She duplicated the response her husband had shown at the door when she saw Jack, then she looked as if she might cry. But she eagerly shook his hand and expressed her gratitude for their visit.

While Jack was wondering when he'd get to meet David, Brother and Sister Henderson looked at each other and laughed as if they shared some private joke. Then Sister Henderson *did* cry.

"I'm sorry," Jack said, "did I miss something?"

"Oh, forgive me," Sister Henderson said. "It's just that . . . the move has been so hard. But we *knew* we were supposed to be here; that somehow everything would work out. On top of all the usual complications, David has been such a challenge. But now I think we can see that we're being looked out for."

Jack nodded, appreciating the theory, but he still felt lost. The bishop said, "I didn't have a chance to explain to Brother Hayden the full extent of the situation."

"Oh." Brother Henderson looked suddenly enlightened. "Well, the thing is, David was born with spina bifida. He's usually dealt pretty well with it, but becoming a teenager combined with having to move has really thrown him off."

Jack absorbed what they were saying, but he had no idea what spina bifida was. Everything fell into place, however, when Brother Henderson went to get David, and the boy begrudgingly entered the front room—in a wheelchair. He looked as surprised to see Jack as Jack was to see him. Only then did Jack make the connection to Ammon's building a home that was wheelchair accessible.

"David," his father said, "this is Brother Hayden. The Young Men's president."

"Hello, David," Jack said. "It's good to have you in the ward. We'll be—"

"This is some kind of joke, right?" David interrupted cynically.

While his parents seemed appalled and embarrassed, Jack said to the bishop, "You set this up, right, Bishop? It must be a joke. You're just trying to make me feel better since I couldn't go rock climbing with the guys last week, right?"

Jack didn't know if his attempt at humor had lightened the mood or intensified it. But David's expression was more curious now than skeptical; perhaps he was even slightly embarrassed.

With no hint of malice in his voice, Jack added firmly, "I can't walk, David. Do you think that's a joke? Because if you do, we need to get things straight between us right now."

David slowly shook his head, and Jack added with a smile, "It's been a pleasure meeting you, David. I'll expect to see you Wednesday at seven." Jack pointed a finger at him, saying lightly, "If you're not there, I'm coming over here and we'll have Mutual one-on-one. Understand?"

"We'll make sure he gets there," his father said. David said nothing.

David arrived at the church a few minutes before seven on Wednesday evening. During opening exercises, Jack discreetly observed him. The boy's expression alone could scare off any attempt at hospitality from the other youth. Some of them courageously ventured to greet David in spite of his angry demeanor, but they got nothing in response.

The different age groups split up to do their separate activities with their leaders. Jack went with David's group into the kitchen, where the boys were learning some basic cooking skills so they wouldn't have to survive on hot dogs and cold cereal the next time they went camping.

While Jack was demonstrating how to drain the grease from browned ground beef, one of the boys asked, "Do you really cook at home, Jack?"

"I sure do. When my wife works, I cook. When I'm working, she cooks. On the days we both work, we eat hot dogs and cold cereal."

"No way," one boy responded, and they all laughed—except David.

Jack observed him through the activity and was filled with compassion. The child was obviously angry, and Jack knew why. He only hoped that with time, he could reach the boy and appeal to something in his character that could help him get beyond this. Jack had resigned himself to be patient when a couple of the boys began politely asking David questions. The others gradually joined in, and Jack felt proud of them for including David and trying to make him feel welcome. Everything seemed fine until David actually yelled and told them to shut up and leave him alone. He left the kitchen and Jack promptly followed, leaving the boys all looking stunned.

Jack caught up to David in the hall and grabbed him by the back of the shirt collar. "Just leave me alone," David snarled.

"What are you gonna do? Walk home?" Jack growled back and put a strong arm around the boy from behind, preventing him from using his hands. David became angrier, but Jack just calmly said, "I'm not letting go of you until you settle down and listen to what I have to say. If you want to have it out, fine. I'll take you on, kid. If it'll make you feel better to beat up on somebody who can't run away, go for it. But don't you go taking out your bad moods on my guys. No one has been anything but kind to you since you came in the door. It's apparent you're determined to make enemies, and you're doing a good job of it. But you know what? One day you're going to have to find a way to be happy in that chair, or you might as well just shrivel up and die right now. And I don't think you want to do that."

"How do you know what I *want?*" David growled.

"I'll tell you how I know. I know because I've been there. I've been angry and scared, and I've had to learn how to make it in a world where everyone can do things I can't. But I've also had people who cared about me, and so do you. If you want to just give up and end it all, David, nobody can stop you. But you'd leave a big empty space in a lot of people's lives. And you know what? There's a lot you'd miss out on."

"Yeah, like what?"

"Well, if there are ten thousand things a person who walks can do, then there are at least nine thousand things you and I can do. And we don't have time in a lifetime to do all of them."

"Oh, yeah? Prove it."

Jack smiled. "You come to Mutual every week and do your best to get along with the others, and I will."

Now that David had calmed down and was listening, Jack took him into an empty classroom and they talked for nearly an hour. David said little, but Jack was able to say some things he hoped would leave enough impact to at least get that chip off his shoulder. He told David how he had moved to Utah from Texas when he was thirteen, and how he'd been teased about his accent. He told him about Jeffrey, who had taken him in and accepted him, and how Jeffrey had been killed. And he told David that he was really hoping they could be friends, since he'd never had a friend who used a wheel-chair, except some people he'd been acquainted with in the hospital.

When Jack figured he'd said more than enough, he asked David, "Wanna shoot some hoops? The gym is empty right now." David reluctantly followed Jack to the gym and watched as Jack briefly demonstrated his dribbling technique, then he made a long shot. He attempted another and purposely missed. "You try it," he said, passing David the ball.

David tried over and over to make the shot, while Jack retrieved the ball and tossed it back to him. When he finally made it, he actually laughed, and Jack applauded. David kept working at it until the boys all gathered in the gym following their other activities. David's father showed up to get him a few minutes later.

"I'll see you next week," Jack said, and David nodded.

Jack told Hilary all about what had happened that night as they lay close together in bed. And the next day, he told Ammon he needed a favor.

"Sure, what?"

"You know that house you did with the ramp in the garage?"

"Yeah."

"I need a basketball standard put up there—one that can have the height adjusted. I'll cover the costs if you'll put it up."

"That shouldn't be too hard. We're pouring concrete in that neighborhood day after tomorrow."

"Good," Jack said. "I appreciate it. Oh, and don't tell them who sent you. Just tell them . . . it came with the house."

Ammon grinned. "I understand. It's one of those *the Lord works in mysterious ways* things."

"That's right."

The following week, David came to Mutual. He was quiet, but he wasn't belligerent. When the other boys were busy, David quietly asked Jack, "Do you know anything about that basketball hoop at my house?"

"What about it? Is there something wrong with it?"

"No, it's . . . cool. But . . . did you have something to do with it?"

"Me?" Jack asked with exaggerated surprise. Then he laughed. "It came with the house, I think."

"But my dad said he didn't order one, and—"

"It doesn't matter where it came from, David. Just so you enjoy it."

"That's what my mom said."

"Your mom is a very smart woman. And she's lucky, too."

"Why's that?"

"She's got you for a son. Hey, wanna go for a walk around the block sometime? I'll show you around the neighborhood."

"A *walk?*" David asked.

"Okay, a *roll,*" Jack corrected.

"Sure," David said, "and maybe we can shoot some hoops."

"I'll look forward to it."

Within a few weeks, David was doing considerably better. He was beginning to interact with the boys in the ward more, and Jack heard them talking about things going on at school that David was involved in.

Josh, on the other hand, seemed to be digressing. He'd made some improvement, but Jack could see he'd lost his enthusiasm. He suspected that his parents weren't making it easy for him to meet goals that clashed so strongly with their lifestyle. He knew well enough how difficult that could be.

While Jack was discussing his concerns with Hilary over the dinner table, he noticed that she didn't look very good. "You okay?" he asked.

"Yes," she said with a smile, "I'm just tired. Please go on with what you were saying. The lasagna is really good, Jack. I think you're a better cook than I am."

"I've improved a little." He chuckled and kissed her, then he continued with his concerns for the young men he worked with.

He stopped in mid-sentence when Hilary clamped a hand over her mouth and slid her chair back. "What's wrong?" he asked.

She slowly moved her hand and swallowed carefully. "I just feel nauseous all of a sudden."

"You just said the lasagna was good."

"It is, but . . . oh, my gosh!" Hilary ran to the bathroom and slammed the door. By the time Jack got there, she was sitting on the bathroom floor with a wet towel against her face.

"Are you okay?" he called from the other side of the door.

"No!"

"Can I come in?"

"I suppose."

Jack pushed the bathroom door open, and she looked up at him. "Good heavens, you're white as a ghost," he exclaimed.

"That's funny. I feel more green."

"Can you make it to the bed?" he asked, offering his hand.

Hilary came to her feet with his help and only teetered a little. "Just don't make me eat any more lasagna."

When she was lying down, he checked her face to see if it was warm. But it felt more clammy. "Whatever you've got, I hope I don't get it," he said lightly. "I'm not as good at running to the bathroom as you are."

"We'll put a bucket by the bed," she said, her face pressed sideways to the pillow. "We've done it before."

"Yes, I know," he said with chagrin. "But having the flu is not my idea of . . ."

Hilary cut him off as she ran to the bathroom. After she'd thrown up again, she sat on the floor, trying not to feel dizzy. Having the flu did not fit in with her plans this week, and she groaned at the thought. Then something occurred to her that sent her scrambling through one of the drawers in the bathroom vanity, searching for a particular little box she'd purchased several weeks earlier. It was still good according to the expiration date, and she quickly read the instructions while she could hear her heart beating in her ears.

"Jack!" Hilary practically shrieked. He hurried to the bathroom, fearing that something was horribly wrong. She was sitting on the closed toilet seat, her hand pressed to her chest. It was difficult to tell if she was laughing or crying as she held out a little plastic thing he'd never seen before. "Look! Look at this!"

"What?"

"It's a pregnancy test, Jack!" She laughed and flung herself into his arms. "It says I'm pregnant. Oh my gosh, I can't believe it."

All Jack could do was hold her and laugh . . . until she had to throw up again.

The following day, Hilary had an official test at the doctor's office. She was most definitely pregnant. After she went to see Jack at work and tell him that the good news had been verified, she spent the remainder of the day at Janna's, discussing how to cope with all the symptoms she was feeling.

Through the next few weeks, Hilary felt so sick that she could hardly function. She was grateful to have people she could turn her dance classes over to, and to have Jack making enough money that paying the substitutes wouldn't be a problem. But no matter how miserable she got, she only had to remember the reality that she was going to have a baby, and she knew it would be worth it.

Hilary was released from her church calling when she couldn't even make it to her meetings for several weeks. But Jack always sat on the bed after church and recounted all of the talks and lessons. And since he took some of his boys around to the homes of sick and elderly members to give them the sacrament each Sunday, he also brought them by for Hilary's benefit.

"You take such good care of me," she said on a Friday evening after she had declined going out to dinner, not certain she could keep it down.

"I'm only returning the favor," he said, leaning an elbow on the bed and smoothing her hair back from her pallid face. "I'll go to the store in the morning. Be thinking what sounds good to you."

She groaned. "Anything but—"

"Lasagna, I know. I'm going to be fasting tomorrow, but I'll fix you anything you want, since I don't have to work."

Hilary looked up at him. "Why are you fasting? May I ask?"

"Sure. It's no secret. It's Josh; I'm worried about him. He's been coming to church most of the time, but his heart isn't in it. I just sense that I'm losing him. He's getting discouraged."

"Well, I can't fast," Hilary said, "but I'll remember him in my prayers."

Jack smiled and kissed her. "Thank you." He touched her nose. "And I'll remember you in mine." She looked baffled and he clarified, "I'm worried about you."

"I'm fine," she insisted. "Some women just get sicker than others. Janna said that some of her pregnancies were worse than others. And the doctor told me that as long as I don't lose weight or get dehydrated, there's nothing to worry about."

Jack sighed. "I guess I'll have to take your word for it. But you take care of yourself, okay?"

"I promise."

The following day Jack shopped for groceries and waited on Hilary, while his thoughts were with Josh. He remembered a time in his youth when he'd been wavering, but the right person had said the right thing at the right time, and it had made a difference. If Josh was at that crossroads, Jack wanted to be the right person to help him. If only he knew what might be the right thing to say.

He went to bed that night with no answers. But he was barely awake the following morning when an idea came to his head that filled him with excitement. He could hardly wait to get to priesthood meeting, and he pulled the bishop aside for a minute to be certain he wasn't doing anything out of line. The bishop enthusiastically approved the idea, and Jack waited anxiously for the boys to arrive. As usual, David arrived early with his father. The boy greeted everyone with a smile. He was doing much better, and Jack had learned that David had a strong spirit and always tried his best to do what was right. He simply had trouble with feeling different, and Jack sensed his usual underlying melancholy. But he believed he now understood something that might help—something he'd never even considered. With a little luck, or rather, some help from above, Jack hoped he could help David feel a little more like he belonged. And at the same time, he could hopefully help Josh.

As usual, Josh sauntered in late, looking haggard and smelling of cigarette smoke. When priesthood meeting ended and they separated for Sunday School classes, Jack asked Josh to wait for a minute. "What's up?" the boy asked.

"Nothing. I just want to talk. Can you spare a few minutes?"

"Sure," Josh mumbled, and Jack motioned toward an empty classroom.

With the door closed, Josh slumped his large frame into a chair and tipped it onto its back legs.

"I've been thinking about you a lot lately," Jack said.

"Boy," Josh chuckled, "you need to get out more."

Jack laughed in response. "Maybe I do, but . . . well, I like you, Josh. The truth is, you remind me a lot of me."

Josh snorted. "You're joking, right?"

"No. When I was your age, things were a lot different for me."

Jack was hoping Josh would ask some questions, or at least appear curious. But he seemed completely indifferent. Jack decided to get right to the point. "So, I was wondering what's keeping you from passing the sacrament."

Josh furrowed his brow in obvious irritation. "I talked to the bishop about that. I'm not worthy. I already told you that."

"Okay . . . you told me you'd quit drinking and smoking, but—"

"I did!" he said angrily. "The smell is from my house. I can't help that."

"I know, Josh. I understand. My dad smoked—a lot. So did my older brothers."

Josh's expression softened a little and Jack continued, "So, if you've stopped smoking, what's the problem?"

Josh was silent for more than a minute. But he seemed thoughtful rather than upset. "Well," he finally said, "it's mostly the swearing, I guess. I quit seeing Shawna, and I talked to the bishop about that. But those words just fly out of my mouth, and I . . . well, I just don't know if I've got what it takes to be here, Jack. It's like I told you, I'd really like to be able to pass the sacrament and stuff, but . . . maybe it's just better if I don't even worry about it."

"I think you're doing great, Josh. You have to take things one step at a time. As I see it, you're moving in the right direction. But . . . well, there's something else I wanted to talk to you about. It's David."

"Yeah, what about him?"

"Well, the two of you have a lot in common, you know."

Josh laughed. But Jack knew it wasn't from comparing himself as a strong, handsome young man to a disabled boy who wasn't much to look at. Josh was thinking of David's strong spirit in comparison to his own continual struggle to do what was right.

"I'm serious," Jack insisted.

"Yeah, like what?"

"He wishes he could pass the sacrament, too."

For a moment, Jack thought the boy was going to cry. But his expression quickly hardened and he asked, "So, what's that got to do with me?"

"Well, I know you have a little ways to go to be able to pass the sacrament, but the bishop and I both agree that you would be the right person to help David do it."

Jack could almost feel Josh's mind working, and he allowed him the time to think it through. When he looked up at Jack, the glowing spirit that occasionally showed through was evident. "You really think so?" Josh asked.

"Sure. All you need is a white shirt and tie, and I just happen to have some extras with me." Jack pulled a shirt carefully out of a bag, adding lightly, "I ironed it myself."

"Really?" Josh chuckled. "That's cool."

Josh was hesitant but excited to put on the shirt and tie. Jack offered him a comb and then followed him to the men's room, where he smoothed his hair back off his face. "Hey, you look great," Jack said.

"Like a real Mormon?"

"Yeah," Jack shook his hand firmly, "like a real Mormon. Shall we go find David?"

"Okay." Josh held the door open for Jack to pass through.

* * * * *

Hilary felt downright depressed when Jack left for church. She knew she couldn't sit through three hours of meetings without feeling sick, but she prayed for strength and decided to get ready. The ward had recently changed their schedule so that sacrament meeting was last, and she decided if she was careful she could at least make it to that. Even if she had to leave early, it was better than nothing.

She was sitting at the end of the pew where Jack always parked his chair when she saw him enter the chapel. Just seeing his obvious delight at having her there made the effort worth it. During the sacrament, Hilary studied her scriptures intently, oblivious to her surroundings until Jack nudged her. He pointed discreetly up the aisle, where Josh was pushing David Henderson's wheelchair from one pew to the next so that David could pass the sacrament. Hilary glanced at Jack in question, but he was absorbed in watching the boys, his expression serene.

"Did you have something to do with that?" she whispered.

"Maybe I did," Jack whispered back. "Or maybe I was just the mouthpiece."

Five weeks later Josh passed the sacrament himself, and in another month he was ordained a priest and was able to bless it. Jack couldn't help feeling gratified to see the changes that came about in Josh's attitude, and in his aura. He began talking about a mission, and Jack told him that if he went, he would pay half of the monthly cost.

"You'd do that for me?" Josh asked.

"I went on a mission because someone I hardly knew was willing to do that. This will give me a chance to pass that blessing along."

Later, when he told Hilary how far he'd seen Josh come, he was astonished himself to realize that he had actually made a difference. He looked at his own life. He had a beautiful home. A good job that he enjoyed. An incredible wife. And a baby on the way. "We are so blessed, Hilary," he said.

She nuzzled up close to him and agreed. "Yes, we are."

CHAPTER EIGHTEEN

*H*ilary was nearly four months pregnant when Jack came home from his Mutual activity to announce, "Guess what? I'm going camping with the boys."

He'd perhaps expected her to remind him that such an endeavor could be a challenge—to say the least. But she responded enthusiastically, "That's great! When?"

"Next weekend," he explained. "It's just for one night, but . . . well, we were planning this camping thing, and I could tell that David was having a hard time. He was handling it great, but I could see through him, you know. So, I decided I was going. And if I can go, he can too."

"I assume you've got it all figured out."

"Well, not *everything*, but we're working out the details. The guys said they'd help me. And David's father is going. He was so excited, we had to threaten him to keep him calm." Jack chuckled softly. "It'll be great."

"Well, after you've conquered next weekend, maybe *we* could go camping sometime."

Jack took her hand and kissed it. "Now, *that* would be great."

While they talked through the other events of the day, Hilary observed her husband more closely than usual. Wearing boots and jeans, he looked the same as he always had. In a way that had become typical, he lifted one leg up with his hands and crossed his ankle on his knee. His eyes sparkled as he repeated the antics of the young men he worked with and whom he'd grown to care so much for. Then, holding her hand and playing idly with her hair, he told her what was going on with the construction business.

Four days before the scheduled camping trip, Hilary called Jack at work to tell him she was bleeding and cramping—and frightened. "I called the doctor," she said tearfully. "He said it was significant enough that I should go to the hospital to be checked, but I—"

"I'll be right home to get you," Jack interrupted. "Will that be fast enough, or should I call for an ambulance and—"

"No. Of course not. Just hurry."

Hilary cried all the way to the hospital, while Jack attempted to convince himself—and her—that everything was going to be all right. He knew how long she'd waited to get pregnant. Losing this baby now could be devastating for both of them, but especially for Hilary.

At the hospital, Hilary was cared for efficiently and the bleeding quickly stopped. Following some tests and a thorough examination, they were informed that the baby was fine, but the problem would not go away. The condition of Hilary's uterus would make it difficult for her to carry a baby full term. The only hope of making that happen was for her to stay flat in bed until the baby was big enough to be delivered without complications.

Hilary was understandably upset. Jack did his best to console her, but he found it difficult to know what to say. He called Janna, and she and Colin came to the hospital as soon as Colin got off work. Jack explained the situation while Janna held Hilary's hand.

"So, how long are you staying in the hospital?" Colin asked.

"She can go home in the morning as long as nothing changes," Jack reported. "But she's going to have to stay down flat. I can be with her except when I'm working. We've already talked to her parents; Millie's going to come and stay as much as possible. And her sister can come and help some."

"And I can be there whenever you need me," Janna said. "Even if I have to bring Jake and the baby with me, I'll be there to see that you have what you need."

"Well, I'm not that helpless," Hilary said. "I'm sure if Jack leaves what I need close by, I can manage."

"Maybe," Janna said, "but it would still be better not to leave you alone."

"I agree," Jack said firmly. "That's why I'm going to stay home this weekend and—"

"Oh, you can't!" Hilary insisted.

"What's this weekend?" Colin asked.

Jack quickly explained the situation, adding that he wouldn't think of leaving now, under the circumstances. Hilary argued with him until Janna interrupted firmly, "Kick me if I'm butting in here, but as I see it, you really should go, Jack. I can stay with Hilary. It's only for one night. We'll rent some romantic movies or something." She winked at Hilary. "Sometimes we girls just need some time without the men around, right?"

"Sure," Hilary said, grateful for Janna's offer. She didn't want to be without Jack, even for one night, but she knew his plans were important. For himself as well as for David, this was a great milestone.

With plans made for the coming week, Colin assisted Jack in giving Hilary a priesthood blessing. In it she was promised comfort and peace, but no specific assurance was given as to whether or not this baby would make it.

After three days of being down, with only the scenery of her bedroom, Hilary already felt as if she'd go insane. Before Jack left on his camping trip, Ammon came over and helped move the television and VCR into the bedroom. Janna came for the weekend, and Hilary thoroughly enjoyed the company. They never ran out of things to talk about, and Janna had good taste in movies. In fact, she brought several that she owned to leave with Hilary, and she made a list of good movies that Jack could rent for her.

Jack returned from his camping trip to report that it had been a success. After Janna left he told Hilary every detail, laughing over the challenges they'd had, and the way they'd worked around them. David had enjoyed it as well, and Jack felt certain it was a big step in helping this young man see that he could do a lot more than he'd once believed.

"And the same applies to you," Hilary said. Jack just smiled and went to the kitchen to fix some dinner.

The weeks dragged by for Hilary as she faithfully tried to do exactly as the doctor had told her. A nurse came into the home occasionally to make certain everything was all right. She was showered with help and support from friends and family, and Jack took very good care of her. He found that with a computer and a telephone at home, he could do a good share of his work there and be close to Hilary. And she had everything imaginable to occupy her time. Books to read, and books and talks on tape to listen to. Video tapes of everything from good movies, to General Conference, to documentaries on anything that even remotely interested her. Still, she felt discouraged. She read her scriptures, and prayed more than she had since Jack had been in the hospital. She read the *Ensigns* from cover to cover, as well as every Relief Society lesson she missed. The young men in the ward brought the sacrament in for her on Sundays, and she was grateful. But she still missed attending her meetings and being able to get out.

Hilary was about six months along when Jack came home from work one day to tell her that Ammon had offered him a partnership. "What exactly does that mean?" she asked, sensing the solemness of his mood.

"Well," he said thoughtfully, "it would mean splitting everything fifty-fifty. Rather than getting a salary, I would take fifty percent of the profits, which at this point, would technically give us more income. It would also mean fifty percent of the problems; half of the bills, half of the debts. If the company ever failed, I would end up with half of the responsibility."

Unable to guess what Jack was thinking, Hilary asked, "So how do you feel about it?"

"Well," he drawled, "I must say his offer is terribly flattering. He insists the business is doing better than ever, and he says he owes a lot of that to me."

"That can't help but make you feel good."

"Yes, it does," Jack admitted. "And you know I really enjoy my work. Ammon's track record is good; construction can be a fluctuating business, but he knows how to plan well, and he's always made it work. I have no reason to believe that it won't continue to work. But unpredictable things can happen, and it's something that has to be considered."

"Then as I see it," Hilary said, "this is a decision we need to fast and pray about. I can't fast under the circumstances, but I'm certain we can go to the Lord and get an answer. He's the only one who knows the long-range repercussions of such a decision."

"Yes, I know that's true."

"Looking at it logically, what do you *want* to do?" she asked.

"I think it's right," Jack said. "I look at it this way: if something went wrong and Ammon's business *did* fail, I would do everything in my power to help him anyway. After all he's done for me, I'd be more than willing to put my neck on the line for him. I think if we pay our tithing and try to do what's right, and if we know the Lord is behind us, we'll be okay one way or another."

"I agree," Hilary said firmly.

Jack took her hand and kissed it. "You have incredible faith, Hilary Hayden."

"Do I?" She chuckled, but her eyes revealed the doubt she was feeling.

"You've always believed in me, even when I couldn't. I never would have made it to where I am now without you."

"Oh, I think you would have."

Jack shook his head firmly. "You saved my life, Hilary. You loved me unconditionally. I think back and know that even as difficult as it was for *me* to believe you would love me that much, you never once flinched or wavered in letting me know that your love and commitment were real. At times I wondered if you were just being noble, but I think I sensed your heart was really with me. I know in my heart that you saved me. Without your faith in me, and your example of faith in God, I might have just shriveled up and died."

Tears trickled down Hilary's face. There were no words to explain what that meant to her. But she had to ask, "Then why can't I find any faith inside of me now to believe I can get through this? I feel so helpless, so useless."

"Hey," Jack said, putting his arm around her as much as possible, "you are anything but useless. Listen to you, giving me the feedback I need in making a big decision. I couldn't face life without you. This is just a temporary setback, Hilary. And creating a life is certainly not useless. Your sacrifice means more to me than you could ever know. And I'm certain your Father in Heaven appreciates your sacrifice—not to mention my daughter here." He rubbed her rounded belly affectionately.

"You don't know for certain it's a girl," she said. "Those ultrasound things aren't perfect."

"Close enough. Besides, I just *know* it's a girl."

Fresh tears brimmed in Hilary's eyes. "And what if your little girl doesn't make it—in spite of everything I can do?"

Jack touched her face. "Then you'll know that you did everything you could."

"I'm so scared," Hilary admitted. "If I thought all of this time in bed was for nothing, I think I'd go insane."

"It won't be for nothing," he insisted. But they both knew there was no guarantee that this baby would make it long enough to survive.

"I don't know what I'd do without you, Jack." She squeezed his hand tightly. "Promise me you'll always be here for me."

"Forever," he said, kissing her brow softly.

Through the following days, while Jack continued to do his best to keep Hilary occupied and cheerful, Hilary did her best to have faith and be positive. After much prayer and consideration, Jack accepted Ammon's offer with Hilary's full support. They both knew it was the right thing to do. To celebrate, Ammon and Allison brought in a nice meal for the four of them to share in Hilary's bedroom. The following week everything was made legal, and Mitchell-Hayden Construction Company was formed. Hilary was pleased to observe Ammon's obvious pleasure over the partnership, and even more so to see how far Jack had come, and the fulfillment in his life as he achieved still another milestone of accomplishment.

As time continued to drag for Hilary, she developed a new understanding and compassion for how Jack must have felt through his months of depression following the accident. Of course, the circumstances were very different; there was nothing she *could* do about this, and she also knew it was temporary. But she did have a new comprehension of how useless and helpless he must have felt.

For Jack, the time Hilary spent in bed gave him a new understanding of himself. It had been a long time since he'd considered himself useless, but caring for Hilary's every need made him realize how very capable he actually was. Not only was he completely caring for himself, he was running their household on his own, with only a little help here and there from Janna and Hilary's mother. And he was taking care of Hilary most of the time. He also developed a new comprehension of what love really meant. As he cared for Hilary, never once begrudging a moment of it, he found peace in knowing that her efforts in the past to care for him had been no more or less of a burden to her. The love they shared balanced out as they were able to help each other through the low times. Their commitment went beyond any petty differences or earthly struggles. He found true joy in serving her, and he vowed never to resent his need to be served in the future. The balance of giving and need taught him something about Christlike love, and he was grateful for the struggles that had strengthened his relationship with Hilary.

Late on a Friday evening, as they approached Hilary's seven-month mark, Jack sat on the bed beside her, watching a movie. When it was over, he turned off the TV with the remote control, then turned to look at her. "How you doing?" he asked.

"I refuse to answer that at the risk of either being dishonest or crying hysterically."

"You can cry any time you want."

"I know, but . . . I think I'd rather not."

"Another month or so, and the baby will be strong enough to make it without you."

Hilary sighed. "I honestly wonder if I can make it that long. It already seems like I've been here forever."

"I can see how you'd feel that way, but . . . well, in the eternal perspective, it's not so long."

"I know," she said softly as he kissed her face. "Keep telling me that, and maybe I'll get through this."

Following a long silence, Hilary said, "I wish I could dance, Jack. I miss it so much."

"I know," he said.

Hilary hesitated to voice her next thought, but it wouldn't go away. "And I wish we could dance together."

He looked into her eyes, but he wasn't upset as he would have been in the past. He touched her face and actually smiled. "We could do that ballet thing, where I hold you up and help you keep your balance. I could do that."

Hilary smiled, unable to keep from admiring his attitude. "I'll look forward to it," she said and snuggled up close to him. "And tell me how we'll dance together, when forever comes."

Jack tightened his embrace and spoke softly of dancing with her in a heavenly setting, with no physical restrictions to hold them back. Hilary cried silent tears as she listened to him, silently thanking God for giving her a man with so much faith—especially at a time when her own faith seemed so fragile. At this point, it was difficult to imagine actually getting through this and having a baby to compensate for her efforts. On the other hand, thoughts of losing the baby were more devastating than she could even imagine. She'd heard stories of women who simply couldn't carry babies full term, and finally had to resort to adoption. And she wondered how they could bear it. She decided that being unable to get pregnant at all would be less agonizing.

As negative thoughts only fed her discouragement, Hilary tried to be positive, looking to Jack as an example. Still, it took great willpower not to be depressed with her confinement—and worse, not to be afraid that this baby wouldn't make it at all.

Hilary's fears rose dramatically when she showed signs of going into labor more than six weeks before the due date. Jack rushed her to the hospital, while she prayed continually that her baby would live to be healthy and strong. She told the Lord she'd be willing to go through anything to make that happen, which made the months of being bedridden not seem so bad. The hospital staff was efficient and compassionate, but after all they could do, it became evident that this baby was coming.

Jack stayed at Hilary's bedside, holding her hand while they both paid close attention to the monitoring of the baby's heart. "I'm so scared," Hilary admitted.

"Everything's going to be fine," Jack said. "No matter what happens, we'll get through this . . . together." She still looked afraid. Though he couldn't blame her, he touched her nose, saying, "Hey, if you and I have made it this far, we can make it through anything."

Hilary smiled, albeit tensely. "You keep telling me that, Jack. I couldn't do this without you."

"I'm here," he whispered, kissing her softly. "I'll always be here."

Labor progressed so quickly that Hilary became even more frightened, and Jack never left her side for a minute. Soon after midnight, a beautiful baby girl was born. Hilary was crying too hard to speak when the doctor announced, "She's tiny, but she looks perfect."

Erin Hilary Hayden weighed in at four and a half pounds, but the doctor later confirmed that they could find nothing wrong with her.

She was kept in the intensive care nursery for observation, with the hope of going home very soon.

While Hilary slept peacefully, knowing it was behind her, Jack sat beside his daughter in the nursery, watching her closely, marveling at the miracle of her life. One of the nurses talked freely with him, answering his questions, filling him with excitement at the prospect of caring for this child.

Because of her friendly demeanor, Jack wasn't the least bit offended when the nurse said, "Your disability must be a real challenge."

"Not as much as I thought it would be," he admitted.

"It's obvious you're going to make a great father."

Jack smiled down upon his daughter. "I hope so."

The nurse left him with his thoughts. He watched the baby stretch and move her little thumb into her mouth, as if it was a familiar habit. Then it occurred to him that he'd hardly given his *disability* a thought for a long time. He'd become accustomed to a certain way of life that no longer seemed a daily challenge. It was just life. He simply wasn't conscious of being different, or of being held back from things he'd once considered vital.

"Hey there, Daddy." Hilary's voice interrupted his thoughts, and he turned to see her in a wheelchair. A nurse pushed her close to the baby's little bed, then left them alone.

"Look at you," Jack said, patting the arm of her chair. "That's quite a mode of transportation you've got there."

"Yes, well . . . it's standard hospital issue. It's not nearly as high-tech and fancy as yours."

"Well," he grinned and kissed her, "you have to work hard to get one like this."

"One per family is enough, I think."

He laughed, then asked, "How are you feeling?"

"A little sore, but better than I expected. It's nice to at least be sitting up for a change."

"You'll be dancing in no time—and you'll have your daughter dancing before she even walks, I'll bet."

"Maybe," she said, and they both turned their attention to the baby. "Oh, she's so beautiful," Hilary said.

"She looks like her mother."

Hilary laughed. "She didn't get those curls from me."

Jack took notice of how the baby's dark, wispy hair had dried into little curls. He had to admit, "No, I don't think she did."

"There's no question that she's your daughter."

Jack grinned. "That could really impress some people—people like me, who didn't know such a thing could be possible."

Hilary looked into her husband's eyes, so filled with relief and contentment that she couldn't hold the tears back. "We are so blessed, Jack. I've never been so happy in my life."

"Amen to that," he said and kissed her again.

Little Erin came home from the hospital to a warm welcome. Hilary's parents came to stay for a few days, helping to coach the new parents through the first steps of caring for an infant. On her fourth day home, Jack insisted on bathing the baby by himself after he'd watched Hilary and her mother do it a few times.

For the first month of her life, Erin remained at home, and visitors were kept to a minimum to avoid exposing her to a possible infection. But Hilary was so grateful to have the baby here, and to be up and around, that she hardly noticed the confinement. Jack took turns staying home with her so Hilary could go to church and get out to do errands. She felt like a whole new person. *She was a mother.*

When Erin was finally old enough to be appreciated publicly, Janna put on a shower for mother and baby. Hilary didn't realize she had so many friends and relatives until they were all gathered in her front room, overwhelming her with gifts and good wishes. A few weeks later, when Matthew returned from his mission, he was able to stand in when Erin was blessed and officially given her name.

Through the first few months of Erin's life, Jack felt as if he was observing the world in a new light. Nothing gave him more joy than to take part in this child's care, and to just delight in his sweet wife and the love she had for their daughter. This new family relationship strengthened the love they shared as husband and wife more than he had ever imagined.

Looking back over the years since the accident, Jack could see that he'd accomplished more than he'd ever dreamed possible. In truth, he could see that his own testimony and character had become much stronger, and he'd probably made a more profound difference in the lives of those around him, than he ever could have without the challenges in his life. Yes, he'd accomplished much, and he felt good about it. He had a good marriage, a successful career that he enjoyed, and his work in the Church was fulfilling and kept him busy. But nothing in his life could compare to the reality of having this beautiful little girl, and the opportunity he had to help care for her and watch her grow. Knowing that many men with spinal cord injuries were unable to father their own children, he wondered if he might feel the same way if this child had been adopted. Of course, it was impossible for him to compare when he only knew his own experiences. But observing little Erin and the way she grew and changed so quickly, he believed in his heart that he would love her no less if she weren't his own flesh and blood.

"You're such a good daddy," Hilary said one evening as she plopped onto the couch in exhaustion. Jack held little Erin against his shoulder, patting her back to encourage a burp out of her.

"She's easy to love," he said.

"She's got her daddy's curls—and that same little sparkle in her eyes, too."

The baby burped loudly and Jack added, "And she's got her daddy's refinement."

Hilary laughed. "You're not going to teach her to chew on toothpicks, are you?"

"No, but I might teach her to say words like *criminantly.*"

"You can teach her how to spell it, too."

Jack held the baby where she could see him, talking dramatically to her until she smiled, which made both her parents beam with pride. Hilary observed Jack with the baby, marveling at what an incredible man he was. She often thought of the time when he'd temporarily lost sight of who he was; but he had risen above that, and it was long in the past. It was easy for her to say, "You know, Jack, you're going to be Erin's hero."

There had been a time when Jack would have responded cynically to such a statement, his mind fixed on the concept that heroes were a composite of supreme strength and physical capabilities. But he only smiled and said, "You really think so?"

"I know so. Well, she might have a little trouble with it during her teenage years, when it's not cool to like your parents. But eventually she'll come around to the fact that her father's an incredible man." She touched Jack's face and looked into his eyes. "You're *my* hero, because you are a *real* man."

"Really?" He laughed, distracted by the baby's continuing smiles. "How is that?"

"It's like I told you a long time ago—long before I even considered marrying you . . ."

Surprised by the direction their conversation was taking, Jack's attention turned fully to Hilary as she continued.

"I meant it then, and I mean it now—more than ever. I think a real man has a sensitive heart and a listening ear. A real man is someone who can respect a woman, even if he doesn't agree with her. And it doesn't matter whether he can change the oil, or drive a tractor—or even walk. It doesn't matter what he wears, or how he talks, or what he does for a living." Her voice quavered with emotion. "That's what makes you a real man, Jack. You always have been. You always will be. And let me add that I think a real man isn't afraid to be a nursemaid to his invalid wife, or to change diapers, or to bathe babies. And a real man's not afraid to cry or admit he can't do everything alone. That's why you're my hero, Jack. Because you understand what's *really* important.

"Back when we were just friends, you were the one who taught me that I could believe in myself; that the good inside of me was the only thing that really mattered. It was because of you that I went on a mission, and I didn't give up on my dancing. And through our years together, you've taught me a great deal about faith. You once told me you believed love could overcome any earthly obstacle. You've proven that to me. And that's one of many reasons I love you." She kissed him and repeated softly, "You're my hero."

"Well, you're *my* hero," he said with an intensity in his eyes that chilled her. "You've carried me through times when I couldn't carry myself. You loved me in spite of myself, and you taught me to believe in my potential and reach for it; to find the qualities in myself that really mattered."

Hilary laughed softly and he asked, "Is something funny?"

"No, but . . . in a way it seems like you taught yourself those things. I mean, if you taught me to believe in myself, and then I helped you get through, then . . ."

"I see your point, but I still wouldn't be where I am now if it wasn't for you." He touched her nose with his finger. "And I'm not the one who sacrificed months out of my life to give this child life."

Hilary laid her head on Jack's shoulder to admire their baby. "It was worth every minute."

Jack pushed one arm around Hilary and held the baby close, saying with an exaggerated southern drawl, "Amen to that."

Photo by Nathan Barney

About the Author

Anita Stansfield published her first LDS romance novel, *First Love and Forever,* in the fall of 1994, and the book was winner of the 1994-95 Best Fiction Award from the Independent LDS Booksellers. Since then, her best-selling novels have captivated and moved thousands of readers with their deeply romantic stories and focus on important contemporary issues. *When Forever Comes* is her ninth novel to be published by Covenant.

Anita has been writing since she was in high school, and her work has appeared in *Cosmopolitan* and other publications. She views romantic fiction as an important vehicle to explore critical women's issues, especially as they relate to the LDS culture and perspective. Her novels reflect a uniquely spiritual dimension centered in gospel principles.

An active member of the League of Utah Writers, Anita lives with her husband, Vince, and their four children and two cats in Alpine, Utah. She currently serves as the Achievement Days leader in her ward.

The author enjoys hearing from her readers. You can write to her at:
P.O. Box 50795
Provo, UT 84605-0795